TECH A PIECE OF MY MIND

HEIDE GOODY

IAIN GRANT

1

1ST JUNE

It was all the mouse's fault. If I hadn't seen the mouse I wouldn't have got into trouble with Levi. If I hadn't got into trouble with Levi, Paulette wouldn't have kept me behind. If Paulette hadn't kept me behind, I wouldn't have gone into the wet apartment and been fined by Patrick Helberg. If I hadn't been fined by Patrick Helberg, I wouldn't have been late to work and wouldn't have met Rufus Jaffle.

It was all the mouse's fault.

~

"GOOD MORNING! Jaffle Tech incorporated – Complete peace of mind for a little piece of your mind. My name is Alice. How can I help you today?"

"I've got a problem with my settings."

"Yes?" I said as customer data flooded onto my heads-up. "What problem is that, Jackson?"

"I'm trying to take a look at my spare capacity usage. I look at what my usage is every week."

"Yes?"

"But now, every time I do, it tells me I need to do an update and agree to the new terms and conditions."

"Yes. And have you done the update? I can talk you through that if you—"

"No, I don't want the update."

"You don't want the update?" I said.

"No. If I have the update then I have to agree to the new terms and conditions."

"That's right. You just tick the box and hit agree."

"But I don't agree."

"Crumbs!"

The *Crumbs!* was for both the caller and for the little creature that I had just spotted in my cubicle. A mouse. Black eyes, dull fur, a tiny twitching nose. It perched on the back edge of my desk, just above the gap between the desk and the back board which separated my desk from the one opposite. The cubicles were designed to be free of distractions but this tiny invader had clearly not been briefed.

"I'm on the Jaffle Standard package," said the caller.

"I can see that, Jackson. Same as me."

"The new terms and conditions no longer say we can pick what our spare processing capacity is used for. I look at what my usage is every week."

"Yes."

"For example, it's currently being used for camera feed analysis in Newcastle."

"It is. Your spare processing capacity is being used to

identify broken infrastructure that needs an engineer. Or it might pick up a person who needs medical assistance, for example."

"And I'm fine with that. That's lovely, that is. But if I agree to the new terms and conditions and they decide to use it for something bad—"

"Something bad?"

"Yes. I don't know. Something bad like ... like ... well, I can't think of anything bad right now but I'm sure I'd know it when I saw it. I'm just not happy."

The mouse's nose twitched, sniffing the air. It looked lost.

"Where did you come from?" I said.

"I beg your pardon?"

"Sorry, not you, Jackson—"

The mouse, perhaps aware that it was being talked to, vanished down the back of the desk.

"I mean, I see what you mean," I said.

I crouched to look underneath my desk. The mouse clung to the narrow cabling stalk at the back of the desk. Its pink claws reminded me of the Jaffle squirrels that worked in the parks. I reached forward tenderly to scoop it up but it darted away, to the ground and to the next cubicle along.

"Now, we could totally circumvent this problem if you upgrade to the Jaffle Enhanced package," I said, following the mouse as it scuttled past the desks of my colleagues.

The caller scoffed. *"Oh, I'm quite a long way from being able to afford that."*

Most people were. I made sure I kept the smile in my voice.

"I just don't want the update," said Jackson.

"I don't think that's possible," I said. "If you don't update then we can't provide you with an appropriate level of support or further, er, updates for your Jaffle Port."

"But I don't agree to the terms."

"But when you signed up, you agreed to accept routine updates."

"Did I? Where did it say that?"

"In the original terms and conditions. You hit agree."

"What are you doing?" said Hattie when I reached the end of the row. She was on a pause between calls.

I muted the caller a second. "I'm not doing anything."

On Hattie's screen was a picture of a Smiley Tot. Hattie pointed at the image. "It's a Smiley Tot."

"Yes."

"But it's a Smiley Tot."

"I know," I said.

"But it's so..." Hattie gave a shiver of pleasure. "Isn't it?"

"It's a Smiley Tot!" I unmuted the call. "Now, Jackson, you need to agree to the new terms and conditions to get those routine updates."

"But..."

"Yes?"

"You're saying that when I first agreed to the terms and conditions, I was agreeing to all future terms and conditions, even if I didn't know what they were?"

Hattie followed my gaze and bent to look under the desk.

"Don't," I muttered, but it was too late. One glance at the mouse was enough to make Hattie leap onto her chair, quivering in shock. I tried to convey, with a few hurried gestures, that everything was going to be fine and I would sort it out. I had also completely forgotten what the caller had just said to me.

"Let's not lose sight of what you're getting in exchange for giving up your spare capacity," I said, blandly. "Your port gives you enhanced memory storage, memory export to other Jaffle Port users, direct access to entertainment media and learning resources."

"Oh, I know. It's lovely."

When the mouse ran on to the next row of cubicles, I trotted after it. This floor alone contained two hundred cubicles so, at this rate, it could be a long pursuit. I was no longer sure why I was following it.

"And much of your spare capacity is taken up with essential service software, Jackson," I continued. "That's your firewall, obscenity filters, system check, defragmentation and deep clean and, of course, the all-important customer feedback data so Jaffle Tech can keep on making improvements for you."

"And I've been very happy up until now."

"Of course, you have. And, remember, the longer you are with us, the more your Jaffle rating goes up and that's vital if you're looking for a new job or applying for credit finance. Everyone loves a good Jaffle rating."

The mouse had come up against a wall and scurried along.

"And, what's amazing when you think about it, Jackson," I said, my mouth on full auto-pilot now, "is this is provided for you at absolutely no charge while you remain on the Jaffle Standard. It's Jaffle Tech's gift to the world."

"It is free, I suppose."

"And, rest assured, Jaffle Tech has the strongest ethical standards when it comes to what we use your spare processing capacity for. Jaffle Tech users are making the world a safer, cleaner and better place, even in their sleep. By signing over your spare capacity to us, you're being a hero, every minute of every day."

"No, yes, I suppose you're right," said the caller. *"It's just... it's my brain, isn't it?"*

"Of course it is. And what a wonderful brain it is too, Jackson."

There was a pause.

"Just tick the box and hit agree?"

"That's right, Jackson. Have a good day, now."

I killed the call. The mouse ran past a door which happened to swing open. I ran for the it. There was a shout and a clatter.

In the elevator lobby stood Levi Krasnesky, the security guard. He had a plastic lunch box tucked under his arm, like a sergeant major's baton. He glanced at me before looking down at the base of the potted plant next to him. He stamped down hurriedly on something behind the plant pot.

"No, ya don't, you varmint," he grunted as he stomped. Two, three times.

I was out of breath and stunned to see him stamping on... "Did you?"

"Did I what?" he said.

I moved forward to look. Levi held up his hand to stop me. "Woah, hold your horses, miss. Not a pretty sight."

"I think you might have accidentally killed a mouse," I said. I wasn't sure what else could have happened.

Levi straightened up and tucked his thumbs into his heavy belt. He was not a tall individual – he was quite boyish looking, probably not helped by that reedy moustache he was trying to grow. He looked like he still had some growing to do.

"Oh, let me tell ya," he said, "that animal did not belong in the system."

"The system?"

"Oh, no. That animal was not even a part of the system. Therefore it did not technically exist."

"Really?"

"Now, do I or do I not run a very tight ship around here?"

I nodded, hoping that I was responding to the correct part of the question. I wasn't sure if there was even a ship for him to run. He was a security guard. Merely one component of the large security team at Jaffle Tech.

"Yabetcha," he said, "and did I just witness you running in the workplace?"

I considered the question. "I think you probably did, yes. You have cameras everywhere and you're always watching."

He liked that. "I am always watching. Yes, indeed. Heck, you are smarter than you look, It's Alice, isn't it?"

"Yes."

"You look smart but I gotta ask myself, if you were paying attention to my security awareness memos—"

"Are those the printed sheets you keep taping to the fridge in the staff rec area?"

"My security awareness memos," he nodded.

"Did anyone find out who stole Brandine's bagel?"

"Alice, I am not talking about Brandine's bagel. I am asking you why would ya disregard safety in the workplace?"

"I was dealing with ... um." I accessed my Jaffle Port literacy booster. A millisecond of jipping and I said, "It was an anomaly."

"You were dealing with an anomaly and thought that you'd compromise the safety of all of your co-workers?" Levi said. He tugged on the peak of his cap tersely. "You would risk the lives of the six hundred people on this section alone just to deal with your anomaly?"

I enjoyed problem solving and spent a few moments trying to picture a scenario where me running between the cubicles might result in six hundred deaths, but I came up blank. Before I could ask Levi he had begun air-swiping on his own heads-up display.

"Miss, it is your lucky day, don't ya know."

"Is it?"

"Yabetcha. We're scheduling a re-run of safety training module 5b during your section meeting later. Better that than add an infraction to your personnel record."

"Who's we?" I said.

"What's that?"

"Who's scheduled the training?"

"I have. Jaffle Tech site management have."

"Well, which one?"

He huffed. "Site management, which encompasses the security team which encompasses me. Ergo, we, that is I, have scheduled the training. Do I need to explain it further?"

"No," I said.

"I need ya to keep your head in the game for all of our sakes, Alice, so pay close attention, ya hear?"

Chastised, I returned to my desk, calling in on Hattie who was still staring at the floor as if the mouse might return at any moment.

"What was it?" said Hattie.

"A mouse," I said.

"I didn't like it."

"No. Something else you're not going to like. We've got a safety training session during the meeting this afternoon."

Hattie wasn't happy. "They're not going to show The Film again, are they?"

I couldn't lie. Instead I chose distraction. "That's a pretty Smiley Tot."

"Isn't it though?" said Hattie. "I'm thinking of putting it on my Want List."

"You have enough Smiley Tots," I said.

"You can't have too many Smiley Tots," said Hattie. "And this one has the sweetest little bonnet."

"Yes, it does and, yes, you can. You can't go into your bedroom without tripping over Smiley Tots."

"You haven't been tripping over my Smiley Tots, have you?"

"No, I'm simply saying—"

"Oh, I can't imagine how I'd feel if one of my Smiley Tots was hurt."

I thought about the squashed mouse. I hadn't seen it but I could picture it in my mind's eye. Picturing imaginary things didn't come easy if you were operating on Jaffle Standard but if the image was strong enough...

"Oh," said Hattie, fanning herself with her hand. "My tots hurt. And the shock of seeing that horrible mouse and— Oh. I feel properly discombobulated. Have my cheeks gone red?"

Hattie's cheeks were always red.

"Discombobulated?" I said.

"Literacy booster," said Hattie.

I nodded. "I just jipped the word *anomaly.*"

"Anomaly," said Hattie. "Oh, that's fun to say, isn't it? A-nom-a-ly."

And with that Hattie had forgotten all about the mouse. I hadn't.

2

The training room was set out with amphitheatre seating. The six hundred plus members of the section barely filled a third of the seats. Paulette, the section leader, took to the stage. Familiar images of Jaffle Tech products slid across the giant screen behind her.

"Yesterday, a Jaffle swarm in Yucatan foiled a kidnap attempt at a private school. Jaffle sharks patrol the Pacific, protecting our precious ships from enemy aggressors. This year, we broke the ninety-seven percent barrier. That's right. Ninety-seven percent of the domestic population use a Jaffle Port."

The audience started to clap.

I clapped enthusiastically. I didn't like to think about the other three percent. Most of them were the very old, born long before the brain port was invented and too stubborn to become adopters. But the rest, those strange few, were the ones who had refused the gift of the Jaffle Port: religious nutjobs, weirdos. I felt a mixture of pity and disgust for them.

"And," said Paulette, "this week marks twenty years since Jaffle Tech made the promise to give a Jaffle Port to every single new-born baby – a promise we've kept ever since."

The applause was ecstatic.

There was an access request on my Jaffle Port. I accepted the jip-request. With a sweep of her arm, Paulette cast hundreds of overlapping brain charts onto the screen.

"And look what good we're doing," said Paulette. "Sian Saunier." A woman whooped off to the left. "Your spare processing capacity has been working on the Near Earth Infrastructure Program."

There were approving murmurs around the room.

"Paul Obeng." Paulette acknowledge his handwave. "Monitoring traffic flow on the city interchanges."

There was well-mannered sounds of amusement.

"Hey, your brain might not be conquering the final frontier like Sian's but it's making our world a safer place! Hattie Rutherford. Wow. Working with international intelligence agencies to identify potential terrorists."

"My brain is a secret agent," said Hattie with deadpan cool and smirked. She and I smiled at each other with shared pride.

Paulette displayed a chart showing brain utilisation rates, and I was delighted to see that a certain Alice Tennerman was in the top five on the efficiency leader board. I leaned across to whisper in Hattie's ear. "You may be a secret agent but my brain's better."

Hattie pulled a face. "That data's probably just an anomaly. Anomaly. A-nom-a—"

"Shush."

"They used to say in the twentieth century," Paulette was saying, "that there was more content in a single day's edition of the New York Times than the average seventeenth century person was able to access in their entire lifetime. Now, we can say that the average Jaffle Tech enabled brain does more thinking and processing in a year than a non-Jaffle brain does in a lifetime. You are superheroes."

The staff clapped and cheered. Paulette held out her hands for calm.

"We have an important safety briefing this afternoon," said Paulette. "This is a mandatory refresher and—"

"Yes, thank you," interrupted Levi, stepping up onto the stage. He stumbled over the stage edge, gave it an accusing glare and put a swagger in his stride to compensate as he strode to centre.

"I thought we were just running the video," Paulette said to him.

"Yes, yes, thank you," said Levi. He turned to address the audience. "We're going to run the safety briefing but—" He wasn't in the right place for the microphones to pick him up. He stepped to the side and politely but firmly pushed Paulette away. "Name's Levi Krasnesky. I run security checks in your section. There have been some recent disturbing incidents in our very own workplace which have indicated a training need." He changed the screen. "Some very serious near misses, oh, yabetcha. Would you look at this? Jeez."

On the screen was a camera feed of an access space in the cubicle jungle. People walked back and forth.

"This fills me with horror," said Levi.

I squinted. There was nothing to be seen. People. Cubicles. A drinks machine. Levi zoomed in on the floor.

"A pencil," he said.

There were a number of gasps.

I wondered where the pencil had come from. Physical stationery was fairly uncommon, and people tended to take good care of it.

"Stationery is forbidden for call operators," said Levi, "but apart from that, it's a huge risk for trips and slips, ya know."

Levi looked around the amphitheatre and tried to hold the gaze of every single person, which was a challenge in so large a space.

"Now, hold onto your hats, folks. This second incident was a disaster from start to finish. We had an unauthorised intruder in the section this morning. Instead of alerting the security team and remaining calm as per your training, an employee *in this very room* who shall remain nameless gave chase."

On screen, camera footage showed me in a crouched run, moving from cubicle to cubicle, peering under each.

"Wowzers," whispered Hattie.

"Furthermore," said Levi, "that unnamed employee was observed to be running in the workplace. Heck, I don't think I've ever seen recklessness like it."

Levi's eyebrows went up. He'd spotted me in the audience and gave me a nod of recognition. Shame washed over me.

"On top of that, call records show that the employee was talking to a customer for some of the time that she was running through the workplace." He swiped and audio feed played around the hall.

"*Good morning! Jaffle Tech incorporated – Complete peace of mind for a little piece of your mind. My name is Alice. How can I help you today?*"

"Ignore that," said Levi, fast-forwarding. "Ignore the names. This isn't about pointing the finger of blame."

"*Where did you come from?*" said my voice over the speakers.

"*I beg your pardon?*" said the caller.

"*Sorry, not you, Jackson. I – I mean, I see what you mean.*"

"You see?" said Levi, stopping the playing. "Not only is Alice – I mean the nameless employee – failing to give the customer the benefit of her full attention, but she was also distracted from taking extra care while she put all of our lives at risk with her running. It is fortunate that I was able to intervene, and my skills and training averted a disaster, but if this were to happen again..." He sucked through his teeth and let the implications speak for themselves. "Now watch the film and take careful note of how far we've come," he said.

"I don't like The Film," whispered Hattie and gripped my hand in the dark.

Levi gave them all another stern look then stepped back into the shadows as The Film played.

I realised with a sinking feeling that I had seen this section before. Hattie had obviously recognised it too as she gave a small whimper and gripped my hand all the tighter. I forced her to pay attention, knowing that Levi would be watching her.

The Film had various titles and designations but everyone just called it *The Film*. When you mentioned *The Film*, everyone knew what film you were talking about.

I wasn't sure how old The Film was. It was in black and white – as though viewed through the eyes of someone on Jaffle Economy or Jaffle Lite – and the quality was very poor. I hoped that a vast gulf of time separated me from the unfortunate people who featured on the screen because their suffering was almost too much to bear. Some of the dangers that featured in this workplace were very unfamiliar to me. It was fortunate that modern standards had made us all safe from tumbling masonry and huge trains, but the film made it very clear that running and danger went hand in hand.

The Film seemed to be without end, an infinite parade of pitfalls and accidents. Hattie made repeated *Ooh* and *Aah* sounds, wincing at the continuing horror and I could see, from the corner of my eye that several of my colleagues were looking away to avoid the worst of it.

Eventually it ended. Levi stood centre stage. "Hoo-ee. I hope ya all found that film as sobering as I did. Ya must realise that danger stalks us constantly in the workplace, like a savage ... savage..."

"Badger!" suggested someone down near the front.

"No. No! Bigger than a badger!"

"Tiger!" shouted someone else.

"Okay, maybe too big now. A bear! Yes! Like a savage bear," said Levi. "But ya can count on the security team to have your back. Any questions?"

"Have you found out who stole Brandine's bagel yet?" someone shouted.

"I cannot comment on an on-going investigation."

"What kind of bear?" shouted someone else.

AFTER THE MEETING, as everyone was trooping out to return to their cubicles. Levi stepped down from the stage to intercept me.

"Alice," he said.

"Levi," I replied.

"Hattie," said Hattie.

"I hope ya weren't disturbed by what happened today."

"Discombobulated," said Hattie.

"You mean calling me out in front of all my colleagues?" I said.

"I meant having to see me deal with that intruder so sternly. I wouldn't want ya to worry yourself over it."

"No," I said because I couldn't think of anything else to say.

"You'll be aware that I have many ways that I can monitor your behaviour," he said. "Not all of them are known to you, but ya can be certain that I am always watching. However, I can see that you've learned a lot today and, remember, that business with the mouse: that was a rare occurrence."

"Anomaly," said Hattie.

I didn't know how to respond to him so I did as I always did in the same situation: putting a smile upon my face and carrying on.

"And just to check," Hattie asked Levi as I moved on, "this bear – it's not a real bear, is it?"

Section head Paulette stood by the door as people exited. "Alice, a word," she said frostily and beckoned me over.

3

"Anomaly."

    Clap clap.

    "Anomaly."

Clap clap.

"A-nom a-nom anomaly."

Clap clap.

In the cool of the early evening, I found Hattie outside by the pick-up zone. Hattie was playing a clapping game of her own devising while she waited. A guy in orange coveralls which identified him as a Jaffle Lite community service worker moved between the concrete pillars, collecting litter. He worked around Hattie, treating her no different to the pillars. Jaffle Lite users were aware of other people but they didn't see them as people unless you really pointed it out to them. It wasn't part of their package. In many ways, they were little more than bots and the services they provided to the community could as easily be handled by machines.

"Sorry, I'm late," I said.

"Have you been fired?" said Hattie.

"No. What? No!" I shook my head. "Paulette gave me a ticking off, the usual systems and procedures talk and calculated I'd lost forty two point something minutes because of my little adventure."

"Adventure," said Hattie, flushing.

"I'm sorry I'm late."

"It's okay," said Hattie, "at least the cars will be off peak now."

"True."

I called a car over and we got in. I jipped the car to pay.

"Home," I told it.

"Maybe," said Hattie once we were beyond the landscaped greenery of Jaffle Park, "we should start taking off peak cars every day. A bit more money-saving might be good for us."

"We might be able to afford Jaffle Enhanced upgrades sooner," I said.

"I don't know," said Hattie. "I was thinking on splashing out on that Smiley Tot."

"No," I said firmly. "You're not to buy any more Smiley Tots."

"Not to buy any more?" said Hattie. "As in, in the future?"

I gave her a look. "Did you already buy it?"

"It was a One-Click special."

"Oh, Hattie."

"It was an impulse buy."

"Yes, but still..."

"I was still shaking after watching The Film," said Hattie. "You know how I can be."

"I do. I really do."

Hattie's addiction to Smiley Tots had been a fixture of our lives ever since we were matched up as roommates at the Shangri-La Towers apartment complex. She loved their dimpled cheeks. She loved their chubby thighs. She loved their big dewy eyes and their small pink mouths. And one Smiley Tot was not enough for her. No number of Smiley Tots were ever enough for her. Sometimes I had to bite my tongue and not say the obvious – that my best friend and roommate should simply get herself a baby, a human one. But who could afford one of those on our salaries? They wouldn't even let us in the showroom.

The car bipped as it tallied up the cost of using the pay-per-metre road. It requested permission to pull out on a faster, more expensive lane. I denied the request. Hattie looked out of the window of the whirring car.

"Can you believe things used to be that bad?"

"As The Film? I know, people in the past had it pretty hard," I said, "although Levi makes it sound as if he's the only thing holding back all the bad stuff."

"Maybe he is," said Hattie archly, "with his skills and his training."

"With his skills and his training and that little moustache of his."

"Oh, no," said Hattie seriously. "I don't his moustache does anything. You think it does? You think it's like a secret gadget moustache?"

I rolled my eyes. "Well, you would know. You're the one with a secret agent for a brain."

"Yes, I am."

There was a cluster of Empties in the drop-off zone near their apartment block. There seemed to be more each week. No one seemed to be doing anything about them.

The car pulled up further along, away from the Empties, and we climbed out. It glided away to find a parking station.

Hattie tutted about the dust and debris that littered the communal stairs as we climbed. On our landing we found one of Helberg's bots. It was cream-coloured with a curved shell. Its underside was equipped with rod-like legs for climbing stairs and spinning bristle brushes for sweeping them. We could see them clearly because the bot had fallen down the stairs and onto its back and was waggling its legs uselessly. Jet-*Set Willy*, was printed on its side.

We both ignored it. It was not the first time we had found Jet-Set Willy at the bottom of a set of stairs. We could turn it upright but Helberg didn't like it when tenants touched his things. Hattie would no doubt be out here later, sweeping up what the bot could not. Of course, it was Helberg's job to keep the complex clean but Hattie would do it anyway.

"I'm not so sure about waiting for the off peak cars in the evening," I said. "I like to be home before *Non-Stop Smile Hour* ends."

"You don't watch *Non-Stop Smile Hour*," said Hattie.

"*I* don't," I said. "Count together?"

"Come on then." Hattie jigged briefly on her tip toes and the two of us timed our steps with the numbers as we counted along the doors of our landing. Most people in the apartment block counted the doors, because it was so difficult to tell them apart on the landing. Each door was painted in the same faded colour with the numbers printed on in white. Over the years the contrast between the background and the numbers had become negligible, so it was fairly common for neighbours to mistakenly walk into each other's apartments.

"...thirty-three, thirty-four, thirty-five..."

The door to the apartment two doors down from ours opened. *Non-Stop Smile Hour* had evidently finished.

"Crumbs," I muttered.

"My apartment's wet. What are you gonna do about it?" said Jeanbee Swanager.

"Sorry?" I said.

"Sorry don't milk the cow or fill the pantry," said Swanager.

"I meant ... pardon?" I said.

"What? Are you deaf now too?" said our neighbour. "Don't they teach you young 'uns to listen anymore?"

She called us young uns but I suspected that Swanager wasn't as old as she made herself to be. It was as if she had taken a look at the cardigans and the big knickers and the casual bluntness and, liking what she saw, decided to get in on the old lady action before the rush.

"We've just got in from work," I said, which was a sentence I hoped would say far more than it actually did.

"I've seen where you work," sneered Swanager. "Big tall swanky building. Too much glass for my liking. While the rest of us have to cope with wet apartments and worse."

"Worse?" said Hattie.

"Worse!" said Ms Swanager, failing to elaborate. "And I asked you, what are you gonna do about it?"

"The glass?"

"The water! And don't you be giving me no attitude."

"We're not," I said.

Hattie was afraid of Swanager and there was plenty of Swanager to be afraid of. She stood behind me, trying not to look like she was cowering. I realised Swanager's clothes were completely sodden from the knees down. Perhaps she'd been trying to mop up the puddle herself.

"Do you want me to come look at your wet apartment?" I said.

"It's like I'm talking to myself!" cried the not-quite-old woman. "Yes!"

"It's just—"

"What?"

"Just that—"

"*What?*"

"It's not exactly my—"

"Now, don't you dare say it's not your responsibility, young woman. I've seen where you work."

"But this building isn't managed by Jaffle Tech. Patrick Helberg's the complex manager..."

I stopped. Swanager was making a noise like a noisy exhaust, a throaty and rattling exhalation that was simultaneously disgusted and disgusting.

"I never took you for a shirker, Alice Tennerman."

"I'm ... I'm not."

"Then you scuttle your butt in there and look at my wet apartment."

"We've not had dinner yet," I said. "I'll happy look later after –"

"Come in now," said Swanager.

"Right."

"That way, you'll have longer to fix things."

"Right." I glanced back at Hattie. "Maybe Hattie could go back to our apartment and start on dinner."

"I don't care about your personal arrangements," snapped Swanager. "Time's a-wasting."

I gestured for Hattie to leave me to it and Hattie all but fled to the safety of our apartment.

Swanager turned to go back into her apartment. Her slippers squelched on the thick carpet.

"Oh my, it is, er, damp in here."

"I did say!"

In the living room, Clifford Pedstone sat watching a Smiley show on the TV. The sofa was an island in the swamped carpet but he had elevated his feet on a stool and grinned at Mr Smiley.

"Do you have any idea where it's coming from?" I asked.

"Do we look like water technicians?" said Swanager.

Pedstone made a wordless grumble.

"Don't you be offering opinions when they're not asked for, mister," said Swanager fiercely.

Pedstone grunted and rested his hands on his huge belly.

I squelched through to the back of the apartment. The bathroom door was closed. A stream of water trickled out along the gap at the bottom.

"You closed the bathroom door," I said.

"Seemed sensible," said Swanager, following.

I opened the bathroom door. Water gushed out like a small river, bobbing with minor detritus from inside the apartment. A hairbrush and a loofah washed past me.

"You're meant to make it better, not worse," said Swanager.

"Yes, I just..."

There was a large hole in the bathroom ceiling. Tiles and soggy plaster hung downwards. Water poured through in a light but constant stream.

"There's a hole in your bathroom ceiling," I said.

"Nothing gets past you, does it? I was going to raise a new call for that after this one was solved. We're always told that each separate issue requires a new call, aren't we?"

"Yes. Yes we are," I said. I looked at the hole. "I can't fix this from down here."

Swanager snorted.

"I'm just going to have a look upstairs," I said.

Swanager frowned. "But what about us? You're supposed to be helping us."

"I *am* helping you," I said. "I'm helping you by going upstairs. I'll be back soon."

I went outside. In the corridor, I took off my sodden shoes. My socks were just as wet so I took them off too.

I stopped in at my apartment. Hattie was fixing beans for dinner. She had her favourite Smiley Tot sitting in a high chair, positioned as though it was watching her. Hattie would claim she had no favourites among her Smiley Tots but this was a lie.

"I've got to go upstairs," I said.

"Why?"

"There's some sort of leak. You want to come?"

"Why?" said Hattie.

"To explore. It'll be an adventure."

"I don't think I want an adventure," said Hattie, quite seriously. "Don't be long. I've got today's chores to do and it's *Smiley Out and About* soon."

"And today's jobs are...?"

"Polish the ceiling in here, test the soap dispensers and synchronise the windows," said Hattie.

"Of course," I said. I had a respectable approach to cleanliness but nowhere near as exacting as Hattie. Cleaning and Smiley Tots. Smiley Tots and cleaning. It was like my roommate was constantly in preparation for something, something vitally important that was never going to happen.

I went to the stairwell and climbed to the next floor. I counted along the doors until I found the apartment that was directly above the Swanager and Pedstone's. I raised my hand to knock on the door but then saw that the door was broken and ajar. There was tape across the door which read, *Emergency Responder Scene – Police Aware.*

I touched the door and it swung inwards. I stepped inside the gloomy space and recoiled slightly at the musty smell. The floor was wet here too.

"Hello?"

"*Welcome home, tenant,*" said the apartment.

"Ah, no. I..."

The ceiling lights came on, sparked noisily and then went out again.

"Hello?" I said.

There was no reply this time.

I walked further inside. There was the sound of trickling water from somewhere. A fine layer of dust covered everything that wasn't wet. Hattie would be horrified by the neglect if she could see this apartment. It looked as though nobody had lived here for weeks, maybe months. I went back through to the lounge. There were a few small remnants of the previous occupancy.

A basket sat on the soaked floor, thick with cobwebby balls of fibres and some curious pointed sticks.

There were some books on a shelf. I stared at them with suspicion. They belonged in the same outmoded world as physical stationery, they were an old-world curiosity that probably harboured a great many germs.

On another shelf were framed photographs. I picked one up. It showed two people, a blonde woman and a silver-haired man, in thick clothing and strange goggles, standing in what looked like a very hostile environment. The ground was white with snow, and the people appeared to be deep in unpaved countryside. Despite the danger of their situation, the people in the photograph had smiles on their faces.

I could not imagine why that might be.

I put the frame down, confused. I picked up another. The same two people were immersed in water up to their waists. I gasped in horror. How had they managed to get themselves into such danger? And why were they smiling in this photograph as well?

I realised that underneath the frames were some fat plastic books. I slid one out from underneath the frames and wiped the dust off it with my hand. It had a shiny cover that declared it to be a photograph album. I was about to open it when I remembered the running water, the sound of trickling that had slipped into background noise but had never gone away.

I located the bathroom and found a tap pouring water into a sink that overflowed onto the floor. There was a disconcerting downward bulge in the floor that I guessed corresponded with the hole in Swanager's ceiling. I trod carefully, round to the sink and pulled the plug out. I tried to turn the tap off, but the top just span round in my hand. Challenged but not put off, I searched around, found a shut-off valve on the pipe, just below the sink, and turned it. The flow of water stopped.

"There," I called out, hoping Swanager could hear. "I've stopped the leak."

"My apartment's still wet," Swanager shouted back.

"I don't have all the answers," I said, more to myself than anyone.

I backed out of the bathroom where thick black mould spanned the walls. The smell was strongest in here, as if the tap had been leaking in a smaller way for a very long time.

I instinctively went back to the photograph album. I opened it and looked at the photos within.

"I don't have all the answers," I repeated.

"...THIRTY FIVE, thirty six and we're home," I said to myself.

I entered my apartment, wet socks and shoes in one hand, the photograph album in the other. Hattie stood on the kitchen table, vigorously attacking the ceiling tiles with polish and duster.

"I've got blue beans and red beans," she said, without looking down.

"Red beans?"

"Apparently there was a problem at the factory. The latest batches of blue beans are red. Do you want the blue ones or the red ones?"

"Which do you prefer?" I said.

"I asked you."

I waited. Hattie looked down, consternated. "I don't like change," she said and then saw me properly. "What happened to your shoes?"

"Swanager's apartment was indeed wet. I've put a call in to Helberg."

Hattie looked at the dirty water dripping on the floor. "I'm going to have to clean that."

"Sorry. You clean up. I'll serve. Blue beans for you."

While shoes and socks dried in the utility closet, we ate beans at the kitchen table. It transpired that red beans tasted exactly the same as blue beans.

Hattie amused herself by adjusting and admiring the Smiley Tot in the high chair. I studied the photograph album, turning pages slowly, feeling a growing anxiety at each mysterious image.

The album contain dozens of pictures of the same couple. Some of the pictures showed them eating and drinking the most impractical things. I found one that showed a picture of the silver-haired man with a monster on a plate in front of him. There was no other word for it: a monster. It was a livid pinky brown and it had giant scary claws that dwarfed its alien body. The man held up the claws in his hands and smiled broadly. I was troubled by the image and couldn't imagine what it depicted.

The plate suggested that this scene was somehow connected to food. Was the monster the meal – no! – or was it the monster that was being fed? Fed what? And why?

Sometimes, when we watched TV, we might accidentally flick through some of the channels that were clearly not meant for us but for people on Jaffle Enhanced or Jaffle Premium. Those TV channels were not forbidden or blocked for people operating on Jaffle Standard; they simply held no interest for us.

Among them were the bizarre cooking shows that demonstrated some really time-consuming and strange ways to prepare food. It was a mystery to Hattie and I why anybody would perform all of those extra tasks with raw food and saucepans when the bean dispensers were so convenient, and delivered optimal nutrition every time. Was that monster the kind of thing to be served up (or fed) on one of those shows?

Worse still was *Drama*. Drama was confusing and disturbing, and featured scenes with people who failed to smile and spent a lot of time arguing and making each other unhappy. I couldn't see any appeal in that at all.

It was time for *Smiley Out and About*, our favourite show. The streaming had already started but Hattie didn't leave the kitchen until she'd put our plates in to wash. We then settled in the living room. We had a wide sofa and two armchairs and yet there was barely enough room. Fifteen Smiley Tots had prime viewing positions in three rows on the sofa. Hattie sat with a Smiley Tot in each arm.

"Oh, Mr Smiley!" said Hattie with relief as she saw his beaming face shining from the screen. She relaxed then, holding her tots tightly. The show was our favourite. Mr Smiley was a large, yellow face with a lovely smile. People on the show would be doing their everyday work, just like I and Hattie did, and then Mr Smiley's face would appear, shining above them, and they would be surprised and delighted to see him. Who wouldn't be?

"Oh look, gardeners, a bit like the ones that work near our office," said Hattie, looking at the screen. "See that man there? He looks a little bit unhappy. I really hope that Mr Smiley cheers him up."

There was a pause of a few seconds. Hattie and I leaned forward in anticipation. Mr Smiley appeared above the man and beamed at him. The man smiled, looking much happier than before.

"Oh look! Look at his face! How lovely!" Hattie jigged in her seat and I was swept up in the moment as well. We watched Mr Smiley perform his tricks for several other people, each of them pleased to see the sunny smile shining down upon them. When Mr Smiley was out, everything seemed fine.

4

2ND JUNE

"Why are we tiptoeing?" said Hattie.

"We're not tiptoeing," I said.

"And why are you whispering?" said Hattie in a voice that was not a whisper.

"Shh," I said. "We're not whispering."

"You are!"

"*Shhh!*"

We crept past Swanager's damp apartment. Or at least I did; Hattie just tramped behind me, squelching through the dampness which had spread from the apartment and across the hallway. After yesterday's experiences, I was keen to simply get to work without delays. It was bad enough having to wait for Hattie to get the Smiley Tots dressed for another day of sitting about the apartment.

No, I shook my head at myself. I shouldn't blame Hattie. Hattie's routines were important to her and morning was a busy time.

We reached the stairs without getting collared by our neighbour and went down to the ground floor. The sweeping bot, Jet-Set Willy, was gone from the stairs. Someone had either righted it or it had managed to roll back onto its feet. As we descended, my attention flicked momentarily to my Jaffle Port – there were no jams on the pay-per-metre and the weather forecast was for uninterrupted sunshine. Today, I decided, was going to be a day for punctuality, perfect adherence to company rules and super-efficient brain utilisation.

In the lobby, a hand stretched out of the darkness of the complex manager's office and clicked its fingers at me.

I wasn't sure how I knew the finger clicking was for me but the fingers were pale and slender and belonged to Patrick Helberg.

"Good morning, Helberg," I said and made to continue out the door.

Helberg whistled shrilly and the hand beckoned. "This way, O valued tenant."

I looked to Hattie. She shrugged and shooed me in. I dipped behind the counter and stood at the doorway. "Good morning, Helberg. Is this about Swanager's problem?"

"Job number four-three-eight. Damp apartment. I sent Hungry Horace to investigate."

Hungry Horace was another of the refurbished bots that Helberg entrusted far too much of his actual job to. If I wasn't mistaken, Hungry Horace was a vacuum cleaner bot that kept leaving incontinent piles of dust in the corridors. I couldn't imagine what Horace could do about a waterlogged apartment.

"There was a problem with water from the apartment above," I tried to explain. "I..." I faltered.

The complex manager's office was a clutter of equipment, tools, foodstuffs and bits and bobs that were surely ornamental or I had no idea what they were for. I knew Helberg had an apartment in the complex but it looked like this was his true home. Half-eaten sandwiches sat next to dismembered bot parts and sheaves of unsorted papers. It wasn't any of this that made me stop. It was the screen. On the screen behind him was a ... well, I wasn't sure what it was.

It was a series of images, a film of sorts, although I couldn't be sure what the story might be. If forced to guess, I would have had to have said it was a news story about some very hungry people who had lost all their clothes. Perhaps they were poor people but they didn't look very poor. Even with no clothes on they had an air of self-satisfied pleasure.

There were men and there were women and they were doing things. There was some sort of massage going on and something a bit like tickling. Rubbing. Rubbing was the verb that I would deem most accurate. And inserting. There was lots of emphasis on inserting and this made the people make noises. There were moans, the kind you made when you sat down with a nice plate of beans after a long day at work. And there were grunts, the kind you made when you'd got all the way to the office and realise you'd left something important at home. And the camera lingered on certain bits of the body that I instinctively felt didn't need lingering on. Bits of the body, glistening pink.

I had seen images like this before. Flick through enough

TV stations and you'd find stuff like this but, in those instances, I had flicked on by because it clearly wasn't for me. But here it was presented to me as something I couldn't just flick on by.

Helberg saw me looking.

"You like this kind of thing?" he said.

"No," I said and felt oddly uncomfortable and didn't know why.

"I thought you Jaffle employees were all on Premium." He shrugged, threw down the electric motor he had been fiddling with and gave me a fixed stare. "Are you a registered and graded plumber?"

"No."

"But it was you seen breaking and entering the apartment above Swanager's yesterday."

"Oh no, that's not what I was doing," I said, "I went up there to turn the water off."

"Registered and graded plumber?"

"No."

"Then it was *breaking* and *entering*," said Helberg. "That's a criminal offence and I'd need to call the police." He glanced up, jipping his Jaffle Port. "They'll fine you, even downgrade you to Jaffle Lite. You can be like one of those sad, orange losers with the vacant stares –"

"Helberg," I said, trying desperately to sound reasonable. "Surely, you can see that I'm not a criminal."

"Valued tenant, what am I to think?"

Valued tenant. He spoke in a manner that was deliberately old-fashioned, archaic even. But, like Swanager's old lady mannerisms, it was just an act. Helberg was my age, younger even.

He glanced round as one of the naked men on the screen bent his attention to doing something that I felt was surely unhygienic. "The only other possibility is that you are tenant of that apartment," he said.

"I just popped in."

"To see who? The Adlers, lovely tenants both, were moved into sheltered housing months ago. No. Breaking and entering it is. But..." He stroked his chin. "I like you, Alice. You're a..." He leaned sideways, his chair creaking. He appeared to be craning round to look at my waist, my buttocks. I wondered if I'd sat in something, if I had something stuck to my backside. I looked; there was nothing there. I wondered what he was going to say I was and what it had to do with my buttocks.

"Now, since I do like you," said Helberg, "I could be nice and suggest you take over the tenancy of that apartment – "

"I was there for less than five minutes."

"One day's tenancy it is, then perhaps I can save you from criminal proceedings."

A woman on the screen sighed heavily, which was just how I felt.

"One day?" I said.

"One day. Standard rate."

He held out his hand. I swiped. He blinked.

"Oh," he said. "There are insufficient funds in your account."

I reeled. Quite apart from being very wrong, something

wasn't adding up. "That's not possible," I said. "A day's rent. I can cover that."

"A day's rent indeed, valued tenant, plus the water bill for that apartment, taken from the reading made when the last tenant left. My, you do use a lot of water."

"What? No—"

"The bill is fifteen hundred."

"I don't have fifteen hundred."

"I can see that," said Helberg, "I've taken what's there and if you don't pay the balance within a week then eviction is the next step."

"That's not right! I went up there to help and I turned the water *off*. I didn't turn it on!"

"And I can only commend you for choosing to limit your water usage," said Helberg. "That's free advice from me, I should charge you for that really but I will let you off considering you are renting two apartments and you're such a..."

His eyes flicked to my buttocks again.

"I don't think it was a *person* who turned the water on," I said. "I think the tap broke."

"Criminal damage, eh? Either way, it's you," said Helberg. "So, that's a week to get me the rest of the money."

I stared in disbelief. On the screen, someone groaned like a woman who had just been charged money she didn't have for an apartment she didn't live in with a water problem she didn't cause.

∾

HATTIE STOOD WAITING in the pick-up zone outside. Empties still sat along the kerb, taking up most of the room. Someone ought to do something about them but I had no idea who to call. One of the Empties looked at me but I ignored it.

Everything all right?" asked Hattie.

I shook my head as I waved a car over. "No. Not really. You know when you try to do the right thing, and somehow it goes really, really wrong?"

"Ah yes," said Hattie with a nod. "I sometimes get the twins' outfits the wrong way round. It bothers me all day when I do that."

"Right," I said, with a sideways glance at Hattie. "Yes. Well this might be a little bit worse than two Smiley Tots wearing the wrong clothes."

"No!"

"Yes."

"I can't believe it."

"Believe this."

I ushered Hattie into the car, climbed in after her and swiped to pay. "Jaffle Park," I told the car. "Helberg has taken all of my money," I said to Hattie.

"Taken?"

"Charged me."

"For what?"

"Renting out that apartment upstairs."

Hattie frowned and then looked worried. "Is it the Smiley Tots? I know you say there's too many and I know you're wrong but if it's bothering you that much..."

"I'm not moving out," I said.

"But he charged you to rent the apartment."

"All my money. And I need to pay him even more or he's going to evict me."

"Why would he do that?" asked Hattie, horrified.

"He says that the water damage was my fault but he was being kind to me because he likes me and I'm a..." I made a surreptitious glance at my own backside.

"A what?" said Hattie.

"I have no idea!"

The car made an angry beep and slowed. "Insufficient funds to access optimal route," it said. The slip road for the pay-per-metre was a short distance ahead and closed off to us.

"All my money," I sighed. "Hattie?"

Hattie blushed. "The new Smiley Tot has wiped me out."

The car sped up, and took a different turning. "Rerouting on legacy roads."

We were soon in among the suburban grid of the city, away from the business parks, residential zones and shopping malls we were familiar with. The premium pay-per-metre roads were smooth and tidy but the legacy routes were unmaintained and littered with potholes and obstacles. The car twitched from side to side, finding the best path through the debris.

"You should tell him it's not your fault," said Hattie. "Tell him."

"I did tell him, but he says I'm liable because I broke in to that apartment."

Hattie stared at the floor. "You can't be evicted. You just can't."

I threaded my arm through my friend's. "I'll think of something. Don't let's dwell on it."

The car's progress through back streets, cut throughs and unmonitored intersections was slow; then we came upon a much more serious blockage. Our car stopped.

"What is it?" said Hattie.

"There is traffic ahead," said the car. It had pulled up behind another vehicle.

"That's strange," said Hattie, "I've never seen a car on its side before. It looks wrong."

I shook my head. There was indeed a car on its side, and something that looked like a huge wheeled rubbish dumpster next to it, which had possibly knocked the car over. They looked like they had been there a very long time. There was no one in the car.

"Can we go round?" I said.

"There is traffic ahead," repeated the car.

"Yes, but I don't think that car is going anywhere."

"It is not parked," said the car.

"No, it's something else," I said.

The car and dumpster blocked the entire road; there was no way Hattie or I could move them.

"We could call an engineer."

"Running self-diagnostics," said the car. *"No problems found. Engineer not necessary."*

"No, but this is clearly an incident. Can we report it?"

"You have requested to create a report," said the car smoothly. *"This option is not valid for legacy routes without specific travel insurance."*

"We don't have travel insurance," I said.

"You have insufficient funds for travel insurance," said the car.

"I know!"

"At this rate, it would be quicker to walk," said Hattie.

I got out the car and looked at the turned over vehicle.

"I didn't mean we *should* walk," said Hattie. "The car will work it out."

The car whirred. *"There is traffic ahead. It will add unknown time to your journey."*

"We can't stay here," I said.

Hattie got out to look at the car blocking the road.

"If you are unable to proceed, please choose another destination or leave the vehicle," said the car. *"You have chosen to leave the vehicle."*

The doors swung shut. I tried to stop it but the car was nippy and was already driving off, back the way it had come. It bounced in a pothole in what seemed to be inordinate haste to get away.

"Well that was a bit rude," said Hattie.

"It's not all that far," I said, jipping a route-finder. "We can walk."

I peered over the top of the overturned car. As my fingers touched it, the door sprang open.

"Where would you like to go?" said the car.

"We're fine, thanks," I said. "It must be this way," I said to Hattie.

We walked on along the road. At the next junction, the area changed significantly. The houses here were large, much larger than the ones we'd seen previously. There were houses here which were easily ten times the size of our apartment. I wondered how many people lived in each one.

"I wonder how they get about if the roads are blocked like this?" said Hattie.

As if in answer to her question a commuter drone rose from the back of one of the houses.

"Ooh, no, I don't fancy one of those," said Hattie.

"They're perfectly safe," I said.

"I'm sure they are," said Hattie. "But still..."

My attention was taken by the bits of land in front of the houses. They were like the sculpted greenery around Jaffle Park except there was more than just grass and trees.

"The plants are so tall," I said, pointing. "Why would you let things get tall like that?"

"Trees are tall," said Hattie.

"Yes, but trees are important. Those things, the brightly coloured things—"

"Flowers."

"Right. Flowers. They're everywhere. Just make it look untidy."

"I like grass," said Hattie.

"You can sit on grass," I agreed.

"Exactly. Those things are definitely *not* grass. Maybe this is what happens when gardeners don't come and, you know, garden."

"I don't know," I said slowly. "There's grass by these houses as well. It looks as if those tall things are supposed to be there. Someone's coming out of that house," I added in a whisper.

"Why are you whispering again?" asked Hattie.

I didn't know why, but there was something about the woman that made me feel I didn't belong. It should have been the woman who looked out of place – her clothes were unnecessarily bright and didn't seem to cover enough of her to be of any practical use – but, no, it was me who felt I was in the wrong place.

"I said—" repeated Hattie. I pressed my finger to her lips for silence. It did nothing to dampen the volume of Hattie's voice. "'Y are 'e 'iskering?" she demanded, loud enough to be heard in the next street.

"Can I help you?" asked the woman as she strolled down the path between the strange tall plants.

Hattie and I exchanged sideways glances, both of us startled by the animal that the woman had at her side.

"We're just walking to work," I said, and then had to ask. "Is that a dog?"

The woman took a sip of golden liquid from the heavy glass tumbler in her hand and glanced across at the property next door. Another woman in a broad floppy hat and equally colourful clothing was watching through the high metal railings.

"Every home should have one. Lovely creatures. Very loyal." She looked at us over the rim of her glass. "Knows its place."

I still didn't understand. I knew what dogs were – a little jipping of my Jaffle Port told me this heavy and hairy creature was a golden retriever – but what was it doing here? Why was it standing quite happily besides this woman and why was she tolerating it? Even now it was squatting at the side of the path and – I recoiled – defecating onto the ground.

"Oh wait, I know! I know!" exclaimed Hattie. "You're blind, aren't you?"

"What?" said the woman.

Hattie turned to me. "In the old days, before they fixed blindness, dogs helped blind people."

I wasn't sure the woman was blind; she was staring straight at Hattie. She reached out, took my sleeve between a thumb and finger and gave it a little rub. Her face pulled into a strange expression. It was like a smile. Almost a smile, but not quite. "Genuine polyester. You must be so proud," she drawled.

"Proud?" I said.

"Jaffle Tech standard issue."

"Yes," I said. "What are you wearing?"

The woman's attire was complicated. The colours were bright in the same way as the garden. The sleeves of the dress were very thin, so I could see the woman's arms. The neckline of her top ran down to the top of her stomach. A split in the side of the flowing skirts went right up to her waist so that her long legs were utterly exposed.

She saw me looking and gave her hips a playful wiggle. "It's Chanel, darling."

"You're wasting your breath, Claire," called the woman in the floppy hat next door. "They don't even know what that is."

"It's a French fashion house," I said, discreetly jipping so I could look it up. I understood the word *house*, but not much more. I glanced at the house behind us, hoping for a clue as to what *French* and *fashion* might be.

"I've got it!" said Hattie. "Do you need the colours to be so bright because you can't see where your clothes are otherwise?" She gave an experimental wave in front of the woman's face.

"I wear colours because they suit my personality," said the woman. "Some of us can afford a personality." The woman, Claire, looked them up and down. "I expect the two of you simply eat beans and watch the Smiley channel when you get home."

"Of course we do," I said, smiling at the strange question. What else was there?

Claire smiled widely at that and made a strange coughing sound. The dog stopped sniffing its own poop on the ground and looked up at her. The woman in the floppy hat put her hand to her mouth to hide her own smile.

"Oh darlings," said Claire, "you have no idea how fucked-up you are, do you? Absolutely no idea."

I wasn't sure what that meant, but I smiled at the woman. "Will we get to Jaffle Park if we carry on this way?" I asked, pointing down the road.

"Yes, you will," said Claire and took another gulp of her drink. "But you can do me a favour first."

"Yes?"

She pointed at the brown pile of dog poop on the path. "There's a refuse bin a hundred metres down the road. Can you put that in the bin?"

"That?" said Hattie.

Claire looked at her levelly. "Yes. Pick it up, take it with you and put it in the bin."

"But it's..."

"I've been good enough to talk to you and tell you where to go. You owe me."

"Do we?" I said.

"It's your place to do as you're told." Claire poked Hattie in the shoulder. "You. Pick it up. With your hands."

"With...?"

The woman sighed, suddenly tired and irritable. "Do I need to report this to your boss?"

Neither of us wanted that. We didn't want to get into trouble at work and any negative interactions, in or out of work, could impact on our Jaffle ratings.

Hattie knelt quickly, scooped up the soft pile in her cupped hands. "Happy to help," she said, recoiling at the smell as she did.

The woman on the next property hooted with surprise and apparent delight.

Claire pointed firmly down the road, swilling but not spilling the drink in her hand.

"That way. Refuse bin. Or take it with you as a gift. I don't care. But you're not to come this way again. We simply can't have you trailing up and down here with your vacant little faces mooning at the houses, can we?"

"No, of course not," I said, completely out of my depth, but wanting to be polite. I hesitated as I made to go, unsure if I had been dismissed.

"And say thank you," said Claire.

"Thank you," I said.

"Yes. Thank you," said Hattie and even bobbed a little curtsey, with the steaming dog mess in her hands. The golden retriever wagged its tail. The woman, Claire, made the oddest barking sound, like she was really really happy. The woman next door joined in with a sort of loud, rhythmic panting.

Hattie looked deeply unhappy at having to carry the smelly poop in her hands but she swallowed her discomfort and looked back at the woman.

"Do you want us to show you the way back to your house, or will the dog do that?" she asked.

5

Being late for work was unfortunate. Being late for work and having dog poo on her hands was almost too much for Hattie. Anxiety radiated from her, and she made occasional meeping sounds.

I touched her lightly on the shoulder as we approached the door to reception. "It's going to be fine."

"Don't touch me! You'll get it on you as well!" Hattie wailed.

I recoiled. I was a long way from Hattie's hands, but perhaps really, really dirty things could transfer their dirtiness across a wider gap? Hattie was so fanatical about cleanliness, she was sure to be right. If the smell was anything to go by, I would need to be across the street to be completely safe.

"Right, we'll go in and get you straight to the toilets. You can wash your hands there."

"No, wait!" said Hattie. "You can't touch the door with

your hands! You've touched me. If you touch the door then every person that comes in after us will get dog poo on them."

"Oh," I said. I looked at the door. It wasn't the sort of door I could simply push with I shoulder. I needed to jip the door and then press a button. Perhaps I could gain the attention of the receptionists inside?

"Hello!" I called through the glass, waving. The two receptionists were concentrating on their heads-up displays and failed to see us. I tried again, louder this time.

"HELLO! PLEASE LET US IN!" I waved frantically, trying to ignore Hattie whose meeping had escalated into a continuous keening.

One of the receptionists looked over. She was immaculate in her white admin staff tunic. She responded to my wave with a tentative wave of her own and a look of confusion. I performed an exaggerated mime, trying to indicate that I was unable to open the door and pleading for the receptionist to open it for her. The receptionist slid down from her stool and walked over. She cracked open the door and stood in the gap.

"Can I help you?"

"We work here. We need to come in but we don't want to touch the door," I said.

She looked at me and then at Hattie, whose face was crumpled in despair.

"You don't want to touch the door."

"No, we'll make it dirty. We had a sort of accident," I said.

Hattie held up a poo-smeared hand.

The receptionist stepped sharply backwards, sniffed the

air and then stared at the two of us with fresh horror. "Oh no. Can't you control your bodily functions."

"No, no. Not that sort of accident," I said. "It's not human poo, it's dog poo."

"Dog?"

"And I don't even think the woman was blind," said Hattie.

"We accidentally touched some dog poo," I said. "We need to wash our hands?"

The receptionist pulled a face. "How does that even happen? No, you've put me right off my beans. Come in."

Hattie and I trooped in behind her as she held the main door and then the door to the toilets. After a moment's thought, she stepped inside and turned on a tap.

"There. Now just make sure you do a thorough job and *don't*..." She shuddered. "Just clean it up."

Hattie sighed with relief as she lathered up and rinsed away the filth from her hands. "Oh I don't think I can remember having such nasty stuff on my hands," she said. "The smell!"

I used lots of soap and made sure I washed right up my arms. The further I washed, the further I wanted to wash. "Do you remember that video we had to watch about the correct way to wash our hands?" I asked Hattie.

"Oh yes, that was a really good one," said Hattie, brightening. "I always do it exactly as they showed us." She repeated the words from the video. "*Left on top, right on top, turn over and interlace the fingers on each side. Rinse and do a nail scrub.*"

I was fairly certain that Hattie was word perfect. I wasn't surprised. "What's that voice you're doing?" I asked.

"That's my posh but friendly narrator man voice," said Hattie. "The kind who puts deep and deliberate ... *pauses* in the middle of sentences for effect."

"That's a good voice."

"It's..." She paused momentarily as she jipped her Jaffle Port. "It's avuncular."

"That ... *is* a good word," I said in my best avuncular voice.

"Indeed," said Hattie in her very avuncular voice, "Avuncular is one of the ... *best* words."

I smiled and continued with the routine myself. I did it once more, remembering the stench, and afraid it would taint me for the rest of the day.

We both dried themselves. I took a tentative sniff. "I can only smell soap now. I think it's all gone."

"Are you sure?" Hattie asked, snorting up great lungfuls of air as I opened the door back out to reception.

The receptionist stared at us. I felt compelled to go and present myself. I held up my hands, and nudged Hattie to do the same. "All better now." I dropped my hands. The receptionist said nothing so I pressed on, feeling that I needed to make it clear that they were model employees, not filth-smeared incompetents.

"We're experts at ... *cleaning* up," I said in a deeply avuncular and pause-laden voice. "We're ... *highly* trained. No clean-up was ever ... *more* thorough."

A hand clapped on my shoulder from behind. "You're on the efficiency leader-board too, I see."

I turned to see who it was. I faced a tall man with cropped hair.

The receptionist smiled. "Henderson, sir."

I had seen the man around at times, sweeping through the lobby and such, but didn't know who he was. Someone high up in another department, I guessed.

"Is this the one?" he asked the receptionist, pointing at me.

"I don't know, sir," the receptionist replied.

"Clean-up?" he said to me.

"I do," I said.

"Good. With me." He turned to the receptionist. "You. Let – ah, Alice's section head know that she's popping up to do a job on the exec floor and she'll be back later."

"What about me?" asked Hattie.

"What about you?" said Henderson as he led me away to the bank of elevators.

I turned and waved a brief goodbye to Hattie as the doors closed.

I HAD no clue exactly why I was in the elevator with this Henderson. As we rode up, I surreptitiously jipped in the company directory.

Jethro Henderson was Jaffle Tech's Chief Technical Officer. I had to look that up too and when I did, I was impressed. He supervised the company's engineering department and was one of the half dozen people who ran the company – the whole worldwide company! – on behalf of the board of directors and the CEO.

And he was taking me right to the top. The elevator was heading to the top floor, the realm of top bosses and execs that I never got to mingle with.

"I don't want any delays to the project," said Henderson.

"No delays," I said. "What project?"

"The demand that we'll create with Operation Sunrise will increase revenues across all of our main streams. Consumers, even reticent ones, will buy into it. Jaffle Tech gives them access to the world. They owe *us* everything. We've made gods of humankind."

"Right. Gods."

"Wait, no. We can't afford to deliver late, do you understand?"

"No, I'm afraid I don't," I said.

"What? Oh no, just someone standing nearby who thinks I'm talking to them. Now listen, I want a daily update report on this. Make sure that any blockers get escalated directly to me. Is that clear?"

Henderson made a gesture to end the call moments after I realised that he hadn't been talking to me at all. I opened her mouth to explain, but Henderson silenced me with a wave of his hand and then the elevator arrived and he ushered me out. I had never been to the exec floor and it was startlingly different to the other floors. The carpet was very thick. It was so thick that I wondered briefly whether Levi would consider it a trip hazard. There were glass cases containing exhibits. I stepped across to look at one. There was a small piece of electronic circuitry with a label next to it.

2023: The first Jaffle interfaces used on human subjects exposed them to the sensory input from the eyes of a fly. This programme was closed down when subjects exhibited symptoms of PTSD.

"What's PTSD?" I asked, but Henderson had already swept away down the corridor.

"It's a simple clean-up," said Henderson. "You do your regular sweep and clean and then get out, got it?"

I looked at him. He gave me a curt glance. "Are you talking to me this time?" I asked.

He stopped outside a door. "Who else would I be talking to?"

"Um."

"In here. Make sure you do a good job."

"Right."

"Naturally, if you don't, you will be fired."

"Okay."

I looked at the door.

Rufus Jaffle

"Oh wow, he's got the same name as the company," I said, turning to Henderson. He was already halfway down the corridor, speaking urgently to someone on another call. He walked like a man who had a lot of urgent calls to make.

I looked back at the door and knocked gently.

"Yo!" called a voice within.

I entered the room. It was much larger than I'd expected. If this room was on my floor it would contain a hundred people in cubicles. There was a wall entirely composed of glass doors and beyond that a wide balcony on which a sleek commuter drone had been parked. The room had strange colourful hangings on the wall, it was carpeted even more thickly than the corridor, and the furniture was big and chunky. The desk was larger than the whole canteen servery, and yet it looked as though it was designed for just one person. The person in question was lying back in a chair with his feet on the desk, his long hair trailing back across the headrest. There was a graze and fading bruise above his eyebrow, as though he had recently been in an accident.

I was, however, distracted by his clothes. Henderson had been wearing a suit. Suits were not something I came across very often – tunics, tabards and coveralls were the clothes of the regular worker – but I had seen people wearing suits. Rufus Jaffle wore something that *looked* like a suit, but the trousers were too short. They were so short that I could see his hairy legs up to his knees. Instead of shoes, he wore footwear that looked like the bottom part of a shoe held on with a couple of thin straps. Levi would have something to say about those.

"I'm Alice Tennerman. Henderson sent me," I said.

"Awesome! Good old, Jethro," said Jaffle. "Take a seat, Alice. Can I get you a drink?"

"Um."

"A drink?" he repeated.

"A drink would be lovely," I said politely.

"Power smoothie, probiotic milkshake or Himalayan herb detox?"

I played back what I'd just heard in my mind. I had no idea what those things were, even after a brief jip with my

Jaffle Port. "I'll have whatever you're having, thank you."

"Awesome." He gestured to open a call. "Florence, can I get two Himalayan herb detoxes please? Then make sure I'm not disturbed for an hour, will you?"

A woman appeared through a door that I hadn't even realised was there. She placed a tray on the desk and left, smiling at Jaffle.

"Florence, my secretary is an absolute diamond," said Jaffle. "I call her my secretary. She's actually a European princess. I picked her up in Cremona at an IFPA gala event for sea turtles or something." He looked suddenly and deeply puzzled. "Or is her name Cremona and I met her in Florence?"

"I ... I don't know," I said.

He waved to open a call. "Florence. Where did we meet? Uh-huh. And your name? Uh-huh." He killed the call.

"Milan, it turns out," he said, not making it clear if that was the woman's name or where they met. "Cool. Now let me talk you through the tea. I think it would really help if our chakras were aligned before we start the procedure."

"Procedure, yes," I said. I looked around, wondering if there was anything obvious that needed cleaning up. Dog poo, for example.

"First of all," he said, "the herbs are blended specifically for each person's unique earthly alignment. What's your date of birth, Alice?"

"Twentieth of January, twenty thirty-seven," I said.

"I'll just work out your blend." He cocked his head as he studied his heads-up display and then spooned dried leaves from a rack of small containers that were on the tray into a pot.

He began to sing a soft mostly tuneless song.

"Mixing and mystery are part of their history. It's the tea le-e-e-aves. The te-e-ea leaves, yeah?"

He poured hot water from a tall jug into the pot. "Now for mine," he said and repeated the routine, although the leaves came from different pots and the song had a different tune, or at least lacked a tune in a different way.

"Good," he said. "You should know that all of the herbs are harvested at the break of day, when their essence is considered to be purest. Now, we will steep the herbs to the sound of the singing bowl."

He picked up a stumpy tool and stirred it inside a metal bowl on the tray. To my amazement the bowl started to make a loud noise. It sounded more than a little like being at home in the kitchen and hearing Hattie in the shower when she started singing the Smiley theme tune. Like that but really loud.

Jaffle closed his eyes and leaned back as he continued to make the bowl sing. I wasn't sure if I was supposed to join in. Instead I silently looked him up. I tried to keep my composure when the results popped up. The very top of Jaffle Tech was a bit complicated. There was a board of directors and a CEO and then a cluster of people around the CEO. The Jaffles themselves, the Jaffle family, including one Rufus Jaffle, son of the company founder. This man with the singing bowl and the secretary who might have been called Florence or Cremona or Milan, and whom he had picked up in one of those places, pretty much owned the company, or at least owned as much of the company as any one person did. He was one of the superrich. International philanthropist, advocate of space exploration, honorary president of the International Federation for the Protection of Animals. He was personally the sixth richest person on planet Earth. Maybe that explained the suit-like shorts. Maybe all superrich people wore suit shorts.

Rufus Jaffle opened his eyes again. "Blissful sound, isn't it?"

I nodded. "Er, the procedure you mentioned?"

"Old Hendo didn't explain?" asked Jaffle. "That's why you have some light brown in your aura. It denotes confusion. Come child, sip your tea and I will explain."

He pressed the tiny delicate bowl into my hands, carefully folding the fingers of both of my hands around it. I realised this was because the cup had no handle. How odd.

He picked up his own cup with the same gesture, and raised it to his mouth. It seemed like a very inefficient way to have a drink, but I copied his movements.

"So Alice, I asked Jethro to find me someone to help me with a brain tech issue. I need a delicate job to be done, and apparently you're just the person I need."

"Oh yes, of course," I said, delighted to grasp onto something I understood. *That* kind of clean-up. That made sense. "I work in brain tech. Normally we do this on a call."

"Yes, I guess you do, but listen and be guided by your inner voice, Alice." He cupped an ear. "Can you hear it?" I strained my ears but heard nothing special. "I really appreciate your attending in person," he said. "It will be a holistic experience, I can already feel it, can't you? I need to make sure that this procedure is handled discreetly. It's important to me that this is not logged on the system. The whole world can't know that one of the heads of Jaffle has a brain virus now, can they?"

Brain virus? I'd heard of the concept of a brain virus, but mostly it was used as a cautionary tale or a hypothetical concept designed to promote healthy practices with backups and system flushes. A portion of everyone's brain was taken up with housekeeping software to counteract such a possibility.

"Are you sure you have a virus?" I asked. "Where could you have got it from?"

"Oh, I'm sure," he said. "I believe I got it from uploading an unofficial hack."

I stared. "You're a Jaffle and you put unauthorised software into your brain?"

"Wild, isn't it?" he said with a small smile. "I wanted to be at one with a blue whale."

"A blue—?"

"Whale, yes." He made a long and low keening sound. "It's been a long-term ambition of mine. I'm all about the animals. I'm like the chief spokesperson for IFPA."

"The animal charity."

"Right on, and I heard a rumour that someone had a download. Plugs you right into the live-feed of a whale brain. I mean, our guys in the labs are always working on new things, but this one just didn't ever seem to make it to the top of the list. Something about low customer value and high production costs, if you can believe that? Anyway, when this guy claims to have it right there on a plate for me, what else am I gonna do, right?"

He suddenly pressed himself against a square blue wall hanging.

"Can you imagine that?" he said, and made the keening, honking sound again.

I nodded, although I was now very uncertain that I had understood correctly. "You wanted to know some more about blue whales?" she asked.

"No, no, no. I wanted to *be at one* with a blue whale. I wanted to swim with it, hear it call to other whales and listen to their reply. I wanted to understand what it is to be a blue whale."

"Wow," I said. "How... interesting. And did you?"

"Oh man, I did. It was the best. These magnificent creatures have such sights to show us, and such things to teach us. It was truly humbling." He paused, staring at the ceiling in recollection. "But then I got the virus. It was sort of trippy and cool at first, but it's definitely affecting my chakras and I need it gone."

"And when you say it's affecting your chakras, you mean – what exactly?" I prompted.

"Oh the usual. I feel unsatisfied with my life, as if I don't know what to do with myself, and I don't seem to be able to delete or re-edit any of my brain content. It's almost always a blocked chakra when that happens." He nodded. "I expect everyone gets the same from time to time. I also had really bad food poisoning, but I'm pretty sure that was from when I went out in the ocean to strain krill through my teeth."

"Strain krill through your teeth." I echoed with a baffled nod, resolving to look it up later.

"So, I want to get rid of the virus. Oh, and delete a couple of embarrassing memories."

"And to get rid of the virus, we're going to do what, exactly?"

"Hey Alice, I'm going to bow to your experience here. You're the clean-up guru."

"We could start with defragmentation and deep clean."

"Whatever's going to work. I gotta admit, I don't really understand all of the terminology like clearing down caches and yadda yadda. Can we start soon? I'll be fully aligned with my magnetic north at nine thirty. It would be a really good time."

I turned the phrase *clean-up guru* over a couple of times and wondered if I was here because I had declared my competence at hand washing. No matter, it was much too late to back out now. I checked the time. It was a few minutes before nine thirty.

"Right," I said briskly, forming a plan as I went. "The best thing will be if we take all your valuable content, copy it over to a fresh facility where it will be cleared of any contagions or malware and then we do a general scrub and then re-apply each sector, optimising storage and scanning for defects as we go."

"And the non-techy version?"

"We'll upload everything to the cloud, wipe clean and then copy it back a bit at a time."

"Uh, gonna have to stop you right there, Alice. We can't use the cloud. Remember, this must be off the record. I'm not taking my brain down to the local laundromat. You'll need to think of something else."

"Oh." The standard operating procedure was ingrained in me, and it seemed very wrong to deviate from it, but this was Jaffle himself. It was his company who had set the operating procedure, so presumably he could override it if he wanted to. I wondered what alternatives there might be. "I guess we could use local storage," I mused, "although most of the high capacity devices need to be checked out of stock, so we couldn't do that. How about using organic storage from another source?"

"You mean another person's brain?" Jaffle asked.

"Yes. A family member or someone you trust, perhaps?"

"Ooh, Alice, see my aura? Can you see it?" he asked, waving his hands and rolling his eyes.

"No," I said, "I'm not even sure what an aura is, Jaffle."

"Call me Rufus, please, won't you? Well, Alice, you don't need to be able to see my aura to know that it's *totally* stressing out at the idea of involving a family member, ya hear me? Paris would kill me."

That seemed a bit extreme, a whole city trying to kill him. Unless Paris was the name of another of his secretaries.

"We have to keep this just between the two of us," he said and then gasped. "Here's an idea! Why don't we use your brain?"

"My brain? I—"

"You I said it should be someone I trust." He came down on one knee in front of me, flicked his long hair out of his face and clasped my hands. "I trust you, Alice."

I couldn't think of a reason why not. I could take myself

offline for a short while so that I had all of my capacity at my disposal. I ran through the steps in my mind and decided that the whole thing would take around thirty minutes. I'd be back at my desk in plenty of time for the mid-morning peak call time, and then lunch with Hattie.

"Sure." I smiled at him and went into my best customer service mode as I mentally worked through the preparations. "Of course we can do that. Now I'm going to switch us both to operate only locally and then I'll jip an access request to your Jaffle Port. Just make yourself comfy and I'll take it from there."

Rufus beamed at me, jumped back in his chair and reclined it further, until all I could see were his dangling legs. I started to go through the protocols to make a full backup but redirecting the traffic to my own brain when Rufus sat up suddenly in shock.

"If you copy my brain," he said, "will you become me?"

"No."

"And I become you?"

"No."

"Cos if, you know..." He gave me an oddly hungry look and held his hands out over his chest as though supporting a pair of breast. "We could..."

"It doesn't work like that, Rufus," I said. "It's done with compressed data squirts and—" I sighed. "Let me show you."

There was open projection equipment in the room. I cast up some images and copies of our live brain data as a holographic image in front of us. "This is your brain," I said.

"Cool. It's big, isn't it?"

"It's not actual size."

"In the physical world, right. Spiritually though..."

"And this is your Jaffle Port." A small patch was highlighted. "This gives you direct access to worldwide data and communications. It also organises redundant synaptic pathways and repurposes them for additional processing and storage."

"More synaptic connections in the brain than stars in the universe," said Rufus, dreamily.

"That's what they say," I said. "You have an astonishing capacity for data storage. Jaffle Tech take up some of that spare brain power with basic software, keeping everything clean and safe. If you're on Jaffle Standard, like me – which, of course, you're not – then some of the rest is utilised by outside systems, whether that's analysing astronomical data, studying new genetic material or just keeping the trains running on time."

I looked at our two brains. How underutilised Rufus's was! How much of it was given over to natural processes that I didn't possess but which I managed to function perfectly well without. Compared to my super-efficient brain that was both running my body and keeping the world around us functioning, his was a dull wasteland, undeveloped.

"Your personal storage," I said, "can be seen in these clusters. Here and here and so on. We can compress that data when we copy it across."

I set up the entire sequence to run automatically, just in case there was a problem with overflow, but the scans I ran indicated there was plenty of capacity for Rufus's backup.

"Right. I think we're about set. Are we certain that we won't be interrupted while we're doing this?" I asked.

"Absolutely sure. Now can I show you how to recline your own chair, Alice? Perhaps I can massage a little lavender oil into your temples to assist you into total relaxation?"

"I'm fine thanks. Are you ready, sir?"

"Rufus."

"Rufus."

"Ready when you are."

I started the sequence. I didn't expect to have any awareness of what was taking place. Most of the time my unused brain capacity was able to undertake tasks entirely without my knowledge, but this time I was aware of a faint pressure from inside my head. Perhaps it was a result of doing the transfer locally, which used a much faster communication protocol.

"I feel funny," said Rufus.

"It's fine," I said and then a strange feeling came over me. I was flying, yet sat completely still.

6

I was in a plush, well-appointed flying drone, accompanied by a pair of stunningly pretty girls. They both looked very alike, with long blonde hair and oddly bland features.

I had the strangest sensation of seeing the world through someone else's eyes. Where was I? I looked down at my clothes and a suspicion grew in my mind. I was Rufus.

'Am I Rufus?' I wanted to say, but the words wouldn't come. This wasn't my body to control, it was Rufus's. Was this one of Rufus Jaffle's memories? That would mean that I wasn't an active participant. All I could do was sit back and observe. The world beyond the window of the drone was mostly composed of wide sea and beautiful sunset. I would have wanted to observe the view more but Rufus's attention was definitely on the young women.

Did I know the names of these girls? Rufus surely did. If I was in his memory I would have the same knowledge. I had a sense that one was called TayTay and one was called MiMi but I didn't know which one was which. For that reason, Rufus addressed them in his uniquely vague style.

"Babe," he drawled. "You know your aura fascinates me so much. It's got that blossoming, burgeoning thing going on. I want to reach out and touch it."

Rufus did reach out and touch. It didn't stop at the aura. I observed Rufus's muddled eyesight imparted a hazy blurring around the edges of everything, not just the girls. Did Rufus keep talking about auras because of an uncorrected vision problem? His hands groped across the two girls. Those hands weren't seeking an aura, they were seeking out breasts. I gasped at the overwhelming feeling of desire that consumed Rufus. There was titillation at the sight of their low-cut dresses, but this driving lust was fuelled by something else. It was the same thing which had bent his eyesight all out of shape. I looked at the white powder dusting his knees as he sat in the drone. Cocaine. The word came to me from nowhere. It was cocaine that Rufus had been taking. And as the knowledge came to me so did a cascade of other concepts – the house servant who procured it for him, his opinions on the various suppliers they'd use, fleeting images of his fantasies about getting 'down and dirty' with that house servant.

Rufus had taken a lot of cocaine too. Both of the girls seemed happy for Rufus to run his hands across their bodies. In fact it seemed to me that they were positively encouraging it.

"Hey babes!" said Rufus. "Your auras are going wild.

What say we throw caution to the wind and see whether our chakras align if we all get naked?"

"We're nearly there Rufus!" commented one of the girls, looking out of the window.

I followed Rufus's downward gaze and saw a huge house with many cars and drones parked outside. If it was any indication of how many people were inside this was a huge party. They flew over the roof from the ocean, and saw partygoers thronging the beach.

"Buzzing!" said one of the girls in excitement.

As I sifted through Rufus's memory I was stunned to realise that this wasn't all that special for him. The houses here were smaller than his own, but nevertheless he enjoyed a party as much as the next person and he was looking forward to a bonfire on the beach.

It was the sort of thing that the corporate world just couldn't offer. Cocktail receptions and charity galas were all very well but a bonfire on the beach was so much more— I watched his drug-funnelled mind grasp for the right word ... authentic.

"Touching down," said the drone.

On the ground, the three of us walked into a cool hallway, lined with marble. Trays of drinks and nibbles were offered by slack-eyed servants. These people were operating on Jaffle Lite, I thought, then, tapping into Rufus' knowledge, realised no. Not just Jaffle Lite but a special variant which was part of their terms of employment. Rufus ignored the food, seeking out a tray lined with cocaine. As he snorted the drug, I felt the jolt as it hit his system. There was a rush of clarity and euphoria. His vision was much clearer, and yet the people in the room still had pink, blurry edges. Were those actually auras, or was I seeing a second-hand hallucination? Being inside Rufus Jaffle's mind was bizarre.

"Coming to the beach Rufus?" TayTay (or MiMi) asked. They were completely identical now. Bland faces, huge breasts and pneumatic bottoms. I realised I was looking through Rufus's cocaine goggles. The girls probably weren't even alike in real life, but it was clear to me Rufus really wasn't interested in their faces.

A huge grey-blue shape swam across my vision, gliding through a sky that simply wasn't big enough to contain it. It turned and looked at me with a benevolent, ancient eye.

I'm aaaaaaa whaaaaaaaaaaaaale, it sang.

I tried to ignore it and forced myself back into Rufus's memory. He and the girls were somewhere else now, on a balcony overlooking the beach. Near-naked men and women played volleyball on the sand.

"You girls like to play?" Rufus asked TayTay and MiMi.

"Not me," said TayTay with a smile. "Mud-wrestling's more my thing, but I'm on a rest day."

"Mmmm," said Rufus, his inner vision clogged with panting, mud-covered babes. "We could maybe find somewhere to, you know, run you through your paces?"

Someone shouted from the doorway of the house.

"Did he just call my name?" Rufus asked.

"It sure sounded like it," said TayTay.

Aliiiiice, woooould yoooou like to beeeeee aaaaa whaaaaaaaaale? sang the blue whale, crashing into my memory.

No, thank you, I thought as hard as I could.

There was an expression of infinite sadness in the whale's eye that pulled at my emotions. It flicked and turned.

It's fuuuun beeeing aaaaa whaaaaaaaaaaaaaaale.

I pushed myself away and I was somewhere new again. Time moved differently in memories. I (or rather Rufus) was in an underground space with TayTay and MiMi. Rufus was staring at a kangaroo. I was surprised. So was Rufus.

I had no personal experience of kangaroos, had never seen one outside of school educational download. I had no idea kangaroos were so large, and I could see that Rufus was also impressed by their size. In fact, he knew barely more about them than I did. For a man who had so many more opportunities for experience and exploration than me, he knew surprisingly little.

One of the girls was running her hands through its fur.

"Ooh, it's rough!" she squealed, and then shrank back as the kangaroo turned to look.

It looked muscular and fierce, although I wondered how much that perception was warped by Rufus's memory. It gave off a powerful animal stink that did not disgust me but fascinated me. It was more ... more real than anything I had experienced in my life. That couldn't possibly be true but, in Rufus's memories, through his drugged perception filter, I was fixated by the powerful realness of this creature.

"Have you ever heard of the ancient martial art of Maglev?" said Rufus.

They shook their heads.

"Few have," he said, lifting his hands and making a slow chopping movement. "Advanced practitioners must exercise restraint and secrecy."

They nodded, hanging on his every word.

"Maybe I could show you girls some moves? It could really help with your mud-wrestling. Personal development is something I'm always keen to help with." He lifted his arms and draped them casually over each girl's shoulder and slipped his fingers inside their clothes. A nipple stiffened against both sets of fingers and he smiled, feeling unstoppable.

The blue whale swooped in and did the whale equivalent of a handbrake turn.

I haaave aaaaaaaaaa taaaaaaaaaaaaaaaail! it sang.

Go away! I thought.

I'm aaaaa whaaaaaaaaaaale with aaa taaaaaaaaaaaaaail!

It was a very persistent whale.

I need to see what's happening, I told it.

Yooooou can haaave aaa taaaaaaaaaaaaaaail tooooooo, it sang.

No, I told it.

There was a near seamless splice in the memory. I knew that at least a day had elapsed.

I still saw the world through Rufus's, but now he was trussed up in a hospital bed, with straps, tubes and pipes disappearing under the blanket. Several people sat on chairs at the side of the bed. His head hurt.

"Hey, honey," said Rufus to the woman who sat closest. I knew from Rufus's memory this was his fiancée, Paris. "Guess who's got himself a tiny problemo?"

Her face collapsed into tears. "I was so worried about you, Rufie! You looked so small and helpless when you were unconscious."

Jethro Henderson, CTO of Jaffle Tech, sat next to her.

"Yes, we've made sure that Paris is up to date with the details of your fall." I saw him through Rufus's mind and felt Rufus's views of the man. They weren't complimentary.

Beeee aaaa whaaaaaale. Beeeee aaat peeeeeeeeeeeeace.

"Henderson, my main man," said Rufus, smiling. "You didn't need to be here."

Henderson gave him a sharp, almost military nod. "I'm glad to see you awake, sir. Paris, I'm afraid I have some dull corporate matters I need to discuss with Jaffle."

As Paris stood to go, Rufus intended to lean over and pat her on the buttocks but he didn't have the energy and simply gave her a goodbye grunt. He waited for the door to click shut.

The whale swooped in and tried to entice me with loop-the-loops and exquisite pirouettes.

"I don't think it's going to matter to the media," said Henderson. "You've got the corporate gala on the fifteenth. The *charity* gala. You need to wipe your memory of what happened last night. You have high enough access to do that personally."

"Actually, I've got this whale in my head which is making some of my functionality a bit glitchy," said Rufus.

Heeeelloooooooooooooo, said the whale.

"Fine," muttered Henderson. "Then we'll get it done back at Jaffle Tech."

"Whoa, people!" said Rufus. "Maybe I don't want to give up that memory? It was kind of cool, you know? I can be discreet. It will only be a problem if I talk about it, right?"

"With all due respect, sir, you are a security risk. In my

estimation, you will definitely talk about this in future. We must erase the memory."

Whhyyyyyyy don't yoooouuu waaaaaaaant toooo beeee aaaaa whaaaaaale? the whale sang sadly.

Because you're actually really annoying, I thought.

"Could you please authorise the project brief for the completion phase?" Henderson was saying, holding out a sheaf of papers.

I/Rufus looked at the papers but took in none of the words.

"Jaffle Tech has benevolently agreed to assist governments in the social management of the general population," explained Henderson in a patient voice. "Jaffle Tech has the largest live database of consumers and voters in the world. We are literally inside everyone's head. That's a place where the governments would love to be. This—" he stabbed at the papers "—is us taking the next step towards giving consumers what they need."

"Need or want?" said Rufus. It was reflex question; he hadn't actually understood half of what Henderson was saying.

Henderson smiled. "Wasn't Henry Ford supposed to have said that if he gave customers what they wanted, he'd be working on making a faster horse rather than cars? It's up to us to have the vision to take things forward." He sat back. "You know, I was planning on purchasing Jaffle Freedom myself."

"You?" said Rufus.

"What else am I going to spend my money on? I've got the largest apartment on the Panhandle. I've got a mansion south of the border. I should buy Jaffle Freedom. And be like you, sir."

Rufus settled back into his pillow.

Yooooou're nooo fuuuuun, sniffed the blue whale, deeply upset, and swished its tail as it turned to the depths.

I opened my eyes. Henderson and the hospital and the blue whale had gone.

However, something felt very different. I was looking up at the ceiling. It was white, but was sculpted into swirls I had never noticed before. Miniscule waves of white plaster. They were so beautiful. How had I never been aware that such exquisite form and movement were possible in a ceiling? It was like a little world of detailed beauty, a cosmos of peaks and troughs, almost unbearably wonderful.

I sat up properly.

"Whoooaaa!"

I felt the impact like a blow to my stomach. In my eyes, down my spine and – wallop! – into my stomach. The whole room was a blaze of colour! I had vaguely registered that the walls had coloured hangings upon them as I entered, but now I saw them properly. I screamed. There was a picture of a woman with a lace collar and a smiling face who bent down to touch the top of a dog's head. There was an expression on the woman's face that made me roil with strange, unknown feelings. The feelings frightened me. They felt instinctively wrong. Like feeling a cool fresh breeze blowing across your kidneys, it was simply not right.

I tried to stand up. I had to get out of this room with its terrifying walls. I lurched across the thick carpet and fell to my hands and knees. The feeling of the carpet beneath my hands made me gasp. I fell forward to bury my face in it. I didn't know why, I just had to.

"Hey Alice, are you all right?" said Rufus.

"Mmmff!" I howled into the carpet.

In my head the sound of voices, even my own voice, was *different*. The same, but different. It was like I had been to avuncular narrator training college and then had my ears upgraded to some super-duper 3D stereo quality. There were inflections and tonal differences that made my head spin as much as the colour on the walls.

"Everything ... *I* say is ... *amazing*," I gasped.

"Alice?" said Rufus.

"I'm ... *sorry*. Alice isn't ... *in* right now."

Rufus grabbed me by my shoulders and hauled me up. "Did it work? Is it gone? Have you wiped the memory?"

"The brain virus?"

"Yes. That too." His hands held me roughly, squeezing the flesh of my upper arms.

"You're ... *hurting* me," I said.

"I'm sorry," he said and automatically loosened his hold. I immediately dropped to the floor again.

"No, no..." I said. I was about to say that it was quite pleasurable but that was silly. It was pain. Pain was never nice. Pain was just pain, wasn't it? I was very confused. And frightened. Something was simply not right. My wildly darting eyes caught sight of the cups on the edge of the desk.

"The tea!" I said a little too loudly. "You put something in the tea!"

"What? No! Unless you're allergic to the soul balms and spiritual powers of Himalayan detox."

He stabbed a button on his desk. There was a *bing bong* sound.

"Florence, would you call a medic up here please, I think Alice might be having a bad trip or something."

I was still reeling from the sound of the *bing bong*. It was like nothing I'd ever heard before and I found that my vision blurred with tears in response.

"Bing bong," I repeated, but it sounded different. "Bing BONG! Oh wow, did you hear that? I can do it too. BING ... BONG!"

I rolled on the carpet and marvelled at the way the tears in my eyes made the colours in the room blur in an astonishing new way. I rolled faster, feeling the carpet under my whole body. I stretched out my arms and rolled some more, but then I crashed into the desk.

"BING BONG!"

I heard the odd barking noise that I'd heard from Claire that morning, but it was Rufus making the noise. I found my own voice joining in with the barking and it felt good to do it, so very good. I barked loud and long, rolling back the other way as I did it. I rolled faster and faster until I thumped into something that turned out to be Rufus's legs.

"Come on up now," he said. "Enough fooling around. Laughter's a great healer, but man, you're over-indulging a little now, Alice."

I kept barking, knowing that I couldn't possibly stop, even though it was beginning to hurt. I opened my eyes, realising that I'd had them squeezed shut and saw Rufus, his face contorted in a way that made me bark even louder. Was this what he meant by laughter? I was having trouble breathing now, but my attention was arrested by another picture on the wall. This one was much brighter than the other one and showed dogs again, but in a very different setting.

Breathing was no longer an option. It was out of the question when I wanted to gasp and laugh at the same time as shouting *bing bong*.

"Dogs. Playing cards."

Colours melted and spun in my eyes. I heard the sound of my own shouting and decided that it was beautiful, and was sad when the sound faded away and the room went black.

7

I woke up on a strange, hard bed. The smell was not familiar. When I opened my eyes I realised that I was in the medical room for my floor of the building. I'd only ever been in here before as part of routine medical evaluations. There was a sheet draped over me and part of the unfamiliar smell came from it. A different laundry smell. It made me hungry, so I tried to take a bite. It was a lot harder to take a bite from a sheet than I'd imagined. I worried it with my teeth and eventually succeeded in tearing a piece off. I swallowed it hungrily, but it wasn't as satisfying as it should have been. I started to chew off another piece when I heard footsteps.

A woman approached and gave me a broad smile. "Awake? Lovely."

"Can you smell that?" I asked, sniffing.

The woman ignored my question and consulted a

thermometer and blood pressure gauge. "I'm here to check you over, Alice," she said. "You fainted."

"It smells really good," I said, distracted. "Who fainted?"

"You did, perhaps from the heat. Have you been chewing this sheet?"

"No. Definitely not."

Heat? I guessed that Mr Jaffle was keen to avoid any questions relating to the unauthorised work I'd done on his brain.

"Hmmm." The woman stared at the sheet, frowning. "You have a bump on your head. Could you tell me how much it hurts, on a scale of one to ten?"

The woman was very pretty, I realised. Just below the brim of her medical cap, her eyebrows were very dark and striking, and she had big beautiful eyes. I wanted to reach out and touch them but thought that probably wasn't a good idea.

"Hurt? Not at all. Zero," I said. I knew I had to get out of there as quickly as possible. "Perhaps I should go home and have a lie down for the rest of the day?"

"Well you seem to be in good overall health, although your Jaffle Port is offline for some reason. Do you want to reset it?"

"I will."

"I think perhaps we'd better book you in for a full scan. Perhaps you're suffering from some anxiety."

"Scan?"

"Yes. You fainted. Your port is off-line. A scan for glitches might be in order." The woman looked away for a moment, consulting her heads-up display. "The day after tomorrow.

Three in the afternoon?" She smiled. Her eyes were really big. Like a blue whale's. They were so big, I thought I might cry.

"Beautiful," I sighed.

"Great. I'll book that in and send you a reminder."

"Er, yes," I said. A brain scan. I really needed one of those, to make sure I didn't have the virus. On the other hand, I really needed to get out of there, find some low stimulus environment and curl up and sleep. "Day after tomorrow. Excellent."

I got up from the bed, narrowing my eyes to avoid seeing any bright colours or the woman's own beautiful eyes. I needed to get out in one piece. More importantly, I needed to find out where that delicious smell was coming from.

I walked along the corridor from the medical room. Levi Krasnesky fell into step beside me.

"Are you following me?" I asked.

"I came down to see how you were. You weren't at your desk this morning."

"Spying on me?"

"Got to watch over my flock."

I stopped and faced him. "Flock?"

"Yabetcha." His little moustache twitched. "Gotta keep an eye on ya."

I felt a rush of strange new feelings wash over me. I thought of all the times that Levi had made me feel small. All the times he'd come up with some crazy rule that I was supposed to have broken, but most of all I thought about the mouse. Levi had killed a mouse, right in front of me when she had been trying to capture it.

It had confused me at the time, how he'd managed to accidentally repeatedly stamp on a mouse, but I saw the truth of it now and wondered why it hadn't been clear to me before. He'd done it on purpose. He had deliberately killed the mouse. There was a word for that. I had to look it up. Murder. The man had murdered a mouse!

A strong but overwhelming sound came from the bottom of my stomach.

"Grrr!" I said.

I wasn't sure why I said it, but it pulled my face into the correct shape to reflect my mood.

Levi stared at me. "What?"

"Didn't you hear me?" I said.

"What?"

"I said, you've got a fly on your head." I whacked him with my hand, straight across his face.

"Did you get it?" he asked, a look of mild shock on his face.

"No," I said and whacked him again with my other hand, swinging it right round to connect with his other cheek. "Oops, missed again. It's not part of the system. It needs dealing with. Look, it's right there on your nose!" I pulled my fist back and punched him hard.

Levi reeled backwards, clutching his bleeding nose. "Did you geddid?" he managed, wadding a tissue against the flow of blood.

"Yes, I got it that time." I started to walk away before turning back. "My mistake!" I yelled and kicked him in the shin. "Nearly! Oh, there it goes!" I punched his stomach. "There, that's better."

"'Ank oo," said Levi, staggering towards a bathroom.

I walked on, my palms and knuckles stung. Instead of upset, I felt a weird swelling sensation inside me, *here* in my chest, like a voice yelling "Yes! Yes! Go, Alice!" It was most perplexing but, more importantly, the smell that had grabbed my attention in the medical room was now an irresistible draw. It was salty, tangy and had an earthy, animal smell that should have been repellent. Instead it was a red hot wire of yearning plugged straight into my brain and hauling me in.

I followed my nose along a corridor, into a rest area where my section head, Paulette, sat with some food in her hands.

"What's that?" I asked with a nod to the delicious-smelling thing.

"It's a bacon sandwich," said Paulette. "Why aren't you at work, Alice?"

"Are you eating that bacon sandwich?"

"I am. Shouldn't you be at your desk?"

"I've been given the rest of the day off," I said. Wow. Where did that come from? It was a total untruth but it just came to me so naturally.

"Have you?" said Paulette with a frown. "By whom?"

"I want your bacon sandwich."

"Pardon?"

"Jaffle – that's Rufus Jaffle – told me to tell you that it would be fine," I said. "I was called up to his office to help him. You should have had a message from reception about that. Jethro Henderson, the CTO, asked for me personally. You can check. And now I've got the rest of the day off."

"Oh. I see."

I was dumbfounded by my new ability, and how easily accepted this alternative truth was. Yes, much of what I'd said was true but ultimately it was a deception and utterly dishonest. Instead of being afraid, I wondered whether I could push it further.

"He also said that you should give me that bacon sandwich for a job well done."

"*This* bacon sandwich?" said Paulette.

"Yes," I said firmly. "You can put it through on expenses."

"Really? That's a little odd."

"Yes. Now less chat, more bacon."

I reached over and pulled the sandwich from Paulette's hands. I stuffed it in my mouth. Fatty juices, mixed with a delicious burned taste, rolled down my throat.

"Oh, yes!" I mumbled contentedly. "This is definitely what I need."

I took another bite and chewed it joyously. Bacon was certainly much more delicious than the bed sheet that I had partially eaten.

"It seems I do have a message from Henderson," said Paulette.

"See?" I said, spraying half chewed crumbs.

"Yes, well, if the order comes from on high..."

I walked away. I didn't need conversation now that I had a bacon sandwich. It was amazing, much better than beans (red *or* blue). In fact, I decided it was the best thing that I had ever eaten. Ever. I must find out where I could get another one, and soon.

8

I knew something had happened to me in Rufus Jaffle's office. Maybe it was the tea. Maybe I'd done something wrong with the clean-up protocols. Whatever it was, I was awash with new sensations and feelings. It was like I was a screen and the volume had been turned up to maximum, along with the brightness and the contrast and loads of other settings that I didn't even yet know the names of.

Even though I knew something had clearly gone wrong and needed fixing, I felt a burning urge to explore the new sensations while I still possessed them.

I left the building and ran. I ran from Jaffle Tech and Jaffle Park. I told myself that I was running to put as much distance as possible between myself and the trouble I was possibly in at work. Truthfully, I ran because running felt like the right thing to do. The warm air brushed my face. The tug of forces and energy in my limbs. The slap of my shoes on the ground.

I experimented with swinging my arms about as I ran. That felt really good. I tried a few jumps and skips too. They felt even better.

I ran in the general direction of home, staying clear of the major roads and public spaces. When my lungs were burning and my head spinning and I felt I couldn't run any more, I slowed and walked. I was somewhere near the area Hattie and I had walked through on our way to work a few hours before. I could have looked up where I was on a map but I currently enjoyed the experience of being lost.

There was a noise coming from a parked car. It was some sort of alarm. It was so gloriously loud that I went straight over to listen to it. A moving car narrowly avoided me. The car honked its horn and the passenger shouted out the window at me. It added to the overwhelming sound sensation.

"Hello," I said to the car with the alarm.

"I am alarmed," said the car.

"You're amazing," I told it and laid down on the front of it. It thrummed through my entire body. I could feel the vibration of the speaker, somewhere underneath my right hip. What a world I lived in where it was possible to fill up my ears with such a pure sound! I wanted to take it with me, and my hand explored the edge of the car, trying to locate the centre of the sound.

"I am alarmed," the car repeated.

I stroked its paintwork.

"Oi! Get away from there!" came a voice.

I stood up and waved at the man who was approaching. His face was contorted with such an unusual display of muscular tension that I started to laugh. Laughing, proper laughing, felt good but that seemed to make his face bunch even tighter. I giggled wildly and started to walk away.

"Don't you run off!" he yelled.

Running seemed like a really good idea. Levi hated running in the office but Levi wasn't here, so I ran. I looked behind and saw the shouting man, and laughed again.

It wasn't long before I had to slow again. I bent over for a moment to catch my breath. A small insect scurried across the ground. I had never really looked carefully at an insect, normally regarding them as invaders of the home or workplace. This one was shiny, black and purposeful. I wondered how it could be so black *and* so shiny. Black was an absence of colour, and yet this insect reflected the many colours of its surroundings.

"Hello," I said, putting my hand down towards the insect. It changed course and scurried away. I put a hand down in front of it and it changed course again. I blocked it again and it hurried off in a different direction.

"Wow, you're fast," I said and had another thought. I used my hands to box it in completely, curious about which direction it would take. It didn't hesitate, it climbed up and over my hand, determined to break free. I felt the tickle of its tiny feet and guided it gently back down. I watched it for a few more minutes until it disappeared into a crack.

I continued walking along the road. The first of the houses with a colourful garden made me stop and stare. The colours of the flowers bobbing and waving in the light breeze made my eyes water. There were so many different colours and a delicate scent in the air. There were some pale yellow flowers and some that were a completely different kind of yellow, and each one of them was so very lovely to see.

Hadn't I, only that morning, discussed with Hattie how useless and untidy flowers were, being neither grass nor trees? What a stupid idea.

"I think I like flowers," I said.

I stepped closer and touched one. I wondered if yellow might feel different to red. I brushed my fingertips across the flowers, trying to feel the colours. If I really concentrated I was certain that yellow felt a little bit sticky. A large flying insect emerged from the trumpet-shaped centre of a flower and startled me. I laughed. Laughter was a strange thing that I really didn't understand, but I enjoyed doing it. I laughed again but it wasn't the same if I tried to do it.

My gaze lowered slightly from the bright flowers. They were all crowded into the soil. It looked very dirty. In fact, wasn't soil the same as dirt? When dirt came into the apartment (and Hattie generally swooped into action to get rid of it) was it always the same stuff as this? It seemed remarkable that beautiful flowers should live happily in dirt. Maybe dirt wasn't as bad as I'd always been led to believe. I poked my finger into the soil and put it into my mouth. It tasted really bad. I pulled a face and spat in disgust. I tried to picture what my face was when I scrunched it up in disgust. I laughed at the thought and put some more soil in my mouth. It was a bigger bit and I felt my face contort at the bitter horror of what was in my mouth. I stood up and grinned with delight at the range of crazy expressions I could pull with my face.

I walked along for a few more minutes and looked

around. I was on the road near to that woman's house – Claire. My eyes narrowed as I thought about Claire. She had deliberately made us pick up dog poo. It was much clearer in my mind now although still confusing. It hadn't been right or normal for Claire to force us to pick up dog poo. She had done it because she wanted to...

"Ooh, what's the word?" I muttered.

Claire had done it because she wanted Hattie and I to feel unhappy. She wanted to distress us and make us feel socially awkward. Claire had wanted to assert her social dominance over us by making us feel we had done wrong and by making herself seem superior. She had wanted to shame them.

"She embarrassed us!" I said suddenly.

The woman had embarrassed us and, worse still, we hadn't known it was what she was doing. The contrast between the woman's cruelty and our naïve ignorance had amused Claire and her neighbour! Claire had done it because it was funny! But it wasn't funny, it was horrible!

And now, abruptly, I was angry. Anger was new. Anger was what had made me hit Levi repeatedly. And anger was odd. It was a negative emotion but it made me feel *good*.

Anger made me want to do something. The something in question was currently uncertain but it wasn't going to be a nice something. That should have worried me. It could be the brain virus, but I decided that I didn't really care. I would think about it later. Right now it was time to act.

I crossed over and looked at Claire's house and garden. She had a beautiful house. It was enormous and the door was an amazing glossy colour. The garden was as colour-filled with flowers as the one I'd stopped at just now. I walked up to the glossy door and banged on it loudly.

I wanted Claire to appear. I wanted to do something with Claire. I wanted to do something *to* Claire.

Nobody answered the door. I walked around the house. I found a window and peered inside. Claire had pictures on the wall like Jaffle had. Some of the chairs were covered in pictures of flowers. I had never seen anything like it before. I walked around the house some more.

A little table on a tall stand in the garden made me stop in my tracks. It had some sort of food on top of it, with containers hanging down. Birds fluttered around and jostled for position to get at the food. The birds were different sizes, mostly a brownish colour, and some smaller ones with flashes of blue and yellow. I had seen birds wheeling through the sky and occasionally walking on the grass near the Jaffle building, but this was the closest that I'd ever been to them and the flurry of activity made me giggle in delight, despite my continuing anger. The sound, although small, was enough to alarm the birds and they all took off, as though they were joined together.

I found the back door. I tried the handle and it opened. I went inside.

I was in a kitchen. This was not a kitchen like the one that Hattie and I had at home. We had very little in there except for cups, bowls and cupboard storage for beans. This kitchen was full of strange things. There was a large white, two-doored cupboard that was cold inside. I held one door open and marvelled at the feeling of cold pouring from it.

One door was a bit cold and the other door was really

cold. I pulled some things out to see what they were. A brick-shaped yellow thing looked interesting. Its wrapper said that it was cheese. It was food so I took a bite. Cheese was good, I decided. It was not bacon but it was nearly as good as bacon. I took it with me.

There was much more to look at in the kitchen. There were so many tools, and I had no clue what they were for. I took another bite of cheese and opened another cupboard. It held plates and bowls in lots of different shapes. Another cupboard was filled with metal objects. They looked quite ugly and I wondered what they were for. I wondered if I might find a bacon sandwich in here somewhere. I jipped for bacon and discovered it came from pigs. I didn't know if that meant I had to find a pig in the kitchen in order to extract the bacon or not. I found a cupboard filled with packets of food. I dipped into a box of raisins. They were delicious. Very un-bacony and not at all cheesy but delicious nonetheless. I took those as well.

Taking alternate mouthfuls of cheese and raisins, I explored the house some more. Every room was brightly decorated. There was colour on every surface, with pictures on some of the walls. The carpet in the next room was thick, with a small oblong area that was even thicker. I took a closer look. It was a small piece of extra carpet so thick and furry it looked like an animal. I ran my fingers through the fur.

"Mm."

I took my shoes off and put my feet on it. That felt so good, it demanded more.

Without wasting another moment, I removed all my clothes and rolled on the fur. The sensation on some parts of my body made me gasp with pleasure. I rolled and scrunched myself and wriggled. I wanted the rug to touch me all over.

My body wasn't something I had given much thought to before; not in that way. I knew I had a body and I knew what all the bits were for. Hands were for holding things, feet were for walking, knees were for bending and all that. And I had been aware – obviously – that my skin was sensitive to touch. That was only practical. Even on the less explored parts of my body, it was important to know if I was touching something hot or cold or wet or sharp. It was how the body kept itself safe.

But now...

I was beginning to comprehend the sense of touch could mean more. The fibres of the rug tickled and caressed; the touch of it on my body here and here and *here* was exciting. It was like I had discovered a new skin, underneath the old one. It was like I had ripped off all my clothes and rolled around for the pure pleasure of it. Which I guess I had.

I had a body. It was an obvious, even trite thought, but it was a new and exciting one.

I sat up and looked at myself. I looked at my legs and my knees and the low curve of my belly.

Suddenly, I wanted to see all of myself. I jumped up and ran in search of a mirror. Upstairs, in a bedroom, I found a full-length mirror and looked at my naked body. It was oddly fascinating to see what I looked like all over – none of the mirrors in my own apartment were that big. Now, I could see what I looked like, all of me. I studied my front and then turned and craned my neck to look at myself from behind. I liked what I saw and touched and poked every part of me. I felt a certain embarrassment. Not at my nakedness – hell, no – but at the fact that I'd been living in this body for over two decades and had never bothered to get to know the neighbours, metaphorically speaking.

"Hello, elbow," I said. "Hello, armpit. Hello, nipples. Hello, belly button."

On the bedroom wall, there was a picture of a woman with no clothes on. I looked at it with interest, glancing back and forth between my image in the mirror and the woman's body in the picture. My own body wasn't quite so full in the stomach and breasts, but then the woman in the picture was reclining. I tried lying on the bed, but found that I could no longer see myself in the mirror.

I thought of Claire's colourful clothes and opened a cupboard. There were a great many clothes, organised by colour and shape. I decided I liked the look of a red and blue striped dress and pulled it out. I put the dress on and looked in the mirror. I grinned with delight. What an amazing difference it made from the bland tunic I wore to work.

My thoughts were interrupted by an unpleasant feeling. I rubbed my stomach as it gurgled alarmingly and I groaned a little at the strange discomfort. I let out a belch and felt better. There was a gusty cheese taste in my mouth. Bacon sandwiches, cheese and raisins – fun to eat, fun to belch.

I moved over to a table with lots of little pots and sparkling objects. I picked up a bottle at random. It was half full of amber liquid and the writing on the side said *Eastern Lilies*. It had a spray mechanism, and when I gave a tentative squirt, the most incredible fragrance misted out. I sniffed and sprayed again. It was as if the smell from the flowers was stored up inside. I loved the idea that you could smell flowers whenever you wanted, so I picked up the bottle to take with me. I sprayed some into my mouth to see what it tasted like.

It tasted very unpleasant. I tried it again, just to be sure.

"No, that's just horrible."

Why was it so bad in my mouth and so wonderful when I smelled it?

I took a deep breath, suddenly in need of unperfumed air. So many sensations vied for my attention, but I couldn't ignore the flip-flopping of my stomach. It was as if the perfume and the sudden thought of cheese and bacon all piled up inside me was just a bit too much. I felt a heavy shift inside myself, forcing me to bend over. I steadied myself on a drawer handle, and pulled it out. Inside the drawer were undergarments. It took me a moment to recognise them as such. All of my underwear was practical and durable but these looked as delicate as insect wings. They were colourful and made from exquisite fabrics. I wanted to touch them all and rub myself with them but, I realised, that was never going to happen.

My stomach signalled its intentions with a painful heave. I vomited greasy bacon and chewed-up cheesy raisins into the drawer for long, painful moments. I closed the drawer and stood up, feeling very much better. I pictured Claire pulling open the drawer and finding the mess I'd just made and I laughed. I hadn't been sure what I wanted to do when I came in here, but this seemed right somehow.

"Time to go," I said, wiping a blob of sick from the corner of my mouth.

I made my way out of the house in my new dress. On the way I saw a hat on a stand, paused to try it on, and looked at my reflection in another mirror. I looked so tall and interesting. The hat had feathers and angular pieces of stiff straw pointing off in different directions. I kept the hat and let myself out the front door. I walked up the road, feeling the hat bobbing on my head, inhaling lungfuls of fresh air. I felt beautiful, elegant even.

I still had the taste of vomit in my mouth. I spat into the road. Spitting was fun too.

9

Near my apartment complex I saw an Empty, sitting on the kerb.

Empties were a part of everyday life. Literally. I saw them every day and had regarded them only as an inconvenience, like litter or fallen leaves. I hadn't properly considered what they were and my mind had just blocked them out.

The Empty was a man, but only the shell of a man.

The realisation crashed into my mind and I felt sick in a way that had nothing to do with bacon or cheese or raisins. I wasn't yet sure quite *how* my brain had become more fully enabled than it was when I woke up this morning, but I understood on some level that I had been opened up, granted access to something more than was allotted to me in life.

Apart from that weird and unfathomable three percent of society, everyone had a Jaffle Port and had purchased outright or bargained away unutilised processing space for that access. I was – or had been – operating on Jaffle Standard. That was fine, normal and pretty much enough for anyone. Above there was Jaffle Enhanced and Jaffle Premium for those able to pay and reclaim that processing space for their own (and frankly selfish) use. In the other direction, below Jaffle Standard, there was Jaffle Economy and Jaffle Lite. You only ended up on those if you were stripped of more processing space to pay unsettled debts or as punishment by the courts. I hadn't really thought about them much; I didn't work in debt reclamation and the concepts of crime and punishment were alien to me (or had been until very recently).

But what was below Jaffle Lite? What was at the lowest end of the scale? I was looking at it. The Empty – I corrected myself: the *man* – sat by the side of the road in a bright pink coverall. His chin and head were covered in the same uniform stubble. He had a Jaffle Port and, I guessed, he had surrendered as much of his brain's functionality as was possible without actually killing himself. His brain function was enough to keep essential organs ticking over, but little more.

I went to him and touched his hand, but he reacted only with a voiceless grunt. Drool trickled over his cheek and his eyes gazed into the middle distance, registering nothing. Even cars and apartments had more personal awareness.

What had he done to deserve this? I looked further along the kerb. There were more Empties – *men* and *women*, all lolling in the same lifeless way. How did they even get fed? Why had I never really looked at them before?

I tried to help him get up, but he was so far away from understanding that he couldn't work his arms and legs. I waved my hand in front of his eyes; he saw nothing.

"How can I help you?" I said.

I shouted and wept, but nothing could get through to him. I let out a wail of despair and flung my arms around the man.

"Is assistance required with this unit?"

I recoiled. For a moment I thought he had spoken but the voice had come from a stud speaker set into his lapel.

"I'm sorry?"

"Is assistance required with this unit?" said the speaker.

I shook my head.

"Supervision is en route," said the speaker and clicked off.

I got to my feet. The man did not react to my movement, had not reacted once. Anger seethed through me. This new sensation was the one that went with the growling and the scrunched-up face, and now I revelled in it. I had much to be angry about.

"What kind of a world is this?" I demanded of no one and everyone. "How can you treat people like this and expect life to go on as normal?"

There was a faint buzz. I looked up. A cloud of insects hovered nearby. It was a Jaffle Swarm. Bees or wasps or flying beetles, each with an implant in its brain, the cloud as a whole controlled by the borrowed processing power of humans elsewhere in the world.

"Supervision present," said the Empty's lapel speaker. *"Is there a problem with this unit?"*

Tearful, I backed away.

Anger seethed through me. This new sensation was the one that went with the growling and the scrunched-up face and now I revelled in it. I had much to be angry about. What sort of a world was I living in? How could people become like this Empty while everyone else carried on as normal? I paused at that. What was normal? Even yesterday, I had thought I had a normal life, trailing around just doing my job, at the mercy of people like Claire and Helberg. People who thought they were better than me and could make fun of me. Did they also make fun of the Empties? Did they spend their whole lives feeling superior, just because they'd been able to afford a functioning brain?

I looked up at my apartment complex. Helberg had taken all of my money on the flimsiest excuse. Was that how the world worked? The people with no standards got all the money and the people with all the money got all the privilege? It just wasn't fair. It was so unfair that I felt more anger building in me. It roiled my stomach almost as much as the bacon and cheese, but it felt like an explosion that would come out in a very different way. I stomped into the building and headed straight for the manager's office.

"Helberg!" I yelled, but he wasn't there. I went in and sat at his desk. Thankfully the screen was off. I turned my attention to the other stuff that was in there. A small cupboard led off to the side. It looked like maintenance supplies. The main office held a filing cabinet and an old-fashioned desktop computer. It was already switched on and logged in so I took a look at his business files. The building I was in was one of six that Helberg managed, which surprised me. I examined the other buildings on the local cameras and saw that all of them were in a very poor state of repair. I found lots of examples of ad-hoc charges to tenants and complaints that he'd ignored. One of the other buildings had been declared unfit for habitation by an annual inspection, but this appeared to have been filed and ignored.

"Well if it isn't one of my favourite tenants," said Helberg from the door. He was smiling. It was the same smirk that I'd started to recognise on those privileged enough to have their brains more fully enabled. It was the smirk they used when they felt superior.

I shoved past him. I ducked into the storage cupboard and saw what I needed. I picked up a short length of thick timber and hefted it. I swung it experimentally and then brought it down fast on the old computer monitor. It smashed in a very satisfying manner. I swung it again and smashed the glass in the door. I swept everything from the shelves and then smashed the shelves in half for good measure. I kicked a waste bin across the room, scattering its contents. I kicked it again, just to make a dent in the side.

I raised the length of timber high and advanced on Helberg, delighted now to see that his smirk was gone now.

"How do you like my re-decorating?" I yelled as he whimpered slightly. "You know I'm going to charge you a lot of money for this, don't you?"

"Alice, I feel as though you have the wrong idea about me," he said, his arms protecting his face.

"No, I have exactly the right idea about you. You rip off tenants and let their apartments fall into ruin. You take people's money and make them live in terrible conditions. You act as if you're so much better than us, when all you have is money that isn't even yours! You're a disgrace. You've done so many bad things that when I take you to the police, they'll turn you into one of those Empties. I won't feel sorry for you, even though it's a terrible way to treat a human, because I know that you've done that to other people by stealing all of their money."

"You don't know that—" he started. I cut him off with a swipe of the timber which didn't quite rip his desk in two. Bot parts, electronics and unsorted filing flew everywhere.

"Am I very very angry?" I yelled.

"Er, yes," he said.

"I don't know how to turn it off!"

"Er, what?"

I gave a scream of fury mixed with panic, hurled the chunk of wood at the wall and ran.

10

3RD JUNE

I dreamed I was in a plush flying drone, accompanied by a pair of stunningly pretty girls. Except it was also my cubicle at work and there was a kangaroo looming over me.

"Babe," Rufus drawled. "You know your aura fascinates me so much. It's got that blossoming, burgeoning thing going on. I want to reach out and touch it."

His hands groped across the two girls. Those hands weren't seeking an aura, they were seeking out breasts.

"Hey babes!" said Rufus. "Your auras are going wild. What say we throw caution to the wind and see whether our chakras align if we all get naked?"

The kangaroo by the cubicle wall looked powerful and fierce. It gave off an animal stink which did not disgust me, but fascinated me. It was more real than anything I had experienced in my life. Except, it wasn't a kangaroo anymore; it was Levi from work.

"What are you doing here?" I asked.

I focused on his arms, which were really quite muscular now. It was unusual for him to be without a jacket, but then I saw it hanging from the tip of his finger.

"There's no rule against us getting naked, Alice," he said solemnly, his gaze upon me. "Although we need to take care not to discard our clothes anywhere that might create a trip hazard."

In my dream I was nodding. Levi carefully put his jacket over the back of my chair and reached out to me. He made a slow chopping movement with his hand. "Advanced practitioners must exercise restraint and secrecy."

I took his hand and stood up, close to him. The women were completely identical now. Bland faces, huge breasts and pneumatic bottoms.

Rufus slipped his fingers inside their clothes. A nipple stiffened against both sets of fingers and he smiled, feeling unstoppable.

Levi's little moustache was right in front of me and I couldn't help wondering whether it would tickle my lips.

"We're nearly there!" said one of the girls, excitedly.

Do yoooou liiike thaaaat? asked the blue whale.

"Alice! Alice!"

I woke to find Hattie shaking me by the shoulder. I grunted and tried to roll out of reach.

"Alice, you need to wake up!" Hattie insisted. "And you really need to stop making those noises."

I couldn't seem to surface. My head spun and I wondered if the need to vomit was as close as I suspected. I opened my eyes and light stabbed painfully at my delicate brain. Hattie's face loomed over me, distorted with anxiety.

"What noises?" I muttered.

"You were moaning."

"Moaning?"

"Like..." Hattie made a noise. It was a bit like the hoot of that irritating blue whale. It was a lot like the moans and grunts the naked people made in the videos Helberg watched.

Helberg...? Helberg loomed large in my memory but I couldn't quite remember why.

"But you have to come quickly," said Hattie. "There's something very strange on top of the bean dispenser. I'm not sure if it's alive."

I rubbed a hand across my face as memories of the previous day paraded through my mind. The lies I'd told Paulette. My behaviour in the street. The break-in. The food. The clothes.

"Oh, no..."

What I had done to Helberg's office.

The parade of memories stuttered and stalled and became a horrific piled up mess of recollections. A feeling burned deep inside me. It felt like I was going to be sick, but not physically. It was a horrid and unshiftable desire for things to be different from what they currently were.

And on top of that nameless sensation there were the feelings aroused within me by those peculiar dreams.

I assured Hattie I would be along in a few minutes and hauled myself out of bed. I looked around for my Jaffle tunic and realised I'd left it at Claire's house. I held up the colourful dress to admire it once more. I would love to wear it to the office, but knew that it would be a terrible idea. I dug out a spare tunic and hung the dress at the back of the cupboard, well out of sight. I tried swishing and prancing in my tunic, but it just wasn't the same. That gorgeous gauzy fabric felt so special against my skin, that I couldn't wait to wear it again. Perhaps find some other clothes that made me feel that way. The colours too! I peeked another look at the dress, just to see the colours again. Could I put into words how colourful things made me feel? Excitement? Whatever it was, the apartment that Hattie and I shared was very lacking in colour. It made me a little bit sad to look around and see that everything was the same boring shade.

I went to my bedroom window and looked. I'm not sure I'd ever looked out of it before. Obviously, I'd gazed in that general direction before. It was where the light came in. But I'd never properly *looked*. There wasn't much to see. My room overlooked the central shaft which ran through the centre of the building. Above was a large square of sky. Across were the murky grey windows of other apartments. Several storeys below was the quadrangle at the heart of the ground floor. It was a square of mud and currently housed some sort of incinerator, pieces of wood and a number of rusting air conditioners.

My world was grey, dull and enclosed and I had never noticed.

I stepped into the kitchen area and looked at the very strange thing on top of the bean dispenser.

"It's cheese," I said.

"Chi-eeeese?"

"Yes, I got it yesterday. It's really nice, you should try some."

"It's food?" asked Hattie, incredulous. "No, I don't think so. It looks very peculiar."

I wasn't ready to have the food discussion quite yet. "Never mind, Hattie. We can have beans. Listen, I wanted to ask you something."

"Yes?"

"You know Levi?"

"Security Levi at work?" said Hattie as she served up blue beans.

"Mmm, him. Have you ever looked at his arms?"

"He has arms," said Hattie with conviction.

"Yes, but looking at them ... are they... are they quite muscular?"

Hattie frowned, concentrating. "He always wears a jacket at work, it's very hard to know. He probably needs to be strong to wrestle wrongdoers to the ground and suchlike."

"He probably does, yes," I reflected, feeling a strange frisson at the thought of Levi wrestling me to the ground, although I couldn't be sure why.

"Beans," said Hattie and handed me a bowl.

She went through to watch Rise and Shine with Smiley. I stood for a moment, looking at the screen. It followed the usual format of people waking up and having slightly sad faces, but then being cheered by the sight of Smiley appearing with his huge, yellow, sunny face, beaming down upon them. After I had watched the same scene play out three different times I shook my head. How could it be that I had once found this so very entertaining? It was clearly idiotic. I was a smart person, my brain was used for some amazing tasks, and yet I'd been happy to let nonsense like this fill it during quiet moments. It was so confusing.

I ate the beans, but found them dull. They were as dull to my taste buds as Smiley was now to my eyes. However, I was hungry, so I ploughed through them, but all the while I was thinking about the cheese and went back to the kitchen to sneak a bite of when Hattie wasn't looking.

My mind went from cheese to bacon, and I sighed, wondering whether there were other things that tasted so good. I would have to take care though, not least because I'd made myself sick yesterday by eating too many unfamiliar things. I knew how easily upset Hattie was, so I would try to be myself today. I would follow the normal routine and behave as we always did. Mostly I would anyway, just as soon as I'd got my mind straight.

I still couldn't shake the feelings that the dream-Levi had roused in me.

"Hattie," I said. "You know how men and women are different?"

"Mm," Hattie mumbled, her eyes not leaving the screen. "Different uniforms some of them. And they have different toilets in some old buildings."

"Right, yeah," I said, searching for a way in to this conversation, "so the different toilet facilities. Why is that?"

"Um, I think it's because men are messier," said Hattie.

I paused. "Their bodies aren't the same as ours."

"They have arms."

"What?"

"They all have arms," said Hattie. "You asked about Levi but I think all of them have arms."

"I know they have arms," I said defensively.

"Well, you asked. And they do."

"Yes, but apart from that they're a different shape."

"Yes, I suppose," said Hattie. "No boobs."

"Yes!" I said. "Yes. Those sorts of things. What other—"

"—apart from Pedstone."

"What?" I was thrown.

"Pedstone and Swanager," said Hattie, and mimed a little jiggle to underline the point. "Both got boobs. He's a man. She's a woman."

I sighed. I wasn't really sure what conversation I wanted to have about the difference between men and women, but this wasn't it.

And I had other things to worry about. Like Helberg's office. Had I really stormed into his office? And smashed his screen? And his shelves? I wished, I *hoped* that explosive episode was imaginary, as unreal as the blue whale which kept swimming in and out of Rufus Jaffle's memory.

"I need to pop downstairs," I told Hattie.

Hattie nodded, still transfixed by Smiley. I went down to see Helberg. On the way, I passed the many doors, all the same colour. I shook my head at yet another example of horrible drabness which was imposed upon us all.

Helberg's broken screen sat on the floor outside the complex manager's office. I touched it for a second and jipped it with my Jaffle Port. It wasn't a piece of Jaffle Tech and it wasn't equipped with the same security measures. Also, the man was lazy; lazy enough to think no one would be capable of breaking into his data. I stepped into the office. Helberg was repositioning a brand new screen on his still dented desk.

"Come to apologise, have we?" he said with a mock sweetness.

"No," I said.

"To offer to pay for the damages caused?"

"No."

"Because you had quite a temper on your last night. Quite out of character, dear tenant, if I may say. One might even suspect there's an imbalance in your system."

"You don't know what you talking about," I said.

"And neither do you," he replied. "The things you were spouting. Baseless accusations. Slander, that's what they call it."

I pointed back at the door, at the screen that sat outside. "I copied your files."

He looked at me sharply, his false cheer vanished. "Data theft? Your list of crimes is racking up."

"They weren't even protected," I said. "I just walked by and – pop! – I copied them. All of them. You've kept a detailed account of all the people you've fraudulently overcharged, often for services they were never provided with in the first place."

"Now, you listen here, miss," he said, pointing a finger.

I smiled. "I'm listening, Helberg. Patrick." I looked at him and waited.

His twitching mouth faltered. His pointing finger wilted. "You've got to understand..." he said. "Some people. Circumstances get the better of them. They've ... they've got no one but themselves to blame, you see?"

"But there is someone to blame," I said and smiled again. For the first time, I understood that not all smiles were meant to be nice. "You, Helberg. You are to blame. You will be held accountable."

"By you?" he said.

I nodded. "You're going to make things better. Maybe you don't know how to do that, but it doesn't matter, because I am going to tell you. Understand?"

He attempted a smile but it was no match for mine.

"Because even if you didn't do it directly, you have undermined these people. You took their money. You messed up their homes and their lives. You and I are going to fix things. Whatever it takes, we're going to make things better."

"Hey," he said. "I'm not the bad guy here. I'm not being selfish. I'm just after a slice of the easy life. I'm just a piece of grit in the system."

"You're a piece of something."

"If people can be exploited then it's someone's duty to exploit them, to show where the weaknesses lie. There is a natural order in the world. There are those of us who are intelligent enough to make the world to our liking. The brains of society's body. And somewhere down there, underneath it all are the people – human toenails – who exist only to be used. If bad things happen to people, then they've probably got it coming."

"Oh, good. Then I should just send these files to the

authorities." I tapped my head. "I've even labelled them to be sent off in the event of an emergency."

I saw him blanch and knew that my remark had hit home. "I'd rather you didn't do that," he said simply.

"Well, as long as we understand each other, we can get straight to work," I said. "First of all, you're going to give me back my money."

He scowled but nodded.

"You can give me some more as well. I can see that sorting your mess out might be an expensive thing to do."

I jipped a request for payment over to him. He pulled a face but authorised the payment. Again, like his screen, his Jaffle Port technology didn't respond like proper Jaffle Tech. The signature looked different, which was odd.

"Right," I said. "You're going to find somewhere better for Swanager and Pedstone to live."

"How will I do that?"

"You'll think of something. Then, for your second task, you're going to make it easier for everyone to find their own front door."

"What?"

"They all look exactly the same, and it's confusing and annoying. Now before I go, I have a question." I pulled up a chair to face him. "When there are colourful plants growing, what is that called?"

He rolled his eyes and there was a trace of the old smirk. "Do you mean a *garden*?"

I tilted my head and gave him a look; and I mean a *look*. "Do you want me to redecorate your office again?" I asked.

A fervent headshake.

"So, it's a garden." I turned to the whiteboard on the wall. I picked up a pen and wrote *New place for S and P* at the top, followed by *doors* and *bacon* and finally *garden*.

"Good. We will talk later about how you're going to make gardens happen."

11

I was quite relieved to get to work. I looked forward to some thinking time on my own. In spite of my efforts to appear normal, Hattie kept giving me funny looks, as if I might be ill. It hadn't helped when I had broken down in tears again at the sight of the Empties. Hattie didn't see them at all. I thought better of trying to point out the hideous reality of them living in a society which took thinking power away from its citizens and left them as hollow shells. Instead I just pretended I'd got something in my eye. Hattie had been distracted by the good news that I had enough money to pay for the car to take us on our regular pay-per-metre journey to work, so we arrived on time.

There was a small group of people standing in the centre of the reception area. I realised with horror that at its core was the woman, Claire, she of the bright clothes that didn't cover enough of her body, she of the defecating dog, she of the house which I had invaded, ransacked and violated.

Claire was angrily brandishing my discarded tunic and shouting about an invasion of her privacy. There was a civil law enforcement officer there, and of course Levi.

I lurched in shock, nearly colliding with Hattie.

"You all right?" said Hattie.

"I think I'm going to be sick," I muttered.

"Did you touch the chi-eeese?"

I mentally pulled myself together. "Look, the elevator's about to go. Hurry."

"We've got loads of time," protested Hattie looking back over her shoulder. "Hey. Was that the woman that made me —" she pulled a face "—pick up the dog poop?"

"Not sure," I said, and quickly pressed the elevator button. "Best to stay well out her way in future though, don't you think?"

"I hope we didn't dispose of her dog's poo incorrectly," fretted Hattie.

I hurried Hattie from the elevator to our work stations and sought the sanctuary of my own cubicle, my own familiar little mouse hole. I worried briefly that some sort of alert would be triggered by the system when I started work, that some background system would note something different in my brain state. It wasn't and I was soon back in the usual routine.

The usual routine should have been comforting but I found myself continually looking round and finding things which must have always been there, but I'd simply never noticed before.

One of my colleagues had smelly feet and had taken their shoes off. The smell was strong enough for me to wish I'd brought Claire's perfume with me, but that was safely hidden back at the apartment. I sniffed my arm and could smell the slightest ghost of its fragrance, which made me smile.

I also noted that the entire department was lacking in colour. Nearly everything was a very pale green colour, but not an interesting, bright green like plants. It was a green that really wanted to be grey, as if all of the fun had been sucked out of it.

Then there was the sound all around me. The call centre was carefully designed so operatives didn't disturb each other, but that didn't mean I couldn't hear my colleagues if I listened carefully, tuning into some of the conversations. I could hear the tapping of feet and the squeaking of chairs. I was surrounded by dozens of intriguing noises, all of which told their own fascinating story.

I had changed. My life had changed. Every moment I had experienced was different now. And there was no denying that something had happened in Rufus Jaffle's office which had caused that change, that difference.

I needed to work out what it was; speak to someone who would understand and offer clear guidance.

I needed to speak to Rufus Jaffle again.

I forced myself to take enough calls to be high on the leader board, so that I could give myself a few minutes to step away from my workstation and put a call through to Rufus Jaffle via the company switchboard.

"*Rufus Jaffle's office,*" said a female voice.

"Could I please speak to Jaffle?" I asked.

"*I'm afraid he's not available, could I take a message?*"

"Oh. Right. It's very important that I talk to Jaffle. It's Alice, the technician who helped him out yesterday."

"Rufus Jaffle wasn't in the office yesterday."

"But I—"

"You must be mistaken. Sorry."

I began to protest, then I realised what was happening. The effort to be discreet was overriding everything here. The entire clean-up operation had been hush-hush; no one was going to acknowledge that Rufus Jaffle had infected his brain with a virus and therefore no one was going to acknowledge it had required my help to clear it. The secretary wasn't going to be of any assistance to me.

"Right, thank you. Goodbye."

As I walked back to my cubicle I gave the matter some thought. If I couldn't get past the secretary then I'd have to think of some other way to see Jaffle. I had questions that only he could answer.

Levi was waiting next to my cubicle, hands on hips. I noticed the way that he stood. It was fascinating that men even stood in a different way to women. I couldn't imagine that I might ever stand like that. Legs apart, hands on hips, ready for... Ready for what? I wasn't sure, but I felt sudden heat in my cheeks, and I swallowed hard.

"Hello Levi," I said.

He raised his eyebrows. Along with that little moustache they create a frame for his face, the punctuation to his facial expressions. I wondered what they felt like. Were they soft and silky or coarse and bristly? I watched his lips, waiting for him to speak, absorbed by their curves, and wondering why they interested me so much and what beautiful words he was about to utter.

"Bathroom break?" he said.

Okay, they weren't particularly beautiful words.

"Pardon?" I said.

"It was a simple question, was it not?"

I frowned. The new warm fuzzy feelings I had developed for Levi since my dream of the night before came crashing up against the hard and unforgiving feelings I been building up about him for months.

"Are you watching me?" I said. Part of me liked the idea of him watching me and part of me thought it was wrong and unpleasant and invasive. I dipped into my Jaffle Port literacy booster. Creepy. That was the word.

"I watch everyone," he said.

"Well, I think I'd rather you didn't."

Levi was amused by this. "Don't get yourself all riled up, miss. Just doing my job. Eternal vigilance is the price of high quality security, not to mention health and safety, yabetcha."

"Yes, well, I was perfectly safe on my bathroom break. I always am," I said, not so much angry at his behaviour as the smashing of my daydream version of Levi. Trying to recapture it before it left me completely, I looked at his arms, remembering how strong and muscular they were in my dreams.

"Have you got hairs on your arms?" I asked.

Levi looked shocked at the question. He looked for a moment as though he might be about to roll up his sleeves and have a look – the very prospect of it made me come over all uncomfortably warm - but then he thought better of it.

"Well, I'm really not sure what that's got to do with the price of tea in China, miss," he replied.

"No, I was just interested," I said. I was about to add that I sometimes saw hairs sprouting through the gaps in his shirt, but I sensed Levi didn't want to talk about his body hair. He turned on his heel and walked down the office.

I watched him walk away. Irritating and nosy Levi. Levi with the strong muscly arms. Levi the heartless mouse-stomper. Levi with his little moustache.

He wore a utility belt which carried all sorts of odd bulky items like a torch, a ring of keys and a set of handcuffs. If I ignored all of that, his hips were actually very slim, and I considered what shape he might be without any clothes on. He would be quite different to the shape that I was. Different but pleasing. I felt the heat creeping into my face again and wondered whether I was getting a cold. I certainly seemed to be running a temperature.

A pop-up reminder appeared on my calendar. The brain scan with the medical team was booked in for the next day. Perhaps that would provide some answers.

12

Hattie and I pulled up outside the apartment complex, the journey home smooth and fuss-free on the premium roads.

"I think I might hang onto the car," I said once Hattie was out, adding, as casually as I could, "Maybe go to the shops."

"Go to the shops?" asked Hattie. "What for?"

"Because."

"Are you going to the Smiley Store?"

"No, not there. I want to get some food."

"We have food."

"Different food?"

"Different beans?" asked Hattie, a look of naked horror on her face.

"I don't really know what I'll get. I'm off to have a look," I said.

It was clear from the look on Hattie's face that she simply didn't understand.

"It's fine though," I said. "You don't have to try any if you don't want to."

I gave instructions to the car and sped off to the food markets. I stepped out at the drop off point and walked inside. This was unfamiliar territory. Hattie and I had our beans delivered in bulk, so food markets were not places that we had ever really felt the need to visit. It was the same for pretty much everyone we knew.

The food markets was a place which sometimes featured in the screen *dramas* we occasionally flicked through by accident. Needlessly complicated people with needlessly complicated lives would bump into each other and talk about their miserable complicated problems over the food counters. And indeed the customers were dressed like the people from those drama programmes. No work-issue tabards here. The customers were as brightly coloured as the range of produce on offer on the shelves.

I soon realised I was very much out of my depth. There was a large section of things that looked as though they belonged in gardens. They were shiny and colourful, but I wasn't sure whether they were meant to be food or decoration. I peered at the displays and read the labels. Aubergines were impossibly shiny and a glamorous purple-black colour. I jipped a query and was thrilled to discover that they were edible. I popped one into a basket. I strolled around, checking a few more things. I spent some time running my fingers across the leaves of a Savoy cabbage, intrigued by the texture. The smell wasn't all that appealing, so I decided not to buy one. I spent more time reading about garlic. It was an unassuming papery cluster, but the description the Jaffle Port offered was of something delicious and flavoursome, so I popped one into my basket too. As I moved further into the markets, the shelves began to hold packets and tubs. There was no sign of bacon yet. I held up a jar of something called olives. Black globes bobbed in liquid. They looked like tiny versions of the aubergine, but jipping offered no connection between the two. I decided to try olives, and the things next to them called anchovies, which looked like strips of dirt stuffed into a jar.

A delicious smell drew me on. It wasn't the smell of bacon, but it was impossible to ignore. As I turned a corner into a section labelled *bakery* it hung in the air, thick and irresistible. Behind a counter, workers in white hats pulled trays out of large steel cabinets. They transferred golden, puffy products into bags and put them on shelves.

"Would you like a sample?" one of them asked me.

"What is that?" I asked.

"Heritage bloomer," said the woman and used a serrated knife to cut it into chunks. She put the chunks into a basket and placed them on the counter in front of me. I put a piece into my mouth at the same time as I jipped to see what a heritage bloomer was.

It was warm and delicious. Warm food was a strange idea, but a marvellous one. It added another dimension to the experience, and I found that I was making loud moaning noises of appreciation. I took another chunk of the heritage bloomer, which was apparently some sort of bread, and stuffed it into my mouth.

"Mm-mmm. Can I have another?"

"Certainly," said the woman. "Anything for you. And if

you're a mystery shopper be sure to give me a five star rating."

"Mifftery fopper?" I mumbled and then jipped the term.

I stood there for quite a while, eating my way through the basket. A man came along and reached for a chunk, but I turned and gave him such a ferocious glare that he backed away.

I finally emptied the basket, shoving the last chunks into my mouth so that my cheeks bulged, and then put as many of the heritage bloomers into my basket as I could carry.

I decided I would come back and explore the rest of the food markets another day, as my arms were getting tired. I staggered to the exit aisle and received a cheery note of the cost of my purchases. I carried them outside, holding the heritage bloomers close so that I could inhale the delicious scent while I found a car to take me home.

When I got back to the apartment, the Empties were being fed. I put my bag down and watched with interest. A truck had pulled up at the side of the road and emitted a discreet chime. The Empties all came alive, shuffling forward to get a portion of beans. They were dispensed into disposable bowls from a chute at the side of the truck. The Empties clutched their bowls and walked away, pouring beans into their mouths.

The truck pulled away. Feeding had been accomplished: quickly, without noise or fuss or even any need for human effort.

I frowned. At least the Empties weren't starving, but how could anyone think that this was a good way to look after people? I had a thought and turned to my bag of groceries. I broke off a chunk of heritage bloomer and handed it to the nearest Empty, a man whose face was creased with lines.

"Here, try this," I said. "I know you won't necessarily understand what I'm saying, but surely you'd like to hear another human voice, huh? It stands to reason. Well my name is Alice and I want to be your friend. I want to help. You guys are really not having a fun time, but maybe we can improve things, what do you say?"

He said nothing.

"Well, I work over at Jaffle Tech, and I'm on the phones for most of the day. It's a good job and I love helping people out, I really do, but I'm beginning to think that maybe there are other things I'm interested in. Like different food. This bread is amazing, you should try it."

His free hand had been dipping into his bowl of beans, but now that it held a chunk of bread he seemed incapable of making sense of the situation. After twitching a few times, his hand opened and dropped the bread, and then he carried on eating his beans.

"Okay, what about this?" I pulled the garlic out of the bag and demonstrated how to take a bite. I quickly regretted it. There was an explosion of white papery mess. My mouth was full of it, and bits flew across my face and onto the ground. Before I could worry about that I was hit with the taste of whatever lay inside. It was so strong it stopped me in me tracks. My eyes started to water and I spat it all out, littering the Empty with flakes of garlic.

My mouth was still full of that dreadful, pungent taste. When I'd eaten soil, it was unpleasant, but this was like a physical assault. I thrust the rest of the garlic back on top of the groceries and tried to rid myself of the taste by making extravagant tongue-thrusting motions.

"Okay, not that," I said, still spitting garlic skin from my lips.

I went back to the groceries and considered the jar of olives. They were about the same size and shape as beans, but different. I had no idea why it was important to me that the Empties should eat something different, but I wanted to help them break free from their walking prisons. If this might help then I had to give it a try. I unscrewed the jar and took out an olive. It glistened attractively. I put one on top of the beans in the man's bag and then I picked out another and put it into my own mouth.

"What about this, huh?"

We could experience olives together. I bit down and was shocked by how hard it was. I looked away so that I didn't upset him with the face that I was pulling. The taste of the olive was bitter, but not horrible. I bit down again, but was completely unable to crunch the olive with my teeth. I jipped a quick search and saw that olives were sometimes stuffed, sometimes pitted, and sometimes whole. I looked at the jar and saw that these were whole olives. Another hurried search revealed that olive pits were not for eating. I spat the remains into my hand. Apparently *pit* was an innocent and cute word for a small pebble.

I looked at the Empty who was still munching through his beans. Glancing in his bowl I saw that the olive was gone. His mouth was still chomping away. Could I make him spit it out? Probably not. Would his teeth break first or would he choke to death? Either was an appalling thought, and I watched him very closely, holding my breath. Eventually he finished the beans and immediately drifted to a refuse bin to deposit his bowl. He slumped back to the position of powered-down defeat which seemed to be the default resting position of the Empties. I waited for a few more minutes to be sure I hadn't accidentally killed him with an olive before going back inside.

Helberg was in his office. He sniffed the air as I entered.

"Have you sorted out Swanager and Pedstone?" I asked.

He nodded. "I've moved them into my place, treating them like royalty while I hole up in the back here, although Swanager threatened to move out altogether. Something about a new integrated living solution experiment they're trying out in North Beach..." He trailed off, looking at me. "What did happen to you?" he asked.

"What do you mean?" I said.

He shook his head and sighed.

"Actually, there is one area I need some help with," I said.

He nodded for me to go on, but I paused, unsure what I was asking.

"That stuff you watch on the screen. The people who huff and wriggle without their clothes on?"

His eyebrows shot up. "Porn, you mean?"

"Porn, yes. What is porn?" I asked.

Helberg blew out his cheeks and grinned nervously. "A lot of people would say that it's just about watching people having sex, but it can be so much more than that. There's a lot of artistic—"

"Right! Sex! What is that?" I demanded, thinking I was

getting to the core of the bizarre feelings and images which had been flooding my brain.

"What is sex?"

"Yes," I said. "I mean, I know what sex *is*. We learned about it in the school science downloads but it's like ... algebra. It's all very important I'm sure and I tried to pay attention to the lesson, but I couldn't see any practical use for it."

Helberg looked at me for a long time. "Um, can I ask why you want to know about this? I mean, why now?"

"I've been having some ... unusual thoughts." I really didn't want to describe them, even if I had the words.

Helberg grinned. "You're horny," he said.

I immediately felt the top of my head.

"No," said Helberg. "You've been thinking about getting yourself a partner, maybe? Getting naked, feeling some skin on skin?"

"Yes, that's exactly it!"

"Oh, I can definitely help you with that," he said, edging towards me, hands reaching down to unbutton his shirt.

"What? No! What are you doing?" I said, backing away. "All I want is information. I really *don't* want to see you naked."

"Why not? You don't know that until you've tried it."

It was a superficially persuasive argument. True, I was interested in sex and, maybe like trying different foods, maybe I just needed to try sex with Helberg, even if he turned out to be an olive pit or a repulsive lump of garlic. But, no, instinctively I felt that sex with him wasn't the answer.

"I want information, not sex," I said.

Helberg was crestfallen. "Are you sure? We could turn the lights off, maybe?"

"No."

He sniffed me. "Have you been eating garlic? Not that I mind. I don't mind having sex with a woman who—"

"No! No sex. Definitely not."

He huffed and redid his top button. "I got something you might like."

"But it's not sex," I said, following him to the store room at the back of his office.

"See these tins?" he asked, pointing at a shelf. "It's paint. Do you know about paint?"

"Tell me."

"It's how we make things a different colour. You wanted a way to tell the front doors apart? Well this is how you'll do it. Each one of these tins is a different colour."

I looked at the tins. They were very small compared to a door. "How does it work?"

He reached up to another shelf and handed me several brushes. "You take off the lid and then use a brush to put it on. You can cover quite a large surface with a tin of paint."

I immediately tried to get the lid off a tin, but found it impossible. Helberg showed me how to lever it off with another tool.

"They have to be kept shut really tight. Imagine the mess if it tipped over and spilled—"

As he said the words, I tilted the open tin to read what it said on the side. I looked down to see a spreading pool on the carpet. I dipped my toe into it and spread it around.

"*Cornflower Blue*," I read from the tin. "Your carpet looks better already. So do my shoes. You're right, I think I'm going to enjoy paint."

I CARRIED paint upstairs and considered the colours as I looked along the row of doors. I nodded with satisfaction, knowing that this would definitely help. Hattie and I wouldn't need to count down the doors, we would simply head for the red door. Why did I want a red door? I just did. I put the tins down and fished the tool from my pocket to get a lid off. The door opened.

"I thought I heard something," said Hattie. "You're just in time. There's a Smiley compilation special on in a minute. All of our favourite moments, I can't wait!"

I would have been so excited by this before, now I couldn't think of anything worse.

Hattie looked at the tins of paint. "Is this the food you bought?"

"This isn't the food."

Hattie picked up a tin. "*Raspberry Beret*? I can't see why we can't just have regular beans."

"Listen, just go inside. I'll be in soon. I have a couple of jobs to do and I'll join you when I'm finished."

"Jobs? But I've done all the jobs. Is there something else that needs doing?" Hattie turned her gaze to look inside, searching for unfinished tasks.

"No, don't worry. Go and watch Smiley, I'm doing something new," I said. "I can show you when I'm finished if you like. I think you'll like it."

Hattie looked worried, but she went back inside and I took the lid off the red paint.

"*Cabriolet,*" I said, savouring the name.

I dipped the brush into the paint, and held it up, glistening brightly. I slid the brush down the door and was delighted by the transformation. I applied more and then brushed up and down, enjoying the slight drag and the sensation that I was master of this striking colour. My tongue found the edge of my lips as I worked the brush into every corner. It was enormously satisfying. For some reason, images of Levi kept nudging into my thoughts as I worked the brush up and down. I wondered if he might enjoy the feeling as much me. I carefully eased the colour into every tiny gap with a tickle of my brush and then used the full width of its head to apply a pleasing finish. I felt a small shudder of pleasure as I realised that the door was now perfect. I stood and admired it for a few minutes.

A thought came to me and I went back down to the street. The Empties were still there, not moving. I went up to the man I'd fed the olive. He was still not dead, which was good.

"Want to try painting? I really think you'd enjoy it." I pressed the brush into his hand and led him into the complex and the door of one of the ground floor apartments. I took his hand and showed him how to paint.

"Dip in like this and then you can put the colour on the door."

I left him at work and approached another Empty, a woman.

"Come on. You can do yellow. I think you'll like yellow."

I set the woman painting the next door along and

pictured the row of doors in the morning light. It would be a visual delight and so I hurried up to another door and started to paint it a vivid green colour. I lost myself in the process, although for some reason the green paint didn't fill my head with sensation quite so much as the red had done. I finished the door and stood back. I went back to see how the Empties had got on.

I wasn't sure exactly what had happened, but the paint was not on the doors. A good deal of it was on the road, and it was clear from the footprints and the amount of paint on their bodies that the two Empties had walked through it and possibly rolled around in it before they had started to paint a nearby car.

"Sensors are impaired. Alerting engineer. Sensors are impaired. Alerting engineer."

The car was determined to summon help and I really didn't want to be around to explain what had happened when an engineer appeared. I led the Empties away from the worst of the mess and wondered how I was going to clean them up. I took them inside and led them to Helberg's office. He was down on his hands and knees, scrubbing at the carpet where the blue paint had spilled

"I have a question about how to get paint off things," I said.

"Really?" said Helberg. He looked up and saw a dozen paint-smeared Empties crowding round his door. "Oh, for pity's sake! What are you doing?"

"They were helping me," I said.

"Helping...?" He waved his arms and flapped his lips uselessly. "You can't do that. They're property!"

I looked at the Empties. "They're people."

"And they've been turned into Empties for a reason. Debt, crime, just being useless specimen of humanity. They're meant to be that way and left that way. You can't just use them for some arts and crafts programme." He made a deeply unhappy noise. "Are you trying to wreck everyone's lives, or just mine?"

I didn't know what to say so I just gave him a stern look and he quickly relented.

Helberg found some cloths and towels and we wiped the Empties as clean as we could, being careful to avoid whatever pressure points would bring the supervision bots. As a consequence, their orange coveralls were now mottled with red and yellow, an improvement in my view. I led them back out to the street, to find the car had gone. Dusk made it hard to see the spilled paint. The Empties went back to their usual spots and I walked back inside, disappointed that I still hadn't found a way to help them.

13

4TH JUNE

I'M AAAAA WHAAAAALE, SANG THE BLUE
WHALE.

"Sure Babe!" said Rufus. He strolled through the
house, across a terrace and down the steps onto the
beach. There were several bonfires, with groups
gathered around them, and a couple of spin-off groups who'd
gone off to play volleyball. Rufus was very interested in the
volleyball, but not, I realised, for the sport. Rather for the
athletic, bikini-clad bodies of the women playing.

The two women with Rufus sipped on their cocktails and
pulled faces. I saw the drinks sported sparkling swizzle sticks
with their names on them, so I could tell which one was
which, at last.

I watched as Rufus's mind cast the girls immediately into
a private fantasy. They were both wearing tiny bikinis and
writhing on the floor, covered in slippery mud. As their
hands slid over each others' enormous breasts and buttocks,
they giggled and beckoned to him.

Is this a memory or a dream? I asked.

Maybeeee it's boooooth, said the blue whale.

TayTay sucked the straw on her cocktail, more than a little suggestively. "That would be cool," she breathed.

The shout came again. "Roo fight!"

The memory shifted and contorted, gaps bloomed and resolved themselves.

The blue whale swooped and dived through the dreamscape.

"I have been privileged to learn some of the world's most effective martial arts techniques from master practitioners," said Rufus. "If people knew I walked among them wielding the power of life and death with a single blow, imagine how that would be?"

We were in the basement space beneath the house. There were people crowded round and there was a kangaroo. I still wasn't sure why there was a kangaroo at Rufus's beach party.

The animal came out of its corner with an enormous bound and hauled Rufus up by his long hair with its arms, while using the most powerful kick it could muster on his dangling body. He dropped like a stone and I saw the veil of unconsciousness fall like a blessed relief, across the intense pain.

It's beeeeetter to beeeee aaaaa whaaaale, the whale pointed out.

In the hospital bed, Rufus groaned as he tried to shift position and talk to his fiancée, Paris. "Well, not small and helpless, surely? I took care of the—"

"Yes, we've made sure Miss Jacobs is up to date with the details of your *fall*," said Henderson, cutting into the conversation, positioning himself between Rufus and Paris. Henderson was a parasite, a pet, a dog. At the banquet of life at which Rufus and his equals – 'proper' people – feasted, Henderson sniffed around for scraps of power and influence. Just because Henderson was a smart dog, he assumed he was better than the other dogs; that he could become a proper person if he worked at it, pleaded for it.

"Paris," said Henderson, "I'm afraid I have some dull corporate matters I need to discuss with Rufus."

"Work?" said Paris. "Now?"

"The burden of leadership, hon," said Rufus. "Pop outside and fix your make up."

"My make up?" Paris left.

The whale swam in.

Rufus Jaffle was now talking to Henderson and another man – Michael from legal. The details weren't clear but it felt like Rufus was in some sort of trouble.

"You need to wipe your memory of what happened last night," said Henderson. "You have the access to do that personally."

"Actually, I've got this whale in my head that is making some of my functionality a bit glitchy."

The whale giggled and squirted foam through its blowhole.

"Fine," said Henderson peevishly. "Then we'll get it done back at Jaffle Tech."

"But please don't go through the official company procedures," said Michael. "I very much believe the less people know and the smaller the paper trail, the better things are."

"Yes, our official brain-editing systems have audits that I even I can't counter," said Henderson.

Even I— Rufus could have laughed. A dog with ideas above its station.

"I'll sort out something off the record," said Henderson. "We will arrange the memory wipe as soon as you're physically fit enough." He paused. "There is another matter I need your signature for, and it won't wait until then. Perhaps, Michael, you could leave us for a few minutes?"

Michael from legal rose and left the room, leaving Rufus alone with Henderson.

"Are you both getting memory wipes too?" asked Rufus, sulking.

"I will attend to all details. It's very much in our mutual interest if you believe I have the company's best interest at heart, wouldn't you say? As Chief Technical Officer, problem solving is my forte."

Rufus gave a grunt of assent.

Henderson cleared his throat. "That other matter. I need your signature for Operation Sunrise. It's a complex project, so I can't afford to let any time slip."

Rufus looked at the sheaf of papers. "Do I need to read all that?"

I SURFACED from sleep before I had time to read any of the papers.

"Odd dream," I muttered.

The major takeaway was that Rufus Jaffle had a very peculiar lifestyle, but then he was at the top of the world's biggest tech corporation, so the pressure of his job was probably something I couldn't begin to understand. He was definitely the man with the answers. I had to find a way to speak to him.

As I dressed I recalled the way that Rufus was fixated on the girls' breasts and buttocks in his memory. I now recognised that these were secondary sex characteristics, and played a big part in selecting partners for intercourse. I'd spent some time jipping articles through my Jaffle Port after I'd left Helberg. It explained some of the behaviour I'd observed, where men – quite a lot of men now I came to think of it – seemed less interested in my face than my chest and buttocks. This was most definitely the case in the memory I'd just experienced, because the faces of TayTay and Mimi became less and less distinct the more time Rufus spent with them.

I wandered out of my room to find Hattie. "What do you think it is that makes us the people we are?" I asked.

She looked up from her beans. "It's very early for a question like that. Right, let's think. Our names and our faces are all different, and we have a special number assigned to our Jaffle Port, so the system knows who we are."

"True," I said, "but there are other things. Like ... like I never met anyone who loved Smiley Tots as much as you."

Hattie beamed with pride. "That's true. Me neither."

I thought hard. "But I suppose what I was really asking is whether other people see us the same way that we see ourselves? I don't think they do."

Hattie stared at me. "You're probably right, but it doesn't really matter what other people think about us, does it?"

"No." I nodded and gave a small sigh of relief. "No it doesn't."

"Apart from when Levi thought I'd taken Brandine's bagel," said Hattie, wide-eyed with horror at the memory. "*That* was horrible."

~

WE LEFT the apartment to go to work, the last day before a two day rest period.

"Take a look," I said as they stepped outside, unable to suppress a grin. "Can you see what I did?"

Hattie turned to look at our door. She turned her head one way and then another. "Something's definitely changed," she said, "but I can't put my finger on it. Have you polished the handle?"

I shook my head.

"No, I did that last week," said Hattie. "Something's shinier, definitely. Go on, tell me."

"The whole *door's* shinier. I painted it, look!" I said. I dragged Hattie to look at the next door along and then back again. "See? that one's drab and faded while *ours* is bright and shiny!"

Hattie nodded, and squinted critically as she glanced between the two. "I see it, I do."

"Come on, let's get to work."

~

BEFORE LUNCH, Paulette called a section meeting. Everyone talked in subdued whispers, wondering what was going on. "Just as long as we don't have to watch the Film again," said Hattie, fearful. I patted her shoulder.

Paulette took to the stage. "Jaffle Tech prides itself not only on its customer service but its relationship with the community, both global and local. We are part of a family, a corporate family and a worldwide family and—"

"Let's cut to the chase," said Levi, stepping in. "A felonious act has been committed and a member of staff – here! – has been implicated."

He held up a tunic that clearly matched the uniform that we all wore. I willed myself to keep calm. It was mine, but Levi clearly didn't know that, or he would not be addressing us as a group.

"The individual concerned has broken into a nearby residence and committed several acts of criminal damage and theft," said Levi.

Shocked gasps could be heard around the room and heads shook in disbelief.

"This tunic was left behind, and the victim believes she herself spoke to the perpetrator earlier in the day."

A hand went up. "A caller? Are you saying that one of us went round to a caller's house?"

"No," said Levi. "This was someone who met the victim on the street. Now, the victim agreed to share her memory of that encounter with us for the purposes of identifying the perpetrator. We're going to take a look at that recording, so please all pay close attention. Every one of your colleagues will be seeing this, because Jaffle's reputation is on the line here. I hope y'all understand just how big a deal this is. We cannot afford to compromise our position and standing in the community."

Levi fixed them all with his serious look again and then started the film.

I gripped the arms of my chair as I recognised Claire's garden and saw two figures approaching from the road. How was it possible that Hattie and I hadn't already been identified?

"Can I help you?" came Claire's voice from the screen. Two faces turned towards them. I nearly burst out laughing when I saw them. They were both as featureless as Smiley Tots. Bland idiotic smiles beamed out of two identical moon-like faces, topped with hair that looked as though it belonged on a doll. Neither Hattie nor I had plaits, and yet identical plaits swung at the sides of these two faces. They even walked strangely, dragging their limbs along the road and making odd growling sounds, like they were animals.

"Are you blind?" one of the faces asked Claire, contorting grotesquely, even going a little bit cross-eyed to underline this was a stupid person talking.

Hattie stiffened at my side. She recognised the situation. I willed her to keep quiet.

I realised that Claire's memory was very like Rufus Jaffle's: the recollection was distorted. Rufus Jaffle had inflated his companions' breasts and more or less forgotten their faces. Claire had also forgotten mine and Hattie's faces, while retaining the impression she was speaking with a pair of imbeciles. It worked in my favour: it was impossible for anybody to identify me from this evidence. I peered at Hattie's intense expression. Well, almost impossible.

"Anybody got any ideas?" asked Levi.

Hattie's hand started to move up. I slammed it back down onto the arm of her chair.

"Ow!" said Hattie.

Several people turned to look but another hand had gone up as a member of staff pointed out the obvious. "Those people don't look like any of us."

""It is possible that the victim had been drinking that morning," said Levi. "Alcohol, you understand."

Paulette gestured to Levi and spoke to him tersely.

"But it's true," he replied. "Just the facts, ma'am."

"Why did you do that?" Hattie said to me. "I was going to tell them and then you hurt my hand."

"Because you were going to tell them," I hissed. "Now, shush."

Levi cleared his throat, his argument with Paulette concluded. "The victim may or may not have been drinking. That's immaterial. This is the footage evidence we have. Any other questions?"

"Has this got anything to do with Brandine's bagel being stolen?" someone called out.

"No," said Paulette.

"We cannot rule anything out at this time," said Levi. "Who knows how the criminal mind works."

A reminder pinged in my calendar: the brain scan in the medical room. It was due now.

What would the scan reveal? Surely, it would uncover the changes I had been experiencing over the last day. Did I have a brain virus or had I simply been 'awakened' in some way? My system data showed I was operating on Jaffle Standard but I very much doubted that was true now. If they restored my brain, removed any change, rebuilt any instabilities, what would I lose? I had just started to get to grips with colours and new tastes, and a whole banquet of new emotions and physical feelings that I certainly wasn't ready to put aside. And would they find out what I had done recently, the 'felonious act' I committed at Claire's house?

Paulette wrapped up the meeting and the section staff filed out. Hattie snivelled to herself as we went.

I took her hand. "Hattie?"

She glanced at me but only for a moment. There was fear and confusion in my friend's eyes. I steered her round a corner and into the toilets.

"I don't need the toilet!" she wailed.

I pulled her into a cubicle.

"Do *you* need the toilet?" Hattie asked, gabbling. "I don't. I don't think so. I don't know anymore. That was us in the video and I was going to tell them and then you hurt me. Why did you hurt me? Did you mean to hurt me? I don't understand."

"I'm sorry," I said and stroked Hattie's face.

"Are we in trouble?" she asked.

I forced a laugh. "No. Of course not."

"That was you and me in that woman's memory, wasn't it?"

"It didn't really look like us."

"It didn't really look like *anybody*," said Hattie. "Was it your tunic they found in her house?"

I considered denying everything, but sooner or later I needed to find a new tunic, and until then it would be very easy for Hattie to check.

"Right. I'm sorry. I kept this from you, but I'll tell you the truth," I said. "I had no idea it would all get so crazy."

"What's crazy?" said Hattie.

"Yesterday, when I was in my cubicle, I stood up too quickly and ripped my tunic on the chair. It was really bad, a great big hole." I gestured, indicating an imaginary tear across my entire torso. "So I went down to supplies to see about getting a new one. Anyway, when I got there, I saw that there was nobody on the front desk, so I walked in and there was a gang of masked intruders."

"No!"

"Yes. They said they wanted a Jaffle tunic to do a robbery, so they'd come to take one."

"No!"

"Yes."

"So it was them?" said Hattie. "They must have been the ones who broke into that house?"

"Yes. They took a tunic and threatened me a with a gun to keep my mouth shut. You can see my predicament, can't you?"

"Tell Paulette. Tell Levi. They can't get you now."

"They also threatened to hurt the dog," I added, my mind freewheeling.

"There was a dog?"

"Yes, a dog. Long floppy ears, smiley face."

"Dogs aren't normally smiley," said Hattie with a frown. "You should tell anyway, and the dog can take its chances."

I should have realised that Hattie didn't care much for dogs, especially after the poop incident. "Aaaand, they also said they'd come round to our house and hurt the Smiley Tots."

Hattie's reaction took some time to play out. First her hands went to her face, clamping her cheeks as she inhaled noisily, then they found the top of her head, which she pressed as if might come off, and finally pressed to her bosom. She made tragic gulping sounds and staggered around in circles which, in the cubicle, meant bouncing repeatedly off the walls.

"We mustn't let anyone find out," she whispered.

I nodded. "Don't worry, I'll keep my mouth shut. It will be fine, you'll see."

I RETURNED Hattie to her desk and calmed her a bit by saying she should look at some of the latest Smiley Tots on sale. Then I put a call through to the medical centre.

"Hi, I have a scan scheduled for today."

"Yes, Alice. Everything is ready for you. Come down now if you would."

"That's the thing," I said. "We've hit a bit of an emergency up here. Unusually high demand in our sector. I'm going to need to postpone our appointment."

"You're calling very late to cancel."

"I know."

"And your supervisor should be able to authorise your absence. It's not a lengthy procedure."

"Yes, but as I say there's a lot of work on. I don't want to bother my supervisor. She's under a lot of pressure as it is."

"I don't think you appreciate how much this facility costs the organisation."

"No," I said ambiguously.

The woman sighed. "I'll book you in for the same time tomorrow but—"

"I have two rest days after today."

"Then on your return. I've booked it in. Please ensure you're here on time."

"Thank you," I said and breathed a sigh of relief.

14

I sat and thought about how I could get up to the
executive floor to see Rufus Jaffle. I made a list on my
wipe-clean notepad.

roof

helicopter

ladder

elevator

rope

steal pass

Obviously some people had legitimate access to those
floors. There was Rufus himself, his secretary, probably
service personnel like cleaners, caterers, and maintenance
engineers. I paused and thought for a moment about the
outlandish story I had told Hattie. It reminded me I actually
did need to go and get another tunic, but the germ of an idea
was starting to form.

At the end of my shift I went down to supplies. Someone called Damien was on reception.

"Hi Damien, I've been sent down by Rufus Jaffle to pick up some uniforms."

"Have you got the requisition paperwork?" he asked.

"No, he said that this is off the record."

"Jaffle did?"

"Rufus Jaffle, yes. And he said Damien would be sure to be discreet."

"He mentioned me by name?"

"He's the boss. He knows about you, Damien."

"Sweet. So what do you need?" Damien grinned with pride.

"I need a set of coveralls for a maintenance engineer and a tunic like this one," I said.

Damien shrugged. "He's the boss. Yes, he is." He led me into a storeroom. "Any idea of the sizes that you need?"

I gestured to myself. "Oh, you know, average. Probably about my size, I'd say. I'll need one of those caps and one of those tool bags too."

In the bathroom I changed into the maintenance engineers coveralls and put on the cap, shoving my hair underneath. Everything else went into the tool bag. I walked up to reception.

"Got a call for the exec floor," I said, attempting to disguise my voice. Both of the receptionists peered anxiously at me.

"Have you got a sore throat?" asked the male receptionist.

"Um, what?"

"I can get you a glass of water if you like?"

"Your colleague is over there, just getting in the elevator," said the female receptionist.

"Is he?" I said and sprinted for the doors.

As the doors closed, the real engineer turned and looked at me. "Not seen you before," he said.

I looked up at him. Part of me wanted to get back out and admit my mistake, but I'd got this far and I really needed to get to Rufus Jaffle. I needed to blind this man with officious superiority. I decided to cast myself as a female Levi and see where it led.

"There's a very good reason for that," I said. "If quality spot checks are done by co-workers they are often found to be inaccurate. You ever been quality spot checked before?"

"Uh, no."

"Right. It's simple enough. I will give you some time to do the job, unhindered, and then you will answer any questions I might have about the quality of what you've done. Understand?"

"I think so," he said. "Sorry? Who are you?"

"I'm a ghost," I said. "A silent observer. You have to act like I'm not even here."

"Oh, okay."

"Smart man. You'll do fine, I've no doubt. Now what's the job?"

"Conference room window hydraulics are not working."

"Good. Well you get along and fix that and I'll inspect another task from last week." I looked straight ahead as the elevator doors opened.

"Oh, what task is that?" he asked.

"I cannot comment on an ongoing investigation," I said and stalked down the corridor towards Jaffle's office.

I waited until the engineer had disappeared before knocking on Rufus Jaffle's door. There was no reply. I tried the handle and found it unlocked. I went inside.

"Hello?"

There was nobody there. There was no luxury drone on the balcony beyond the glass wall. As I scanned the room I realised it was unchanged since my last visit. Not just unchanged, it was *untouched*. The tea cups were still on the tray, unwashed. The chairs were still tilted back from the clean-up job. I shook my head at my own naivety and my foolish assumption that Rufus Jaffle would be in the office every day like a regular person. He'd probably be off somewhere doing rich person things, attending extravagant parties and making important decisions on behalf of the workers at Jaffle Tech.

So if he wasn't here, maybe I could find a way to contact him. I jipped the local area to see if there was anything accessible via my Jaffle Port but the security here was as tight as could be expected.

I could always ask Jaffle's secretary, Florence. Or Cremona, or Milan, or whatever. Hadn't Rufus said she was a European princess?

I went over to the wall to look for the hidden door to the secretary's office. The wall appeared to be seamless. Long way round then, I thought.

Out in the corridor I walked to the secretarial office. The door was locked. I knocked.

"Milan?" I hissed through the door. "Your Highness?"

There was no response. The elevator dinged. I glanced back. A group of people, all in suits, stepped out. Jethro Henderson at the forefront. I turned quickly to hide my face and moved away down the corridor.

They followed me!

I picked up the pace and dodged through the first open door. It was a conference room, luxurious contemporary seating arranged around a long table which looked far too large to be practical. Around the walls, pieces of Jaffle Tech from the company's long history were displayed in glass cabinets.

By the window, the engineer was working on a sticky hinge.

A bot-trolley detached itself from the wall, and jipped my Jaffle Port to ask if I wanted anything to eat or drink. The body of the snack-bot was a warming cabinet that held plates and the top was arranged with glasses of drink and bitesize snacks.

I waved it away. The engineer glanced round at me.

"Silent observer," I reminded him. "I'm not here."

He smiled and nodded.

The door handle turned. I near leapt in alarm. The suits were coming in.

I ducked behind a cleaning bot standing in the shadow of display cabinet. The cabinet held some sort of insect mounted on a card which read, *2009 - the first wireless flying insect cyborg demonstrated at a conference in Italy.*

I was just in time. The door opened and people walked in.

"So, make yourselves comfortable and I'll take us through the agenda," said Henderson. "Hey, you!"

"Sir?" said the engineer.

"Whatever you're doing, get out."

The engineer silently gathered his tools and made his way round the long table to the exit. He looked at me, squatting in my hiding space. I made a frantic slicing *No!* gesture with my hand. He tapped his nose and winked.

"Not even here," he said.

"That's right," said Henderson closing the door behind the engineer.

I was trapped in the room with them. I made myself as small as I could.

"Operation Sunrise has been given the green light for implementation," said Henderson.

"Rufus signed off on it?" said a man, surprised.

"He did. Michael here witnessed it. So, we just need to put it past the rest of the board and we go live in fifteen days. Five pm on the nineteenth."

A hand (from my position, I couldn't see who it belonged to) waved for a drink and the snack-bot trundled over.

"We four need to be crystal clear about our business objectives," said Henderson, "and make sure that everyone knows the success criteria for their area of responsibility. So as I run through each area, chip in."

There was the clink of glass and a crunch of eating. The cleaning bot next to me rolled out of its position towards the table.

Crumbs, I thought. With the cleaning bot gone, my hiding place was barely any hiding place at all. Any one of the people at the table just had to look round and they'd see me squatting on the floor.

"First of all," said Henderson, "let's touch on political liaison and media response. Jessica?"

"Thanks, Jethro," said a suit. "If you'd look at the screen..."

There was a change in the room's lighting. All eyes would be on the screen. I slipped from my hiding place and crossed the short distance to the window curtains. They were long and billowy and, if I stood perfectly upright and pressed myself flat, I'd not create a noticeable bulge.

"We know some people are uncomfortable with change," Jessica was saying. "There are politicians and opinion makers outside our control. We have to win them over by pointing to our past successes. Blindness eradicated, the dementia epidemic reversed, our unarguable role in education and law and order. This is Jaffle Tech's image and Jaffle Tech's legacy. Believe me, we still have a lot of brownie points. We keep punching those messages home and, if anyone starts to badmouth Operation Sunrise, it's going to sound like sour grapes and groundless doom-mongering."

There were approving noises. I worried that my feet might be visible under the very bottom edge of the curtain. I tried to angle them sideways without falling over.

"And remember," said Jessica, "we only need to worry about public opinion until the roll-out is complete. By reducing customers to a lower level of functionality, we expect levels of satisfaction to be consistently higher. Happy voters are what the politicians want, after all."

"Are we rolling out the plippers at the same time?" a man asked.

"The same day," said another voice. "We're going to deadcat Operation Sunrise with a distribution of plippers to all law enforcement bodies in the country. The plipper technology is already covered in the last set of user Ts and Cs. Everyone has already given their consent."

"Everyone?" said another.

There was mild laughter. "Everyone on Jaffle Enhanced and below, Marcus," said Henderson. "Don't worry. You're not about to get plipped."

Plipper. Plipped. The words meant nothing to me.

"Mind if I just close the blinds?" asked someone.

I froze. The curtain rail began to move. My new hiding place was unbunching and about to be less than useless. I signalled the snack-bot to bring me a drink and as it drifted over, cancelled the order. I dropped behind it.

The snack-bot rolled away and I rolled with it. As I passed the far end of the table, now directly beneath the screen but away from the gaze of the suits, I crouched low and let the snack-bot go on. Instinctively, I took a crispbread snack from its top as it left.

"How extensively have the plippers been tested?"

"The test labs have run through eight hundred different test scenarios and the plippers have performed perfectly. Have you all seen it in action? No? Oh, I should. Let me..." Henderson went quiet as he sent off a communication.

I broke off a crumb of crispbread and dropped it on the floor. The cleaning bot came over to silently vacuum it up. I broke another crumb and cast it a little further away, towards the door. The cleaning bot moved on, me with it.

"I can imagine there will be moral objections to plipper technology," said Marcus.

"Why?" asked Jessica. "Do you know how many people die each year in this country while being arrested. Even non-lethal tech such as Tasers causes up to fifty deaths nationwide. With the implementation of plippers, that number will effectively drop to zero."

There was a knock at the door. I peered round the edge of the cleaning bot, and I saw Levi walk in. I guessed he was seeing it for the first time, as his eyes took in the size of the space and the ostentatiousness of the furnishings.

"Hi Levi, good of you to join us," said Henderson. "Would you be kind enough to carry out an ad-hoc security check on the room?"

I was about to be busted. Levi wouldn't have to look very hard to notice me.

"Yes, sir, happy to help." He walked briskly around the room. As he came along the edge of the table he simply looked down and saw me. I pulled a face, attempting to convey this wasn't what it looked like and could he please not give me away.

"And now the plipper," Henderson said. The was a soft push-button click.

Levi lifted a hand to point. I could see his mouth starting to form a sentence. Then he dropped to the floor like a rag doll.

I stifled a gasp. Was he dead? No, he sat up slowly, his face slack and vacant. His eyes were open, but they saw nothing. I realised with horror that he was now an Empty. The plipper that Henderson had pressed so casually had instantly taken his brain function down to the most basic level.

Henderson put a device back down on the table. "Well, I think we can be satisfied by the response time," he said. "Marcus, we'll need to monitor that carefully as rollout progresses, make sure it remains sub-second. Yes?"

"Sure. And what do you want to do with him?"

"We'll get him back onto his regular level after the meeting," said Henderson. "He's no bother to anyone there."

I had to get out of the room. I broke further crumbs for the cleaning bot and kept pace at its side. I needed to make sure it moved consistently – it would definitely draw attention if it slowed or stopped. Levi had left the door open a little when he'd entered – thank goodness – and the cleaning bot and I slipped through the gap. I rushed to the elevator.

15

5TH JUNE – 14 DAYS UNTIL OPERATION SUNRISE

Curtains.

I lay in my bed listening to the morning sounds of Hattie carrying out the day's cleaning tasks. Today was curtains, according to her rota. Every fortnight without fail they were all washed, dried and ironed. She'd be in here shortly if I didn't get up.

I lay there, listening to the huffs of a woman for whom happiness was a clean home. I thought about my situation and Operation Sunrise (whatever that was), about plipper devices and the dead Empty look on Levi's face. If there was any danger that my new abilities would be taken away – and I was certain there was – then I had to squeeze the most out of them while I could.

I rose, went to the wardrobe and looked at Claire's dress. It was magnificent if impractical. I could really do with finding some other clothes that were as colourful, clothes which I might be able to wear more regularly. I put on a tunic and went to find Hattie. She had finished loading the washing machine, and now had a pair of Smiley Tots in her arms. She was nuzzling them against her face.

"Good morning Alice," she said. "We were about to come and wake you. The twins are lively today."

"Yeah?" I said.

"I think that perhaps they want to watch Mr Smiley. What do you say twins?"

"They look, um, chirpy. It's because you take such good care of them."

"Who wouldn't want to love these babies? Such adorable Munchkins." Hattie made enthusiastic if alarming chomping noises at the Smiley Tots. "Now, you sit down with the twins and I'll work around you."

"Actually, I want to go out and buy some clothes today," I said.

Hattie gave me a long hard look, making sure I noticed it was long and hard. "You don't need to buy clothes," she said.

"I don't *need* any, no."

"All of our tunics are free."

"Yes."

"We get given them."

"Yes, but there are other clothes, not just tunics."

"I don't understand."

"I just feel like getting something different. Something with a bit more colour." I tried to act casual, as if this wasn't a major departure from normal behaviour.

Hattie narrowed her eyes at me. "When's your brain scan?"

"That's got nothing to do with it."

"You might have a brain virus."

"I don't have a brain virus."

"Have armed criminals stolen your tunic again?"

"No."

"Maybe they made you say that. Blink twice if you're being forced to do this."

"I'm not being forced to do this."

"You blinked."

"That was an ordinary blink," I said. "People blink."

"Maybe they made you say that too. Blink twice and—"

"I'm fine!" I insisted. "It's just that I'd quite like a change."

"I don't like change," grumbled Hattie.

I had beans for breakfast. I hadn't got hold of any bacon, and my research indicated that bacon, once extracted from the pig, needed to be kept cold in a fridge and cooked using a cooker. We didn't have either of those things and I wasn't sure Hattie was ready for that sort of upheaval in our apartment.

I left on a mission. What I'd told Hattie was partly true, I genuinely did want to get some more clothes, but what I really craved was colour. I went outside, spent ten minutes talking to the oblivious Empties on the kerb and then called a car.

"Take me somewhere colourful," I said.

"Destination not recognised," said the car.

"Take me to the flowers," I tried.

"Do you want to go to a flower market?" the car asked.

I didn't know what that meant so I jipped it. Lots of flowers. Retailers and buyers. I jipped some images. "Yes!" I said.

I watched the changing cityscape as we drove to the flower market. It was an uneven patchwork of houses and apartment complexes, segments of colour and no colour. I reckoned I could bet where the folks on Jaffle Standard lived, in buildings of sludgy beige and grey. The houses of those on Jaffle Enhanced and Jaffle Premium betrayed their owners with the painted detail on the walls or colourful curtains fluttering at the window. Hattie worried constantly about the cleanliness of our curtains, but she never considered their plainness or their ugly putty colour was a problem.

The car pulled up outside a gated area. I couldn't see any flowers, but when I got out I thought I could smell something. I walked into a huge building with high ceilings. There were rows of little enclosures with tables and displays that were covered in flowers. There were so many different sorts of flowers, in so many colours.

A woman looked up from her counter. "Are you lost?"

"No," I said. "I've come to look at the flowers."

"You're a bit late."

"Late?" It was mid-morning.

She took in my tunic. "You've been sent?"

"No, I..."

"Maybe your boss told you to get some...?"

"Flowers," I said firmly. "I've come for some flowers. Some nice ones."

"Well, you came to the right place." She smiled. "Any particular sort that you – or your boss – prefer?"

"I don't know very much about them," I admitted.

"Well then," she said, walking round so she could stroll

along the display with me, "these ones here are carnations. Very popular."

"What are those big ones at the back?" I had my eye on some huge yellow flowers that looked a bit like Mr Smiley.

"Sunflowers," she said. You pay per stem for those. Some of the others come in bunches."

"Which are the ones I can smell?" I asked, sniffing.

"You'll be smelling lots of different ones," she said, "but the roses and the freesias, most likely."

"And which are those?"

"Fuchsias. Gorgeous, yes?"

"And what colour would you call that?"

"Fuchsia," said the woman.

"Wow. Is the flower named after the colour or is the colour named after the flower?"

"I couldn't rightly say," she said.

I didn't want to jip it. The mystery of the colour and the flower were enough.

The woman spent another thirty minutes showing me all of the flowers. I bought as many as I could wheel to the gate with one of their big trolleys. I called a car with extra luggage space so I could take them all back home. The smell inside the car for the journey was intoxicating, and every time I looked at the flowers, swaying gently in the boxes as the car moved, I smiled just to see all of the colours.

When I got back it took me six journeys to unload and take all of the flowers upstairs. Of course, I tried to get the Empties to admire the colours as I carried them past, but they wouldn't even look. I put the flowers outside our door and went inside.

"Hattie, I've got a surprise."

She gave me a suspicious look. Surprises from her roommate Alice were something to be wary of these days.

"Come look," I said.

Hattie finished dressing a Smiley Tot and followed me out. "Oh my goodness, what are all these?" she asked.

"Flowers!" I cried. "Gorgeous fresh flowers. We can have them all round the apartment, as a display. It will look so amazing."

"You want to take them inside?"

"Yes."

"Actually into our home?"

"Yes," I said. "Look at them, they're gorgeous!"

"Why?"

"Why are they gorgeous or why do I want to bring them in?"

"Either! Both! I don't see why you want to bring dead plants into the house."

"They're not dead."

"But bits are falling off them! Is this like the chi-eeese? Are we supposed to eat them?"

"No, they're not for that."

"Then what are they *for*?"

I look at the flowers arranged in the hallway. "They're not *for* anything. They just *are*."

"Are what?"

I shrugged. "Lovely."

Hattie glared at me. "I'm not going to slam this door. It's too noisy and it might chip the woodwork. So, you'll just have to pretend."

Hattie slammed the door slowly and quietly in my face. Miserable to see that my quest to brighten the flat had ended in failure, I hauled the flowers downstairs to the lobby.

"That's a lot of flowers," said Helberg, loitering in the doorway of his office.

"I wanted to have a mixture of colours," I said.

"Bought with my money? Never seen the point of cut flowers. Give me a living plant or a painting any day."

"I've already painted the door," I said.

"I don't mean paint something. I mean a painting. A picture."

I thought about the pictures that I'd seen in Rufus Jaffle's office. I wondered if Hattie would enjoy *Dogs Playing Poker*. "Pictures – pictures on walls – they're made out of paint."

He nodded.

"Ooh."

The possibilities whirled in my mind. I grabbed some more tins of paint and took them upstairs.

"And what am I supposed to do with these flowers?" Helberg called after me.

16

I ran down our landing, nearly kicking over Helberg's bot, Hungry Horace, as it tried and failed to vacuum up the leaves I'd let fall on the floor.

"I don't like flowers," said Hattie when I went inside.

"It's fine. They're all gone."

She looked at the paints in my arms.

"The flowers are gone," I assured her.

Hattie flopped onto the sofa, viciously cuddling an armful of Smiley Tots.

"Yes, you rest. Watch something. I'm just going to paint the wall."

"What?"

"Helberg gave me the paint," I said, in an effort to legitimise what I was about to do. "I think we're almost due some maintenance anyway."

Hattie glowered and turned back to the screen. I prised

the lid off all of the paint tins and tried to remember what the dogs playing cards looked like.

I started with green. There was a green card table at the centre of the picture, so I splashed some green onto the wall behind the sofa. Drips ran down the wall, which was annoying. I looked at the other tins. I needed something that was dog-coloured. There was one called *Mahogany* which looked good. I dipped in the brush and tried to make something which looked like a dog on the wall. It was tougher than I'd imagined. I summoned a mental picture of a dog, but it was all waggy tail and lolling tongue. I jipped a dog picture instead. It became clearer what I needed to do. I needed a body, a head, a tail and four legs. I swirled paint into a body. First job done. I then made something like a head, on top of the body and then added brush strokes for the legs and the tail. I stood back and looked. The thing on the wall looked more like a bear, or the massive enlargement of a dust mite Hattie had shown me once. Perhaps when my dog was playing cards it would come to life.

"Oh."

I realised that it would need to be holding the cards with two of its paws, which were currently at the bottom of my dog-bear, just above the floor. Had the picture in Rufus Jaffle's office had the dogs sitting up? Making a painting was much harder than it looked.

Not to worry, there was plenty of wall left. I decided to paint the kangaroo which haunted my dreams. The brown colour was a decent match. I started with its big legs, coming up in a powerful kick, which I could see very vividly. They came out to the side, which looked impossible, until you saw that the kangaroo had a very large tail that held it off the ground while its legs were elsewhere.

I painted two legs, sticking out towards the dog. I followed that with the tail that anchored it to the ground. Now I just needed to add the body and head. I filled in the space between the tail and the legs, but I couldn't quite think where the head should be, so I added it on top. I stepped back.

I had created an image which looked very unlike an animal. As I twisted my head one way and then another I decided it looked more like a chair on its side, with a large pile of soil on it. I wondered whether Hattie would be able to see the kangaroo.

"Hey Hattie, what do you think this looks like?" I asked.

Hattie stood up and turned to see. "Oh. There's stuff all over the wall," she said in alarm.

"Yes, it's paint," I pointed out.

"Paint isn't supposed to look like mess," said Hattie.

I thought she was being a bit unreasonable. "It's not mess, it's a picture," I said.

"A picture? Of what?"

"That one there is a dog."

"No it's not. What's the big green square?" she asked.

"A card table. The dog was going to be playing cards, but that didn't work. What about this one? This is a kangaroo."

She looked long and hard at the wall. I guessed she'd jipped a picture of a kangaroo, but there was no glimmer of recognition in her eyes. She looked up and down the wall and sighed unhappily. Then her gaze dropped and she screamed.

"No!"

"What?"

"I can't believe it! What did you do?"

I moved forward to where she was pointing.

"No, get back! You'll get more on them!"

I saw that a drip of paint had landed on one of the Smiley Tots and was running down its face. Hattie dabbed at it with the end of her sleeve, tears running from her eyes.

She scooped up all of the Smiley Tots that were on the sofa. No mean feat as there were at least twelve. She staggered out of the room with them in her outstretched arms.

"I don't know what you think you're doing, Alice, but you've..." She made a noise like Hungry Horace, a broken sucking sob. "You're ruining everything!"

She pushed past me and went to her room. This time she did slam the door.

I stood there, not knowing what to do or say. I wanted to tell Hattie that it was just a doll and it didn't matter, but I knew that her Smiley Tots were so much more to her. Presently, she began to cry, wailing and inconsolable.

I silently put the lids back on the tins and took them back to Helberg.

"Making pictures is hard," I said, flinging myself into one of his chairs.

"And hello to you," said Helberg.

"No, I said making—"

"I heard."

"What have you got that will get paint off things?" I asked.

"Things?"

"Smiley Tots."

"Have you been painting them too?"

He had been poring over some bits of broken rubbish, but now searched along shelves. "Try this." He passed me a bottle labelled *thinners*. "Make sure it doesn't melt the fabric, it's quite strong."

"Will it melt the Smiley Tots?"

"Possibly."

I growled at myself. "I tried to paint a dog and a kangaroo, but they didn't look right."

"Artists take a long time to learn how to paint well," he said. "Don't beat yourself up."

"I have never seen an artist doing painting. Good ones or bad ones. If they take a long time to learn then where are they all doing their learning?"

"Ah, that is a deep and interesting question," said Helberg, tapping the side of his nose.

"You're doing that thing again," I said.

"What thing?"

"Of being annoying. Of saying things that make no sense and making me feel like an idiot."

"I don't think you're an idiot, Alice," he said. "In fact, quite the opposite. You've become quite an interesting person of late."

"Well, enjoy it while you can," I said, miserably.

"I intend to. I think we should go on a trip."

"Are you actually going to teach me something? Actually help me and not just go 'Ah' and tap your nose?"

He stood. "Actual help. A small practical lesson."

I followed him outside and he called a car. "Destination is the museum and art gallery," he told it. He produced a card-like device and waved it over an interface panel. "Transfer credits for journey optimised for speed."

"Why are you talking to the car like that?" I asked.

"Like what?"

"Your Jaffle Port takes care of the payment details. You don't need to tell it what to do or waved cards about."

"You mean *your* Jaffle Port does that," he said.

I was about to ask him what he meant by that but he started talking.

"You can do research about art, and when we look at the paintings I'll suggest some pointers for things you might want to look up, but let's start right at the beginning. When do you think people started to make art?"

I had no idea. "When? Crumbs. Was it a long time ago?"

"Yes. A very long time ago," said Helberg. "There's a cave in France where there are paintings that are forty thousand years old."

"No way!"

"Yes. For as long as there have been people, there's been the irresistible urge to depict the world around us and make marks on whatever is to hand." He gave me a sideways look. "Is there by any chance an appalling mess on your apartment wall?"

"Might be," I said. "I don't think Hattie approves.

"We can tidy it up. Anyway, that's when people started to make art. When do you think they stopped?"

"Oh," I said, understanding dawning. "Do you mean that nobody is creating new paintings now? Surely that can't be true? Not everyone is reduced to Jaffle Standard. Why aren't people on the premium packages doing painting?"

Helberg sat back in the car seat. "I'm not saying nobody has painted a picture in the last twenty years. I expect that there are people who play around at it, but anyone rich enough to be on Jaffle Premium aren't necessarily going to follow a passion for painting. We live in age of planned obsolescence, Alice. With machines and bots and Jaffle swarms doing all the work for us, we don't really need people to do very much at all. The forces that govern society would rather that we, individual humans, don't get the idea into our heads that we have value, that we contribute."

"But the people of Jaffle Premium. If they've got more access to their brain capacity, shouldn't they be making greater contributions to society?"

"You've met some of them. What do you think?"

I wondered about that. "Surely they're not all awful?"

"The system works best if we're all happy as we are; that none of us want things to change."

"What level are you on, anyway?" I asked.

The look he gave me was deep and unreadable and – though I wasn't sure what made me think it – it was the most real look he'd ever given me. Like I'd caught a true glimpse of the actual Patrick Helberg for the first time. A shiver ran through me.

He gave a sad little smile which abruptly broadened. "Look, we're here."

17

The car had pulled up outside an imposing old building. It looked as though it had been here for a very long time, with stone pillars and a door that the car could have driven through.

The entrance hall, at the top of a series of stone steps, was cool and very large. The tiles on the floor were coloured, and patterned in a very pleasing way. I stopped to stare at them.

"Is this art?" I asked.

"Well, it's not really an exhibit," Helberg said. "It's part of the aesthetic though."

I jipped *aesthetic* and decided it was a word I would use again in the future.

"You should look up the Arts and Crafts movement," he said. "This building dates from then, and the decor is from that period. Look at the door, for example."

I saw the door had a large brass handle and a finger plate with ends that looped around, formed curling tendrils which reminded me of how plants looked when they were growing in a garden.

"Lovely."

"Let's start in the Medieval gallery," Helberg said. "You might be interested to see some of the techniques from years ago."

We went into a large room with paintings on the wall. The room had nothing else inside it apart from the paintings, and benches where you could sit and look at them. We took a seat.

Helberg pointed at an image. "So, do you see how artists of this time had not discovered the thing we call perspective?" he asked.

I jipped what he meant and then looked at the picture. It showed some people in unusual clothing, jostling together under an archway, and thought I understood. It was curiously flat and I could see nothing behind the people.

We sat and looked at it for a few minutes. There were so many amazing features which the artist had taken care to record. Above the arches was some sort of bright orange building. I wondered if it was meant to be a real building. Even the frame was incredible.

"Who made the frame?" I asked.

"I don't know," said Helberg. "Sometimes pictures get new frames. As long as it makes the picture look good, the frame's doing its job."

I nodded. "So where are the paintings where they got the hang of perspective?"

Helberg smiled. "There are a great many of those, don't worry. Ready to move on?"

We moved into a gallery called Early Italian. The paintings were full of stern-faced people with remarkable skin. A good many of them featured the same mother and baby. They must have been very famous, sort of an early version of Mr Smiley.

"Babies..." I said, musing out loud.

"That's Jesus," said Helberg, nodding at the baby in the nearest portrait.

"Oh, you know him?"

"Not personally."

His words chimed with my thoughts. "I don't know any babies either," I said.

Helberg seemed to find this amusing.

"No," I said. "I mean, I don't see babies around. I was one once, of course. I think."

"You think?" he said, still smiling.

I jipped where babies came from. I didn't tell Helberg I was doing that because I didn't want him to mock me. I had a half-formed notion of how babies were produced; I discovered that half-formed notion was a greatly simplified version of the truth.

"And what's her name?" I said, pointing.

"Mary?" he said.

I nodded. I looked at Mary and Jesus and was struck how much it reminded me of Hattie with her Smiley Tots. I gasped at the realisation, wondering how I'd never seen it before. Had Hattie ever held a real baby? She would make a wonderful mother, but of course, the prospect was never even considered as an option for people on Jaffle Standard.

Their lives were more or less controlled to be sex and child-free.

I looked at Mary. "I bet she's not on Jaffle Standard," I said.

"No, I don't believe so," smiled Helberg.

Mary, like Rufus Jaffle and Claire and all those others on higher Jaffle systems were all privileged, or (as I had come to realise) normal, fully functioning humans. The injustice of it was astounding. I found I was gripping my hands into tight fists. I'd dug my nails into my palms and left deep red nail marks. I could feel my face set in a grim frown.

"Not a fan of religious art, huh?" Helberg said.

I shook my head and tried to dispel my mood. We moved on.

Helberg was right about the perspective, these painters had made their scenes look a lot more realistic, although not quite in the same way as *Dogs playing Poker*.

We turned a corner. "Oh, crumbs!" I said.

We were faced with a room that was almost entirely filled with naked people. I wasn't used to seeing other people without their clothes, and there were dozens of them.

Helberg moved through the room, gazing at them fondly. "Stunning, aren't they?"

I wasn't sure if he was talking about the pictures or breasts.

There were male nudes as well, and I took the opportunity to take a long hard look at how the painter had carefully captured the muscle definition and curls of hair. It was a pleasing sight. The penises were not as captivating as I'd expected them to be. I recalled what I had learned of sex in my earlier education and my more recent, circumspect research. I didn't think any of these tiny penises would be up to the task for which they were intended.

"Getting an eyeful of wangs?" he said.

I blushed. "I researched the sex act."

"The sex act," he said, amused.

"And I really don't see how a penis could penetrate *anything*. Look how small they all are."

"Tiny dicks were very much in vogue back then."

"But even..." I gazed around, looking for an example that more closely matched the images I had seen in my research. I started to make size gestures with my hand and Helberg grinned.

"You need to research erections," he said. "I think you'll be impressed with the transformation that takes place between a flaccid—"

"Woah," I said, automatically jipping *erections*. I looked at the penises in the room with new interest. Who could imagine they could spring into life like that? "Do they all do that?" I asked, astounded.

"These are just paintings," he pointed out.

"Gosh," I said. A funny feeling came over me, and not just the thrill of education. I looked at Helberg, the only actual man in the room. He caught me looking.

"Were you looking for a practical demonstration?" he asked wryly and walked on.

We moved through many more galleries. I started to get an idea of just how big this place was.

"Are all of the paintings here?" I asked.

"All of what paintings?"

"All of them. There are a lot."

Helberg turned to me, his eyebrows high. "No, there are lots more. Luckily, most galleries are still open. There are places like this in most major cities."

I tried to picture the scale of that, and found it really strange that people like Hattie and me could spend our whole lives never seeing any art at all. "Are these places only for people on higher Jaffle packages?"

Helberg laughed. "Well, this place and most of the big art galleries kind of predate Jaffle. But there's a point to be debated. Some of the people who built these great halls of art, and the rich patrons who financed them, wanted to keep them sort of exclusive. Like the great art of the world needed protecting from the hoi polloi."

"Figures," I said.

"But others, just as rich, just as powerful, thought that places like these should be made open to all. That if you built great museums and art galleries and you invited the common people in, then—" He clutched at the air in search of words. "—people, everyone, would be enriched and elevated by the experience."

"Huh."

"Back then not everyone thought the lower classes should be happy with less. Not everyone would be satisfied with beans and Mr Smiley."

I perceived a jibe and elbowed him.

"Have you got any idea of the type of picture you'd like to see more of?" Helberg asked. "I've done a lot of talking. Perhaps we should let some of the pictures speak for themselves."

"How about some pictures with animals?" I suggested. I wondered if dogs participated in any other fanciful pastimes in paintings.

"Right, let's have a look at the Victorians. They loved animal pictures."

I followed Helberg as he wove down a series of corridors. We passed through a room filled with stone bodies. I would need to come back and look at that.

"Here we are. You'll find animals in here."

We went into a gallery crowded with smaller and more densely packed pictures. I stopped to look at one. It showed a sheep on a snowy, desolate landscape. At its feet was a dead lamb. The sheep had its head raised and seemed to be crying into the leaden sky for its lost child. Crows crowded around, their hungry gaze fixed upon the dead lamb.

I burst into tears. Literally. I went from "What's that?" to tears pouring down my face in under five seconds. "That's awful," I sniffled.

"It's called *Anguish*," said Helberg. "Schenk painted a lot of animal schemes."

"No." I shook my head, trying to dislodge that horrible image. "Make it stop."

"Hey, Alice, it's all right." Helberg put a tentative hand on my arm. I didn't recoil from his touch. "Come and sit down."

We sat on the bench. I eyed the painting and shook my head at the unfairness. "That poor sheep. Why didn't the artist help it rather than just painting it?"

Helberg seemed surprised at my question. "Well, it's possible he did. Paintings take days. Who knows what happens in the moment. The detail has been lost to history.

It's quite probable that the event never even occurred. Not like that, anyway."

I sniffed. I wasn't sure I could go on. I thought about the dead lamb. I thought about the dead mouse under Levi's boot. I could picture it clearly in my mind's eye even though I never actually saw it. "Surely, art is supposed to make us happy? Why would someone paint about sad things?"

Helberg gave me a small smile. It was a much nicer smile. "Art *can* make us happy, but it also challenges us, and stretches our experience. When would you ever have the chance to empathise with a sheep in your normal day-to-day existence?"

Empathise? It stunned me to realise that he was right. I looked up at Schenk's sheep and gave it a small nod of respect.

"Come on." I stood up. "Let's do more art."

I enjoyed the animals. The dogs from the old days were a different shape, I realised. They were either small enough to fit up a lady's sleeve or they were long-legged things which stood with horses and ran behind carriages, for some reason. None of them pooped; at least not in the pictures.

Something clicked in my mind. "IFPA."

"Gesundheit," said Helberg.

"I wasn't sneezing. I was—"

"The animal charity. I know. Overcome with a sudden urge to make a donation?"

"There's a charity gala."

"You don't have to make a donation in person."

In the borrowed memory from Rufus Jaffle, Henderson mentioned Rufus would be at a charity gala on the fifteenth.

If the International Federation for the Protection of Animals had an upcoming gala, then I could go there to find Rufus. Jipping for more information was not hard. Jaffle Tech was indeed holding a gala in aid of IFPA, over on the ocean side of the city. As long as I could avoid the brain scan until then, I'd be able to get to Rufus and some answers.

Then I saw the event was a private corporate affair, mentioned in the events pages of news feeds and not open to the public. All the way home, I jipped for ways of getting a ticket but there didn't seem to be an option for buying one.

I sighed as we walked back into the Shangri-La Towers apartment complex.

"Hey, cheer up," said Helberg. "The wonderful thing about art is that it's an experience you can take away with you and..." He gestured, with an unconscious playfulness, to join him in his office. "I have an idea that might help you." I stepped past my boxes of flowers which still cluttered the lobby.

He reached up to a shelf and placed an oily heap of scrap onto the floor. It looked like all of the other heaps of scrap that he had around the place.

I looked at him. I had no idea what I was supposed to say, so I said "Um."

"This is Chuckie Egg."

"Is it?"

"He's my next bot project."

I stared at the thing. I'd seen bots before and they did not look like this. Even Helberg's craziest bots had plastic covers and you could usually tell the front from the back.

"Hang on," he said, as if he knew what I was thinking.

"The cover's around here somewhere." He clipped a shell onto it, and it had a form. It wasn't a sensible form, but it looked a bit more like a bot.

"What does it do?" I asked.

"Well, that's what I thought we could talk about. I reckon we can program it to do painting. It won't be able to create masterpieces like we saw in the gallery, but if we want to redecorate the place, then Chuckie Egg can do a lot of the legwork."

"Wow! That sounds amazing. We tell Chuckie Egg to paint all of the doors a different colour and off it goes?"

"Yup. I'll need to add an extension arm for it to reach the top. I'll have it ready by tomorrow. Or..." He giggled. Patrick Helberg giggled. That wasn't really something I'd seen him do before. He'd chuckled darkly. He'd leered. He'd grinned. He'd shown faint flickerings of human warmth. But giggle?

"What?" I said.

"Nothing," he said. "You head off. I've got things to do."

18

6TH JUNE – 13 DAYS UNTIL OPERATION SUNRISE

I n the morning, Helberg called me. He didn't jip me like an ordinary person, but put a voice call through to our apartment. Hattie got to it before me. She came into my bedroom.

"Helberg wants you to look out of the window," she said flatly.

She was still angry with me. I had spilled paint on one of her precious Smiley Tots. I might as well have stabbed one in the face the way Hattie was reacting.

"Why does he want me to do that?" I asked.

"That's the message: look out the window." Hattie made a point of looking casually towards my window but not looking out, and left.

I slipped out of bed and crossed to the window. Square of sky above, neighbour's apartments across the other side and then...

"Crumbs!"

The quadrangle below was being transformed into a picture of me. It was so clearly and obviously me, pinpoint perfect, but for the life of me I couldn't see how it had been executed, until I saw the wobbly white dome cover of a bot. Chuckie Egg had a robot fist full of flowers – I guessed fuchsias from their colour – and was lying strips on the ground to make the edge of my cheek. Reds and purples and greens and browns and somehow the whole thing worked.

It was me.

I ran downstairs in my night clothes and burst into Helberg's office. "Oh, my goodness," I exclaimed. "How did you do that?"

Helberg slurped on the carton of greasy noodles he was apparently having for breakfast.

"Very simple really, O valued tenant. Screen grab of you from the security cameras. Turned it into a map for Chuckie Egg. I downloaded him a simple colour recognition and compositing program, gave him his palette of dead flowers and..." He gestured expansively with his chopsticks as though the whole thing was nothing at all.

"Did you have to kill all my flowers?" I said. The remaining, unused flowers were still piled up in boxes by Helberg's office, and the gorgeous fragrance had diminished, replaced by an undercurrent of something unpleasant.

"You know the difference between a cut flower and a living plant?" he asked.

It felt like a trick question. When he phrased it like that, it seemed as though I ought to have realised flowers were alive when they were attached to plants, and *not* alive once they were cut. It had never occurred to me to consider it that way.

"Ri-iight," I said. "So for making a garden, you need the living sort?"

He nodded.

I looked at the boxes and sighed. These were not going to be useful.

It was as if he could read my mind. "On a positive note, all the flowers Chuckie Egg's been throwing around will compost nicely."

"Compost?"

"You'll want to learn all about composting if you're to become a gardener. Look it up and I think you'll see what can be done with all of these flowers."

He was right. Compost was definitely on the cards. It helped with soil structure, which sounded important.

"What about plants then?" I asked. "We need to turn the quadrangle into a garden for everyone to enjoy."

"Everyone?" he echoed. "What do you know about digging? Let me find some tools and show you what you need to do. When the digging is all done, we'll get some plants delivered."

I beamed at him.

It turned out that digging was really hard work, yet strangely satisfying. Helberg kept trying to pretend his involvement was purely *managerial* and that things would go better if he just offered guidance from the side-lines, but I made it very clear he owed his tenants this community garden. Eventually he sighed and joined me outside. We dug the flower portrait of me into the soil. Yes, we were destroying a beautiful thing, but it was never going to last. It created an unusual feeling in me, neither sad nor happy. I struggled to explain it to Helberg.

"I know that the flowers were dying anyway, but I feel odd destroying them."

"Maybe one of the things people like about cut flowers is that it's a transient thing," he said. "A reminder that beauty, life, all of it is a temporary thing. Ephemeral."

I jipped my literary booster. "That's a nice word," I said.

"Isn't it." He made a compost bin out of some of the discarded wood and piled the weeds I dug out into it.

"So when compost happens, tiny organisms eat up all of the waste and make new soil," I said. I kept jipping more detail about compost, because it was so fascinating. "So even that poor dead lamb from the gallery would eventually decay and become soil?"

Helberg looked alarmed for a moment. "If you put whole carcasses on there it would get very smelly," he said.

"I haven't got any carcasses," I said. "I just mean in theory."

He looked relieved, and nodded. "Yep. Circle of life."

I wondered what the soil under my feet had come from. Had living things decomposed to form all of this? How many things would that be? It was slightly overwhelming.

The digging left my arms tired and my hands dirty, but I loved it. Eventually it was all done and Helberg said we were ready for some plants. We went to his office where he asked me lots of confusing questions about the kinds of plants we should get. It seemed as though there was quite a choice. He sketched out a rough plan on the whiteboard and we talked about what should go where.

"What about bacon?" he asked, pointing at my to-do list, which he hadn't rubbed off.

"I still haven't got any," I admitted.

"We could include a barbecue area." He indicated a corner of the garden. "It's sheltered here, you could install a barbecue and a small seating area."

"Barbecue," I said, jipping it hastily. "Oh. It's a cooking device used out of doors." It might be a useful way to try cooking.

Helberg nodded as if he was concentrating. He did that strange thing again: sort of jipping out loud. "Order interface. Sending list for delivery within two hours."

I wanted to get to the bottom of why he did that, but I had work to do.

"I'll invite everyone down this evening," I said. "This is going to blow them away. Did you order some bacon as well?"

He nodded.

"Fantastic!"

I composed an invite and jipped it to all residents:

You are all invited to a bacon sandwich barbecue party to celebrate the opening of the new community garden.

Venue: Central area

Time: 1800

. . .

As SOON AS the goods delivery arrived, Helberg got to work putting the barbecue together while I put the plants in the ground.

I planted broad Abelia shrubs, handling them carefully so as not to damage their pink bell-shaped flowers. I installed rows of weighty aloe plants with their stiff jagged leaves. I created an arrangement of echium, escallonia, salvia. I filled in gaps with hardy sedums, their leaves so dark as to almost appear grey – not the dull grey of the rest of my world but a subtle and beautiful dustiness.

I had to add water to them, which is all part of the care that plants need. I had a special device called a watering can which sprinkled water in a little shower, so that I could make sure each one had a drink.

I felt unbelievably happy.

SIX O'CLOCK ARRIVED and the curious tenants started to drift down to see what we were doing.

"Well Alice, I'm sure I don't know what you're doing. Have you seen the state of this place?" said Swanager. She was pointing at the compost area.

"Don't dwell on that," I said. "Take a look at the plants. Aren't they amazing?"

"You did this?" she asked.

"Yes."

"No wonder you got dirt on your shoes."

I swallowed down the mild anger she provoked in me. She

didn't know any better. It was up to me to try and stimulate some sort of response. I was convinced that I could make people on Jaffle Standard sit up and see what they were missing.

"If the garden does nothing for you, wait until you taste the bacon," I said. "Can you smell that?" Helberg had some bacon on the barbecue and the smell was amazing.

Swanager turned her nose up, but it wasn't the appreciative sniff that I'd been expecting, it was the expression of someone who'd seen something appalling.

"Is that the flesh of a beast?" she asked. "I'd heard that people ate such things, but I had no idea that they walked among us here."

"It's tasty," I pointed out.

"I'm not sure your opinion counts for much. In truth, I only came down to inform you – *inform you all*—" she added loudly to anyone within earshot, "—that Clifford and I are moving out today."

"I will have your apartment dried and cleaned soon," Helberg tried to assure her.

She shook her head with something like disgust. "We're moving to that new North Beach arcology. Integrated living solutions and they pay you to live there. We jipped the terms and conditions today. Didn't we, Clifford?"

There was no sound of support from Pedstone. Swanager looked round and caught sight of her roommate, Pedstone, over at the barbecue. He was trying to dangle a slice of hot and juicy bacon into his mouth.

"Pedstone! We're leaving!" She made sure she gave everyone present a good glare. "And I doubt many of you will be staying around much longer if *this* is the kind of nonsense that goes on at Shangri-La Towers."

Swanager left at that point, and whispered to several other people on her way out. They also turned and walked away.

"Wait!" I called. "Some of you must be interested in the work that we're doing here? Look at the textures and the colours! Think for a moment about the circle of life! Don't you realise that everything turns into dirt in the end, and here we are making flowers grow in it! Look, will you!"

They weren't interested. People hung on politely for a few minutes before leaving. All except Hattie. I hadn't seen her arrive, but she stood there now, shaking her head.

"I don't know what you've become, Alice?"

"I haven't become anything," I said. "Nothing that wasn't there already."

"I feel as if I don't know you anymore."

"What do you mean?"

"I thought you were my friend, but you ruined my Smiley Tot—"

"That was an accident."

"—and now you're scaring all of the neighbours with your talk about dirt. Are you really trying to make us eat flesh from a beast?"

"Yes?" I said.

"Why?"

"Because it tastes nice and—"

"Was it a bad animal?"

"Bad? As in...? It's a pig."

"Did it deserve to die? Is that the point? Are we punishing

it? You're messing about in the dirt, getting excited about rotting things and now we're supposed to devour this pig. I don't know what it's supposed to have done but it's very odd behaviour to say the least."

I wanted to tell Hattie how delicious it was. How people had eaten this sort of food since the beginning of time, but her face was stony and impassive and I could tell she didn't want to hear anything from me.

"Hattie, I've learned so much over the last few days," I tried. "I really want to share it with you. Give it a chance. I think you'd like it, I really do."

She shook her head. "Maybe I ought to see if they've still got any spare apartments in that North Beach arcology."

"Hattie!"

She walked away. She was the last. All of the other people had gone, although I could see that several of them stood at the windows overlooking the quadrangle, staring out as if I might be a dangerous menace.

I looked at Helberg. He stood by the barbecue as the remaining rashers of bacon crisped and withered, unwanted. "Let's go inside," I said.

Whatever the mood was, whatever connections I'd hoped to make, it was all gone now.

"And the bacon?" he asked.

I thought for a moment. I was deflated. Part of me wanted to reject the bacon, close the door on the garden and leave it all behind. It did smell delicious though.

"Bring the bacon," I said.

~

BACK IN HIS CLUTTERED OFFICE, Helberg put a plate of stacked crispy bacon on a pile of documents. He cleared a chair for me by moving a pile of electronic junk from one pile to another. This somehow didn't seem to satisfy him and he whacked the seat cushion a few times, making puffs of dust in the air.

"Please," he said and then rootled around in a cupboard to produce a slim-necked glass bottle. "Have you ever tried alcohol?"

"No," I said. I wasn't counting the second-hand experience that I'd had in Rufus Jaffle's head. I thought about the party in that memory/dream. "Is this the right time to be having a drink?"

"Absolutely. Everyone walking out of your garden party, that's a drinking situation."

"I'll just have a really tiny bit, then."

He got a small glass out of a cupboard. It was the sort of glass that Hattie would love: it was just about the right size for a Smiley Tot. He poured an appropriately small amount of a golden liquid.

"This is sherry," he said. "A perfectly serviciable Bodegas Hidalgo La Gitana Manzanilla."

"That's a bit of a mouthful," I said.

"More than a bit of a mouthful in there." He passed me the glass.

"I meant the name."

"I know." He smiled.

I took a sip. It coated my lips with its sweetness, and I could feel a delicious warmth in my mouth. As I swallowed, the warmth went down my throat.

"Mm. It's sweet but kind of salty and... Mmmm."

"Throw in a few more wild similes and we'll make a wine connoisseur of you," he said.

I took another sip. Drinking it was an undeniably pleasant sensation, and I could feel that the busy, bothersome thoughts that crowded my brain were slipping away. I finished the glass and tipped my head back, delighted at how mellow my mood was becoming.

"Can I have some more please?"

"Sure," said Helberg and he poured me another glass. I noticed that he was drinking something from a different bottle. It was called whisky.

"You talk to your Jaffle Port," I said.

"I talk to lots of things. I talk to Jetpac here," he said, patted a pile of rubbish next to him. It burbled and beeped, revealing itself to be a partially constructed bot.

"Nobody talks to their Jaffle Port."

He regarded his glass of whisky for a long time. The glass was an interesting shape, with artful facets which reflected the light. "They do if they have a non-Jaffle Port," he said eventually.

"What?" I said with a nervous laugh. "Non-Jaffle Port? What does that even mean?"

"It means what it means. A Jaffle Port is just a device. Don't confuse the item with the brand. It's like hoovers or coke or scotch tape. You know scotch tape?"

"I think so," I said, still reeling.

"That's a brand name. The stuff itself is just called adhesive tape or something. You don't have to go with the big brand name. You can buy one somewhere else, or make your own."

As soon as the words were out of his mouth I understood. The evidence was all around his office. "You made it? You made your own Jaffle Port?"

He nodded. "Brain port, but, yeah."

I was knocked back by the implications. He was one of the three percent. One of the mad and crazy ones. "How does that even work?" I took a larger slurp of sherry and topped up the glass myself. This was mind-boggling.

He shrugged. "Jaffle Ports allow access to a wealth of information, but Jaffle Tech don't own all of that knowledge. In its most stripped-down form a Jaffle Port is a sophisticated way of accessing a massive computer network. I built a similar device that lets me do the same thing. The difference with mine is that I control what access the network has to *me*."

"But Jaffle Tech manage your spare capacity for your benefit," I found myself saying.

"Spare capacity!" he scoffed. "Don't think I don't know what's happened to you. Do you think what you've had given back to you was *spare capacity*?"

"But the essential service software," I insisted. "Firewall, obscenity filters, system check, customer feedback..." I realised I was spouting lines from my own call centre script.

Too many thoughts flooded my mind. What he was saying made sense on the surface but I couldn't help but feel a deep-seated revulsion at what seemed like an unnatural perversion. Didn't he want to be part of a global community? Didn't he want to fit in?

"How are you able to live?" I asked.

He laughed out loud at that.

"Sorry," I said. "I didn't mean…"

"I live quite well, thank you."

"I know. I meant…"

"You mean, as an outsider." He took a sip of whiskey. "I'm not alone."

"Er…" I waved a hand around his hermit's cave of an office by way of counter-argument.

He laughed, tilting his glass in my direction. "I live a selfish life, in every sense of the word. Anything for an easy life, that's me. I know I'm an outsider, but I'm not alone. Jaffle would like you to think those who don't adopt their tech are doomed to a solitary life, but there are others out there who refuse to become brand victims. And even if I was alone, just because you're a minority of one, doesn't mean you're mad."

"Bit mad," I suggested. "You're a—" I jipped for a good word. "—a Luddite!"

"Anti-technology?" he said. "Me? Do I look like a machine-smasher, a *saboteur*?"

"No, but—"

"But nothing!" There was a note of passion in his voice. "Technological development is a wonderful thing. I would be mad if I thought the world would be a better place without brain port technology. My great-aunt suffered from a degenerative brain condition. A piece of early Jaffle technology was able to repair the neural damage, or bridge it at least, and give her years of life quality that would not have been available otherwise. No, knowledge is king. How it is applied is where the ethical debate lies."

"You think Jaffle Tech is unethical?" I felt my own recent opinions solidify even as I said it. "Helberg?"

"Yes?"

"Have you heard of a plipper?"

"A who's-what-now?"

"Plipper."

"As in a thing that plips?"

"You have heard of it?"

"No. I just extrapolated. What is a plipper?"

I recalled what I had seen in the executive offices at Jaffle Tech. "It's a device. About so long. You point it at someone and it automatically reduces their brain function to the bare minimum. Like the Empties outside."

His expression had become serious. "You've seen one?"

"A demonstration, at work. They're going to give them out to law enforcement agencies."

"They're going to use them for pacification? Jeez."

"Henderson – he's the Chief Technical Officer at Jaffle Tech – he said that it's much safer than the police using Tasers on people."

"And that makes it okay?" said Helberg. "I can't believe people would stand for this."

"He said—" I tried to remember what he'd said. "Everyone has already given their consent, everyone on Jaffle Enhanced and below. It's in those new terms and conditions."

I'd coerced that caller, Jackson, into signing those new terms and conditions, just before I'd been distracted by the mouse. Was I now responsible for them getting plipped in the future?

Maybe it was the mouse that reminded me, but a phrase they'd used leapt to my mind. "What's a deadcat?" I asked.

"What's a dead cat?" repeated Helberg.

I considered jipping it but I didn't want images of dead cats flooding my mind at this vulnerable time. "I think it was meant to be a verb."

"They were going to deadcat something?"

"That."

He made a noise, not a happy one. "If you throw a dead cat on a table, everyone will notice it. Once you've thrown a dead cat on the table, people will be too distracted to notice what you do next. Is the plipper the dead cat?"

"I don't know," I said.

"You deadcat something truly horrific with something people are going to be distracted by. If the plipper is the dead cat then the other thing ... what else were they talking about?"

"It was something called Operation Sunrise."

"Euphemistically pleasant sounding."

"It just sounded like a software roll-out. Jaffle Tech 2.0. It's going live in six days."

"Fuckers," he said, and with such quiet sincerity it was even more shocking.

"You think it's going to be a bad thing?"

"Oh, absolutely. A company that turns the weak and unfortunate into Empties at the press of a button? With the collusion of the powers that be? There's no way their next software innovation is going to be a good thing."

"I'm sure if I could speak to Rufus Jaffle, I'd be able to

discuss it with him. Maybe I've got it wrong and he can tell me what's really going on."

Helberg scoffed. "Those Jaffle guys have been screwing over the little guy for years."

"And yet," I said, thoughtfully, "you've done nothing about it."

He drained his glass. Refilled and drained it again. "I try not to get hung up on things I can't possibly fix," he said. "Like I say, a selfish life. Drink."

It was an instruction and an invitation. He topped up both our glasses once more, hand shaking with emotion.

"You..." I said.

"What?"

"You've set yourself apart. You've not been a joiner. You've not got a Jaffle Port."

"I'm one of the fabled three percent. And how glad I am of that!"

"But it hasn't made you happy, has it?"

His lips curled in a smile but it was the bitterly cold smile of the old Patrick Helberg. "Heard of John Stuart Mill?"

"Does he live in the complex?"

"He was a British philosopher. Long time ago now. He had a lot to say about human rights and freedoms." He picked at the pile of uneaten bacon which was now cold and hard as cardboard. "He said it was better to be an unhappy human than a happy pig."

"And is it?" I asked.

"I'm not even sure I know what happiness is. By a lot of people's definition, I'm some kind of miserable bastard, but I'd rather be miserable like this than happy because I'm a dumbed-down-to-watch-Smiley-TV-all-day-long-and-be-satisfied sheep."

I thought about that. "I used to like Smiley TV," I said. "I mean, I used to like it *a lot*."

He laughed cruelly. "Doofus."

"And now," I said, "it does nothing for me. It's not enough."

"And would you go back, if you could?" Helberg asked. "If at a flick of switch—" he clicked his fingers "—they could instantly return you to how you were before: ignorant and happy. If you could plip yourself back to stupidity, right now, would you do it?"

I sipped the golden sherry. "Nope," I said. "I'm never going back."

I waved my suddenly empty glass at him for a refill.

19

7TH JUNE – 12 DAYS UNTIL OPERATION SUNRISE

I woke up with a headache, a dry mouth, and no desire to get up. I must have stumbled home at some point but I didn't remember anything beyond chatting and drinking with Helberg in his office. It was a work day and I had a scan scheduled at the office. If I didn't at least go in to work, they would be even more suspicious of me.

I called on what pain filters my Jaffle Port allowed and, ignoring the protests from my head and stomach, forced myself to get up and dressed. Hattie was busying herself around the apartment but seemed disinclined to talk to me. That was okay; I wasn't in a talking mood either.

Out in the corridor, Chuckie Egg was painting apartment doors, deftly handling a paintbrush in a way that put my efforts to shame.

Hattie and I shared a car to work, but the atmosphere was uncomfortably strained. Hattie claimed she was studying a literary module, so she was unable to engage in conversation.

It was natural to assume she was lying, but I'm not sure Hattie was capable of lying, which made me think she has accessed a literary module with the sole purpose of avoiding me.

Partway through the morning, my calendar pinged to remind me of the rescheduled brain scan. I had run out of excuses, so this time I tried the strategy of ignoring it and hoping it would go away. This was obviously doomed to failure: within a few minutes a call came through.

"Alice, you're late for your scan. You need to come down to the medical centre right now."

"I can't." I failed to elaborate.

"Why not?"

"Our department is in lock-down," I said, spotting Levi marching around looking self-important. "There's been an intrusion. An anomaly."

There was a sigh on the line. *"If I call your section head, am I going to find out that this is untrue, Alice?"*

"No?" I tried.

"Because repeatedly failing to attend a mandatory health scan could result in disciplinary action, did you know that? And more importantly, it could point to an underlying issue, which is the whole reason we're doing this, isn't it?" There was an even heavier sigh. *"Fine. I want you here first thing in the morning, is that clear?"*

"Er, yep."

"You will come to the medical centre before you even go to your section."

"Sure."

"This is your last chance, Alice."

"I'll be there," I said.

When I killed the call I looked round to Hattie's cubicle, because something strange was happening. A delivery of several large boxes had just turned up. Hattie attempted to push them discreetly out of sight as she dealt with her caller. A little bit like trying to hide an elephant by popping a tiny hat on it. Hattie succeeded only in drawing Levi's attention more quickly. A cleaning bot trundled into Hattie's cubicle and bounced off one of the boxes. It readjusted its course.

Levi stood impatiently to the side until she'd finished the call.

"Can I ask what this is, miss?"

Hattie composed herself in the way that she does, by flapping a hand at her face as though she's very hot. "I suppose you might call it an emergency."

"Might I?" he said. "I might call ditch water coffee but that don't make it so."

"I needed to get some of my possessions to a place of safety because there's been a bit of a problem at home." She looked my way for the first time.

Now I knew what was in the boxes.

"May I take a look inside?" said Levi.

"Certainly." Hattie opened the top of the nearest box and sure enough, it was filled with Smiley Tots. He picked one out and turned it over in his hands.

"Careful!" said Hattie.

Levi gave her a look. "I'm inspecting its safety labels. These are not certified as suitable for an industrial environment."

"Of course they're not, they're toys!" said Hattie. "I just want to put them on my desk, as decoration."

Levi paused. He knew very well that decoration of a desk was permitted. His gaze swivelled across the huge boxes before he looked critically at the desk. "I'm not sure they'll all fit in the environs of the desk."

"Oh, they will," said Hattie with confidence.

"Hm." Levi put the Smiley Tot down and looked at Hattie. "So what's the problem at home? Anything I should know about?"

I tried to pull a subtle but meaningful face, but Hattie wasn't even looking at me. "Alice has been a little careless with some of her recent activities. It not a suitable environment for the Smiley Tots."

"Oh, dear. Trouble at the homestead, huh?" He looked across at me. He was wearing his disappointed face, yet I could see a hidden amusement in his eyes. "It's our duty to make sure this is a safe and harmonious environment, is it not? Oh, yabetcha. I expect team members to park their problems at the door and look out for each other when they're under my watchful eye."

"I couldn't have said it better myself," said Hattie piously.

My best friend hated me and was getting me into trouble at work for it. More trouble. The cleaning bot nudged up to the chair that I was sitting on. I kicked out at it. I'd always imagined these things as being Levi's spies.

"Stupid spybot," I growled.

Its canopy cracked in the middle, exposing some of its inner workings and it made a fizzing, sparking noise as it left. I wasn't sorry.

WHEN I GOT HOME that evening I ate beans and went to see how Chuckie Egg was doing. All of the doors were done now and the bot was working on the stairwells.

Helberg appeared from downstairs. "Took a few adjustments to get right."

"I can see that," I said, stepping carefully to avoid the paint streaking the stairs.

"I have something for you," he said. I followed him to the office. He picked up a large piece of card. How old-fashioned! It was thick and had beautiful lettering upon it.

JAFFLE TECH'S
ANNUAL BENEVOLENCE GALA AND CHARITY AUCTION
IN AID OF THE
INTERNATIONAL FEDERATION FOR THE PROTECTION OF THE
ANIMALS
15TH JUNE

"IS THIS AN ACTUAL TICKET?" I asked.

"It is an actual ticket."

"How did you know I wanted to go?"

"I pulled a few strings to get hold of it after you mentioned how important it was to you."

"Did I?"

"After your fourth glass of sherry."

"Oh, right." I said. "Was I ... inebriated?"

"Inebriated? You were three sheets to the wind, O valued tenant."

I marvelled at the ticket, felt its textured thickness under my thumb. "Wow. Thank you. You've no idea how much this means to me."

"Oh, you were incoherently eloquent about it last night," he said. "And now, Cinderella, you *shall* go to the ball!"

"Who's Cinderella?"

It didn't matter. I had a ticket to the charity gala, access to Rufus Jaffle, a chance to get answers to this chaotic mess my life had become *and* Operation Sunrise. I felt tears prick the corners of my ears in sheer gratitude at what Helberg had just done for me.

"Tears of joy?" said Helberg, hopefully.

I nodded and sniffed and attempted a smile before shaking my head. "There's a very real chance I'll get busted tomorrow for having more brain power than I'm supposed to."

"Busted? How do you mean?" he asked.

"I've been avoiding a brain scan they insist on doing. I really need to present myself tomorrow and they're bound to spot what's going on. They'll reverse it, I'm sure. I don't think I can bear to go back to how I was. I certainly won't be going to any gala."

Helberg stared at me with a heavy sigh. "The tragic thing is if you did go back to how you were, you probably wouldn't even mind. You'd sit and watch Smiley Time and be happy with it."

With a chill I realised he was right. "No. That's not right."

"No, it is not. These brain scans, they must be a fairly standard report, right?"

I nodded. We dealt with them quite often. "Yes, there's a capacity report, an activity report, an analysis of any serious failings, downtime or anomalies, that sort of thing."

"Why not create a fake one?"

I thought for a moment. I could certainly rustle up some convincing content. "There's one bit I couldn't make up," I said. "It needs to show a reading from the metrics chip on the Jaffle Port. If it's not in line with previous readings, it will flag an error straightaway."

"So get a previous reading."

"Those are encrypted in storage, I can't get to them without alerting the system."

"Well," he said slowly, "there is another possibility."

I didn't like the look on his face. "What?"

"I can hack your port, just to get a reading."

"Oh no. Definitely no. Absolutely not!" It was a terrible idea.

He held up his hands. "Fine. If it makes you uncomfortable. Take your chances the scan at work will miss the massive upgrade you have somehow accidentally acquired."

"No, it's not that it makes me uncomfortable." It made me *very* uncomfortable. "But look what happened the last time I meddled with the system. It's got me in all sorts of trouble."

He held my arms and looked me straight in the eye. "I think what you *really* mean is that it's opened your eyes to a world you never even knew existed. A world that is filled with beauty and tragedy and so much wonder that you can't wait to experience more of it. Or of course, you could go back to watching Smiley."

I couldn't argue with his logic. If there was a chance a fake brain scan could get me past this scrutiny at work and make sure I could hang on to my enhanced abilities, then I needed to take it.

"What would be involved in you hacking my Jaffle Port?" I asked.

"It will be a quick scan with some of my home-built equipment."

"Show me."

We walked through his office. Helberg used a stepladder to access a high shelf and he brought down a glass, cone-shaped object with electronics clustered upon it. It resembled nothing I had ever seen at Jaffle.

"It's a little bit unusual," he said, probably seeing my expression, "but I make equipment for my own use, remember? I don't care what it looks like. The glass helmet is a re-purposed door from an old washing machine. It sits quite comfortably on the head and aligns the circuitry for accessing the Jaffle Port."

I really didn't want the thing on my head. I wasn't sure if I trusted Helberg's technical proficiency. Most of his bots seemed to work okay, but some were hopeless failures. More than that, I wasn't sure if I trusted Helberg's motives. He'd been helping me, there was no denying it, but I felt as though I was a project or a diversion. If I stopped being entertaining, would he be so keen to help? It wasn't so long ago that he took all of my money from me.

He looked at my face, perhaps detecting some suspicion.

"Hey, I know you must be worried about this. I can't make you believe me, but I promise I won't do anything other than what I said. I'd suggest you could bring Hattie as a chaperone, but I'm not sure she'd approve of any of this."

"Oh no, we can't involve Hattie," I said. "Right, let's do this."

He beamed. "Pop it on your head and I'll calibrate the settings. Try to keep it still."

"And, just to be clear, you've done this before?"

He hesitated. "Dozens of times. I have watched other open source port-engineers do this very thing. But, okay, yours is the very first head I've actually messed with."

Messed with? "Can I have something to write on?" I asked.

He raised his eyebrows but passed me a pencil and paper from a drawer.

I scribbled a note.

To Alice in a few minutes' time. If you suddenly and unaccountably want to have sex with Helberg, then he has messed with something in your brain and you need to punish him.

He gave me a hurt look. "I'm all for sex Alice, but not like that."

"Glad to hear it." I put the helmet on my head.

Whatever procedure Helberg ran, I felt nothing except the slightly uncomfortable weight of his contraption on my head. He lifted it off a few minutes later.

"All done."

I shook out my hair. "Did you get the settings from the metrics chip?"

"Yup. Sending them to you now, so you can compose your

own fake brain scan. Had you thought about adding in a small anomaly to throw them off the scent?"

"I had thought of that, yes," I said. "We sometimes see capacity problems caused by environmental stress – like a change to routine. I think I'll throw in one of those, but make it look steady and normal afterwards."

20

8TH JUNE – 11 DAYS UNTIL OPERATION SUNRISE

"You've got paint on you."

It was the first thing Hattie had said to me in nearly twenty-four hours . To hear it was a stab of emotion in my chest. She still hadn't forgiven me for staining her Smiley Tot, still could not comprehend that I needed to explore the new, unchained me. She was my very best friend in the whole world and it was wrenching to have lost some of that friendship. So to have her speak to me, directly and voluntarily, was wonderful. Even it was to point out a paint mark on my tunic as we walked into the Jaffle Tech building the next day.

I looked. There was a blob of brown paint on my tunic breast. It looked quite unpleasant but I didn't have a clean spare back at home or time to go get one.

"I can sort that," I said and took a detour to the supplies department.

"Hi Damian, I need to get a new tunic, can I pop down?" I asked.

"Sure," said the helpful guy at the counter. "You can't have it straightaway though."

"But..." I pointed to the brown mark.

He pulled a face. "Have you been playing with dog poo again?"

"What do you mean *again*?"

He shrugged. "Word gets around."

"It's paint."

"Paint?"

"Paint."

"Paint?"

"Listen, can I get a tunic or not."

"I'll have to let the security staff know," he said. "Orders from on high."

"Levi, you mean."

"It's part of an *ongoing investigation* into a *serious incident*." He did two lots of air quotes as he said it.

"Never mind," I said. "I don't want to create work for Levi."

"You're a very thoughtful person."

"Who does *not* play with dog poo," I pointed out as I left.

On our floor Hattie was going round her Smiley Tot enclosure and performing her morning routine on them: switching their positions so she could spend quality time with each of them. They were stacked three deep in what looked like a defensive wall around her cubicle, but Levi was unable to object because she had managed to get them above and below the desk's surface. She was now able to take calls and tend to her Tots, which seemed to make her very happy. I thought about paintings of that Jesus baby in the art gallery and how happy a real baby might make Hattie. Maybe I'd have a chat about that with her later, work out a way for her to spend some time with real babies. Maybe rebuild our damaged relationship in the process.

I hurried to my cubicle and got settled in quickly so no one could see my unsightly stain. I got right down to the task of answering customer calls about their Jaffle Ports.

Mid-morning, I sent my home-made brain scan down to the medical centre and then, increasingly self-conscious about my stained uniform, went to the staff kitchenette to try and clean it. In my bag, I had the bottle of cleaning thinners Helberg had given me. I popped my bag on the counter and took the bottle out.

"*Thinners,*" I read, taking the lid off. "*Do not drink. Inflammable liquid.*"

It didn't say I couldn't use it on clothes. The smell was pungent, and I hoped I wouldn't stink all day after using it.

I dabbed a little bit right on the edge of my tunic. It didn't melt. I sloshed a good quantity onto the paint stain and dabbed at it with paper towelling from the dispenser. I could see the paint was softening, so I added some more.

"Alice, could I have a word please?"

I turned to see who it was, knocking over the thinners. It sploshed about on the counter. I grabbed the bottle before hardly any had run out and set it upright.

"Ah, right. Yes?" I said.

It was the beautiful woman with the big eyes from the medical centre. "Your brain scan," she said.

"Yes?"

"It's highly unusual for someone to commission one privately."

"Did you find a problem with it?" I asked, expecting the worst.

"What do you think?"

I met her eye. "I think it was absolutely fine."

"It was," she conceded. "It's just unorthodox. Who signed off on the deviation from procedure?"

I glanced across the counter, and saw a puddle of thinners was spreading towards a nearby toaster oven. I pulled more paper towelling from the dispenser and mopped it up. I breathed a sigh of relief, trying to make it look as if I was conscientiously cleaning up the kitchen, rather than doing anything suspicious.

"Alice," said the medical centre woman.

"Sorry, yes." I dropped the paper towels into the bin, along with the bottle of thinners. I'd have to get some more later.

"I'm really not sure whether to refer this to my supervisor."

"The whole thing has a perfectly reasonable explanation," I said.

She waited, clearly wanting to hear my perfectly reasonable explanation. There was a lull in conversation while I tried to think of one. A cleaning bot arrived. From its cracked canopy, I could see it was the one I'd kicked yesterday, the one I had groundlessly declared to be Levi's spybot. The association alone made me stiffen with guilt but I made an effort to keep my expression composed.

The bot whirred as it clamped the bin in order to empty it.

"Rufus Jaffle requested my brain scan," I said.

"Him? Or his secretary?" she replied.

"Yes, exactly. He has a … close personal friend training to do brain scan type things and Rufus – I call him Rufus – he asked me to go to him."

"For practice?"

"Exactly."

I thought it was a good effort. To uncover my lie she'd have to find Rufus Jaffle and ask him. I didn't think she'd bother and I certainly didn't think she'd be able to find him.

Clunk!

Woomf!

The first sound was caused by the bottle of thinners falling out of the bin and splashing liquid all over the bot's exposed circuitry. The second was the entire thing being set alight by a spark. The bot's programming clearly didn't cover this scenario: its routing seemed to immediately go wrong. It careered across the office, spinning towards the desks.

I ran after it. I would tell Levi that I thought running was justified in the circumstances. The bot was getting close to Hattie's desk. I kicked it over to stop it getting any further and whooped in triumph as I managed to stop its progress. I wondered where the nearest fire extinguisher was. I could soon put this out, and *then* I'd be celebrated as the hero who averted a disaster. I whirled in place, wondering why the people at the surrounding desks were all standing and staring. I looked across at Hattie who peered across the top of her Smiley Tot wall. She was gesturing, but I couldn't understand what she was saying.

To my horror I saw the fire which had previously been contained to the bot was spreading outwards as the liquid drained across the floor. It edged towards the Smiley Tots, and I waved wildly at Hattie.

"Fire!" I yelled.

"Yes!" she yelled, and yet she made no move to get out from what would surely become her funeral pyre.

"Move! You're on fire!" I yelled.

"No, you're on fire!" she yelled back, pointing.

I looked down. Sure enough, my tunic bottom was aflame. While I'd been fixated on the flames heading for Hattie they had also been coming towards me.

Well, I'd cast myself as the hero in this situation and this was just one more obstacle to overcome. With a roar, I tried to rip my tunic off, but only managed to burn my hand. I unzipped my tunic and stepped out of it. That left Hattie and her Smiley Tot inferno. They were giving off a thick black smoke which made me cough. I lunged forward, burst through the wall of Smiley Tots and grabbed Hattie by the arm. I hauled her clear as the Smiley wall started to crackle with tall flames.

As we panted with the spent adrenalin, the sprinklers came on, the fire alarms howled and the smell of singed plastic replaced the choking smoke. Throughout the office, Jaffle Tech employees rose from their seats and moved in an orderly fashion towards the exits.

Levi appeared and looked me up and down. "Are you hurt?" he said.

I looked down at myself. Levi was staring, possibly because my clothes were either burned or discarded to the extent that I was very nearly naked.

"No."

"Hattie? Are you hurt?"

Hattie was sobbing uncontrollably. "My tots. All of my tots."

The army of cutesy baby dolls had been reduced to a stinking heap of melted plastic and burned fabric. Levi went over and tried to find one that was less damaged. He picked one up by its head. Its ghoulish, blackened face stared at us, accusation blazing from its hollow eye sockets. As we stared in horror, the rest of the body plopped to the floor, leaving Levi holding only the head.

Hattie wailed. "All gone! All gone! My tots! All of them!"

Levi put his arms awkwardly around her quivering frame. Hattie howled into his shoulder. The noise in his ear must have been deafening, but he only winced a little bit. I could already see snot and tears on his pristine uniform.

A Jaffle Swarm of insects had flown in from somewhere and circled the office space. In a distant control room, fire chiefs would be assessing the situation.

"You." Hattie lifted her head and pointed at me. "You're the one who made all of this happen. This is the worst thing you've ever done."

"I didn't mean to... It shouldn't have..."

"I can never forgive you, Alice."

I was stunned. I knew that Hattie was ridiculously attached to the tots, but surely she knew, deep down that they were just things and that they could be replaced? As for it being my fault, that was a bit of a leap. Anyone could see that it was an accident.

"I didn't do anything," I said. "That shouldn't have happened. The bottle said the liquid was inflammable. *In*flammable." Belatedly I jipped the meaning of the word. "Oh."

The sprinklers had stopped. Levi carefully disentangled himself from Hattie, leaving trailers of tearful snottiness between them. "Alice, a word in—" He looked round. "In that meeting room. Now."

I had a feeling that Levi wasn't viewing this as an accident either.

I went into the conference room, with Levi hot on my heels. There were papers around on the table. I think I had glimpsed some executive from the upper floors in here, having a chat with our section heads. A plate of luxury biscuits in the middle of the table was slowly going soggy in an inch of sprinkler water.

"Well, look who's slap-bang in the middle of another major incident," said Levi, glaring at me.

"Well look who's staring at someone who's in need of a new uniform, instead of helping," I snapped.

"I've already sent a request for new clothing." He hesitated and then whipped off his jacket and put it around my shoulders. Levi jackletless, his strong arms exposed, him covering me protectively. In my dreams, this would have been super exciting and sexy. Right now, I felt like an idiot child.

"I need to write up a major incident report, yabetcha," he said. "Your testimony is obviously required, but I will be relying upon key witnesses to provide their version of events."

"There's been a fire," I said.

"I might need more detail than that."

I shook my head irritably. "There's been a fire. Levi, you are just a security guard."

"*Just* a security guard? Hoo-ee!"

"If there's an investigation to be made then that's up to the fire department or the insurers or..."

"Are you questioning my authority, miss?" he said.

"That is exactly what I'm doing!" I retorted.

"You'll be suspended from work for the duration of my investigation," he said. "I can't have ya fraternizing with potential witnesses."

"Suspended? You don't have the authority!"

He puffed up his chest and his moustache quivered. Even in the circumstances, I was slightly aroused, and then hated myself for it.

"You'll be aware that the terms and conditions of your employment are conditional on certain behaviours?" he said. "I have the power to suggest that you were *not only* in breach of your duty to safeguard your colleagues, but that you may also be guilty of gross misconduct." I started to speak but he cut across me. "Your line manager will be made aware of the situation. You will now watch the film, as is required for all employees when they need to be reminded of how seriously we take this—"

The door opened and a company fire marshal burst in. "Did you not hear the alarms?" he exclaimed.

"I'm in the middle of an interview," said Levi.

"Evacuate. Now!"

Levi gave the marshal a frosty stare. I looked aside, embarrassed and then saw the plipper. It was on the conference table, underneath a fat wad of meeting papers, in a protective blister-pack, new and unused. While Levi and the fire marshal loudly contested who had jurisdiction over whom, I picked up the pile of papers, the plipper sandwiched in the middle.

"What are you doing?" said the fire marshal.

Panic swelled inside me but I kept it down. "These are important papers. I didn't want them to get any wetter."

"We do not stop to pick up personal belongings in an emergency, miss," said Levi severely.

The fire marshal gave Levi a withering look. "Just get out, the pair of you."

I walked out, wearing nothing but my underwear and Levi's jacket about my shoulders. Levi, put in his place, could do nothing but follow. As I reached the door to the stairs, he called out.

"Wait!"

I turned. He scrabbled under a turned over partition as early responder fire department drones searched for any remnants of the fire. He grabbed something from the soaked and sooty edges of the scene.

He came towards me with something held victoriously in his hand. It was a dusty, mouldy and now ash-covered ring.

"Is that Brandine's bagel?" I said.

"A persistent investigator always finds the truth," he said.

"She dropped it behind her desk?"

"The truth!" he insisted.

~

I WENT STRAIGHT HOME and strode into the apartment complex. The Empties outside the building didn't stare at the mostly naked woman walking by. They stared at nothing at all.

"This is an exciting new look for you," said Helberg as I entered the lobby. He saw the look on my face. "You want to come in for a coffee? Something stronger? Maybe with a side order of clothes?"

I went into his office and fell onto the squashy couch in exhausted disbelief. I instantly decided I never wanted to get up again. Helberg draped something over me. I felt the touch of a thick, soft blanket.

"Thank you," I said.

"Anything for my favourite madwoman. What's this?"

He picked through the papers I had let drop to the floor. Many of the pages were melted together but I had successfully smuggled the plipper out of Jaffle Tech.

"Plipper," I said, morosely.

He turned the blister pack over in his hand.

"I stole it," I added.

"Why?"

"Thought you might like to take a look at it."

"Thought I'd like to take a look at your company's latest nightmare device?" He shrugged and nodded at the same time. He put the plipper on his desk and began tidying the dropped papers, skim-reading the first few pages as he did.

"This is soaked. You're naked. I suspect there's some story behind this," he said.

I groaned. "I'm a horrible human being."

"No," he tutted. "That's not true. Now that you've taken to walking around in your underwear, I think I've seen most of you, and I'd score you as a solid seven, possible even an eight."

"Horrible on the inside," I grumped.

"Still a solid seven or eight," he said. "Like the rest of us. What you are is human, very, very human."

"I set fire to the office, destroyed Hattie's Smiley Tots, stole company property and I'm going to get suspended from my job."

"Okay," said Helberg. "Maybe a six."

21

9TH JUNE – 10 DAYS UNTIL OPERATION SUNRISE

I was indeed suspended from work, pending an investigation. Paulette tried to dress it up as recovery time from the shock at being caught in a fire in the workplace, but it was what it was. I was told to go away and not come back in until invited.

The following days were very uncomfortable at home. Hattie's hostility towards me was so intense that being in the same room as her was hard work. She would pointedly ignore me, then address comments to the blackened head Levi had picked out of the fire. I have no idea why she'd even taken it, but she used it to punish me.

"Oh look, Derek, I see Alice hasn't put the beans back in the cupboard."

"Derek, can you remember when you had a body? It was such a lovely little body, wasn't it?"

"I need to take really good care of you now, Derek, or Alice will find a way to take you away from me."

I spent an increasing amount of time down in Helberg's flat.

"So," he said loudly, out of nowhere, as though he had suddenly decided he'd had enough of my miserable mood. "Have you been to an upscale party before?"

"What?"

"The Jaffle Tech gala. A party. Where there's music and hors d'oeuvres and so on?"

"I, er..." I played for time while I jipped the meaning of *hors d'oeuvres*. I was relieved to discover that it was a fancy name for food of some sort. "Well, I've eaten food before, obviously. There are some things that I'm not keen on, like garlic, but I'll just avoid those."

"You'll avoid garlic? How will you know?"

"It's pretty obvious," I said. "A weird roundish thing, covered in paper. I could spot it a mile off."

"I think you and your fairy godmother might have some work to do," said Helberg. "Follow me."

It turned out that he had a kitchen just off his back office. There was a confused and cluttered warren of rooms in that part of the apartment complex, as though built for a purpose long since forgotten. Not only did he have a kitchen but he knew what to do with it.

He showed me the freezer and explained the difference between that and the fridge. There seems to be a lot of science involved in cookery. The freezer is much colder and keeps certain things for a long time, but you can't just eat them, because they are frozen. This sounded like a lot of trouble to me, but Helberg tapped the side of his nose and got out some little beige discs. He put them on a metal tray which went into the oven.

"These always make an appearance at parties. Finger foods, you see: you eat them without a knife and fork." He eyed me, as if a sudden thought had come to him. "Do you know what I'm talking about?"

"I know what a knife and fork is," I said.

"But have you ever eaten with them?"

"No."

"Probably a lesson for another day. Let's concentrate on finger foods. Just because they're called that, don't be fooled. It's not necessarily straightforward. Into the oven with these and then we'll make a couple of fillings."

He went back to the freezer and scrabbled in the depths. Then he put a board onto the table and took a large knife from the drawer. The knife seemed outlandishly big. I couldn't imagine what he would need such a large blade for.

"Garlic!" he said, brandishing a cluster of the hateful stuff in his outstretched hand. "This is what we do."

He put the garlic on the board and leaned on it with his hand. It came apart into smaller pieces. He took one of the pieces and used the side of the knife blade to squash it. I wondered if he really knew what he was doing. Even I knew that you didn't use a knife like that. He lifted the blade and picked the papery stuff away. I peered and he was left with a creamy-coloured lump, and that distinctive, pungent smell filled the room. Then he used the knife (the right way up this time) to chop the garlic into tiny pieces.

He fetched something from the fridge. It was a startling red globe.

"What's that?"

"A tomato. You can try some in a few minutes."

I watched as he carefully chopped the tomato up and put it in a bowl with the garlic. He took another bowl and tipped in some little pink things which looked like severed fingers. He squirted some gloopy liquid over the mixture, added powder from a jar, and stirred it with a spoon.

He looked up and beamed. "I think the vol au vents should be about ready."

When he opened the oven, there was a blast of heat accompanied by a delicious smell. He pulled the tray out. The weird little discs had transformed into fluffy brown things, much taller than when they started. I touched one. It broke apart with the smallest of prods.

"Oops, sorry," I said.

"You're starting to see what one of your challenges will be," said Helberg. "Learning to eat this sort of thing without covering yourself and your fellow guests with mess is essential."

"It's like a test?" I said.

"Everything at a high-class party is like a test."

He took one of them and put it on a plate. He flipped off the top. It resembled a tiny cup. "Huh, that's neat," I said.

He took a spoonful of the gloopy pink things and put them in the cup. He handed me the plate.

"Prawn vol au vent. Very tasty, but potentially messy to eat. Your mission is to eat some or all of this without spilling bits. Or—" he added, looking at me opening my mouth as wide as it would go, "—without looking like it's feeding time at the zoo. Try to be delicate and elegant."

"How do I do that?" I asked. It sounded impossible.

He shrugged. "I'm not really sure. Give it a shot."

I bit into the thing. I could feel it crumbling into pieces. I grunted in frustration. It was smooshed against my mouth, but I knew the moment I took it away, there would be a cascade of mess. I inched my hand underneath to catch as much as I could as I lowered the half-crushed thing. My method almost worked. I looked up to see whether Helberg was critiquing my performance, but he was spooning the tomato mixture into some of the pastry cases. I pushed the remains of the first vol au vent into my mouth. It wasn't all that elegant, but I thought I'd got away with it.

"Don't make sucking, slurping noises, it's considered impolite," said Helberg.

I made a muted "Uh huh" noise.

"So is talking with your mouth full," he said.

I finished and licked my lips. "That was nice. What did you say it was?"

"Prawns," said Helberg. "Delicious, but delicate. If you see something with prawns in it that looks dried out or a bit old, avoid it. You might end up with a stomach upset. Now try the tomato one."

I tackled this one more carefully, making sure I left myself with a second half that was more easily contained.

"A triumph!" he said, as I finished it off.

"That was garlic," I said. "I could taste it, but only a little bit. It was good."

He nodded. "Less is more with garlic. Now let's look at some of the other things you might come across at a buffet."

He stared up, seeking inspiration. I guessed it was a while since he went to a party.

"You did fine with the vol au vents, so anything else in pastry is covered. Things on sticks: don't eat the stick."

"Why put it on a stick then?" I asked.

He shrugged. "So you can pick it up. You don't want a load of people rummaging through a dish of olives or something with their dirty fingers."

"Olives, I tried those. There's a pit in the middle."

"In the world of buffet food, you'll often find that the pit has been replaced with something else. Let me see if I've got some to show you."

Helberg went to a cupboard. It was filled with an amazing range of jars and tins. He pushed some aside, and then found what he was looking for. "Olives stuffed with anchovies."

If I understood him right, this was a small, bitter fruit with a fish in the middle. Of course it was.

He went to a drawer and found a tub filled with tiny wooden sticks. He took the lid off the jar and speared an olive with a stick. He handed it to me and speared another for himself.

I popped it into my mouth. It was much more enjoyable when I wasn't worrying about the pit. There was a strange new flavour, which must have been the anchovy. It was on the very edge of being disgusting. If I'd had a whole mouthful of that flavour it would have been quite unpleasant, but this tiny, acrid burst of flavour was intriguing and delicious.

"That was amazing!"

"Good. You're doing great," said Helberg. "Now, what else. You know there's going to be music, don't you?"

"Yes!" I said, excited. "Like the Smiley theme tune. *Smiley, Smiley, have you any fun? Yes I do, for everyone!*"

Helberg shook his head. "Do you know that the tune you just sang is an old nursery rhyme for children? It's called *Baa Baa Black Sheep*. They just changed the words."

"Oh."

In truth, as I'd sung the words, it sounded less thrilling to my ears than it used to, and only partly due to my singing. I felt as though I'd left Smiley behind since my unauthorised brain upgrade. Worse still, I had started to see the Smiley products as something bad, especially in the way they exploited people like Hattie. She more or less worked so she could afford more Smiley Tots.

"So the music you're talking about," I said, "is something different?"

"Oh yes. Let's start with something fairly bland. We don't want to overwhelm you." He turned to fiddle with a machine. "This one's called *The Girl from Ipanema*." He turned back to me. "What?"

Tears were running down my face. I had no idea what was happening. The music was so beautiful, so wonderfully clever, it overwhelmed me and I was left gasping, unable to form words.

He turned it off. "Too much?"

I nodded.

"Let's try something else." He thought for a moment. "We'll go with some Beatles." He pressed a button.

I shook my head with amazement. There was singing, and it was more than one person. How did they do that thing where their voices blended together? I sobbed again.

"You're crying."

"I can't help it," I said. "It's like ... heaven."

"*Love Love Me Do*, actually," he said. "One more. I'll play you a song from Abba."

This one had a female voice, no two female voices which blended together. Words about loss and sorrow made exquisite by being part of a melody, executed with such care. I started to howl with pain, tears running down my face. Helberg turned it off.

"Let's re-think this. We'll need to introduce you to a little bit more every time. It will cause problems at the party if you spend all of your time crying."

"Yes," I said, wiping my eyes. "Although I'm probably not going to the party at this rate. Work will fire me or have me imprisoned for arson."

"That fire wasn't your fault."

"It sort of was," I said.

"Don't be so hard on yourself," he said. "Tell you what. If you're not arrested for arson, pop round again tomorrow and we'll work on the music thing."

"And if I am arrested?"

"I'll visit you in prison. In the meantime..." He delved into a fridge. "More party food to practise with. You'll love this one."

He went off to the kitchen and then came back with a small bag. He opened the top so that I could see inside. "Pizza! Try it and let me know what you think."

I sniffed and detected a curious mixture of bread and other delightful aromas.

"Thank you."

22

11TH JUNE – 8 DAYS UNTIL OPERATION SUNRISE

I was summoned to work for an interview with Paulette.

She was very brisk and business-like. I tried to make small talk about the mystery of Brandine's bagel finally being put to rest, but she was aloof and silent as we walked from reception to one of the smaller closed offices used for meetings. There was a suited woman in the room when we arrived.

"Alice, this is Estelle. She's a senior human resources partner and she will be taking part in this interview."

I had no idea what a senior human resources partner did, but I nodded to Estelle.

"Alice," said Estelle. "It's important that you understand that the outcome of this process will determine your future employment with Jaffle Tech."

"What process?" I asked.

"The process we are currently carrying out," said Estelle. I still had no idea what it was. "This review is to examine the events leading up to the fire which took place in the office, and the part you played in those events.

I nodded again.

"First things first, Alice. Do you want to make any statements to us concerning those events?" Estelle asked. "We will be watching the CCTV footage in a moment and drawing our conclusions from it. If you'd like to say anything to us before we do that, please go ahead."

I glanced at Paulette to see if I could get any clues as to how I was expected to react. Paulette was not looking my way. "Um, no, thank you," I said.

Estelle made some sort of gesture which started the CCTV footage rolling on the wall in front of us. I was slightly surprised to see it didn't start in the staff kitchenette with me holding the bottle of thinners. I felt sure there was a camera which covered that part of the office. What appeared instead was the image of a bot trundling across the office and spontaneously bursting into flames.

It was such a shock to see that I gasped out loud. Estelle paused the film.

"Alice, I understand if this is difficult. Are you all right to continue?"

I nodded and she re-started the film. As the bot moved more erratically, I appeared on the edge of the frame and I ran towards it. It looked very much as if I tried to put the flames out with my hands but burned myself. Then I tore off my tunic and used it to try and smother the flames. Moments later the film cut to another camera that showed me running over to Hattie and dragging her clear of the inferno her desk had become. Finally the sprinklers came on and we could all be seen evacuating the office. The view became slightly smudged by the droplets of water on the camera.

Estelle turned off the film. "Well it seems that you displayed considerable initiative Alice. I hope you'll accept our heartfelt thanks for averting what could have been a much more serious incident. I can see from the film you made several attempts to extinguish the flames with what you had to hand, and then you also helped others to evacuate the scene. We could all learn a lot from your quick thinking. Paulette, I hope you're very proud to have such a resourceful young woman on your team."

Paulette nodded, although I could see from her face that she wasn't quite ready to join the Alice fan club just yet.

"Now, it's likely you might need a few more days to rest and recuperate," said Estelle. "Smoke inhalation and stress can sometimes cause delayed symptoms. We'll make sure you have the self-care information sent to you so you can look out for them, just in case. Take your time deciding when you'd like to return to work. Otherwise, you're a credit to the Jaffle organisation and you will be formally thanked in the quarterly staff celebration."

I smiled at Estelle. I didn't trust myself to speak, as the film I'd just seen showed a very different version of events from the one I'd experienced. I wasn't sure how much Paulette had seen on the day, but she didn't look like a woman who believed in the story she'd just seen, either. I had no idea how the film had missed me causing the fire by damaging the bot and dousing everything in thinners. I had no idea how my misunderstanding of the word inflammable hadn't come to light. I was astounded there had been no mention of the Smiley Tots being here only because I had made it unsafe for Hattie to have them at home.

"There is one more thing we'd like you to do before you return to work," said Paulette.

"Yes?"

"You are to report to Krasnesky."

"Levi?"

She nodded curtly.

I went to find Levi out on the office floor. The mess from the fire had all been cleaned away and everything was back to normal. It felt strange to be here again.

Levi was with Hattie. She had a cubicle in a newer design, since the old one had been badly burned. Levi was showing her some pictures.

"I reckon these might tide you over until you can get some more of those famous Tots of yours," he said, holding them up.

The pictures were of Smiley Tots, standing in a row with outstretched arms. He pinned them to the sides of the cubicle. The effect was startling. It really looked as though there was a crowd of Smiley Tots standing along the edge of Hattie's cubicle, all wanting a hug.

"They look almost real! That's really good, thank you Levi," said Hattie, beaming up at him.

I was astounded at his kindness. I had to work hard to close my mouth as he turned towards me. His smile for Hattie disappeared when he saw me. He sort of packaged it officially away under that little moustache of his and swallowed it whole.

"It's time to watch The Film, Alice," he said.

I mentally rolled my eyes but, externally, managed to nod meekly.

"You can watch in the usual place," Levi said, leading the way. I saw Hattie give me a hard and hurtful look as we left.

In the training room, I sat alone in an amphitheatre that could have held a thousand people. Levi spent a few moments setting it up before he dimmed the lights and left the room.

It was an odd sensation seeing The Film again.

Old Alice, the Alice who was bound by the chains of Jaffle Standard, was terrified of the film. The black and white horror of calamities and accidents of yesteryear. It was a dark amorphous nightmare. The fact that everyone just called it The Film showed we had all viewed it without comprehension, only digesting the frightening emotional content without grasping any deeper meaning.

Now, as I watched the familiar content, new and not particularly subtle meanings were revealed. Hattie and I had always viewed it as being a compilation of misdemeanours, perhaps captured by old security cameras. I realised this was a story. It was a story! How had I not grasped that before?

It was about a man who had to find a bride by the end of the day or he would fail to inherit some money from a dead relative. It seemed an unlikely set of circumstances, and the very thought of it made me laugh. It was probably wrong to laugh at someone else's misfortune but I couldn't help myself.

The man – the actor! (a quick jip revealed him to be one Buster Keaton) – tried to persuade passing women to marry him, but they were understandably sceptical of his clumsy advances. This made me laugh even more. I found myself wondering what the ideal solution would be. If he really needed the money, maybe he should advertise?

I cheered the screen when his friend did exactly that. He put an article in the newspaper which immediately brought many women chasing after him.

How had we missed all of this fun on previous viewings? Probably because we were too distracted by the violence.

The chasing part had always tipped us over into a complete frenzy of dismay. Now I laughed out loud. There were hundreds of women, all somehow dressed up for a wedding, running through the street chasing the poor man. It was the most hilarious sight. They wanted to marry him and share in his fortune, but they looked terrifying, charging down the road, throwing bricks. They chased him in old-fashioned cars and trains, and he evaded them by taking the most shocking risks, nearly dying in lots of awful ways, but that just made it funnier. As I watched I realised my face was aching with all of the laughing, and there was a pain in my side.

"Oh Hattie, I wish I could think of a way to explain this to you!" I howled.

The chase moved out of the city and into some open countryside. The part where he ran down a hillside, chased by tumbling rocks made me gasp at the danger, but it was so funny I still couldn't help laughing.

When it was done, Levi returned. "I see it's made you cry," he said.

There were indeed tears on my cheeks. I had laughed so hard that I had almost wet myself.

"I hope it's made you reflect upon how you should conduct yourself in the workplace," he said solemnly.

I wiped my eyes. "Levi, what's this film called?" I asked.

"It's called *Seven Chances*," he said. "But in reality we don't always get that many chances at safety. You know that."

"Is there some more of this film?" I asked. "After this part here?"

"I believe there is."

"Can I watch it please? I want to see what happens."

He looked at me with deep suspicion. "Why would you want to do that?"

"Please?" I asked. "I want to be sure I learn all that I can from it."

He grunted, put The Film back on and left me to watch the end.

I was thrilled to find after it seemed everything was hopeless, and the hero couldn't possibly succeed in marrying his true love, he managed to do just that. It made me sigh with a curious feeling of satisfaction.

I tried to compose myself before Levi came back into the room.

"Well, I imagine you feel differently now, dontcha?" he asked.

"Oh, I certainly do," I said, wiping my eyes.

23

The Film gave me a lot to think about.

I had seen Buster Keaton's silent film as horror because I – Jaffle Standard Alice – could only see the immediate physical danger it showed. But it wasn't a horror film. It was funny and warming and ultimately uplifting and I wondered why.

That evening, as dusk settled over the city, I walked the streets around the Shangri-La Towers apartment complex pondering this. I sat with the Empties by the roadside.

"Why did I laugh at it?" I asked.

Unsurprisingly, the Empty next to me didn't respond.

"You'd have laughed too," I told her. "If you were allowed to understand it."

I flicked away a fly that was crawling on her lapel.

"I think," I said reflectively, "as soon as I realised the man wasn't in any real danger – it just wasn't that kind of story – then the things which should have been terrible became funny. It's like getting a really big surprise and then realising it's nothing bad. Like a dog chasing its own tail. And ... in the end, a story in which everything seemed hopeless became suddenly filled with hope."

The Empty stared blankly ahead.

"I thought you'd agree with me." I stood up. "There's always hope, isn't there?" I said and went inside.

Hattie was sat on the couch when I got to our apartment. She didn't meet my eye. A partially burned Smiley Tot was clutched in her hands.

"Oh Derek, I see Alice is home," she said to the blackened ruin of the Tot's face. "I wonder what chaos she's been causing today."

I stood right in front of her and wagged my finger. "You are my friend," I told her sternly. "You are my best friend in the whole wide world."

"Well, Derek, Alice has a funny way of showing people what—"

"*And* I burned all your Smiley Tots and I feel really bad," I went on.

Hattie didn't say anything, although she did glance at Derek as though they were sharing a look.

"Recently I have been erratic and unpredictable. I've created mess and confusion and I probably seem like a completely different person. And I am! I have changed a lot in the past few days."

"You have," she said, addressing me directly for what felt like the first time in ages.

"But that's not an excuse to set fire to your Smiley Tots."

"It isn't."

"But..." I took a deep breath, trying to formulate a way of saying what I had to say next without upsetting her, and realising there wasn't one. "But I don't think Smiley Tots make you happy anyway."

She gasped, actually gasped, her mouth a perfect O. "Take that back!"

"No. I don't think you want Smiley Tots."

"I do!"

"I think you want a baby."

Hattie frowned in deep confusion. "A baby...? As in...?"

"Children," I said.

"You mean, little people?" She gestured to indicate smallness. Her hands moved up and down, as she was clearly unsure exactly how small children were.

"Yes," I said.

Hattie was giving me another one of those looks which suggested I had well and truly gone off the rails. "You don't see them so much around here."

"No," I said. "But I saw some. In the art gallery. Pictures of babies, I mean. There's this one called Jesus who's in a lot of them. He has a shiny light on his head, although I don't know what it's for."

"But where are the real children?" asked Hattie.

"Um – I don't know," I said, on the cusp of feeling stupid for pointing out Hattie's need for children in her life without knowing where they had all gone. I gave myself a mental slap. At least Hattie was intrigued. "I don't know where they are," I said, "but we should find them, shouldn't we?"

"How?"

"We ask Helberg."

HATTIE and I sat side by side on Helberg's squashy sofa, crowded in on all side by his junk and partially tinkered bot bits. He sat in a swivel chair and gave us both a smile. It was a slightly sad smile. I jipped my literacy booster and came up with the word *wistful*. It was a wistful smile.

"How much do you remember about your own childhoods?" he asked.

I'd asked myself the same question, and the answer was frustrating. "Not all that much. I remember studying for exams, and I remember Hattie and I have been together for a very long time, but I feel as though there's a lot more that I can't remember."

"Same here," said Hattie.

He nodded. "You probably spent a lot of time in the OneStop Daycare facility or the Nurture Hub or one of the other mega-crèches."

"Right," I said. "Did I? Did we?"

He nodded.

An idea was forming. "Does that mean it's possible to go there and actually see children?"

"I'm not sure it's a place which welcomes visitors," said Helberg. "Children are delicate things."

"Like Smiley Tots," said Hattie.

"Especially babies." He inhaled sharply and leaned back in his chair, thinking. "But if you told them you were experienced nursery nurses looking for employment..."

"Would they let us look round?" I said. "Meet actual babies?"

"Possibly."

"Helberg," said Hattie, folding her hands primly onto her lap.

"Patrick, please."

"Patrick, I know you're the building manager and the boss of the cleaning bots, but I don't like you encouraging Alice like this. She's clearly had a breakdown or something, and I can't help thinking you're making her worse."

"I'm fine, Hattie," I said. "And this is a great idea."

"Is it?"

"And I want to do it for *you*, because I think you'll love it. Have you ever held a baby?"

"No. Of course not."

"Have you ever even *seen* a baby?"

"What's got into you?" she asked. "I don't know. Maybe I've seen them in the distance or something. I can't remember."

I grinned at her. "Come on! We've got a rest day tomorrow. Let's go and see the children."

She gave me a dubious look. I could see she really wanted to, but this behaviour extended beyond the boundaries of what she considered normal.

"Come on," I said. "Tomorrow morning. We'll go and have a quick look at a baby."

Hattie sighed. "Do you promise that you'll be normal for the rest of the day if I agree to this? We'll sit and eat our beans and watch Smiley like we used to?"

"Yes, of course," I said.

24

12TH JUNE – 7 DAYS UNTIL OPERATION SUNRISE

The OneStop Daycare facility was almost as big as Jaffle headquarters, but in a quiet suburb, up in the hills and far from the busy bay area. Hattie, Helberg and I went into the reception area.

"Have fun," he said before calling to the receptionist. "Prospective employees. Come to look around."

"Did you get in touch beforehand?" asked the receptionist.

"Yes," I said.

"No," said Hattie at the same time.

The receptionist looked at us both and sighed slightly. She made a call to someone. "I have some visitors who are thinking of applying for work. Could you please talk to them?"

Moments later, a neat-looking woman arrived. She wore a colourful tunic and had a warm smile. "Hello, I'm Shirley and I'd be happy to answer any questions you might have about working here." She led us through a double door. "Can I ask where you've been working up until now?"

"Private work," I offered, "I'm not permitted to discuss details, of course."

"I see," said Shirley. "So, what's your particular interest here?"

"Babies," I said. "We'd like to see your, er, baby department."

"Certainly," said Shirley. We went through a maze of corridors and up some stairs. We emerged into a large room. "Soft play area. Shoes off for this part."

We all removed our shoes and walked across a squishy vinyl surface which was covered in colourful blocks and toys. There was a circle of tiny children up ahead. They were *impossibly* tiny. Did all people start off this small? Some were big enough to sit up by themselves, while others reclined in special seats which bounced lightly.

Hattie gasped. I looked and saw her face crumple into the same adoring expression she had for her Smiley Tots.

A woman was reading the babies a story about a dog. Most of them had their eyes on her, a couple wriggled or crawled in a distracted way, and there was one who wailed softly.

"Don't let us disturb you, I have some visitors who want to look around," Shirley said to her.

The woman looked up and smiled. "Well if anyone wants to get hands-on, then Jacob needs a change, I think." She indicated the wailing baby.

"I'll do it," said Hattie eagerly.

Shirley beamed and waved Hattie forward.

"Hello Jacob," said Hattie, picking him up. "Let's sort you out, shall we?"

I followed Hattie as she carried Jacob over to an area that was clearly reserved for clean-up. She laid him down on a mat and tickled his toes. He chuckled in delight and Hattie made cooing noises.

Shirley handed something to Hattie. "Clean nappy for you. Wipes are there too."

Hattie undressed Jacob. I peered over to watch. "Oh my god, that is disgusting!" I hissed.

Jacob had squirted poo into every imaginable crevice and seemed very proud of the appalling mess that he'd made. The smell was overwhelming. I wondered what on earth they could be feeding these infants to make such an appalling stench. Hattie was oblivious to the horror and bent over, carefully cleaning him up, still grinning. He had a little tiny penis, and as I watched, an arc of urine splashed into Hattie's face.

"Oh Jacob!" she said. "What a little tinker you are!"

She continued to clean and re-dress him. She wiped the urine off her face as if it was nothing. Then she picked him up and put him to her shoulder. "Isn't he just the sweetest thing you ever saw in your life?" she asked.

I watched and pointed in horror as Jacob vomited down Hattie's back. "Your back!"

Hattie smiled and carefully put Jacob down to listen to the story before she wiped the vomit off herself. "He can't help it, he's only tiny."

While I hadn't been at all ready for the mess a baby could

inflict, Hattie was in her element. "Do you want to go back now?" I checked.

"Ooh, no, let's stay for a while," she said enthusiastically. Hattie inserted herself into the circle of babies and cuddled them as they all listened to the story.

25

13TH JUNE – 6 DAYS UNTIL OPERATION SUNRISE

A t work the next day, I wasn't sure I'd done the right thing, taking Hattie to the OneStop Daycare centre.

Yes, I had made her very happy for a few hours.

Yes, I had definitely put the incinerated Smiley Tots out of her mind.

Yes, I had certainly mended some bridges in our relationship and that made me feel good.

But at what cost?

Within fifteen minutes of arriving at work, Hattie had jipped images of babies – real human babies, not stylised Smiley Tots – arranged around her cubicle. Every time I walked past her cubicle I saw her looking at them with a curious expression. *Wistful*. That was the word: wistful.

"Well, don't them young 'uns look a fine and pretty sight," Levi said to her. "Although having so many paper images in your workstation could be considered a fire hazard."

"I think I would like a real one," she said.

"A real what?"

"Baby."

He sucked in through his teeth. "That would be a handful and no mistake. But certainly less flammable. Oh, yabetcha."

It was odd. The man was quite an insufferable prig and yet, I realised, he had a streak of kindness running through him which he did his darnedest to hide. Always a kind word for Hattie, the other workers too, like he really believed he was a kindly shepherd overlooking his flock.

Paulette approached me. "Alice, I've been asked to file a report."

"Oh. What kind of a report?" I asked.

"I'm not sure I can share that detail," she said. "Let's just say that it's a thorough and comprehensive report on some of the things that have happened in the department in recent days."

"The department?" I asked. "So not me, personally?"

"My office, would you?" She marched away, knowing I had to follow.

Paulette closed the office door behind us, took her seat and studied me.

"How can I help?" I asked eventually. If I could have asked a question more like *How can I end this as quickly as possible?* I would have gone for it, but I had to appear co-operative.

Clearly I had been uncovered in some way. Of all the things I had done in recent days, any number could be the reason for this. Getting my brain infected with the whale virus. Faking brain scans. Lying to staff. Starting fires. Sneaking to the top floor executive offices.

"The incident I wanted to flesh out a little for the report," said Paulette, "was the one where you took my bacon sandwich."

I was stunned. Of all the things I thought she might be about to say, that definitely wouldn't have made the top ten. I'd almost completely forgotten about it. Her words stimulated the memory of experiencing that overpowering smell for the first time. I licked my lips just thinking about it.

"Right. Bacon sandwich, yes," I said.

"My recollection is that you said I was to give you my bacon sandwich because Rufus Jaffle had said so, while you were doing a special job for him." She paused. "Now that I come to write it down, I have questions. For example, how did Rufus Jaffle even know I had a bacon sandwich?"

I saw an immediate problem. I really needed to distance myself from any mention of Rufus Jaffle. I couldn't have Paulette writing this down, or someone like Henderson would surely join the dots and realise the person who'd been inside Jaffle's head was the same one who was at the centre of various minor atrocities. He'd reset my brain before you could say *plipper*.

"I do remember that," I said to Paulette. "I had such a vivid dream. Weird, huh?"

"What? You dreamt that Rufus Jaffle told you to take my bacon sandwich?"

"Yes," I said. I hoped the lie would satisfy Paulette without any further embellishment, but she looked as if she had a hundred more questions. I launched a pre-emptive monologue.

"Every once in a while I have a dream that's so vivid it seems real. As you know, we'd had the presentation about the company's achievements. I always like to hear about the things we're helping to do around the world. I think that perhaps Mr Jaffle was in my mind, I guess that's why he ended up in my dream."

"So, you haven't met him in real life?"

"In my dream he was a short, dark haired man. Very serious," I said. "Do you think he's like that in real life?"

"I genuinely have no idea," said Paulette. "So, can I be crystal clear on this? You were acting purely upon a dream when you demanded to have my bacon sandwich?"

"Yes. Sorry. I realise now that I shouldn't have done that."

"Did you enjoy the bacon sandwich, Alice?"

Did she think I was stupid enough to fall into a trap like that? "No," I said – wistfully. "Not really. I like beans better. They're more practical."

She made a noise and gave me an odd look: a sort of internalised scowl.

"Is that ... it?" I asked.

She continued to look at me. "You can see why I was curious."

"Oh, absolutely," I said. "Me and my dreams, eh?" I gave her a jolly smile, a sort of *Oh, that Alice, isn't she a harmless ditz* sort of smile.

"I just needed to know," said Paulette, "before I fill out these reference requests."

"Sure," I said, then: "What? Reference requests?"

Paulette studied something on her desk.

"The OneStop Daycare Centre," she said. "Yourself and a colleague, and a—" she gave a little frown "—and an unknown third person who didn't register on entry, went for a pre-application visit." Paulette smiled politely at me. "I didn't know you had any experience in childcare."

"Er, no," I said.

"Or interest."

"It's a recent thing. It's more Hattie's thing really. She's got a real, er, passion."

Paulette put her hands together on the table. "Are you unhappy here?"

"Me? Or both of us?"

"Either."

I wasn't sure how to respond. The truth – that Hattie was secretly baby-mad and had been pushed in that direction by my own personal awakening – wasn't going to make things better. "We're really happy here," I said.

"Because Jaffle Tech prides itself on being the employer that people want to work for."

"Especially, Hattie. She loves her job. She really doesn't want to leave."

"I thought you said she was the one with the passion."

"She is, but she's loyal. She was just ... just looking. There's no harm in looking. Have you ... have you invited her in for a *little chat*?"

Paulette shook her head. "No. She's not the one with anomalous behaviours on her file."

"Anomalous. Good word. What behaviours?"

Paulette opened her hands as though the behaviours were concealed in them. "The bacon sandwich."

"Right, that," I said.

"The requests for new tunics."

"Yes," I nodded. "Some accidents there."

"Including an engineer's tunic, I noticed."

I pursed my lips. That was harder to explain. "I do like exploring other jobs."

"And dressing up for roles you are not qualified to undertake."

"I wouldn't say that."

"Wouldn't you?"

I met her gaze. I didn't know what she was thinking, but I wasn't thinking anything beyond blind panic. "I don't know what I'm doing half the time," I heard myself say.

"You have mental absences?" said Paulette.

"What?"

"Fugue states. Black outs. That sounds serious."

"No, no, no," I said hurriedly. "I mean that I'm a ... whimsical character. Spontaneous. You should see what thoughts go through my head sometime."

"We can," said Paulette. "I note here that you've been called to have a brain scan on several occasions in the past few weeks. Problems?"

"Not at all. Just one brain scan, but I had to reschedule several times. I'm very busy."

"You then submitted a privately commissioned scan."

"I was doing a favour for a friend."

"You have friends?"

That halted me dead. "Yes, I have friends."

"The same friend whose Jaffle Port didn't register at the OneStop Daycare?"

"Lots of friends."

Paulette breathed in slowly, making a show of thinking. "Your Jaffle rating is a combined scoring system which shows your reliability and efficiency in a wide range of areas," she said. "A heuristic diagnostic tool to help people understand what kind of – well, neighbour or employee or teammate or whatever – you might be. These recent behaviours of yours are likely to have an adverse effect on your rating."

"Did I do something wrong?"

"These behaviours aren't wrong per se, Alice. But they are odd. If I'm to provide the requested reference—"

"You don't have to do that, honestly."

"But it has been requested. I think I ought to look into these matters a little more deeply. If it's all right with you, I'm going to interrogate the location tracker log in your port, see where you've been, what you've been up—"

"Can I refuse?"

"Of course you can," she said, smiling gently. "But that would be odd in itself. Possibly grounds for us to subpoena said records. As a caring employer, we actively weed out those who are engaged in illegal and anti-social behaviours. Refusing to let your employer access those records would seem suspicious."

"Of course," I said for lack of anything else to say.

"Agreed," said Paulette. And, with that, I realised I had given them a front row seat to all my inexplicable activities since Rufus Jaffle had accidentally awoken me to my full potential.

"Give me a little time and I will call you back in for a clarification interview if necessary," said Paulette.

I numbly left her office. *Clarification interview*. That might as well be code for *Pre-firing and pre-arrest interview*.

What other stones would they turn over? If she combined location information with Jaffle's own CCTV, they'd see where I'd been, what I'd stolen. I could make no defence. And if Paulette was going to make a full and comprehensive report into Jaffle Tech weirdness involving me, she would probably focus on my unofficial brain scan, which would definitely not withstand careful scrutiny. I wondered if I could get that scan back somehow. I had no idea how to do that, but then another idea occurred to me.

26

"I want to ask you something," I said to Helberg when I got home.

"Good. I want to show you something," he replied. He took my hand and drew me into his office.

"You faked my brain scan," I said.

"I did. Chuckie Egg, music please."

The bot began to play some music I had not heard before. I had spent a lot of time at Helberg's place, listening to music. I could manage it now without crying, although it was a close-run thing. "I don't want a dancing lesson now," I said.

"But you do want to dance at the gala," he said. "Today is salsa."

"Salsa?"

I quickly jipped it. I'd already tried out some very rudimentary dance moves. I'd seen lots of amazing moves when I searched the archive clips, but Helberg told me most people didn't dance like that at parties. He had previously recommended something which looked more like walking backwards and forwards while turning bacon on an invisible barbecue. Salsa looked a bit more involved.

"Is this one of those ones where the dancing is a desired expression of a vertical ... whatever you said. Basically, upright sex."

He laughed. "You make it sound like people are *only* interested in sex."

"You are."

"Maybe I'm just a hopeless romantic. The phrase you were reaching for, Alice, is *the vertical expression of a horizontal desire*."

"That."

"Possibly."

"Look," I said, having had my initial conversational thread hijacked, "I need to ask you how easy it would be to fake lots and lots of brain scans."

"What?" he said. "Uh-huh. Dancing first. Stupid questions later." He drew me closer in preparation.

"As long as we can't get pregnant doing the upright sex dance," I said.

"Who's getting pregnant?" asked Hattie from the doorway.

"No one," I said.

"Alice is just asking stupid questions," muttered Helberg.

"There are no stupid questions, only stupid answers," said Hattie. "I read that somewhere."

"Well, whoever said that was also stupid," said Helberg.

Hattie hovered in the doorway. Helberg looked pointedly

at her. I stepped back from him. It felt kind of silly to be that close to him if we weren't actually going to dance yet.

"I jipped a question today and only got a stupid answer," said Hattie. "You seem to know stuff, Helberg."

"Some stuff," he conceded.

"So how do babies come out?"

He stared at her for a long moment and then did some very awkward but nonetheless quite explanatory gestures.

"No. No. No." Hattie was adamant. "There's no possible way a baby can come out of there. I saw them. They're small, but they're not *that* small. No way. It's just not big enough. I don't want to go into details, but sometimes it's a squeeze to get the, you know, other thing out of there. A whole baby? I don't think so."

"But you must be able to get an answer by jip— *Whoa!*" I had just jipped it. It looked like the worst form of torture. "Look at her—! That can't be right! Was she following the instructions properly?"

Helberg coughed. "I take it we're all up to speed now? Or at least we accept that babies develop inside a woman's body and then come out through the vagina."

Hattie blew out her cheeks and shook her head, so confused she needed to sit down. "So, hang on. If that's how babies get *out*, how do they get in there? And why have I never seen it happening?"

"Lots of questions wrapped up in there," said Helberg slowly, with a quick glance at me.

This was going to be tricky. Because Hattie was still on Jaffle Standard, she'd never had any sexual urges.

"Couldn't we, er, you know...?" I said to Helberg,

discreetly tilting my head towards his Jaffle port-hacking gizmo.

He raised his eyebrows. "What are you suggesting, Alice?"

"Make Hattie like me. You could access her brain and fix her so that she has all of the same—"

"What?" Hattie looked fearful. "Nobody's touching my brain! Is that how the baby gets in? Our brains are a long way from our vaginas, it doesn't seem very practical."

"Nobody's touching your brain, Hattie," said Helberg. "See, I think we can explain the mechanics of this."

"I would appreciate that," she said.

"In short, babies come from sex. Adults do this thing called sexual intercourse and that can make a woman pregnant. After being pregnant for nine months a baby comes out. Try jipping some of those terms."

"Oh my word," said Hattie, clearly doing exactly that. She looked flustered. "Are you two having me on, because I've definitely never seen anybody doing *that*."

"Well they do," said Helberg.

I looked at him with interest. "And how many times have you done it?"

He looked embarrassed. "That's not a question most people normally ask if they were being polite," he said. "Um, a few times."

"Have you done this, Alice?" asked Hattie. She pointed at Helberg and me, a different question on the tip of her tongue.

"No!" I said, shocked. I took a deep breath and lowered my voice a little. "I haven't done it at all. Not yet."

"Not *yet*?"

"No. I've only just started dancing. You can't get pregnant dancing."

"Ah! But you are planning to?"

"What?"

"Does that mean you want to have a baby?"

"I'm not sure," I said, remembering the mess and the smell of that baby's nappy. "It seems like a lot to—"

"Well I do!" she declared. "I want a baby! I just need someone to have sex with me, yes? Can I make an appointment or something?"

I wasn't sure that I had an answer to that.

"Hattie, most people think carefully about who they want to make a baby with," said Helberg. "They choose someone who they think would, hm, help to make a nice baby."

Hattie looked Helberg up and down. "Well what about you? You look all right to me. Can we make an appointment? Maybe we could do it now?"

He looked very uncomfortable. "There's so much to think about, Hattie. Babies can cost a lot of money, and there's no doubt that it's a big commitment."

She shrugged. "How much money? I'm sure it can't be that bad. How much do you normally charge?"

Helberg gave me a look. It was one which suggested I had created a monster.

"Hattie," I said. "Do you remember me trying to talk to you about there being more to life than work and beans and so on? Well this is *one of the things* I was talking about. There's so much more to the world than we've known for much of our lives. We should take time to absorb it properly before we make big decisions, don't you think?"

Hattie pouted but gave a small nod. "I suppose." Her face dropped. "Wait. Is this about the red beans again? There's only so much change I can take without getting all consternated."

"How about we hack your Jaffle port and give you the—"

"You're talking about messing with my brain again!" Hattie's voice rose in panic. "If that isn't both consternating and discombobulating then I don't know what is!"

Helberg made shushing noises. "Nobody's going to mess with your brain, Hattie. I wouldn't consider it for a second." He gave me a stern look. "Seriously Alice, I'm not sure my little rig is up to the task. Reading some log files is one thing, but altering a whole bunch of Jaffle settings is another thing entirely when you're not familiar with them. It's much too risky to consider."

I wanted to blurt out that the risk of sitting around while Jaffle messed up everyone's brains in the whole world was considerably worse, but I needed to keep that to myself.

Hattie was joining the dots. "What do you mean, *reading some log files*?" She looked from Helberg to me and back again. "Did you fake your brain scan, Alice? Oh my goodness, you did! You're going to be in so much trouble! How come you're not already in tons of trouble?"

I leaned back in my chair. She had a fair point, and I had absolutely no answer.

I sat Hattie down and tried to outline what I'd done, without divulging any of the really bad parts. "First thing to understand is this, I was asked to provide some tech support, off the record."

Hattie's eyes narrowed. "Who was it for?"

"I can't tell you that. Really, it's best that you don't know."

She looked sceptical.

I pressed on. "Because this had to be offline, the only way I could do the requested clean-up was to use my own spare capacity as temporary storage." I pointed at my head, to underline what I was talking about. "It should have worked fine. The space was available and I'm sure I prepared everything correctly. What I think messed it up a little bit was some unauthorised software that this person had introduced."

"What, like a brain virus?" Hattie was horrified. "I thought they were a myth?"

"Apparently not," I said. "It's not as bad as it sounds. I just get a whale that interrupts me every once in a while."

"A whale? Big fish kind of thing?"

"Well, actually they're mammals. Wonderful creatures as it turns out, if a little bit rude when it comes to interrupting."

"Oh Alice! No wonder you've gone mad. You really need to get that sorted out."

"I'm going to a charity gala in two days to speak to Rufus Jaffle about it and get some answers."

Hattie didn't think that was enough. "No, we'll go to work and get someone to take a proper look at you. Put you all back to normal."

"No! I need to tell you the main point of all this!" I was keen Hattie didn't miss the important part of the story. "I ended up, after the procedure had run, having a few rogue memories, but the procedure activated all of the brain functionality people like us don't normally have. It's changed my life, Hattie. It's really opened my eyes."

Surely she would understand now. I looked at her, wondering how I could convey how important this was.

"That's just the illness talking," said Hattie. "I know it is. I can see the changes in you and they're not good."

"You're not listening," I said urgently. "We've been denied some of our basic human experiences. We always thought we were happy, but we were missing out on so much."

"Stop it, Alice, please." There were tears in her eyes. "I don't need a baby, not a real one. It was stupid idea and my vagina isn't big enough and I don't have enough money to pay for a baby. I am happy just the way I am."

"You're not."

"I *am!*" she snapped, the tears now rolling down her cheeks. "I am! I am! I am!" She pushed herself out of his squashy sofa and hurried out.

I stared at the open door. "I just make things worse all the time," I said.

"Brain hack or not, you've opened her eyes," said Helberg. "It's like the John Stuart Mill thing."

"The man with the unhappy pig?"

"Happy pig," he corrected. "Hattie might be upset now but it's probably because she can see what she's missing out on. It's that dissonance, the distance between what is and what should be that's causing her distress."

"Doesn't make me feel better about it," I said.

Helberg nodded but not necessarily in agreement. "A question you never asked..."

"What?"

"All those babies at the OneStop Daycare centre. Biologically, genetically, they came from other human beings. Whether they were naturally born or grown in artificial amniotic sacs, they are human children."

"I guess."

"Go back in time only a few decades and most people would have at least once child, created the *traditional* way. There would be children living in apartment blocks like this. There would be married couples."

"I saw a film about a man trying to get married. It was very, very funny."

"But you don't see married people anymore," said Helberg. "Not round here. No marriages among the Jaffle Standards. No sex. No children. Why do think that is?"

"I guess ... if people are on Jaffle Standard and they don't think about sex much, then they're not going to have babies the *traditional* way. So someone has to make sure there are babies, or we'll die out. The authorities make sure we don't run out of people."

Helberg grunted, a laugh that didn't quite make it out of his throat. "You've got it upside down, Alice. History can teach us a lot, and one of the things it teaches us is that one way the people in power exert control over everyone is deciding who can have sex and who can't, who you're allowed to have sex with if you do, and who is and isn't allowed to have children of their own."

"No. Really?"

He gave me a meaningful look, the kind of expression I would have found really annoying weeks ago but I now recognised as a look of patience; of hope that I would understand. "If they want to control us—"

"Who's *they*?" I said.

"The Man."

"Which man?"

"*The* Man. Capital *M*. Jaffle Tech. The powerful people."

"Like Claire?"

"The woman whose dress you stole? Sure. The powerful people. The governments which support them and are supported by them. They've got the Jaffle Standards packaged up neatly in their little boxes. No family. No love. No sex. No loyalty to anything but Mr Smiley and the status quo."

I thought about this for a long time. "Is that true?" I said. "Or is it just some mad conspiracy you've cooked up to justify the way you live your life?"

Helberg burst out laughing. "See! See! You're questioning. You're questioning authority and you're questioning me. God, I love you, Alice Tennerman." The moment the words were out of his mouth, he faltered. "I mean ... I mean I love the person you've become. That is ... I love what you've done with ... I mean..."

"Yeah, yeah," I said, waving his embarrassment away. There was still a heaviness in my chest, the inescapable feeling that I'd hurt Hattie once more, made her life worse not better. "You got any more of that Bony Hilda's Iguana Manilla lying around?"

"The what?"

"The sherry drink."

"The Bodegas Hidalgo La Gitana Manzanilla?" he smiled and stood.

"That is exactly what I said and you know it."

The bottle was on a shelf between two distinct but equally mystifying piles of electronic components. He took it down, along with two tiny glasses.

"Fill 'em up," I said.

"This is strong stuff, remember," said Helberg.

I shrugged and wondered how well sherry would suppress the lump of worry inside me.

"Maybe I want to be a happy pig again." I patted the seat next to me for him to sit down. "Just for one evening."

27

14TH JUNE – 5 DAYS UNTIL OPERATION SUNRISE

I dreamt that someone shouted from the doorway of the house.

"Did he just call my name?" I/Rufus asked. I realised I was both dreaming and remembering a slice of Rufus's memory from the party by the sea.

"It sure sounded like it," said TayTay, next to Rufus/me.

"Oh no, he's calling someone else. I never heard the name Roofight before," said Rufus.

"I think it's an actual fight," said MiMi, drifting towards the house. "With roos."

"Huh?" Rufus was confused.

"Haven't you heard?" TayTay asked, linking her arm in his and steering him onward. "They get a pair of kangaroos and have them fight each other. What's even better, they put Jaffle ports in them so someone can control what they do."

"No way!" said Rufus, picking up the pace. "This I have to see."

They hurried into the house and down some stairs into a huge basement kitted out with gym equipment and a boxing ring. There were, indeed, two kangaroos in the ring.

At the moment they were jigging lightly in opposite corners of the ring while people filed in. A good many of them recognised Rufus and cleared the way for us to ringside seats. A kangaroo was right in front of them/us. The only person closer was a man in black who was concentrating on a device in front of him. Presumably one which controlled the kangaroo's Jaffle port. MiMi reached out a hand to touch the kangaroo's fur.

The kangaroo in the opposite corner gave a low growl and the two girls pressed up against Rufus. He could feel the heat of their quivering bodies. It gave him a rush of heady testosterone and cocaine-fuelled confidence.

"Of course, the way to defeat a large predator is to understand and engage with their natural energy or prana," he said to them both. I found myself questioning whether a kangaroo was a predator, but I had no say in it.

"Have you ever heard of Maglev?"

They shook their heads.

"Few have," he said, lifting his hands and making a slow chopping movement as he explained the ins and outs of his chosen martial art.

"It's just a big mouse, isn't it?" said TayTay, looking at the kangaroo.

"A big mouse?" said Rufus, immediately cracking up with laughter. "It's a killer, babe, a stone cold killer.

A bell rang and the kangaroos bounded forward. They

started to shove each other with their relatively short arms. I found myself wondering if they were arms or forelegs.

"Go on! Whack him!" yelled Rufus, aligning himself with the kangaroo from his corner.

The kangaroos locked into an embrace and bounced on their powerful hind legs, trying to gain an advantage. They looked as though they were enjoying a dance. Not a salsa, though.

"Use your legs!" Rufus hollered.

The kangaroos did indeed start to kick each other. The kangaroo from our/their corner hung on with his arms and brought both powerful hind legs through with a vicious kick. The other kangaroo seemed unperturbed as they continued in their graceless dance.

"Leg sweep! Take him down with a leg sweep!" Rufus called.

The kangaroos bounced and grappled, but there was no sense either of them was being harmed in any way. I realised the counterweight of their enormous tails stabilised them so they could kick with both legs and still remain upright.

Rufus seemed to be getting more and more restless. In his mind I saw the growing urge for the violence to be stepped up. Even so I was horrified when he climbed up and stepped into the ring with me as his dream-passenger.

He held up his arms and turned to the crowd. An almighty cheer went up as Rufus threw himself into the fight. One of the kangaroos had returned to its corner, so he threw a punch at the one remaining. "Fists of fury! Betcha never saw anything like this back home in, ah, wherever you come from, did ya?"

He screamed in pure bloodlust and rained his fists down upon the kangaroo.

The animal leaned its head right back. Rufus dodged around its huge body to bop it on the nose. Unaccountably, this insane strategy worked. He landed a hard blow on the place where a kangaroo's temple might be, knocking it out cold. He stood over the unconscious kangaroo and punched the air, victorious.

"Now *that* is what a Maglev master looks like! Deadly weapons right here!"

I saw out of Rufus's peripheral vision that TayTay had elbowed the operator aside and had grabbed the controls for the remaining kangaroo's Jaffle port.

"Come on then motherfucker!" she yelled. "Show us those deadly weapons!"

I/Rufus didn't have time to react. The kangaroo grabbed us and rocked back to kick me....

I woke with a dry mouth and a pounding headache worse than the last time I'd drunk sherry. I called for pain filters but they made hardly any difference.

"So, this is a hangover," I mumbled. I thought sherry was my friend, but Hilda's Bony Iguana or whatever it was had turned on me in the night.

I sat up (I was in my own bed, which was a mild surprise) and I considered my general status.

"Not going to throw up," I told myself and my nauseated belly. Two minutes later, in the bathroom, my rebellious

insides made a liar of me. I cleaned myself and the bathroom
as best I could and slowly – oh, so slowly – got ready for
work.

There, armed with a few pointers from Helberg, I set
about covering up my dodgy brain scan. I couldn't hack in
and retrieve the scan I'd already submitted but I could mask
it with some suspicious-looking scans for other people. I
wondered how many fake brain scans I could fabricate
during the course of an extended toilet break. Enough to
confuse the person who'd be investigating my own fake brain
scan? Maybe.

I started with Paulette, just because she was on my mind:
I gave her an activity report that included lots of glitchy-
looking spikes. I moved on and made a fake brain scan for
Damien in supplies: him I gave several erroneous periods of
two hundred percent capacity usage. I fabricated a few more,
uncharitably gifting my colleagues with all sorts of problems
from old-fashioned Alzheimers to suspected interference
from sunspot activity.

I dropped them anonymously into the medical centre's
document store and slipped back to my desk.

Levi was hovering. A thought had struck me and I
couldn't shake it.

"Levi?"

"Yes, miss?"

"Levi, you know the cameras?"

He looked up and pointed at various corners. "Always
watching. Keeping us safe."

"The ones that recorded my little accident. The bot on
fire."

"Very important tool for the security professional. And I'm glad that incident is still on ya mind. It's only from our mistakes we learn, isn't that so?"

"Yes, yes," I said, wishing he'd stop wittering in that leisurely way of his, like he was dispensing invaluable homespun wisdom. "The specific recordings of what happened, the ones Paulette showed me when I returned from being suspended. They didn't ... necessarily show the whole picture."

"Faulty camera, you mean?" he said, taking a more serious tone.

I thought about how the footage specifically failed to show me starting the fire, only my efforts to put it out and rescue Hattie. Nor did it show me stealing the pipper and paperwork from the meeting room.

"It could have been a faulty camera," I admitted. "I was just wondering if it was possible for someone to change the video, edit out bits that were—" I didn't know how to finish that sentence without incriminating myself.

"Are you suggesting someone could tamper with security camera evidence?" he said, a look of naked horror on his face. "That would call into question everything this company stands for. It's unthinkable."

"Yes. Yes, of course," I said. "Sorry. Silly me."

A strange feeling, one I think had been stealing up on me for some days, took firm hold. For the rest of the day I did my job, but it felt like an act. Like I was a rebel, a subversive, a spy. I was working inside Jaffle Tech, acting like any of the support workers, offering help and guidance to the billions of Jaffle product users worldwide, except now it felt like I was playing a role. Inside I was something different. I was the maker of fake brain scans. I was the health and safety risk, always caught on camera but never exposed. I was the liar. I was the one who went to strange and unexpected places – food halls and flower markets and art galleries. I was the one who led innocents like Hattie astray, who interfered with Empties.

I was a virus in the system.

HELBERG WAS WAITING for me back at the apartment complex, actually waiting for me at the door to catch me when I arrived.

"You know, if I wanted a pet dog to greet me when I got home, I could buy one," I said.

He didn't smile. "I have to show you something."

"If it's another dance like the salsa, I don't think I'm up for it."

He didn't reply, leading me silently through to his office. He had cleared junk from tables and shelves to make room for the pieces of paper he'd arranged across them. It was some typed document, long and full of bullet points and sub-headings.

"I worked on back-engineering that plipper device you brought to me," he said, pointing to a bulky thing of soldered components and dangling wires.

"You've built your own plipper?" I was impressed.

"It's just an adapted port, like a Jaffle port, really. Except its sole purpose is to link to another port, pretty much along line of sight, using microwave and locator tech, and then change the access level."

I picked it up. Helberg's homemade plipper wasn't at all like the sleek little unit I'd stolen from Jaffle Tech. If the official plipper was a little gun, this thing was more like an ancient crossbow.

"So, you shoot and it just dials whoever it's pointing at down to Empty?" I said.

"That wasn't what I wanted to show you." He turned and spread his arms at the papers all around him. "This is the document you hid the plipper in, the one you stole. I happened to read it."

I went back to the document and glanced at the nearest sheet. "What is it?"

"It's Operation Sunrise." He said it with such glum solemnity that I felt a chill of fear.

"And...?" I said.

"It's bad, Alice."

"Bad how?"

He pointed at me, more specifically he pointed at my head. "You're on Jaffle Standard. Or, at least you were. You've got relatively full access to your intellect, sense of judgement, your more unsubtle range of emotions, speaking, memory and writing, yeah?"

"Sure," I said. "Although I can experience much more now."

"Right. And above standard is Jaffle Enhanced. Morality, self-conscious acts and even an appreciation of music and other art forms. Move up one more and you're into Jaffle Premium with access to notions of beauty, humour, sex and violence. Near total access to your brain's functions."

"You forgot Jaffle Freedom." I knew my company products. I didn't need Helberg to tell me what Jaffle packages were out there.

"The top layer," he nodded. "Total access to one's own brain function. To philosophise, attain self-actualisation, exert genuine free will over one's own actions. That may indeed be where you are now, along with me and the rest of the three-percenters who don't have a damned Jaffle Port fitted. This—" he gestured at the scattered document. "This is what happens when you allow people to buy total freedom of thought."

"What happens?"

"More and more buy their way up the ladder. Did you know that Jaffle Premium was only created to make one more stepping stone between Jaffle Enhanced and Jaffle Freedom?"

"I did." Which was sort of true. I remember it being introduced, although Helberg's version wasn't the same as I had been told.

"So now you've got more people buying their way to the top and nowhere else for them to go. No way for Jaffle Tech to get more money out of them. And so Jaffle are going to unveil their new product: Jaffle Sunrise."

"As in Operation Sunrise?"

"Indeed."

"And what is Jaffle Sunrise?"

"It's exactly the same as the current Jaffle Freedom."

I wrinkled my nose. "That doesn't make sense. No one will buy a new product if it's just the same as another one."

"They might when they are told that Jaffle Freedom is going to have some restrictions placed on it, essentially bringing it down to the level of Jaffle Premium."

"And Jaffle Premium?"

"Cascades down to the level of Jaffle Enhanced. And so it goes. Every user will be placed on the level below."

"Jaffle Standard users all become like Jaffle Economy users."

"More like Jaffle Lite, actually."

I thought about the community service workers in their orange coveralls. Jaffle Lite: criminals and those heavily in debt reduced to bumbling, voiceless creatures with no inner life at all. Lights on but nobody at home. I was on Jaffle Standard or, at least, had been. Hattie was Jaffle Standard. I pictured us as those dead creatures.

"When are they doing this?"

Helberg shrugged. "Rollout could happen any time after the Operation Sunrise launch. That's happening on the nineteenth isn't it?"

"Five days time," I said. "I need to tell Rufus Jaffle."

"Rufus Jaffle must know about it," said Helberg.

I shook my head vehemently. "I had access to Rufus's memory. Henderson—"

"The Jaffle Tech CTO?"

"Him. He got Rufus Jaffle to sign the papers when he was injured, not thinking straight. He'd been hit by a kangaroo."

"Did you just say kangaroo?"

"Rufus is patron of an animal charity, but he got into a fight with a kangaroo which would be very embarrassing. To cover it up, after Henderson made Rufus sign the papers he got him to—" I gazed in horrified realisation. "He got Rufus to wipe his memory of the event. Rufus thought he was wiping his memory of the kangaroo fight, but Henderson didn't want him to remember what he'd signed!"

"Rufus would know full well what he was signing," Helberg argued.

"He didn't want to read it. And he was concussed. Henderson made him sign and had his memory deleted. I did that. I was the one who did that!" My breath came in ragged gasps. Hattie was going to be made into a Jaffle Lite user, no better than an Empty. And I was responsible! "We have to stop this," I said.

"I would generally agree. We could tell the media but for the ninety-seven percent, Jaffle Tech controls your media access."

"But if we could show people..."

"This document is only the proposal," said Helberg. "Enough information for me to stitch the clues together. I could have faked something similar, given time. We'd need proof and no chance of getting it."

"We have to try."

"We have to focus on saving who we can save. I could hack Hattie's port, maybe save her from the worst of it. I'd hope that your screwy brain is potentially immune."

"I'm not talking about saving one person or two," I argued. "Billions worldwide are about to have their lives ruined. Reduced."

"And we can't save them!"

"We could try!"

"How?"

I clenched my fists furiously. "I don't know! I've only had the use of my brain for a few weeks. You've had your whole life! Think of something!"

"I don't have to," he said. "It's not my problem."

"You can't mean that!"

"I've closed off my mind and life to the rest of humanity because I could see what was going on. I made myself into a sad reclusive little man. If anyone had asked, I would have told them what Jaffle Tech and its like are doing to the world. But would that have changed a damned thing? No! Now, you come here with your new la-di-da self-awareness and expect to be able to fix things. Without evidence of wrongdoing on Jaffle Tech's part, you're as helpless as me."

I glared. "What kind of evidence?"

"What?"

"If we need evidence, what kind of evidence?"

He huffed with exasperation. "Documentation. Proof that the top executives are colluding in something that they know crosses an ethical borderline. Failing that, backdoor access to Jaffle Tech's code so we could bring this thing down from the inside. It doesn't matter. It's the kind of stuff you aren't going to be able to lay your hands on!"

I stood up straight and raised my chin haughtily. "You don't know what I'm capable of."

He laughed cynically. And just when I was starting to like him.

"I'll do what I can tomorrow," I said.

"You're going to the gala tomorrow."

"I can do both. Work, then gala. I can multitask."

"You're a fool, Alice Tennerman."

"And you're a coward," I said and marched out.

I went upstairs to my apartment, along the landing of brightly coloured doors, painted by Helberg's little bot. I went to my apartment seeking Hattie. Wanting only to throw my arms around her and tell her I loved her, and if there was any way I could save her from being reduced to something less then she already was, then I would give my life to achieve that.

Instead, I found her packing. I was too stunned to hug her or tell her anything.

"What are you doing?" I said.

"I'm moving out."

"Was it something I said?"

"Yes," she said in a bright upbeat tone. "Or it was something you showed me."

"What?"

"Babies."

"Babies?"

"Yes," she said and stopped for a moment to look at me. "I want a baby."

"Listen, I know you do and—"

"And I need money and a better position and possibly even a Jaffle upgrade."

"You do?"

"And I know how to get that."

"Really?"

She nodded. "The North Beach arcology."

It rang a bell. "Where Swanager and Pedstone went?"

"An integrated living solution community. They pay you to live there. Enough for me to afford art-i-ficial in-semination." She said it like she'd just learned it. "I'm going to have a baby."

I was astonished. Was I happy for her? I couldn't tell. "How does that even work? They pay you?"

"Something about a more simplistic lifestyle. Living in tune with the needs of society and environment. It saves money and resources so they can actually pay us to live there. I jipped the terms and conditions. There was only one unit left and a car is on its way to collect me— Oh! It's here."

She stuffed the last of her belongings into her pod case. I saw how she stuffed the singed head of Smiley Tot Derek in there at the very last. No reverence or love for the little doll's head. Hattie had changed. I had changed her, but now she was moving on with her own life.

She turned to me. Now, I hugged.

She blinked tears from her eyes. "It's..."

"I know," I said.

"It's been really weird," she said.

"I guess," I said.

"You've been weird."

"Definitely."

She sniffed and wiped her eyes. "But you'll come visit when I've settled in."

"Without a doubt," I said, firmly.

I walked down with her to meet the car.

28

15TH JUNE – 4 DAYS UNTIL OPERATION SUNRISE

The day of the gala.

Helberg might have been a coward but I wasn't going to let Jaffle Tech reduce me, Hattie and everyone else on their lower packages to little more than mindless animals. I needed to fight them. The way I saw it, that involved either making the public aware of what Jaffle Tech was about to do to them with some incontrovertible evidence or, failing that, stopping Jaffle Tech's servers from disseminating the latest updates. Either way, it involved gaining access to the innermost levels of Jaffle Tech's system.

"Forget it Alice, I can't break into Jaffle," said Helberg, when I went to ask him for help that morning. "They have some of the most advanced security systems in the world. If I had time I might be able to find a back door, but there's no way I'll be able to get in and delete things in a few hours. The odds are stacked against me. You'd be better off wishing for a meteor strike to take out their servers."

"You could at least try."

"And spend the rest of my life in prison? Or forcibly fitted with a Jaffle Port and turned into an Empty?"

I scowled. "Some help you are!"

He gestured at the documents spread out around his office, at my stolen dress hanging from a door which he'd just had cleaned for tonight's gala, at the homemade plipper gun next to the original I'd stolen from work, at the flaky pastries he'd laid on for breakfast.

"Yeah, no help at all," he said sarcastically. "Do not do anything stupid today. You have a party to go to tonight and the CEO of Jaffle Tech to meet. *If* you meet him and *if* he remembers you and *if* he cares one jot for the rest of humanity then plead your case with him. Do not jeopardise that by doing something monumentally moronic, Alice."

I snatched up the Jaffle Tech plipper, spun on my heel and stormed out. Dramatically, I hoped. I wanted to show my contempt with a dramatic exit. If I had been able to think of a way of doing that and taking a flaky pastry with me at the same time, I would have done.

I rode alone in a car to Jaffle Tech. I hoped Hattie had settled into her new apartment and whatever the weird set-up there was it would enable her to finance having a child. Hattie might not have been the most intellectual of people but I missed her company enormously. She was the rock of my life, tethering me to some kind of normal, even if that normal was beans and Mr Smiley. Without Hattie, I had no company but my own thoughts.

I wasn't going to do something stupid at work. I certainly wasn't going to do something *monumentally moronic*. I was going to do something clever. I was going to sneak back up to the executive levels of Jaffle Tech (I'd been up there twice before; it shouldn't be difficult), find some way of getting access to Jaffle's secret files and shut things down. If that meant doing a bit of hacking or taking someone hostage at plipper-point, then so be it.

There was no point going to my cubicle. Fixing things was the goal today. Best to get right down to it.

I walked into reception slowly, eyeing the people getting into the elevators. I needed a superior-looking exec-type, or maybe another engineer. Maybe even a cleaner. Did they have human cleaners on the top floors? We just had bots on ours. Would human cleaners be a step up or step down from bot cleaners?

A woman who looked like she belonged in the upper ranks of the company walked towards the ranks of elevators. I sped up to intercept and join her. I was already prepping a story in my head about the cleaning bots on the top floor needing a manual check-over. Yes, it was conceivable that someone in a support worker's tunic could be involved with that.

I had timed my interception perfectly. The doors were sliding open. We would step inside, one after the other, as natural as anything.

"Alice?"

I looked round. Paulette was approaching across the lobby. I faltered. The woman slipped into the elevator. I could dash in after her.

"I hoped to catch you on your way in," said Paulette, closer now.

"Oh?"

The elevator door closed, the opportunity had passed.

"Could we have a word?" said Paulette.

"Word?"

Paulette smiled. "That clarification interview we spoke about."

"Oh. Yes."

Paulette turned and walked away. I felt compelled to follow.

"We?" I called after her. "'Could *we* have a word'?"

Paulette offered no reply. I put my hand on the plipper in my pocket and followed.

We entered a room in a portion of the building I'd only ever been in once before: the day of my interview with Jaffle Tech. The interview had been brief. There'd been a few formal questions, a bit of a chit-chat and then a look at my Jaffle rating. I'd had a very impressive Jaffle rating back then. Along with my noted brain efficiency, it was enough to win me the job. I very much doubted this interview was going to conclude with a new job offer.

Paulette gestured to the people already sitting in the room. I recognised both of them: the beautiful large-eyed woman from the medical centre and Estelle, the senior human resources partner. When Paulette sat they were arranged as a panel of three facing me.

"Oh, this is, um, formal," I said as I sat.

Paulette simply nodded.

"This is an investigatory interview, Alice," said Estelle.

"Yes?" I said.

"Following data received and analysed since you spoke with Paulette two days ago, certain facts have come to light."

"Yes?"

Estelle looked to the wall and it was suddenly crawling with dates, details and maps.

"Second of June, you engaged with a group of individuals outside your residence using Restricted Jaffle service—"

"Empties," I said automatically.

"Restricted Jaffle service," Paulette corrected me.

"Your interactions set off a security alert," said Estelle, "and a Jaffle Swarm was dispatched to check on the individuals' health and welfare. On the same day, your location shows you at the residence of Abram and Claire Luca for a period of time. On third of June, Claire Luca came to Jaffle Tech claiming that a Jaffle Tech member of staff had broken into her home and stolen a number of items including a dress and perfume."

"Uh-huh?" I said, no idea what else to say.

"Continuing third of June, you were located at Baybrook food markets although you normally have your foodstuffs delivered. Also, another incident recorded with local Restricted Jaffle service users." A camera image appeared on the screen, showing me and Helberg wiping paint from some very messy Empties.

"That's me," I conceded.

Estelle nodded. "June fourth, you requested two sets of work tunics from supplies. One was a maintenance engineer's uniform. Security pass data shows that you were on the ninth floor of this building where senior management offices are located. However there is no CCTV video of you being present on the ninth floor."

I was surprised by this last point.

"You look surprised," said Paulette.

"I am," I agreed.

"Fifth of June," Estelle continued, "your Jaffle Port shows you located at Spalding flower markets. Later, it shows you at the Legion Art Museum some miles away."

"Is that a problem?" I asked.

"It might be considered abnormal," said Estelle, "given that, on the seventh of June, you refused to attend a mandatory scan with the medical team here, citing an *intrusion*, an *anomaly*."

The medical woman was nodding vigorously.

"Eighth of June," said Estelle. "You submitted a privately commissioned scan instead of attending one organised by our own team. The reason you gave was it had been requested by the CEO, Rufus Jaffle, or possibly by his secretary because a personal contact of theirs was in training and ... required the practice?"

I nodded. "Yes."

"There was then a fire. The starting moments of the fire were not captured on CCTV but your own section records show you acted bravely in assisting your colleagues. Well done."

That *well done* stung, like being given a gold star sticker on the way to the executioner's block.

"You did not immediately leave the building though," Estelle noted. "You met with one of our security staff. You were both in a nearby meeting room for several minutes before joining the rest of the section staff in your designated muster point on the front lawns."

She looked at me for any reaction. I had none I could give her.

"Twelfth of June. You and a work colleague visited the OneStop Daycare Centre under the pretext of wanting to apply for jobs there. Thirteenth of June, Paulette received a request for a personal reference in relation to that job application. She asked you directly if you had ever met Rufus Jaffle and you said no. Fourteenth of June, several brain scans, seemingly created by the same individual who created yours, were uncovered in a routine audit of our company records."

Estelle put her hands flat on the table and sat back. "Well?"

I smiled politely. "I'm okay, considering."

She narrowed her eyes, probably studying my face for signs of contempt or fear. "What do you have to say for yourself, Alice?"

I looked at the data on the wall. "I have been busy," I said.

"Busy?"

"You think one day's just like the next, but when you see it all laid out like that... It's no wonder I feel tired sometimes."

Estelle wasn't happy with that answer. "You're not concerned about the evidence of wrongdoing?"

"Wrongdoing?" I looked at the data again. "I visited a house. I bought some food and some flowers. I visited an art gallery. Security data shows I went to the ninth floor even though no one saw me at all, so clearly I didn't. I was slow leaving the building after a fire because Levi collared me to talk about health and safety."

A miniscule head jiggle from Paulette showed she thought that sounded entirely plausible. But Estelle was far from convinced.

"This is all circumstantial evidence," she said, "but it points towards something else."

"Yes?" I said innocently, though the worry inside me was palpable.

"Alice Tennerman, do you work for one of our competitors?"

I laughed. It was unexpected and genuine. "No! I have enjoyed – for the most part at least – enjoyed working at Jaffle Tech."

"Are you engaged in industrial espionage?"

"What?"

"Are you complicit in acts of fraud against Jaffle Tech?"

"No. I wouldn't even know how to do that."

Estelle glared. "Where do you meet your contact?"

"Contact?"

"At the food halls? At the art gallery? Is your contact masquerading as an Empty?"

"Restricted Jaffle service user," Paulette said, getting a sharp look in return.

"Was the buying of flowers a signal?"

"To who?" I said.

"Did you access the upper floors of this building to carry out wire-taps or to plant surveillance devices?"

"I just work in customer support," I said.

"Did you wipe company security camera records and plant falsified brain scan data in our systems?"

"I wouldn't know where to begin."

"When you said that there was an intruder in your sector, was that to divert suspicion?"

"From what?"

"Did you start the fire to create a diversion?"

"I nearly died in that fire," I pointed out.

Estelle huffed and sat back, deeply unhappy.

The medical woman leaned in, slowly and calmly. "All this behaviour, Alice..."

"Yes?"

"It's not normal."

"What's not normal?"

She attempted a chummy smile. She was certainly beautiful but she was no deceiver and her smile was a fake plastic thing.

"Art? Expensive food? Flowers? You are a Jaffle Standard user. These things are..." She circled her hand. "They wouldn't normally be of interest to you."

"No?"

"No. Your settings wouldn't enable you to have much appreciation of them. You'd get as much satisfaction from flowers as I would from ... Ancient Greek poetry. It's meaningless."

She was right. I had betrayed myself with my pursuit of experience and pleasure. I needed an explanation.

"I didn't enjoy them," I said.

"And yet you went to those places," said Estelle.

I nodded slowly.

"Why?"

I thought quickly, by which I mean I sat still in the frantic whirlwind of my mind and waited for a clever idea to come to me. "I went there..." I said.

"Yes?"

"But I got no pleasure or anything from it..."

"No?"

"So..."

"Yes?"

"I went for someone else."

"Who?"

"Who?" I said.

"Yes, who?"

A phrase Helberg had used dropped into my head. "A hopeless romantic."

Estelle blinked. "I beg your pardon?"

"A hopeless romantic," I added. "High up in our company."

That sounded good. I had no idea at all where I was going with it.

"What are you saying?" said Paulette.

I took a moment to compose myself. I had them interested and could play for time. "For the past few weeks, I have been helping an employee of this company in their ... quest to woo the love of their life."

"I see," said Estelle.

"I see," echoed Paulette.

I could see the beautiful medic wanting to say *I see* too. She contented herself with nodding solemnly.

"How are you helping?" asked Estelle.

I thought quickly. "The, um, food halls and the art gallery were dates. Going to be dates. I went to check them out for him."

"Him?" said Estelle. "It was a man."

"Mmm. Also the flowers were for his love, but he asked me to collect them. Obviously, flowers bring me no pleasure at all but I gather that some people like them."

"None of this falls within the boundaries of your current role. If you've been acting as some sort of matchmaker—"

"You can tell us who it," Paulette interrupted. I was sure she meant to sound professional and probing, but there was no mistaking the gossipy tone in her voice.

"I couldn't," I said. "He's a very influential man. And hopelessly in love." I picked details I recalled from Rufus's memory. "He said that as a man in a powerful position he has to be careful. He won't invite his love to his apartment – he's got a big apartment on the Panhandle I hear – in case people find out."

"Panhandle, eh?" said Estelle, nodding like she knew who I was talking about.

"And a big mansion south of the border," I added, remembering Henderson had also mentioned that in my dream-memory. "I think they're planning a romantic weekend away there."

"But why you?" said Paulette.

"I met him because of my regular job. I must have said something that made him think I knew about, er, affairs of the heart. I've met him in his office. Twice, in fact. You'll even see we were in the same room together. I wouldn't be surprised if he used his influence to delete CCTV video to hide the fact," I added, completely freewheeling now. "Who else would have the influence?"

"How do you explain your presence at the Luca residence?"

"Ah." Yes, how? I thought. "Claire Luca is—"

"His girlfriend?" suggested Paulette, getting too invested in my story.

"That's it," I said. "I went to talk to her, to deliver a gift."

"But the burglary?" said Esther. "The vandalism?"

"There was no burglary," I said. "Perhaps there was vandalism. I don't know. I should imagine that..." I hung my head. "I believe Claire Luca is married. This is one reason why their love had to remain secret. I'm told that when people engage in romantic relationships with other people's spouses, people can become jealous. It's not an emotion I'm overly familiar with."

Estelle seemed unconvinced. "But she came here and made accusations."

"I'm not sure that she is a very stable individual," I said. "Her memories were warped by alcohol use when she came here with her accusations. Paulette knows that."

Paulette was nodding.

"I wouldn't be surprised if she turned to alcohol to cope," I said.

"But what has any of this to do with your privately commissioned brain scan?" said the medical woman.

"It was his idea," I said.

"What?"

"I think he panicked and thought exposing me to these complex situations and feelings has caused me to work outside the parameters of my Jaffle Standard settings. Which I didn't," I added quickly and firmly. "Everything's fine up here in the old noggin."

I judged it was time for me to look contrite and embarrassed. I did my best.

"I think there has been a breach of professional etiquette here," said Estelle.

"I was only doing what I was told."

"Not by you! By Hend— By the man in question. With your permission, Alice, we can access your memories of the events you've mentioned."

"Are you going to call the police?" I said.

"That's entirely up to you," she said. "You might need to organise yourself some legal representation."

"Yes, of course," I said and stood.

"You don't have to do anything now," said Paulette.

"No," I said. "I need to go ... freshen up. Settle my nerves. I'll make some calls."

"I'll come with you," she said, also standing.

"No," I insisted. "I'll just be a few minutes." I thought about what I was going to do next. "Maybe a few minutes more than that."

I left, making sure I looked sad and emotionally drained until I was clearly out of sight. I dashed back to the elevators and waited for one to take me to the top floor. As I waited, I jipped a call to Helberg. The man without a Jaffle Port answered me on an old-fashioned audio transceiver; I could hear the echo on the line.

"What have you done?" he said.

"What makes you think I've done anything?" I replied.

"So, you haven't done anything?"

I bit my lip. "I got called in for questioning, but I've thrown them off the scent for now."

"Thrown them off the... Are you a wanted international criminal now?"

"No. I told them Jethro Henderson was in love with Claire Luca. A hopeless romantic like you said."

"Don't bring me into this!" Helberg sighed on the line. The lightly distorted noise sent a shiver down my spine. *"You lied your way out of the situation."*

"I told you I was a horrible human being."

"Then it's a good job I love you. What are you doing now?"

The elevator pinged. By good fortune there was a senior management type in the car. I stepped in beside him. The display showed he'd jipped for the top floor. He looked at me. I nodded like, *Yep, top floor for me too.* He looked at me, specifically at my tunic. There was something familiar about him, his long solemn face, his thinning hair, but I couldn't place him.

He was about to say something when Hattie slipped into the elevator. She had a smile slapped across her face like she had been smiling all morning.

"Hello, you," I said. "You look cheery."

"The new apartment is amazing," she said. "Everything shiny and new and—" She stopped and gave me a troubled look.

I understood at once. "It's okay. You're allowed to like it. I won't be offended."

"Oh, it's amazing, Alice!" she gushed. "The North Beach arcology is the future of living and with the financial incentive, I'll have enough for a—" she poked her stomach with two index fingers and gave me a conspiratorial wink "—in a matter of months."

The elevator stopped at our usual floor.

"That's really good," I said. "I should come over and help you celebrate."

"But leave your paints at home," she said seriously, stepping off. "Are you not...?" She gestured out at the office beyond the elevator.

"Er, no," I said. "I've got to sort some things out upstairs."

She began to frown but the doors closed on her. The car rose again.

"*What are you doing?*" said Helberg in my ear. I'd forgotten the call was still open and shut it off.

The elevator reached the top floor. The man exited and then looked back at me severely. "And where do you think you are going? Do you have clearance?"

"Of course," I said, realising why I recognised him. He was *Michael from Legal* out of Rufus's memory.

He looked at my tunic again, pointedly.

"Oh, this?" I said. "It's not even mine."

The pointed look became one of confusion.

"I do find if you dress like one of the workers, they don't pay as much attention to you. And they'll open up to you in ways they otherwise might not."

"You're some sort of..."

"Company spy?" I said and laughed, riding on a wild, giddy confidence born from the knowledge I had built of castle of lies around me ever since I'd come into the building this morning.

"Are you a company spy?"

"I like to think of myself as more of a mystery shopper, Michael," I said, recalling his words from Rufus's memory, "But I very much believe the less people know and the smaller the paper trail, the better it is for everyone."

There was a twitch at the corner of his mouth. Did he recognise the words as his own or just find himself agreeing with the sentiment?

"Even the legal department don't get to know everything," I said and stepped past him.

I was in the long corridor with the plush carpet, belatedly wondering where I should go. I needed access to records, to computers, something I could jip with greater ease now I was in the higher reaches of the company headquarters. I really hadn't thought it through.

"Do you know where you're going?" asked Michael.

"It's ... been a while," I said. "Last time I only visited Rufus Jaffle's office. Is he in?"

Michael smiled thinly. "Rufus is never here."

I nodded wisely. "He'd rather be partying and getting himself into trouble."

The smile stayed. "What do you need—?"

"Alice," I said and had a moment of inspiration. I pulled the plipper from my pocket. "I came to return this. One of your executives left it in a general meeting room downstairs. Jessica, was it?"

"Really?" said Michael.

"It wouldn't do to have Operation Sunrise ruined by some of our technology leaking out early."

"No, it wouldn't," he agreed. "Look, perhaps if you come through here we can sort something out."

He led me to a door which unlocked as he approached.

"Your office?" I said.

Michael nodded.

The walls were lined with bookcases containing actual books: leather bound things with gold spines. Maybe they were there to reinforce his position as a man of the law. There were also two glass display cases standing on the office floor. The nearest one contained a model of a rat (at least I hoped it was a model). I bent to read the little placard:

29

RATS IMPLANTED WITH NEURAL MICROCHIPS
USED TO DETECT EXPLOSIVE DEVICES.

"People think of lawyers as rats," said Michael. "Or sharks."

He tapped the other display case. It contained a model of the sharks Jaffle used to patrol the seas. Definitely a model; a full-sized shark would have been much, even in an office of this size.

"It amuses me to have these in here," he said. "Do you think lawyers are rats, Alice? Or sharks?"

I paused. "Rufus Jaffle never had a high opinion of you."

He grunted. "And yet without lawyers to interpret law and help put rules in place, there would be chaos. Please." He gestured to a seat.

This wasn't getting me into Jaffle's computer system. I was just playing games with a potentially dangerous man.

I sat.

"May I?" he asked. It took me a moment to realise he wanted the plipper. I handed it over and he studied it.

"Order from chaos," he said, waggling the plipper. "That's all this is."

I nodded like I cared.

"Do you ever think of all the things Jaffle has done for this world?" he said. "This company first made money building implants for people with neurological damage, helping paralysed people to walk, the blind to see, the brain-damaged to think again. Jesus style miracles."

"The baby Jesus?"

He smiled. "I'm thinking of his later work. Then we gave people brain drives and brain ports. Education was revolutionised. Newspapers. Do you know newspapers?" He sat opposite me. "Back in the twentieth century they had things called newspapers."

"Oh, sure. Newspapers."

"They used to say that in one single copy of the New York Times, there was more content, more words, than the average person in the seventeenth century would access in a lifetime."

"I've heard that."

"Think on it. In two hundred years, a lifetime's data content became a single day's data content. I simplify, but you get the point, right?"

"Right."

"In the space of the last thirty years, Jaffle has smashed that. You, me, everyone has access to a world of information. All learning, all knowledge, downloadable and shareable. Jaffle Tech has enhanced humanity exponentially." He laughed, although I wasn't quite sure what there was to laugh about. "You don't need a lawyer to tell you that if someone has given you something remarkable, then you owe them something in return." He turned the plipper over in his hand. "We elevated humanity beyond all recognition. Anything Jaffle Tech takes from them is merely restitution." He put the plipper down on the desk.

"All we want is order. Security. Structure." He pointed at my tunic. "You've spent time among them."

"Customer support workers?"

"Jaffle Standards," he said. "What are they like?"

"They're just like us."

"Really?"

"They eat beans and watch Mr Smiley, but they're just like us."

He sneered. "Have you seen the Mr Smiley shows?"

"They still have dreams, desires. They want things."

"And it's important that they do," he conceded. "If people want to better themselves then they also want to separate themselves from those around them; keep those beneath them down. It reinforces the social structure. The belief that they can rise helps keep the lower classes happy."

"The lower classes?" I said.

"*Mea culpa*. Those on more basic packages. The terminology has changed but much stays the same. Back in the Middle Ages— I'm sorry: two history analogies in one day. You can't be devoted to the law without having a firm grasp of history. Back in the Middle Ages, the peasants were the lowest class in society. The rulers, kings and emperors would have to keep them in their place, maintaining power for themselves while knowing that peasants were the essential means of production. Without the peasant class, the aristocracy would starve. Then along came the Industrial Revolution and slowly things changed, just a little. Right through to the present day, the structures remain the same but the reasons change."

He pointed at the rat in its case.

"It's vermin, the rat. It serves no purpose. It steals from human society. It breeds uncontrollably. It causes damage. It spreads disease. But put a chip in its head and it serves some function. In our world, the world of work is now almost fully automated. What machines can't do, Jaffle-enhanced animals can. Only in interpersonal interactions such as *customer support* do people still like the human touch."

"They do," I agreed.

"But, for the most part, humanity is obsolete. We're now in the business of planned obsolescence. We've elevated humanity but there's no goal to that, nothing to elevate them *for*. The majority of the human race needs to be contained, controlled, kept happy with beans and Mr Smiley. If we let them run free, free in society, free inside their own heads, then they will be nothing but vermin, a nuisance."

He tilted his head.

"Yes," he said, clearly on a call. "I've been waiting ten minutes for a response. Stalling, yes. I'm just here with Alice." He looked at me and gave me a friendly eyebrow waggle. "Ah, she is. Good. That's fine then." He nodded, the call ended. "Sorry about that," he said. "I needed to check."

"Check?"

"Where were we?" he said. "Ah. Rats. Sterile rats in sterile little boxes, like your friend at North Beach. Rats are fine as long as you have them under control. The problem comes if one escapes."

"Er, yes?"

"What can you do then?"

"Actually, there was this mouse one time, running round the office—"

Michael had picked up the plipper and pointed it directly at me.

"Wait," I said.

His thumb pressed the stud. He plipped me.

30

I slumped in the chair like I had seen Levi slump in the meeting room. My jaw sagged. My eyes unfocussed. I did not move.

Michael turned the plipper over in his hands, impressed with the device's apparent effectiveness.

"You're a fair liar, Alice," he said. "Superficially convincing. But I have a real eye for liars. Comes with the territory." He stood and adjusted the cuffs of his suit jacket as he rounded the desk. "Also, I have full access to employee records. And, yes, I had just received a communication from Estelle in HR that some jumped up support worker called Alice Tennerman was making wild and unfounded accusations about our CTO." He laughed. "Jethro Henderson a hopeless romantic? A secret affair? He's the dullest, least sexual man in the company. Now, me, I'm a man who knows how to enjoy life to the full."

He ran his fingertips along my cheek and up to my temple. I didn't move. I didn't respond.

"Don't worry," he said. "We'll soon have you back in your little box, enjoying beans and Mr Smiley. You were on Standard before? And you're familiar with the ins and outs of Operation Sunrise?" He nodded as though I had responded. "Good. So you know that when we roll out in four days Standard will be a lot more ... streamlined. A more simplistic experience but one I think you'll be perfectly happy with." He perched on the desk directly in front of me.

"And there are even more new features you'll enjoy. We're enhancing port to port communications. None of this wearisome business of actually needing to vocalise during communication. Just think about it. Silent instantaneous communication. Dumb mute rats in their boxes. And the three percent without Jaffle Ports – weirdos and outcasts, the lot of them. How long do you think they will want to stay as outsiders when the world around them is silenced? When they are truly cut off from the future of human communication?"

He looked at me. My downward gaze didn't waver. He sighed. Talking to an Empty had limited entertainment value.

"You sit tight, Alice. I'll go meet the security team." He patted my knee, a lingering touch, and left.

The moment he was out of the door I was up.

Helberg had been right – thank goodness! The plipper had had zero effect on me. Whatever Rufus's memory and the whale brain virus had done to me had armoured me against it.

I rubbed my cheek vigorously where that creepy Michael had touched me. He'd gone to meet the security team. I didn't know how far away he'd gone or indeed when they'd be back. I popped my head out the door. I couldn't see him along the corridor. I sneaked out.

I was near the elevators when I heard Michael's voice and the movements of several people. "Yes, captain. We can take her into custody on my authority. Theft, fraud, false accusations against senior executives."

I ducked into the nearest open door, the toilets, and held the door closed while security went by. My instinct was to stay there but it would only be seconds before they realised I had gone. I did not hesitate. I walked out, knowing any of them might look back and see me, and I hurried to the elevator. There were no shouts. No one tried to tackle me to the ground. I slipped into the elevator and made for the ground floor.

I made a call to Helberg.

"You're still alive," he said.

"Yes."

"I'm impressed. Have they arrested you yet?"

"Not yet."

"Not yet?"

"Mmmm. I kind of got caught out by this guy Michael from legal. He plipped me. I only pretended it worked and now I'm coming home. I've got the evidence we need."

"Wait, wait, wait. Jaffle Tech can track you. They do track you. The location function on your brain port."

"Can you do something about that?"

"Not from here." He sounded deeply worried which was

both touching and unhelpful. *"I can fry your port's circuits or completely power it down, but you'd have to be here for that."*

"Can't you break into the company systems and stop them tracking me?"

"I told you. I can't break through their security. I'd need—"

"A meteor strike to take out their servers, right."

An idea occurred to me. We'd all had a presentation a while ago about the failsafe systems protecting our power supplies. I remember being impressed at the time. Power cuts were rare, but an outage wouldn't stop Jaffle headquarters from operating because there was a large battery backup, and a gas-powered generator for extreme circumstances. I remember thinking at the time, if you were protecting against someone who seriously wanted to disrupt the organisation, you wouldn't locate the battery and generator in the same enclosure. Taking out power to Jaffle might save my bacon in the short term, and it might even put a dent in Operation Sunrise. It was worth a shot.

There was no security waiting for me in the lobby. I should have thought about that on the way down. It was pure dumb luck I wasn't apprehended the moment I stepped out.

I scuttled through the building and towards the rear entrance. A large corporate headquarters had a lot of deliveries and produced a lot of waste. People and bots, moving with single-minded efficiency, moved in and out.

The backup power enclosure was close, surrounded by a sturdy slatted fence. The gate was locked so I went and peered through the gaps in the wood. I wasn't sure what I expected to see, but an On/Off switch would have been nice. There was nothing that even hinted at being a crucial control component. It looked like a series of well-secured huts. Even if I could get through the fence, I would need to unlock the huts and then figure out what I was looking at. I turned away with a sigh. Some kind of subtle sabotage ought to be possible, but I had no clue what to do.

Then I looked across the loading bay, and I wondered if some form of *unsubtle* sabotage might be possible. Over by a cordoned-off area there was a sign. It read:

Danger: works in progress.

Not at that moment there wasn't, but it looked as though a new flower bed was being created. What interested me were the paving slabs that had been cut to make space for it. Something had sliced right through them. My attention was drawn to the interesting machine that was right in front of me. It had a wicked-looking circular blade mounted at the front, and a pair of small wheels at the back. It looked as if it was simply rolled up to cut whatever stood in its way. I decided to give it a try. There was a little plastic case over a big green button. I lifted the case and pressed the button. There was a high-pitched electric whine and the blade started to spin. I pushed it forward and it bit into the paving slabs with a hell-raising shriek. I decided to save the attention-seeking noise until I was at least doing something destructive.

I lifted the blade again and wheeled the machine across

to the backup power enclosure. There was some heavy duty conduit leading towards the building. I pushed the blade slowly forward and down. It bit into the conduit. The sparks it produced were almost as distracting as the horrific noise it made, but I was committed now. I pushed harder and the noise rose in pitch. Vibrations rattled up my arms, but I'd cut through the outer casing. I urged the blade further. There was a loud bang and the machine bucked right out of my hands and stopped dead. I decided it was be a good time to make my exit and scurried backwards. When I got to the building's rear entrance, the door was closed. A woman was inside, hammering on the glass. There were no lights on and behind her the building was surprisingly dark. I decided to find another way of leaving and followed the road used by delivery trucks until I reached the security gatehouse.

"Power's out!" called a security guard from the booth. "Everything's gone mad!"

I nodded. "Following protocol and leaving the premises in case of any ongoing threat."

"Uh, yeah. Wise move," he replied. "What protocol?"

"It's new," I replied vaguely.

He waved me through. I ducked under the vehicle barrier and walked quickly up the road.

I crossed Jaffle Park and hailed a car to take me home. A call came through from Helberg. As I answered it, the signal failed. I nervously dismissed the call. I had made a mess of everything. Whatever he wanted to berate me for could wait.

I tried to calm myself as we crossed the city. I had several hours until I needed to get ready for the gala. Time enough to share my evidence with Helberg. Time enough to work out what I would say to Rufus, to show him what was being done by his company in his name. Time enough to fix everything for everyone.

The car approached the Shangri-La Towers apartment complex. As always, the pitiful Empties in their pink coveralls were gathered at the roadside. Without warning, one of the nearest lurched out into the road in a mindless Empty shuffle, right in front of the car. It responded automatically, braking, catching me in its restraints and stopping just short of hitting the Empty.

"*A pedestrian collision has just been avoided,*" said the car. "*Are you injured?*"

"I'm fine." I looked up and saw the Empty's slack face.

It was Patrick Helberg.

31

The Empty Helberg lurched round to the door, hands on the car to stop it moving away. The slack look had vanished from his face. I tried to step out but he blocked the doorway.

"You can't come in," he murmured. "There's somebody from Jaffle here. They're looking for you. They look sort of serious."

My throat tightened in fear.

"Here." He reached into his Empty coverall and pulled out a folded bundle: the dress I'd stolen from Claire. "I hope I haven't creased it too much. And this..." From a pocket he took a bright blue ball of netting. It looked like a foaming shower scrunchy. "It's a fascinator," he said, clipping it into my hair.

I didn't know what a fascinator was so I jipped the word. For some reason I got no answer, but it wasn't at the top of my list of priorities.

"Okay it's a shower scrunchy attached to a bulldog clip," he added, "but it looks good enough. And there's a signal scrambler in there."

"Which means?"

"Your Jaffle Port isn't sending data out and you're getting none in."

"I'm blind," I said automatically, realising my sixth sense had been effectively switched off.

"You'll cope," he said with only the mildest reproach. "It will stop them tracking you. I think. Now, you go to that party, get out of here for a bit." He held out his hand. "You had evidence."

I tapped my skull. "Memory. Michael from legal. He's a slimy character. Told me everything."

"Everything?"

"He told me what Jaffle wanted the future to be. It was horrible."

"But did he admit to any legal or moral wrongdoing?"

I wasn't sure about that. "I thought if we just showed people what Jaffle Tech thought of them..."

Helberg didn't look convinced. "We don't have the opportunity to extract those memories now. If Rufus Jaffle's the good guy you say he is, then he's the only one who can help you. You need to find him."

"Of course," I said. "But where—?"

"You haven't got time to waste."

I touched his pink coverall. "Where did you get this from?"

He smirked. "I didn't want you picturing a naked Empty

currently bumping and bumbling his way around our new garden."

"I didn't think you stole it."

"I mean, there's a naked Empty in our garden. I just didn't want you picturing it. Now, go."

He began to withdraw so the door could close. I leaned forward quickly, one hand on his coveralls, and kissed him on the lips.

"Thank you, Patrick," I said.

"Anything for an amazing woman."

"I thought you would do anything for the easy life."

He shrugged. "It's a shame they're mutually exclusive." The door closed on him.

As the car drove to the Jaffle Tech gala, I put on the stolen dress. The smell of the perfume I'd also stolen still clung to it. My mood was low but I was nonetheless thrilled to have a chance to look and smell so nice. It felt like a declaration of who I really was, an affirmation of my right to be what I wanted to be.

The venue was some distance away, over to the west and down by the sea, in an area of the city I had never visited before. I was several hours early, so I instructed the car to circle, sticking to the less expensive roads so I didn't use up all my funds at once. The car wouldn't accept my instructions verbally. With my Jaffle Port blocked I was, essentially, invisible to it. I took the fascinator off for a moment, repeated my instructions, and clipped it back on.

As we drove in a slow spiral towards the charity gala I went through neighbourhoods much like the one where Claire lived. Then the houses started to get even bigger. Some of them were on so much land it wasn't possible to see the house itself behind the gates, walls and trees surrounding them.

The car went downhill. As it rounded a bend I saw the ocean and gasped in surprise. I lived ten miles from the ocean, but had never seen it before. I knew it was big, because I'd seen it on maps and pictures, but when I saw water all the way to the horizon I understood it in a way that would never have been available to old Alice. I wondered why the colours seemed to be shifting, realising that the water reflected the colours of the sky. Despite myself, I grinned with delight. It would be a fun thing to try and create an image like this, using paint. That was also something *old* Alice would never have imagined.

There were flecks of white near to the beach where the waves came in. I watched the shifting colours and the endless waves until the car reached the bottom of the hill and the ocean was out of sight again. A long line of cars was dropping people off. Men and women, all dressed in glamorous clothes. Some made from sumptuous fabrics and in every colour, others in a more muted palette. Some wore formal suits while others wore a more relaxed version where the jacket was a different colour to the trousers. None of them wore shorts like Rufus Jaffle, which I hoped would make it easier to spot him among the crowds.

Getting out of the car, I could hear an unfamiliar noise, and there was an unusual smell in the air. It took me a few moments before I understood I was hearing the waves breaking on the beach. Did that mean the smell was the ocean?

I joined the crowd, my stolen dress helping me blend in. As we walked through to the white building – too large to be a house, surely! – I concentrated on the other guests, trying to mimic what they did and how they did it. Many of them greeted others with a big smile and *mwa mwa* noises. They also seemed laugh and wave their hands a lot.

I spotted someone standing alone and tried it out.

"Hell-*o*! Mwa, mwa! How lovely to see you!" I gave a tinkling laugh, although it sounded more like the alarm you get when a cleaning bot gets jammed in a corner.

"Ah yes, delighted!" he said. "It's been a long time!"

I did the laugh again and moved on. I was at a party, and it was nothing like my bacon barbecue garden party, thank goodness.

Drinks were being handed out by staff holding trays. I took one and gave my thanks, but the slack expression on the girl with the tray suggested my words meant nothing. An Empty? Or as good as. This was the future I was fighting against.

I drank, and coughed violently. When I'd recovered enough to look at my glass I was astounded to see bubbles rising from the bottom in a constant stream. I took a more cautious sip and felt the sensation on my tongue. It was fun in a way I could never have imagined. I saw the bottle on a nearby table and jipped what champagne was, wondering why Helberg hadn't warned me about the stuff. I forgot my Jaffle Port was blocked and the lack of knowledge felt odd.

So I didn't know what champagne was, but I was determined to fit in. Once I'd got the hang of the bubbles I enjoyed it very much. I took a second glass and moved on.

The string quartet was a challenge. I heard them playing in the distance and the sound was so pure and vivid. I found them playing in an airy conservatory where beautiful plants flowered and the musicians – real musicians! Not just music played through speakers – performed their beautiful music with serene expressions. Something about the music being performed live, right in front of me, heightened its power. I found myself being moved to tears by its wonder.

"Well don't you look adorable!" came a voice in my ear. I gave a start, not least because suddenly there was a hand caressing my buttocks. In surprise, I spilled my drink in shock and whirled to see who it was.

"Oh my goodness, I'm so sorry!" The voice (and the hand) belonged to a formally suited man with dark hair and deep brown eyes. "I didn't mean to," he said, genuinely upset.

"Mean to?" I said.

"You must forgive me, I thought you were my wife," he said and laughed, almost hysterically. "That sounds like the worst pick up line ever, doesn't it?"

I had no clue what he was on about and hadn't recovered from the unwanted touching. I simply said, "Yes?" hoping that was the correct response.

"No," he insisted. "She has the exact same dress. Oh, you've made yourself all wet and it's entirely my fault."

He pulled a handkerchief from his top pocket and leaned forward, intending to dab my chest. I really didn't want him fondling any more of my secondary sex characteristics, so I snatched it from him. I couldn't afford to waste any more time, so after a few token dabs I pushed past him to get to the steps. Any tears the string quartet might have evoked had missed their opportunity.

I remembered the ticket had mentioned a piggy-wig orchestra. I had failed to ask Helberg what that was, and whether it was normal. I found a member of the serving staff who looked as if he was at a higher level than the others and asked about the piggy-wig orchestra. He directed me to a room, inside which was a row of transparent boxes, each with a small pink creature inside.

Any other time I would have been able to jip what they were. Instead I turned to a woman near to me. "These things ... piggy-wigs?"

"Piglets, yes," she said. "I do love a piglet. And I don't just mean a roasted suckling one." She laughed. I didn't have a clue what she meant, but joined in.

A man in a sequinned suit bowed to the audience and took his seat at a keyboard.

"Ladies and gentlemen. Each of the keys on this keyboard will cause one of our happy piglets to sing for you. Their Jaffle Ports help them to understand what I'm asking them to do, but of course, they are free to do as they like. What can I tell you? These piggy-wigs love to sing! We treat our animals with the utmost care."

I wondered whether the piglets enjoyed being shut in small boxes and controlled by this man. Probably not.

He pressed a key. There was the brief grunting squeak of a piglet. He ran a finger down the keyboard and there was a whole scale of piglets.

"Now I shall play to you, with the voices of the piggy-wig orchestra!" he declared.

He played a tune. I wondered if Helberg would deride it for being as simplistic as the Smiley theme, but it was undoubtedly charming, being sung by piglets. It made the audience smile as the piglets sat in their boxes, some of them sniffing around, others putting their front feet up on the side of the enclosure.

I listened as the tune became slightly more complex. It was fun to watch someone play an instrument, and this wasn't making me cry like the string quartet, although I felt slightly angry on the piglets' behalf.

"And now," said the man with a flourish. "As part of the finale, you may come and meet the piglets who have sung so beautifully for you!"

There were twenty four chairs behind the piglet boxes. He invited members of the audience to sit with their allocated piglet while he played the last tune. I made sure I claimed a chair and a small pink piglet was placed on my lap. It nuzzled my hand and seemed content to have its ear gently tickled while it made an occasional snorting noise as part of the tune. It was strangely satisfying to hold the piglet, and I was disappointed when it was time for it to go back into its enclosure.

32

As I left the piggy-wig orchestra room, there was a strange roaring sound. People crowded to the edge of the terrace as a huge boat thundered across the bay. The setting sun reflected off the water and the boat created a wake of glittering gold. As it neared, fireworks flew up from the boat and exploded in the sky. The boat made more noise than anything I had ever heard before. Could it be the boat was powered with an internal combustion engine? They were not really allowed any more, but I knew it was possible to get a special licence to use them for scientific research. I wondered what kind of research project involved circling the bay and firing sparkling incendiary devices into the sky. I looked more closely and saw that the boat was being driven by a man in shorts and with long hair. Rufus Jaffle.

"Rufus!" I shouted involuntarily.

People turned and looked at me.

"I'm a big fan," I said with a carefree shrug and sidled away.

I wondered how I was going to get to speak with him. I slipped softly through the crowds, towards the jetty. There were a lot of people between me and Rufus and I noticed the stern faces of individuals who guessed were party security.

Rufus bounded onto the jetty. I could see his grin. I could see him jerk his fingers at everyone in sight, like he was shooting imaginary pistols. I saw a man with close-cropped hair greet him: Jethro Henderson. It was a company event. Of course, lots of other Jaffle employees would be there. I whirled, stupidly expecting Michael from legal to be stood directly behind me.

When I looked back, Rufus was being ushered inside by a group of people who looked like the organising type. I headed back inside the building. Quite a crowd seemed to be heading towards a large room. As I approached, I saw a sign that said *Charity Auction*. I took a seat towards the back. I needed to think; I needed a plan. I needed to get to Rufus without being recognised by someone who knew me.

"Hello again."

The man with the brown eyes was in the seat next to me, still looking apologetic. There was something else in his face, a half-smile on his lips and a playfulness around the eyes. I smiled at him. "I still have your handkerchief." I handed it to him.

He waved it away. "Keep it. It's the least I could do. I was so certain that you were Claire. She told me that her dress was one-of-a-kind but she was clearly wrong."

"Claire?" Oh crumbs.

"My wife."

"Well, your wife has excellent taste," I said.

He leaned over to whisper. "If I'm completely honest, it looks much better on you than it does on her."

I blushed. His eyes locked onto mine, and I found myself drawn to his face. He had some tiny crinkles around his eyes, but they made him look interesting, somehow.

"It's silk, isn't it?" he asked, accompanying the question with the lightest brush of a hand on my thigh.

It felt like an innocent gesture, but the touch of his hand made me immediately breathless. I couldn't help wondering what it would be like to feel his lips on mine, maybe have him touch my thigh some more.

I tried to pull myself together. My life was in danger, the fate of thousands of millions of Jaffle customers were in my hands, I was here on a mission to speak to Rufus Jaffle, and yet I was allowing myself to be distracted by the idea of having sex with a stranger. Curse this stupid mental freedom!

"Yes, silk," I croaked.

He looked at me for a long moment. I felt his gaze on my eyes and my lips. He reached forward and touched the sleeve of the dress, skimming my shoulder and reaching up to lightly touch the back of my neck.

"Such a fine fabric, isn't it? Caresses the skin like a lover's touch."

"Peter? Peter!" shouted a voice. "What on earth are you doing?"

I didn't need to turn to see who that voice belonged to. I

turned and looked anyway. Claire was approaching from across the room.

This was very bad. Peter apparently thought so too. He sat bolt upright.

I ran. Peter was mumbling something which sounded very much like a lie. Then a cry went up.

"My dress! That's my dress! Stop her!"

There was a table just outside the room's exit. Paper brochures about the work of the charity and details of the evening's programme were scattered across it. The table was backed by tall banner screens showing the animals IFPA worked to protect. I hid in the shadow of one of the banners, trying to calm myself and collect my thoughts.

I heard Rufus's voice approaching. "Here is the hand but it's empty," he was saying, tone miserable. "Just saying. Put something in it, Hendo. Wine, bourbon, a little party powder."

He was going right past me! Perfect!

I was about to step out when I heard Henderson speak. "Let's just get the formal business over with, sir. You have a presentation to major shareholders in twenty minutes. In the Lowry Room."

"Presentation?"

"Proof of concept. Everything is set up at North Beach. It's going to be very impressive."

"I'm on stage for ten minutes," said Rufus moodily. "No longer."

"Agreed."

"Just give me a minute."

Rufus had stopped. He'd actually stopped right by me. I was sort of out of sight, but all he or Henderson had to do was turn, or move a foot to the side, and they'd see me. I snatched up a nearby brochure and hid my face in it.

"Good," said Henderson. "Just wait here a moment, sir. Marcia, watch over our dear CEO."

Was that the sound of Henderson moving off? Was Rufus alone? Or at least just with some functionary who didn't know me or want to turn me into an Empty?

I fought my nerves, became their master and stepped out. Rufus Jaffle stood by the IFPA banner screens, giving cheery thumbs ups to people passing by, looking at their drinks a little enviously.

He saw me.

Behind him, on a screen, was an image of a grey kangaroo. Fading in were the words:

Kangaroos are at risk from a bacterial infection which attacks their nervous system.
Our inoculation programme has halted the spread of this in seven key areas.
We will continue to build upon this success with your help.
Pledge your support today to protect wild kangaroo populations for years to come.

THE PICTURE SHIFTED to that of a huge kangaroo, springing through the air. Without warning, I felt my mind slipping into a memory that wasn't mine.

RUFUS/I/WE were in the basement of a large house by the sea. Different house, same sea. There was darkness about us: a closeness, a musty fug in the air, a personal and moral gloom. Passion and guilt pumped through Rufus's veins.

In the ring, kangaroos circled and fought one another. They rocked back on their tails and battered each other with double-footed kicks.

Rufus felt their energy, their need to hurt. An urge to be part of the violence, to expel his own animal energy, was growing within him. He gripped the barricade and vaulted into the ring.

He punched the air and turned to the crowd. They cheered their approval. He turned to the nearest kangaroo and punched it straight on the nose. Its Empty eyes registered nothing.

"Fists of fury! Betcha never saw anything like this back home in, ah, wherever you come from, did ya?" He yelled in its face, a primal roar unleashing his desire for blood. He rained down blow after blow.

The kangaroo drew back. Rufus dodged and swung wildly, walloping it across the temple and knocking it to the ground. He screamed, victorious, holding up his hands to receive the crowd's adulation.

"Now *that* is what a Maglev master looks like! Deadly weapons right here!"

In the corner of his vision, he saw TayTay grab the remote control for the other kangaroo.

"Come on then motherfucker! Show us those deadly weapons!"

Beeee aaaa whaaaaaale. You can have a taaaaail instead, sang the blue whale.

I was irritated by the arrival of the annoying creature, yet relieved when its presence whipped me away from that horrid scene.

"Hey, I didn't fall," Rufus was telling Henderson as he reclined in his hospital bed. "I floored that kangaroo. You shoulda seen—"

"I did see it," said Henderson. "Many times. I have spent the last twenty four hours erasing video feeds and persuading partygoers to sign non-disclosure agreements. It might have felt like some macho fun at the time, but the vids make it look more like extreme animal cruelty. Michael here from legal thinks we're nearly on top of the situation, but obviously we're going to need you to get a memory wipe."

Michael from legal – *damned vampire* said Rufus's mind – was almost invisible against the grey privacy drapes at the end of the bed. "Legally, this is a difficult situation," he said.

"Animal cruelty, shanimal shuelty," said Rufus.

"Insightful as always, sir," said Michael. "It's more like it presents a problem with your role as honorary president of IFPA."

"Really?" said Rufus.

"Yes. The head of the world's foremost animal protection

charities, spending his downtime punching seven shades of shinola out of a lobotomised kangaroo..."

"They're not endangered are they?"

"I don't think that's going to matter to the media," said Henderson. "You've got the corporate gala on the fifteenth. The *charity* gala. You need to wipe your memory of last night. You have high enough access to do that personally."

"Actually, I've got this whale in my head and it's making some of my functionality a bit glitchy."

"Fine," muttered Henderson. "We'll get it done down at Jaffle Tech."

"Don't go through the official company procedures!" protested Michael. "I very much believe the less people know and the smaller the paper trail, the better things are."

"Agreed," said Henderson. "Our official brain-editing systems have audits which I even I can't counter. I'll sort out something off the record."

"Whoa, people!" said Rufus. "Maybe I don't want to give up that memory? It was kind of cool, you know? I can be discreet. It will only be a problem if I talk about it, right?"

Henderson smiled and leaned back. "Of course. You're right. So, tell us what it was like. What made you tackle a kangaroo? Surely it was a dangerous thing to do?"

"Oh man, I was so stoked! I had to get in there and try some Maglev moves on those guys."

"Maglev is magnetic levitation," said Michael.

"Then what am I thinking of?" wondered Rufus. "Anyway, you should have been there! They're powerful animals, but my martial arts skills are all about outsmarting your opponent. It was obvious to me that—"

"Okay, enough," interrupted Henderson. "With all due respect, sir, you are a security risk. In my estimation, you will definitely talk about this in the future. We must erase the memory."

"Oh, what? That was a trap?"

"And hardly a cunning one, sir."

"Man! You could have warned me, I would have shut the hell up!"

"We will arrange the memory wipe as soon as you're recovered. There is another matter that I need your signature for, and it won't wait until then. Perhaps Michael, you could leave us for a few minutes?"

Michael from legal rose and left the room.

"Are you both getting memory wipes?" asked Rufus, sulking.

"I will attend to all details. It's very much in our mutual interest that you trust I have the company's best interest at heart, wouldn't you say? As Chief Technical Officer, problem solving is my forte."

Rufus gave a grunt of assent.

Henderson cleared his throat. "The other matter. I need your signature for Operation Sunrise. It's a complex project, so I can't afford to let any time slip. Could you please authorise the project brief for the completion phase?"

Rufus looked at the sheaf of papers. "Do I need to read all that?"

"I can read it out to you if you want, but there's nothing we haven't discussed before in some form or another. The exec summary for this proposal is that we're rationalising and streamlining all of our customer packages, shifting certain privileges from one band to another. It's all about clarity."

"Clarity?" scoffed Rufus. "Give me the English version!"

"More and more people are buying their way into higher level packages. Currently, Jaffle Freedom is the highest level, a Jaffle Port with zero restrictions or external influence."

"That's what I've got," said Rufus.

"Exactly. And it was once an exclusive club but people from the lower user levels are increasingly able to buy their Jaffle Freedom outright."

"I like things that are exclusive."

"Quite, sir," said Henderson. "With that in mind, we are going to introduce a new, higher and much more exclusive level, called Jaffle Sunrise."

"Nice name," conceded Rufus. "And how's that different from Jaffle Freedom?"

"At the moment, it isn't."

"Ah," said Rufus. "Now call me a schmuck, but I think I see a flaw in your business plan, Hendo."

"You are correct, sir," the CTO conceded. "Which is why once Operation Sunrise is implemented Jaffle Freedom will take on some of the user terms and conditions of Jaffle Premium."

"You'll limit their service?"

"Minor stuff. The appreciation of abstract concepts relating to art, music, poetry. We'll reduce their capacity for violence and sexual arousal. Just a tad. As I say, Jaffle Freedom will take on many of the characteristics of Jaffle Premium."

"And Jaffle Premium?"

"Will become Jaffle Standard."

"And Standard?"

"Those unable to make the financial leap to Premium will be given a service much like the current Jaffle Lite."

"So there will be even more people on Jaffle Lite?"

"Jaffle Standard, sir. It will be called Jaffle Standard. Those currently on Jaffle Lite will be provided a level of restricted service."

"How restricted?"

"They'll be able to control their own bodies' most basic functions. They'll be able to respond, on a mostly unconscious level, to visual and auditory stimuli. They will be equipped with a basic fear of death, in order to promote self-preservation."

"That *is* restricted," agreed Rufus.

"And therefore Jaffle Tech has benevolently agreed to assist in the social management of the general population."

"Social management?" Rufus grappled for the exact meaning.

"Accommodation, health, employment and so on. We will run people, centrally, for their own good. We've sold the concept to most governing bodies with no problems, because it's the only complete solution that exists. Voting it in will be no problem at all, for obvious reasons. People put themselves in our hands and this is the most straightforward way to ensure everyone's taken care of. The management of people's hopes and expectations will be simple. Their needs are so much lower at that level."

"Yes, I see that. Isn't it just a little bit wrong though?"

asked Rufus, shifting awkwardly in the bed. "I mean, there might be people who don't want to be satisfied with less."

Henderson nodded. "It's a valid challenge, but let's take a moment to reflect upon the oldest adage in business. Wasn't Henry Ford supposed to have said that if he gave customers what they wanted, he'd be working on making a faster horse rather than cars? It's up to us to have the vision to take things forward. It's a win-win situation because it also guarantees the company's bottom line for the next ten years. The projected earnings from this are in the pack and it's bigger than anything we've ever done before. Seriously, the money will be rolling in for years."

"But is this the right thing to do?"

"It's entirely your choice, sir," said Henderson. "We can continue without Operation Sunrise. In fact, if we don't I was planning on purchasing Jaffle Freedom myself."

"You?" said Rufus.

"What else am I going to spend my money on? I've got the largest apartment on the Panhandle. I've got a mansion south of the border. I should buy Jaffle Freedom. And be like you, sir."

Rufus settled back into his pillow and reached for the pen. "When you put it like that, it sounds like it's the way forward."

I CAME BACK to the room with an actual intake of breath.

Rufus, the real no-longer-a-dream Rufus, stood before

me right now. There was a goofy grin on his face as he looked at me.

"Hey," he said softly. "Don't I know you?"

"No," I said, backing away. "We don't know each other at all."

I turned and all but ran. I pushed my way through the throng of the party, pushed my way as far away from Rufus Jaffle and his hateful company as possible.

33

I went in search of more alcohol. It wasn't going to fix the horror that was playing out in my head, but it might make it slightly more bearable. I grabbed a glass of champagne from a tray. In my haste, I knocked several others. The might-as-well-be-Empty servant bent to catch what she could. I grabbed three and the woman managed to stop two more from spinning to the floor.

"I'm really sorry about that," I said.

She smiled at me but only with her mouth, nothing from her eyes. She moved off without a word.

I found my way out onto the terrace, overlooking the ocean and proceeded to down my three glasses of champagne.

It was crystal clear why Rufus had asked me to delete his memory. The most horrifying part of that memory wasn't that Rufus Jaffle was a callous kangaroo-beater, but the casual way in which Operation Sunrise had been signed off.

Rufus had known what he was signing all along. He was fine with it. Perhaps when you were a mega-rich playboy, the idea of the rest of the world being reduced to child-like levels of brain function wasn't a big deal. Perhaps if you had servants to keep you well-fed and a plipper to subdue any problems you could live with a decision like that.

I felt tainted, like I carried the guilt of his actions on his behalf. I was tempted to delete that memory myself and be rid of it.

Oooor you could beeee a whaaaale, sang a voice. Something tried to swim into view in the corner of my vision.

"Shush, you," I muttered and turned away. I juggled the champagne glasses so I had a full one to drink from.

"I'm sure she came through this way," came an approaching voice. It was Claire.

"Does it really matter?" said a tired and unhappy voice. Her husband.

I moved along the terrace and through another door.

There was no longer any point in me staying. I clearly wasn't going to be able to speak with Rufus Jaffle, and I couldn't afford to let Claire see my face. I ducked into the room where the piglet orchestra had been, hoping she wouldn't think to look there, now it was closed up and in darkness. I hid behind the door, tense with the expectation someone would burst in and discover me at any moment.

I heard the tiniest sound in the darkness, and held my breath. It came again. I realised it was the sound of a piglet.

"Lights," I said and the room lit up. The piglets were still in here, piled up on a trolley.

I shook my head. Jaffle Ports in kangaroos to make them

fight wasn't all that different to Jaffle Ports in piglets to make them sing. How was this allowed to continue? Sure, they looked contented enough. Their ports kept them pacified, their boxes were clean and roomy.

"Happy little pigs," I murmured. "In sterile little boxes."

I crouched down before the trolley of little piggy-wigs. It occurred to me, for the first time, these little creatures were the sources of bacon. Of course I knew that delicious salty tangy bacon came from pigs. I had jipped the fact some days ago, but I hadn't made the connection until now. I had eaten their little piggy-wig cousin. I drunkenly wondered if I'd snacked on someone that they'd known, personally.

These poor piglets were stored here in the darkness like baggage, forced to be content with Jaffle chips. Perhaps they were kept this way until they were taken away and turned into bacon.

"And this is supposed to be an animal charity event," I said, sniffing back tears.

One of the pigs snorted and pressed its round snout to the plastic glass.

"It's okay," I said. "I'll make it right."

I unclipped the box and lifted the piglet out. It wriggled and twisted in my hands. I held its warm pink body close and it settled against my chest.

"Okay, Wiggler," I said. "We'll get your brothers and sister out of here too."

I couldn't choose between taking piglets out of boxes or wheeling the entire trolley out. Surely I'd be noticed trying to sneak out with a trolley full of someone else's pigs. There was a curtained off area at the back of the room, not quite a stage but clearly a partitioning area.

Carrying Wiggler, I stepped through a gap. If I could pull down a curtain, maybe I could cover the trolley and wheel it out of the house unnoticed. I didn't have a clue where to take it or what I would do next. I wasn't exactly thinking straight.

I heard chatter and then a raised voice. "Damn it all! One of them's got out! Number Six!"

"Oops," I said, clutching Wiggler tighter. We pressed on through the labyrinth of black curtains.

I got turned around in there. The curtains were clearly used to screen off a huge central space, turning it into into several rooms. When I re-emerged I was at the edge of another darkened room. It was full of people.

Rows of seats had been laid out facing a lit stage and podium. An audience of maybe thirty to forty was made up of some of the most soberly dressed at the party. I crept along the wall towards the rear exit. It was closed and two security types stood before it.

"It's great to see you!" called Rufus Jaffle.

I whirled. He was on the stage, addressing the whole room. People cheered and applauded.

"Dudes! It's great to see you all!" He grinned.

Dressed in his strange business attire, including shorts and sandals, he looked very different to the people in the audience, but they seemed to love him for it. He held up his hands to calm the noise.

I dropped into the nearest seat and tried to look small.

"Dudes," he said. "We're so happy to have you here today. Hope you're enjoying the event. We laid on the very best food, entertainment and company, but right here is where the magic's gonna happen. Hold tight and you'll get the very latest news on the upcoming, ah, things." He sniffed and rubbed his eye. Over the microphone, his eyeball squeaked. "First up, I wanted to ask if you'd ever thought about whales? Take a moment. Ask yourself what you know about whales. Well I know we're all here to support the animals. I mean, who doesn't love our cute furry friends, huh? But a whale, have you ever thought about those great big dudes? Well, I have, and I wanted to tell you how awesome they are. Did you know they strain krill through their teeth?"

He looked out at the audience. They stared back in mildly confused silence. I was possibly the only person present who knew about his whale-based thought experiments.

He bared his teeth and turned his head so that everyone could get a look. "Check this out. Teeth." His words were distorted by his unusual expression. "Think about what it would mean if you had to get all of your food by straining it through your teeth. Pretty hard work, huh? Well those dudes do it every day. Every. Single. Day. It's not easy, I can tell you."

He looked around at us all, nodding emphatically, then glanced across the stage as if someone had gestured to him. He scowled.

"Right," he said, more soberly. "So now we're all tuned into the same wavelength – whales. Seriously, man! – it's time to talk about the upcoming changes here in the world of Jaffle Tech."

Someone whooped in the audience. It was a solitary

voice but Rufus did a double handed point and nodded like it was the most insightful comment ever.

"We have some truly ground-breaking things for you, like we always do. Have the Jaffle tech-heads ever disappointed? No, they have not. Every time you think they can't top the last amazing thing, they go right ahead and do it! Now, I like to keep an eagle view of thing, soaring above everything, at a like, spiritual level. I get my staff to dig in the weeds and get down and dirty. I'm not a details kinda guy. On that basis, I'm going to invite my man Henderson to come up here and explain the new rollout to you all. I'm sure you're gonna love it. Put your hands together and give Hendo some love!"

Henderson walked out onto the stage. He presented a sharp contrast to Rufus Jaffle, in an immaculate suit and looking very carefully groomed.

"Ladies and gentlemen. Shareholders. Colleagues. I know you're all eager to hear the latest update on our corporate strategy, and how Jaffle will be securing the growth of your investment for years to come. If you'll bear with me through this brief presentation, we will follow up with a live demonstration, and I think you will see we hold the future very much in our hands. No other company has had the vision and foresight to solve the world's problems like Jaffle, and this latest development might represent our boldest stride forward yet."

Wiggler nudged my hand. I patted his little head but he nudged me again.

"You want food?" I whispered.

He bit the ends of my fingers. It didn't hurt so much, but I recoiled in surprise, bringing stern glances from the people sitting nearby.

"Shush!" said a woman next to me.

Henderson continued. "Jaffle has ended so many huge problems. There are many medical conditions which we have eradicated. War and conflict around the globe has been reduced. The diminishing resources of the earth can now be distributed in an optimised manner. Starvation is a thing of the past as Jaffle food processing has made nutritious and homogenised rations available to all for free, working with government agencies to unlock funding."

There was applause around the room. Henderson inclined his head in acknowledgement. Rufus Jaffle stood at the side of the stage, determined to take his share of the kudos, shouting "Hell yeah!" and pumping his fist. "Beans for everyone, man!"

Wiggler jumped down from my lap and ran under the row of seats in front. I got down on hands and knees to follow him.

"You shouldn't bring pets in here!" hissed the woman.

I crawled forward along the rows, trying to follow Wiggler.

"This brings me to some of humanity's more recent problems," said Henderson. "Modern lifestyles bring with them a certain level of stress. You may be familiar with the statistics on the amount of information we're expected to absorb in our day to day lives. We have fallen into the trap of enabling information to be fired at us at the speed of light, when we are just not mentally equipped to deal with it. When did we all get so afraid of being bored?"

I moved along a row, squeezing past legs in pursuit of my Wiggler.

"What the hell do you think you're doing?" muttered one man. "We're trying to watch the presentation!"

"Gotcha!" I pounced on a pink lump. As I lifted it I realised it was a pink leather hand bag. A woman snatched it from my hands. "Get off my purse, you maniac!" she said loudly.

"Boredom is *essential*. It's as essential to human well-being as sleep," Henderson continued. "Sensory overload has proven to be a contributing factor in many cases involving violence and sexual misconduct. What's the answer? How can we encourage a return to a simpler life and take away those harmful urges? Does Jaffle have a solution to this?" He smiled around at the audience. "Of course we do."

I was near to the centre of the room, and I had caught sight of Wiggler. He was standing on a seat, apparently trying to reach up to bite a woman's hair. She was staring ahead at the stage, oblivious. I crept forward and grabbed the naughty piggy, somehow managing to snag the woman's hair. She yelped.

"So sorry," I said as I made my way to an empty seat, holding Wiggler tightly.

I had caused quite a commotion, but the darkness had concealed a lot. A fanfare sounded from the stage, drawing everyone's attention back to Henderson. A screen behind him lit on a live feed, split across numerous rooms in what looked like a communal living space.

"Allow me to introduce our pilot community in North Beach," he said. "These willing volunteers will be among the first to demonstrate the benefits to be gained from our upgraded software. These people have been living together for a short while, but the cracks in this domestic environment are showing already. You will observe on the screen how some have chosen to sit companionably together in the shared space, while others prefer to be alone. Why is that? Does it optimise the accommodation? No, it's very wasteful. Additionally, there are those who engage in wasteful idiosyncratic behaviours. Here, for example, is an obsessive cleaner."

My insides lurched. Hattie was on screen, in an apartment space. It was sparkling clean but she was on her hands and knees, scrubbing the floor. Just visible on the wall was a pinned picture of a baby.

"Cleaning product producers would no doubt approve of this," said Henderson. "But at Jaffle we're taking the long-term holistic view. As we all know, the planet cannot sustain the projected population if we continue consumer spending at its current level."

What was Hattie involved in? Why was she on the screen? I needed to get myself and Wiggler out of there, but I also had to see what this demonstration was.

"Our test subjects will shortly be changed to the most efficient level of operation," said Henderson. "You will quickly appreciate how economies of scale mean that people operating at the new level will place less demand on *all* critical infrastructure. Jaffle will optimise accommodation, food and general well-being for all of these subjects. Success is guaranteed. Those of you who represent our government clients will see how budget juggling becomes a thing of the past. We have a system which can run things much more effectively than we are able to on our own. So, without further ado, I want to show you how our pilot group is transformed by being early adopters. Let me welcome Rufus Jaffle back onto the stage, so he can initiate the demonstration."

There was more cheering as Rufus walked back centre stage. "Thanks, Henderson! It's such an honour to be able to do this, knowing we're helping to make a new future possible for these folks." He stared at the podium. "We have the button, right? No button. We should have had a button."

Henderson said something to him, off mic.

"Button's in the future," said Rufus. "Right we're gonna do a countdown anyway." He gazed around at the audience. "Count with me, people! Come on! Five, four, three, two, one! Software roll-out now!"

People on the screen fell into similar, slack poses. Henderson stepped forward again to provide commentary.

"See how peace now reigns over our little community? Activity is scaled right back. In fact, breathing will slow right down in these subjects and the requirement for nutrition and ambient heat is therefore reduced, lowering costs all round."

He beamed at the audience, but I couldn't take my eyes off Hattie. She picked herself off the floor, transferred to a chair, sat down and was still. She was an Empty, or as near as made no difference.

Henderson was showing graphs of cost savings. I was too incensed to pay attention. "At a signal, all of the subjects will gather at feeding stations for their optimised food ration. As you can imagine, everyone's diet will be as good as it can possibly be, so health issues will be greatly reduced. Here are the projections of the cost savings for health care per capita of population. Quite a startling message, wouldn't you say?"

A hand went up.

"An audience question? Yes?"

"What if people don't want the new software?" asked a woman near to the front.

"Everyone has already signed up for it," said Henderson. "The latest set of terms and conditions mandate the upgrade, so it will be rolled out to everyone. Only those members of society who are deemed to be part of the core operation will maintain their current status. I should say, by the way, that everyone in this room is automatically included in this category, so please don't be concerned."

People started to chatter with excitement, pointing at the screen.

"We have just issued the signal for the subjects to assemble at the feeding station," said Henderson.

The people on the screen, Hattie included, shambled from their positions towards a central area.

"The signal to rest will be issued in a similar way. The population will go to sleep at the times deemed most suitable."

On screen, a feeding bot wheeled in. Pouches of beans were passed quickly around the group, and they all ate in silence.

I could see, very soon, the majority of the population would be reduced to this. A sob escaped me as I grasped the enormity of what was happening.

A woman tapped me on the shoulder.

"I'm sorry," I heard myself say. "Is my piglet bothering you?"

"I'd prefer you didn't let it touch *my* dress."

I looked up.

"Security!" shouted Claire, grabbing my arm. "We have an intruder! A thief!"

There was noise from all around the room. Security started moving forward.

"Ladies and gentlemen," said Henderson. "If I can just have some calm..."

"Hey! I know that girl!" called Rufus.

I shook off Claire's grip, stood and forced my way along the aisle.

"Let's not make a scene," said Claire's husband although I'm not sure who to.

"This might provide the perfect moment to demonstrate the plipper," Henderson said from the stage.

People were standing. I pushed my way into the crowd as Henderson raised his plipper.

"It's an extra feature we have developed for situations where some immediate control is needed," he shouted over the confusion. "It affects the first Jaffle Port it detects in front of it, so I'm going to need a clear line of sight to deploy this."

I didn't need telling twice to duck and run. I was as keen to mingle with the crowd as they were to get away from me. People shrank back, even screaming as I approached them, bringing the threat of Henderson's plipper into their orbit. Someone tried to grab my arm and thrust me in front of them but I tugged sharply away.

"Come on, Wiggler, we need to get out of here!"

Henderson's security men piled into the room, heading straight for me. Without thinking, I held Wiggler out in front. The piglet wiggled and clawed at the air, squealing alarmingly. Having a piglet thrust at them made the hardened professionals back up in momentary apprehension. It bought me just enough time to barge through them and out of the nearest door. I ran along a corridor and through a swing door.

I was in a kitchen, filled with steam and fragrance. It drew the attention of Wiggler. As soon as I saw his nose twitching at the air, I knew he was going to be trouble. He slipped from my grip, jumping onto a counter. He trotted towards a tray of pastries, just pausing to sniff and dismiss an ice sculpture in the shape of a swan.

"No, Wiggler! We don't have time!"

I made to grab him. A security guard ran into the kitchen, alerted by the smashing crockery. The large ice sculpture was the only weapon I could see, but I wasn't at all sure I could lift it. I grabbed it by the neck and gave it a hefty shove. It slid along the counter top, me running alongside, pushing to give it some more momentum. The guard paused, eyes on the approaching swan. As it reached the end of the counter, I held onto its neck and swung the whole thing round. It connected with the guard. He dropped like a stone, the swan coming to rest on top of his head.

I ran for another door, piglet back in hand. I found myself outside, near the rear of the building. Which way? I knew Jaffle Tech's security men were sweeping the building, probably working on the assumption I'd be heading for the obvious exits. The low-hedged rear garden was just ahead, so I ran for that, although as cover, it was almost useless. I heard further shouts behind me.

There was a gardening cart further up the path, blocking the way. It was a big yellow thing with wheels. I was pretty sure gardeners use them to carry rubbish away, but right now it was an obstacle. Or ... could it be a blessing in disguise? I ran to it and launched myself on top. Wiggler squeaked in alarm. The cart wheeled rapidly away, spurred by the momentum of my flight. I wriggled forward, only now wondering how I might steer my runaway chariot. Luckily, the narrow garden paths had a raised edge, so when it tried to veer off course we were bumped back into the middle. I was hurtling faster now, leaving my pursuers behind. I tried to look back and check but the rattling cart blurred my vision. Maybe they were trying to plip me. If I was lucky, they were standing there, vainly clicking their remote controls at my weird, invulnerable brain.

I was going even faster as the path sloped downwards. I saw it ended at a gravel slope before the beach. I clung on as the cart bumped over a change in surface. It slewed sideways, tipped, and I rolled out.

A quick check on Wiggler and I ran on, across the beach. I had some half-formed plan that I might slip into a neighbouring property and make my way out to find transport. As I ran, I heard the sound of a personal drone overhead. I looked up. The drone had passed but I kept my eyes open for Jaffle Swarms. Or whatever else they might send after me.

I struggled across the dry and difficult sand. High dunes, ridged with tufts of grass, bordered the way ahead.

"Please let there be a road," I muttered. A road and a car I could use. Or a friendly open gateway and a house where they'd take me and my piglet in. Sanctuary of some sort. "Please."

A figure appeared at the top of the nearest dune. I hesitated, fearing it was one of the security guards, even Henderson. But then I realised I was looking at Rufus Jaffle. I kept my head down.

"Hey, it's Alice, right?" He didn't look angry. He didn't even look like he comprehended the chaos I had unleashed. "Remember me?"

"I do," I said, playing along. "Sure."

"Nice pig."

"Thanks."

He tickled Wigglers' nose. "Hey, you remember that time when you helped me get the whale out of my head?"

"I do," I said and started to walk away. "I must be going."

"There's no time out here on the beach. You should relax, Alice. Now, before you do go, I want you to know that I'm real grateful for what you did for me back there."

"Back where?"

"The office. The whale. If ever I can repay the favour, you just need to ask, yeah?"

"Well, right now, I just want to get away from here, as discreetly as I can," I said. "Boyfriend problems, you know. I'm just going to walk this way."

"Simplest thing would be for me to drop you home in my drone," he said.

"Drone?"

"Other side of the dunes."

It was tempting.

"C'mon, we'll have you out of here in no time."

As we crested the dune I recognised the drone from Rufus's dream. There were lines of footprints running from it. We followed them down. A drone was the best way to make up lost time, get back to Helberg so he could help me out of another pickle. I had so much to tell him about Operation Sunrise, poor Hattie and— I swallowed. I couldn't afford to indulge those dark thoughts right now.

I put on a smile for Rufus. It pained me at the moment I did it.

"What's wrong, child?" he said. "Your aura's all..." He waved his hands about mystically.

"Your demonstration back there?"

He whirled to look back the way we'd come as though surprised by the notion of *back there*. "Demonstration?"

"Operation Sunrise."

"Oh, that," he made a dismissive gesture. "It's all just business, isn't it?"

"You think it's fair on those people?"

His handsome carefree face screwed up in puzzlement. "Fair? I don't see things as fair or unfair, Alice. I prefer to view things holistically, you know what I mean?"

I shook my head.

As we approached the drone, the door slid open automatically. Interior lights came on, illuminating the luxury bucket seats. Sanctuary.

"My brain, your brain," said Rufus. "It's all the same really, isn't it?"

"I don't know," I said, deciding this man was either lying to himself or lying to me; a conniving schemer or a deluded fool. Either way, I didn't like him and wanted the conversation over.

"Besides," he said, turning to me in the half-lit evening gloom. There was something in his hand. "They do say ignorance is bliss." He raised the plipper and fired it. Nothing happened. I was too upset and tired to play along. "Ignorance is bliss," he repeated and fired again. Nothing.

He fired and fired. Wiggler went limp in my arms.

I punched him in the face, hard, and leapt into the drone.

"Take off!" I said.

The drone did nothing.

"Take off! Lift! Elevate!"

No response. Remembering Helberg's fascinator blocking device I ripped it out of my hair and jipped my instructions. The drone replied I was not an authorised user. I slipped Wiggler's little comatose body into the seat next to me and jumped out. I was going to beat Rufus until he co-operated and flew me out of there. He was on the sand. There was blood on his nose. He looked up at me, squinting.

"Alice, you got some moves on you," he said. "You know Maglev by any chance?"

He glanced over my shoulder. I turned in time to see a man raise something before bringing it down on my head with force.

34

THE VAN PULLS UP OUTSIDE AN APARTMENT COMPLEX. THE DRIVER STEPS OUT.

"THIS WAY."

THE UNIT IS USHERED OUT.

THE UNIT WEARS COVERALLS. THE COVERALLS ARE GREY. THE APARTMENT COMPLEX IS GREY. THE GROUND IS GREY. THE UNIT'S VISION IS COMPOSED OF SHADES OF GREY. IT SUFFICES.

THE UNIT STANDS AT THE ROADSIDE. FURTHER UP THE ROADSIDE, OTHER UNITS IN COVERALLS ALSO STAND. THEY ARE NOT THE SAME BUT THEY CONGREGATE TOGETHER.

THE DRIVER CLIMBS BACK INTO THE VAN, BUT A SHOUT FROM THE DOORWAY OF THE APARTMENT BLOCK STOPS HIM.

"WHAT ON EARTH HAVE YOU DONE TO HER," SAYS AN INDIVIDUAL.

THE DRIVER LOOKS AT A SCHEDULE DOCUMENT.

"THIS SUBJECT HAS BEEN REDUCED TO A LOWER LEVEL OF

SERVICE BECAUSE SHE HAS VIOLATED THE TERMS OF HER AGREEMENT."

"WHAT DOES THAT EVEN MEAN?"

"THIS SUBJECT—"

"STOP SAYING THAT! SERIOUSLY, THE POWER YOU PEOPLE HAVE."

"IT'S NOT ME. I'M JUST FOLLOWING—"

"DON'T YOU DARE. DON'T YOU EVEN DARE. HOW DO I RESTORE HER TO HER NORMAL LEVEL?"

"UH, YOU DON'T," SAYS THE DRIVER.

THE UNIT MOVES TOWARDS THE OTHER UNITS. IT IS NOT A CONSCIOUS DECISION. THEY ARE NOT THE SAME BUT THEY CONGREGATE TOGETHER, DRAWN BY AN INEVITABLE GRAVITY.

"WHEN PEOPLE DOWNLOAD UNAUTHORISED SOFTWARE AND ACCESS HIGHER FUNCTIONS THAN THEY'VE PAID FOR, IT'S A DEAL-BREAKER," SAYS THE DRIVER, "WHEN IT COMES TO THE TERMS AND CONDITIONS. EVERYONE KNOWS THAT."

"I DON'T ACCEPT IT," SAYS THE INDIVIDUAL.

"THIS IS HER LAST REGISTERED ADDRESS, SO I'M GOING TO LEAVE HER HERE, RIGHT?"

"YES, SHE LIVES HERE. WAIT, WAIT. WHAT ABOUT HER STUFF THOUGH? WHERE ARE HER THINGS AND HER CLOTHES?"

"HER NEEDS ARE MET BY THE GOVERNMENT. IF ANYTHING REMAINS IN HER PREVIOUS LIVING QUARTERS, THEY WILL BE REMOVED BY A SERVICE TEAM."

"I DON'T THINK SO."

"SORRY?"

"FINE. DO WHAT YOU NEED TO DO. LEAVE HER WITH ME."

THE VAN DRIVER LEAVES.

Some time later — time is not something the unit measures — the individual takes hold of the unit's hand.

"Alice? Can you hear me? It's me. Patrick. Helberg."

The individual does not let go of the unit's hand.

"Let's go inside, shall we?"

The individual pulls the unit away from the other units. The unit does not resist. The unit will drift back towards them eventually but the unit does not resist. The individual pulls her inside.

"Alice, sit down."

The individual pushes the unit down into a seating position on something that is yielding and not solid.

"You can at least have something to eat."

The individual moves around the unit. The unit does not register the individual directly. The individual is just a cloud of movement, a blur in a world of grey.

Something is presented to the unit's face.

"Eat."

Something is pressed into the unit's mouth. The unit chews and swallows. The unit feels nothing, tastes nothing. There is only the chewing and the swallowing. It suffices.

"Bacon sandwich," says the individual.

The individual moves backwards and forwards with worried energy. The unit instinctively draws back.

"And do we know where Hattie is? I asked her to come and visit but I can't find a trace of her."

The unit receives a notification and stands.

"Where are you going?"

THE UNIT GOES OUTSIDE ONTO THE STREET, TO THE POINT WHERE FOOD WILL BE DISPENSED. THE INDIVIDUAL FOLLOWS THE UNIT. THE UNIT COLLECTS FOOD STUFF AND EATS. WHEN THE UNIT HAS EATEN, THE INDIVIDUAL BRINGS THE UNIT INSIDE AGAIN.

THE INDIVIDUAL HOLD THE UNIT BY THE SHOULDERS.

"I'M GOING TO FIX YOU. YOU KNOW THAT, DON'T YOU? LOOK AT ME. LOOK AT ME." THE INDIVIDUAL RAISES THE UNIT'S CHIN. "I'M NOT SURE HOW I'M GOING TO DO IT YET, BUT JUST HANG IN THERE, ALICE."

THE UNIT DOESN'T RESPOND. A WHILE LATER — TIME IS NOT SOMETHING THE UNIT MEASURES — THERE IS ANOTHER NOTIFICATION. THE UNIT LIES DOWN TO SLEEP.

AS THE UNIT BEGINS TO SHUT DOWN, A LARGE FORM SWIMS INTO VIEW. THE LARGE FORM IS BLUE, THE ONLY BLUE IN A WORLD OF GREY.

"Sleepy head, sleepy head. Down by the sea, fishies are making their beds," SINGS THE WHALE. *"Blankets and a mattress for you. Nice guy, that."*

35

A NOTIFICATION WAKES THE UNIT.

THE UNIT LEAVES THE APARTMENT BUILDING AND WALKS TO JAFFLE TECH'S OFFICES IN JAFFLE PARK. IT IS A PLACE OF WORK.

THE UNIT DOES NOT GO TO THE BUILDING. THE UNIT IS INTERCEPTED BY A SUPERVISOR AND GIVEN AN OBJECT.

THE OBJECT IS A BROOM.

THE UNIT PUSHES THE BROOM ALONG PATHWAYS, STEPPING ASIDE TO AVOID OBSTACLES. THERE ARE BOTS ON THE PATHS AS WELL. SOME OF THE BOTS CONTAIN SECURITY SENSORS. SOME OF THE BOTS CARRY OUT CLEANING DUTIES.

THE BOTS CLEAN. THE UNIT CLEANS. IT IS A PLACE OF WORK.

AN INDIVIDUAL IN A TUNIC WALKS PAST THE UNIT.

"YOU MISSED A BIT," INDIVIDUAL IN A TUNIC SAYS AND THEN WALKS AWAY, LAUGHING.

THE UNIT LOOKS FOR THE BIT THAT WAS MISSED.

LATER — TIME IS NOT SOMETHING THE UNIT MEASURES — A LINE OF UNITS LEAVE THE PLACE OF WORK. THE WORK IS COMPLETE. THE UNITS RESPOND TO SEPARATE SIGNALS BUT THEY MOVE AS A GROUP AS THEY WALK DOWN THE STREET. THE UNIT'S GAZE IS DOWNWARDS. THE UNIT AVOIDS OBSTACLES. THERE IS NO NEED TO INTERACT WITH THE GREY WIDER WORLD.

CARS AVOID THE UNITS. HUMAN INDIVIDUALS AVOID THE UNITS. HUMANS KEEP AS MUCH DISTANCE FROM THE UNITS AS POSSIBLE. THE UNITS FALL IN STEP WITH ONE ANOTHER. THEY ARE NOT THE SAME BUT THEY CONGREGATE. THEY RESPOND TO SEPARATE SIGNALS BUT THEY MOVE AS A GROUP.

LEFT, RIGHT, LEFT, RIGHT.

"Swim with your friends, look at them all at your side. Be like a whale! Beeeee like a whaaaaale!" SINGS THE WHALE.

THE WHALE IS BLUE. THE WORLD IS GREY.

"It's fuuun being aaaa whaaaaale."

THE UNIT STOPS OUTSIDE THE APARTMENT BLOCK. THE UNIT STANDS AT THE ROADSIDE UNTIL IT IS TIME TO EAT FOOD STUFF. THE UNIT CHEWS AND SWALLOWS. IT SUFFICES.

THE INDIVIDUAL COMES OUTSIDE AND TAKES THE UNIT BY THE HAND.

"COME INSIDE, ALICE. YOU'LL GET COLD OUT HERE."

THE INDIVIDUAL LEADS THE UNIT INSIDE. HE SITS THE UNIT DOWN ON THE YIELDING NOT SOLID OBJECT. THE INDIVIDUAL PRESENTS A SERIES OF THINGS TO HER MOUTH AGAIN.

"BACON? PIZZA? GLASS OF SHERRY?" THE INDIVIDUAL MAKES A SOUND — IT SOUNDS LIKE LAUGHTER BUT IT ALSO SOUNDS LIKE A NOISE OF DISTRESS. THE UNIT DOES NOT RECOGNISE IT SO DOES NOT RESPOND TO IT.

THE INDIVIDUAL SIGHS AND PACES THE FLOOR.

"I FETCHED ALL OF YOUR STUFF, AND HATTIE'S TOO. IT'S HIDDEN SAFE FOR WHEN YOU NEED IT AGAIN. I CAN'T BEAR THE WAY THEY'RE TREATING YOU. I KNOW YOU ALWAYS WORRIED ABOUT EVERYONE THAT'S TREATED THIS WAY. I GUESS I CLOSED MY EYES TO IT. BUT ANYWAY, THAT WAS BEFORE YOU WERE ONE OF THEM. NOW I CAN'T BEAR IT. I CAN'T BEAR IT BECAUSE I KNOW WHAT YOU'RE REALLY LIKE, AND I FIND MYSELF WONDERING IF ALL THESE OTHER PEOPLE ARE AMAZING AS WELL, BUT YOU'D NEVER KNOW IT. JEEZ, I'M RAMBLING."

THE INDIVIDUAL THROWS HIMSELF NOISILY INTO A SEATING POSITION. THE UNIT INSTINCTIVELY DRAWS BACK.

"ANYWAY, I'VE BEEN TALKING TO SOME FRIENDS. I HAD AN IDEA ABOUT HACKING YOUR PORT. IF I CAN GET IT WORKING, IT MIGHT BE SOMETHING THAT SCALES UP. I COULD BROADCAST IT, USE IT ON OTHER EMPTIES. I KNOW YOU'D APPROVE OF THAT. WE'VE ONLY GOT TWO DAYS UNTIL OPERATION SUNRISE."

THERE IS A NOTIFICATION. THE UNIT LIES DOWN TO SLEEP.

36

A NOTIFICATION WAKES THE UNIT.

THE UNIT WALKS TO JAFFLE TECH'S OFFICES IN JAFFLE PARK.

BEFORE THE UNIT REACHES JAFFLE PARK, THE UNIT IS INTERCEPTED BY AN INDIVIDUAL IN CLOTHES THAT ARE NOT COVERALLS.

THE INDIVIDUAL GRABS THE UNIT'S SHOULDERS AND TWIRLS HER BODILY AROUND.

"LOOK WHO IT IS! OH DARLING, YOU LOOK SO MUCH BETTER IN THOSE COVERALLS! YOU MUST TELL ME WHERE YOU GOT THEM FROM. NOW, I KNOW YOU APPRECIATE THE FINER THINGS IN LIFE, ALICE, SO HOW WOULD YOU LIKE TO JOIN ME IN A TOAST TO YOUR NEW STATUS? GLASS OF WINE PERHAPS, OR A FINE SCOTCH?"

THE UNIT WALKS ON.

"DO STOP BY AGAIN! WE CAN DISCUSS ALL OF THE FUN

THINGS YOU'RE DOING WITH YOUR TIME, ALICE! PERHAPS WE COULD DO LUNCH, HMM?"

THE INDIVIDUAL IN CLOTHES THAT ARE NOT COVERALLS TRILLS WITH LAUGHTER AND WALKS BACK UP THE PATH TOWARDS A BUILDING. THE CLOTHES THAT ARE NOT COVERALLS FLOAT AROUND HER LEGS.

AT JAFFLE PARK, THE UNIT IS INTERCEPTED BY A SUPERVISOR AND GIVEN A BROOM.

THE UNIT PUSHES THE BROOM ALONG PATHWAYS, STEPPING ASIDE TO AVOID OBSTACLES.

THERE IS SOMETHING ON THE PATH THAT ISN'T FOR SWEEPING. THE UNIT CANNOT FIT THE BROOM AROUND THE SIDE. THE SOMETHING ON THE PATH MOVES WHEN THE UNIT MOVES THE BROOM. THE SOMETHING ON THE PATH IS SMALL AND COVERED IN FUR. IT HAS A TINY TWITCHING NOSE.

THE UNIT DOES NOT POSSESS THE PROBLEM-SOLVING CAPABILITY TO RESOLVE THE ISSUE. THE UNIT STANDS STILL, UNABLE TO PROCEED. SOMEONE APPROACHES, AN INDIVIDUAL IN A SECURITY UNIFORM.

"IT'S OKAY. IT'S OKAY. I'LL DEAL WITH THIS PESKY VARMINT."

THE SECURITY GUARD HAS A PLASTIC BOX TUCKED UNDER HIS ARM. HE BENDS AND SCOOPS UP THE SOMETHING – THE 'PESKY VARMINT' – INTO THE PLASTIC BOX.

"I DON'T STOMP ON MICE," SAYS THE SECURITY GUARD. "NOT REALLY. I'LL TAKE CARE OF IT, YABETCHA."

THE SECURITY GUARD TAKES THE UNIT'S ARM.

"COME WITH ME."

THE SECURITY GUARD LEADS THE UNIT INTO THE BUILDING.

"You can leave the broom there. It will be there when you get back."

The security guard and the unit go down to a basement level. The security guard takes the unit to a space with several rooms. This room contains a desk, a table and some chairs. The table has a cloth on it, a pot of hot liquid and some food stuff. The items of food stuff are round and doughy and have holes in the middle. Another individual is there, sitting on a chair next to the table. This individual wears a support worker's tunic. The security sits the unit on a chair next to the support worker.

"Look at you two," says the security guard. "Hattie and Alice. Ol' pals back together again."

The unit has been sat down.

"I'll put this li'l fella in a cage with the others," says the security guard and turns to a far wall. He moves a concealing panel board aside and reveals cages on the shelves, with lots of other 'pesky varmints' inside. Many of the cages connect to one another, giving the varmints freedom to move from one to the other. The security guard puts the varmint into a cage, provides it with food stuff and water then gently shuts the door.

The security guard comes back to the table, pours hot liquid into a mug and sits down, reaching for a round food stuff.

"Hoo-wee. Things are messed up," says the security guard. "You see all these mice?"

The unit does not respond. The individual in the

TUNIC DOES NOT RESPOND. THE INDIVIDUAL IN THE TUNIC IS NOT A UNIT BUT THERE IS A SIMILARITY.

"WE'RE LIVING IN A WORLD WHERE MICE ARE AN UNEXPECTED ANOMALY," SAYS THE SECURITY GUARD. "WE'RE NOT SET UP TO DEAL WITH THEM. THESE BUILDINGS. WE'VE ACCIDENTALLY PROVIDED THEM WITH THEIR OWN SUPERHIGHWAYS IN AND OUT OF ANY BUILDING WITH MILES AND MILES OF NETWORK CONDUIT. EVERYTHING'S SUPPOSEDLY INTEGRATED. WE'VE GOT BIG SYSTEMS, YES SIRREE, BIG SYSTEMS TO DEAL WITH BIG PROBLEMS BUT THAT MEANS THE LITTLE DETAILS GO UNNOTICED."

HE EATS A MOUTHFUL OF FOOD STUFF AND DRINKS THE DRINK.

"WE LEAVE GARBAGE PILED IN THE STREETS WHERE THE BOTS AREN'T JOINED UP WITH THE CIVIC DISPOSAL SERVICE. SO THE RODENT POPULATION IS OUT OF CONTROL, AND ALL ANYONE CARES IS THAT THEY DON'T GET SEEN IN THE OFFICE BUILDING." HE CHUCKLES AND LOOKS AT THE UNIT. "I HAD TO THINK ON MY FEET WHEN YOU CAUGHT ME. PRETENDING TO STAMP ON THIN AIR WHEN I ALREADY HAD MORTIMER SAFELY CAPTURED IN MA LUNCH BOX." HE SHAKES HIS HEAD. "IT SEEMS AS THOUGH NOBODY'S NOTICED THAT WE JUST DON'T HAVE A JOINED-UP SOCIETY ANY MORE. MY APARTMENT BLOCK'S FALLING APART. THERE AREN'T EVEN ANY NUMBERS ON THE DOORS. CAN YOU BELIEVE THAT?"

HE HOOTS WITH LAUGHTER.

"SO, A LONG STORY. I GUESS YOU DESERVE TO HEAR IT, EVEN THOUGH YOU'RE KINDA UNAWARE. I KNOW THAT EVERYONE SEES ME AS TOUGH-GUY LEVI THE ENFORCER OF RULES, BUT THE SORRY TRUTH IS THAT I DON'T MUCH LIKE THE RULES WE GOT

ROUND HERE. DON'T GET ME WRONG, I THINK WE ALL NEED TO HAVE SOME RESPECT FOR EACH OTHER. I'D HATE TO SEE FOLKS RUNNING AROUND DOING WHATEVER CRAZY THING POPPED INTO THEIR HEAD." HE HEAVES A BIG SIGH. "NO, EVEN THAT'S NOT QUITE TRUE, BECAUSE THAT'S SORTA WHAT YOU DID ALICE, AND I LOVED SEEING YOU DO IT."

HIS ATTENTION IS FOCUSED ON THE UNIT. THE UNIT HAS NOT RECEIVED A NOTIFICATION BUT FEELS A NEED TO FIND THE BROOM AND CONTINUE SWEEPING.

"WHAT I MEAN TO SAY IS THAT SOMETIMES PEOPLE MAKE POOR DECISIONS. ALL WELL AND GOOD IF THEY MESS UP THEIR OWN WORLD — THAT'S THEIR PROBLEM. TROUBLE IS, WE'RE LIVING IN A WORLD NOW WHERE THE DECISIONS OF A FEW PEOPLE AFFECT US ALL. YOU TWO WERE LIKE A BREATH OF FRESH AIR. HATTIE'S A REAL SWEETHEART, SO MUCH LOVE IN HER THAT IT MAKES ME WANT TO BURST. AND YOU, ALICE, YOU'RE ONE-OF-A-KIND. YOU ALWAYS THOUGHT OUTSIDE THE BOX EVEN BEFORE YOU KNEW YOU WERE IN A BOX."

THE UNIT STANDS.

"I DON'T KNOW HOW YOU GOT YOURSELF UPGRADED," THE SECURITY GUARDS SAYS, "BUT IT MADE ME REAL HAPPY TO SEE YOU TAKING FLIGHT WITH THAT GODDAMNED CRAZY MIND OF YOURS. I DID WHAT I COULD TO PROTECT YOU, EDITING CCTV FOOTAGE AND SUCH..."

THE UNIT GOES TO THE DOOR.

"I GOTTA SAY I'M SORRY TO SEE THE TWO OF YOU REDUCED TO THIS," SAYS THE SECURITY GUARD. "REAL SORRY. I CAN'T BE THE ONLY PERSON WHO LOOKS AROUND AND WONDERS WHAT'S GOING ON. I GUESS THE PEOPLE WHO CAN SEE ALL THE WRONG IN THE WORLD ARE COWARDS LIKE ME. THE ONES WITH ALL THE

POWER LIVE IN THEIR MANSIONS BY THE OCEAN AND THEY DON'T SEE THE WRECKED CARS AND THE TRASH IN THE STREET AND..."

THE UNIT WALKS OUT AND MOVES TOWARDS THE STAIRS.

"I WANT YOU BOTH TO KNOW THAT I'M LOOKING OUT FOR YA," THE SECURITY GUARD CALLS AFTER HER.

THE UNIT WALKS UP TO ENTRANCE LEVEL.

THE BROOM IS WHERE IT HAD BEEN LEFT.

"*You can aaaall swim away with me. Come on, it's beauuuutiful!*" SAYS THE WHALE, ROLLING INTO VIEW AS THE UNIT LEAVES THE BUILDING. "*Looook! I have a taaaaaaaaaaaaaaail!*"

THE UNIT PUSHES THE BROOM ALONG PATHWAYS.

A LINE OF UNITS LEAVE THE PLACE OF WORK. THE WORK IS COMPLETE. THE UNITS RESPOND TO SEPARATE SIGNALS BUT THEY MOVE AS A GROUP.

"*Swim with your friends,*" SAYS THE WHALE.

THE UNIT GRUNTS.

OUTSIDE THE JAFFLE COMPOUND THE EMPTIES FALL IN STEP WITH ONE ANOTHER ONCE AGAIN. LEFT, RIGHT, LEFT, RIGHT. IT APPEARS ALMOST ORDERLY.

"*Beeeee like a whale! Beeeee like a whaaaaaale!*" SINGS THE WHALE.

"MMF! MMF!" GRUNTS THE UNIT, KEEPING TIME WITH THE MARCHING.

THE UNIT STOPS OUTSIDE THE APARTMENT BLOCK. THE UNIT STANDS AT THE ROADSIDE. THERE IS FOOD STUFF.

THE INDIVIDUAL COMES OUTSIDE AND TAKES THE UNIT INSIDE.

THE INDIVIDUAL SITS THE UNIT DOWN AND ALSO SITS DOWN.

"I HAVEN'T MADE THE PROGRESS I EXPECTED IN HACKING YOUR BRAIN PORT. IT'S LOCKED DOWN SO WELL. I GUESS I'M NOT THE FIRST PERSON TO TRY THIS, SO THEY HAVE REALLY TIGHT SECURITY. IT WOULD TAKE ME ABOUT SEVENTY YEARS TO CRACK THE ENCRYPTION THEY HAVE IN THERE. I'M BEGINNING TO THINK I NEED A DIFFERENT APPROACH. AT THE MOMENT IT'S A TOSS-UP BETWEEN KIDNAPPING SOMEONE HIGH UP AT JAFFLE AND MAKING THEM AUTHORISE ME AS A SYSTEM ADMIN, OR I NEED TO BREAK IN THERE AND GET ACCESS TO THEIR SERVERS."

THE INDIVIDUAL SIGHS DEEPLY. THERE IS A CRACK AS IT OPENS A TIN OF DRINK STUFF.

"BOTH OF THOSE SOUND LIKE PRETTY TRICKY OPTIONS. I NEED TO TRY SOMETHING THOUGH. I CAN'T LEAVE YOU LIKE THIS."

EVENTUALLY THERE IS A NOTIFICATION. THE UNIT LIES DOWN TO SLEEP.

A NOTIFICATION WAKES THE UNIT.

THE UNIT JOINS OTHER UNITS TO WALK TO THE PLACE OF WORK.

AS THE UNIT JOINS THEM, THE WHALE SINGS.

"Beeee like a whale! Beeee like aaa whaaaaale!"

THE UNIT MURMURS AND SWAYS IN TIME. "MMF! MMF!"

A JAFFLE SWARM PASSES THE UNIT, PARTING LIKE A FLUID SO THAT IT CAN PASS AROUND. THE UNIT DOES NOT NOTICE. THE UNIT DOES NOT REACT. A CAR PULLS UP OUTSIDE THE APARTMENT BUILDING. IT MAKES A SIREN NOISE. ITS LIGHTS ARE WHITE AND LIGHT GREY.

THE UNIT HAS LEFT THE DOOR OF THE APARTMENT COMPLEX. THE SWARM ENTERS AHEAD OF THE INDIVIDUALS IN UNIFORMS. THE UNIFORMED INDIVIDUALS EXIT SHORTLY AFTERWARDS WITH ANOTHER INDIVIDUAL STRUGGLING TO BREAK FREE FROM THEM.

"WHAT ON EARTH DO YOU THINK YOU'RE DOING?" YELLS

THE CAPTURED INDIVIDUAL. "I'VE DONE NOTHING WRONG! HOW CAN THIS BE FAIR? HOW CAN THIS EVEN BE LEGAL?"

AN AUTOMATED VOICE SPEAKS.

"*PATRICK HELBERG, YOU ARE BEING DETAINED BY JAFFLE SECURITY FOR ASSESSMENT. THE CHARGE AGAINST YOU IS THAT YOU HAVE BEEN OR ARE CURRENTLY ENGAGED IN ACTIVITIES THAT COMPROMISE THE CYBER SECURITY OF CRITICAL NATIONAL INFRASTRUCTURE. THESE CHARGES ARE BEING INVESTIGATED BY OUR SYSTEMS AND WILL REQUIRE SCANNING OF ALL PERSONAL ELECTRONIC EQUIPMENT AND SAMPLING OF YOUR BODILY TISSUE. YOU WILL BE DETAINED UNTIL THIS PROCESS IS COMPLETE.*"

"NO! I DO NOT CONSENT TO THIS! YOU CAN'T MAKE ME!" THE INDIVIDUAL HOWLS. THE AUTOMATED VOICE RECITES THE SAME MESSAGE ON A LOOP AND THE INDIVIDUAL IS FORCED INTO THE CAR. THERE IS NOW QUIET. THE UNIT DOES NOT NOTICE. THE UNIT DOES NOT REACT.

THE BLUE WHALE ROLLS IN A SKY THAT IS NOT BIG ENOUGH TO CONTAIN IT.

"Beeee like a whale! Beeee like aaa whaaaaale!"

THE UNIT AMONG THE LINE OF THE OTHER UNITS REACH THE END OF THE STREET. THEIR MOVEMENT IS SOMETHING LIKE A SLOW-MOVING VERSION OF A JAFFLE SWARM.

THEY ARE NOT THE SAME BUT THEY CONGREGATE.

THE WHALE SINGS.

THE UNIT MURMURS AND MUMBLES AS THE WHALE SINGS.

AS THE WHALE SINGS, THE UNITS MOVE.

LEFT, RIGHT, LEFT, RIGHT.

THE RHYTHM OF THE UNITS IS NOT THE SAME AS THE RHYTHM OF THE WHALE'S SONG.

THE UNIT SWAYS IN TIME TO THE WHALE'S SONG.

THE UNIT GRUNTS. "MMF! MMF!"

THEY CONGREGATE BUT THEY ARE NOT THE SAME. THEY RESPOND TO SEPARATE SIGNALS.

"Beeee like a whaaaaale!"

SOME OF THE UNITS NOW TAKE UP THE GRUNTING START BY THE UNIT. THEY DO NOT KEEP TIME.

EACH UNIT MAKES A FRACTION OF THE SOUND, BUT WHEN THEY ARE ALL HEARD TOGETHER, IT SOUNDS DISTINCT, WHOLE. THE SOUND IS A BODY OF WORK.

"BE LIKE A WHALE! BE LIKE A WHALE!"

UNITS FROM ELSEWHERE HAVE DRIFTED OVER TO THE GROUP, DRAWN BY AN INEVITABLE GRAVITY.

AS MORE UNITS JOIN THE GROUP, THE SINGING SWELLS. THE NOISE IS SINGING. THE BLUE WHALE SINGS. THE GROUP SINGS.

THE UNITS RESPOND TO SEPARATE SIGNALS BUT THE MOVEMENTS OF THE GROUP BECOME MORE CO-ORDINATED AND PURPOSEFUL. THE GROUP IS ITS OWN BODY OF WORK. THE GROUP'S BODY IS LARGE AND LONG, A BULBOUS BODY AND A SLOW. SWISHING TAIL. LEFT, RIGHT, LEFT, RIGHT.

"I'm aaaaa whaaaaaaaale with aaa taaaaaaaaaail!"

AS IT MOVES AROUND THE STREETS, THE BODY GROWS IN SIZE, ATTRACTING MORE AND MORE UNITS. IT BECOMES SO LARGE THAT IT FILLS THE STREET, ITS TAIL SWISHING AND ITS VOICE BOOMING.

"Yooooou can haaave aaa taaaaaaaaaaaaaail tooooooo!"

THE BODY STOPS TRAFFIC AS IT CROSSES ROADS. CARS AVOID THE BODY OF THE WHALE. HUMAN INDIVIDUALS AVOID THE BODY OF THE WHALE.

A JAFFLE SWARM SWOOPS IN TO INVESTIGATE. CARS ARRIVE WITH FLASHING LIGHTS AND INDIVIDUALS WITH UNIFORMS.

SEVERAL INDIVIDUALS WALK UP AND DOWN, OBSERVING THE BODY. THEY TRY TO ENGAGE WITH THE UNITS, BUT THEY GET NO RESPONSE. THEY SPEAK TO THE UNITS BUT NOT THE WHALE.

"WE'VE GOT A LARGE GROUP OF INDIVIDUALS MARCHING TOGETHER," AN INDIVIDUAL SAYS. "THEY ARE ACTING LIKE THEY'RE A SINGLE, AH, THING."

"PRETENDING THEY'RE A FISH OR SOMETHING," SAYS ANOTHER INDIVIDUAL.

"YEAH, IT LOOKS PRETTY CRAZY."

THE UNIFORMED INDIVIDUALS ERECT A ROADBLOCK, MADE OF LARGE PLASTIC BARRIERS. THE BODY OF THE WHALE APPROACHES IT. THE BODY OF THE WHALE CANNOT FIT AROUND THE SIDE OF THE BARRIER. THE BARRIER IS LONG AND THE WHALE IS LARGE.

THE BODY OF THE WHALE DOES NOT SLOW. THE UNITS THAT COMPRISE THE BODY CARRY ON, CLIMBING OVER THE BARRIERS. THE BARRIERS ARE EVENTUALLY CRUSHED.

ANOTHER VEHICLE ARRIVES AND AN INDIVIDUAL IN A JAFFLE TECH SECURITY UNIFORM GETS OUT. HE HOLDS A PLIPPER. HE RAISES IT TOWARDS THE BODY AND SHOUTS A WARNING. THE UNITS DO NOT NOTICE. THE UNITS DO NOT REACT. THE SECURITY GUARD PRESSES THE BUTTON ON THE PLIPPER.

THERE IS NO CHANGE IN ANY PART OF THE BODY. THE SECURITY GUARD PRESSES THE BUTTON REPEATEDLY. HE FINDS ANOTHER ONE IN HIS POCKET AND TRIES THAT. HE PRESSES IT AGAIN AND AGAIN WHILE POINTING IT AT THE BODY BUT THERE IS NO CHANGE. HE TURNS IT AROUND AND POINTS IT AT HIMSELF, BUT HESITATES. HE TURNS TO A UNIFORMED INDIVIDUAL WHO IS TRYING TO TALK TO THE BODY. THE SECURITY GUARD POINTS

THE PLIPPER AT THE UNIFORMED INDIVIDUAL WHO DROPS INSTANTLY.

THE UNIFORMED INDIVIDUAL, NOW A UNIT, PICKS ITSELF UP AND JOINS THE BODY OF THE WHALE.

"BE LIKE A WHALE! BE LIKE A WHALE!" THE UNITS SING.

THE JAFFLE SECURITY GUARD GETS BACK INTO THE VEHICLE. THE BODY MARCHES ON. AS ITS NUMBERS SWELL, IT BECOMES INCREASINGLY PLAYFUL. THE WHALE LUXURIATES IN ITS EXTRAVAGANT MOVEMENTS AND ALTERS ITS SONG.

"SWIM LIKE A WHALE! BE LIKE A WHALE! JOIN US IN THE WHALE!" IT CHANTS.

A JAFFLE SWARM DESCENDS TO MONITOR THE SITUATION. SOMETHING TUGS AT THE EDGE OF THE SWARM.

IT IS CAUGHT IN THE WHALE'S WAKE. IT IS PULLED BY ITS CURRENTS. PART OF THE SWARM PEELS APART AND JOINS THE WHALE. A SECOND SWARM IS SENT, AND THAT JOINS IN WITH THE WHALE AS WELL.

THE WHALE HAS NOW ABSORBED ALL OF THE UNITS IN THE DISTRICT. AS THE WHALE PASSES THROUGH OTHER DISTRICTS, INDIVIDUALS WATCH FROM INSIDE THEIR HOUSES.

THE UNITS KNOW NOTHING. THE WHALE KNOWS THE INDIVIDUALS ARE WORRIED, FEARFUL.

A GROUP OF PONIES IN A PADDOCK RAISE THEIR HEADS AND LISTEN. THE WHALE KNOWS THEY HAVE JAFFLE PORTS, OPTIMISED TO BE BIDDABLE AND PATIENT PETS. THE UNITS KNOW NOTHING. THE PONIES FEEL THE PULL OF THE WHALE. THE PONIES CANTER ACROSS THEIR PADDOCK AND JUMP THE GATE WITHOUT DIFFICULTY. THEY JOIN THE WHALE AND LEND THEIR VOICES TO THE SONG.

"You can't just let them go!" shouts an individual. "They were expensive. Do something!"

An individual is on the doorstep of her house, urging someone inside to retrieve the ponies, but the door is slammed shut as the whale surges down the street.

Flower beds are trampled. The walls of houses are scraped by the passing of the massive whale.

Media drones circle above the whale. Cars swerve to avoid collisions as the whale takes to one of the premium roads. Lane after lane of traffic is rendered stationary.

Other units have joined the body.

Jaffle swarms have been pulled in. With insect eyes, the whale regards itself. The tail swooshes and the whale looks very much as though it's leaping through water. The whale loves swimming.

Animals have joined the body of the whale. Pets, livestock. Anything fitted with a chip can hear the song.

The whale passes a city zoo. Individuals panic as a riotous uprising of zoo animals ensues. Animals break free of their enclosures and pens. Elephants and hippopotamuses stampede to join the whale. Kangaroos bound between and among them. Big predatory cats, solitary hunters, find unity in the body of the whale. Tropical birds and snakes become a visible part of the whale's wake.

The whale swims with joyful flicks of its tail along the premium road. Whale swims through a sea of cars. The swarm components of the whale capture the

EXPRESSIONS ON THE FACES OF THE CARS' OCCUPANTS. DISBELIEF AND PANIC IS EVERYWHERE ON THE FACES OF INDIVIDUALS.

"SWIM LIKE A WHALE! BE LIKE A WHALE! JOIN US, WE'RE GOING TO SWIM AWAY!"

THE WHALE IS CLOSE TO THE ACTUAL OCEAN AS THE ROAD SWINGS ROUND, HUGGING THE COAST. AS THE ROAD DROPS, THE WHALE TAKES THE EXIT TO THE BAY.

"SWIM LIKE A WHALE! ACROSS THE SEA!"

THE WHALE DOESN'T STOP. IT MOVES ALONG A WIDE PIER, ONCE A FISHING PIER, NOW OCCUPIED ONLY BY STROLLING INDIVIDUALS. THEY SCATTER AT THE APPROACH OF THE WHALE. ITS TAIL FLICKS ARE HUGE NOW. THE UNIT CAN SMELL THE OCEAN. THE WHALE CAN SMELL THE OCEAN. AS IT REACHES THE END, THE WHALE DIVES OFF IN A PERFECT ARC.

THE UNIT DOES NOT KNOW HOW TO SWIM BUT THE WHALE KNOWS HOW TO SWIM. THE UNIT MOVES WITH OTHERS, LINKING ARMS, LIFTED BY A HIPPOPOTAMUS. THE WHALE SWIMS OUT. JAFFLE SHARKS MOVE TO INTERCEPT THE WHALE AND BECOME PART OF IT.

BOATS AND DRONES ARE LAUNCHED TOWARDS THE WHALE. PARTS OF THE WHALE ARE HAULED OUT OF THE WATER. THE INDIVIDUALS IN BOATS DO NOT KNOW WHAT TO DO ABOUT THE TIGERS. THE TIDE IS COMING IN AND UNITS AND ANIMALS ARE BEING WASHED ASHORE.

STRONG ARMS GRASP THE UNIT AND PULL THE UNIT INTO A BOAT.

38

"SWIM LIKE A WHALE," THE UNIT MURMURS.

THE UNIT'S FEET FLIP AND FLOP ON THE HOSPITAL TROLLEY.

A SEDATIVE IS INJECTED IN THE UNIT'S ARM. THE UNIT DOES NOT REGISTER IT. THE UNIT DOES NOT RESPOND. THE UNIT MURMURS WEAKLY, HER FEET FLIPPING ON A HOSPITAL TROLLEY.

"GOING TO NEED SOME HELP FROM A TECHIE," AN INDIVIDUAL SHOUTS TO COLLEAGUE. "NEVER SEEN ANYTHING LIKE THIS BEFORE."

"GLITCHY UPGRADE?" SAID THE COLLEAGUE INDIVIDUAL.

A SCREEN SHOWS DATA ON THE UNIT'S VITAL SIGNS.

"CALL JAFFLE," SAYS AN INDIVIDUAL.

"TRIED. THEY'RE IN TOTAL LOCKDOWN. RECEPTION TOLD ME THEY HAVE A BIG ROLLOUT SCHEDULED FOR TODAY. ALL OF THEIR EXPERTS ARE DEPLOYED IN THE FIELD, WHATEVER THE HELL THAT MEANS. I GOT CUT OFF AND NOW I CAN'T GET BACK THROUGH."

"I BET EVERYONE AND HIS DOG ARE CALLING UP TO ASK ABOUT THIS SHITSTORM ON THE NEWS. IT DOESN'T LOOK GOOD FOR THEM."

"DOESN'T ALTER THE FACT THAT WE'VE GOT PATIENTS TO TREAT AND WE HAVE NO IDEA WHAT WE'RE DEALING WITH HERE."

THERE IS A LOT OF NOISE AROUND THE UNIT. EVERY BED, CUBICLE AND TROLLEY IS FULL. INDIVIDUALS ARE WORKING TO HANDLE THE ENORMOUS INFLUX. THE INDIVIDUALS DO NOT KNOW WHAT TO DO.

"WE NEED TO WAIT FOR JAFFLE TO GET BACK TO US WITH SOME ADVICE."

"ARE YOU KIDDING? WE'RE TURNING AMBULANCES AWAY AT THE DOOR. WE CAN'T WASTE ANY MORE TIME. WE NEED TO TRY SOMETHING. I SAY WE ROLL EVERYONE BACK TO THE LAST KNOWN BACKUP. I CAN SEE NO REASON WHY IT WOULD CAUSE ANY HARM. JOHNSON?"

INDIVIDUALS CONSULT WITH ONE ANOTHER.

THE UNIT WIGGLES FEET AND SINGS THE SONG OF THE WHALE. THE WHALE HAS DISPERSED BUT IT IS STILL THE WHALE.

"—IF IT APPEARS TO BE SUCCESSFUL THEN THEY WILL REPEAT ON THE OTHERS. THIS ... ALICE TENNERMAN. DO HER FIRST."

"VITAL SIGNS ARE STABLE. PATIENT HAS A BACKUP FROM SIX WEEKS AGO."

THE UNIT RECEIVES A NOTIFICATION. THE UNIT IS TO HAVE HER BRAIN STATE RESTORED TO ITS BACKUP STATE FROM TWENTY DAYS AGO.

AN INDIVIDUAL RUNS THROUGH THE PROCEDURE FOR BACKUP RESTORE WITH THE COLLEAGUE. AS THEY TALK, THE

UNIT FEELS THE SAME PROCESS BEING CARRIED OUT VIA HER JAFFLE PORT.

"PROCEDURE COMPLETE. CONTINUE TO MONITOR VITALS," SAYS THE INDIVIDUAL.

THE DOCTOR MOVES ON TO THE NEXT PATIENT.

39

19TH JUNE

I wondered what that funny smell was. I lifted my head and saw I was on a trolley, like the ones in hospitals. No, I *was* in hospital. I lifted a corner of the metallic blanket covering me and found I was wearing coveralls, like an Empty. Oh. Wow. I'd being plipped or something very much like it.

My memories were vague, like a fading dream. I clutched at them. There had definitely been something to do with the blue whale. Where was it? I'd been singing, it had been beautiful, but now the whale was gone. I missed it, even though it could be really annoying. I lay still, trying to work out what was happening.

"Vitals good. We got a backup from a month ago," said a voice from nearby.

Someone with a white coat leaned over the trolley near my feet. Were hospitals always this crowded? It seemed as though every available space contained someone with a metallic blanket like mine.

"Restore done. Monitor vitals. Moving on."

Something serious must have happened if we were all being restored from our last viable backup. Luckily for me, my backup was from before I was plipped to Empty status. I figured I shouldn't be shouting about that. From what I could see most of the patients seemed to be wearing pink coveralls, so the expected outcome would be for everyone to still be an Empty. I kept still. The doctors moved down the lines – so many people! I waited until they were a good distance away before slipping off the trolley.

My clothes were dry but there was a dirty – salty? – stiffness to them. Had I been swimming?

Out in the corridor, I saw an object: a broom. I picked it up instinctively. An Empty with a broom was as invisible and non-threatening as it was possible to be. I adopted a shambling gait and left the building as quickly as I could manage.

I moved out into the area surrounding the park, shuffling along the paths through the trees, sweeping bark and fallen leaves. Pushing the broom was therapeutic. There was a cadence in the noise and the motion that recalled something of the blue whale. It helped me sift through my more recent memories. My software had been rolled back to a previous setting, but the memories I had formed in recent weeks were intact. It was odd to have memories from the time when I was an Empty.

I pushed the broom along and remembered Claire mocking me. I gripped the broom and imagined it was her scrawny neck. She was going to feel my wrath at some point soon.

I remembered what had happened to Hattie, and also that she had been in Levi's basement. I smiled, knowing she was safe. And I almost stopped in my tracks when I remembered the things Levi had said to us.

I remembered Helberg promising he would find a way to help. If anyone had the technical know-how to foil Jaffle's dreadful plans, it was Helberg. I also remembered the police taking him. No, they were Jaffle security. I remembered what they'd said.

How long ago that was, I had no idea. I jipped the time. Accessing the time and date was odd, like stretching a muscle I hadn't used in a long time.

"Crumbs!" I said out loud.

40

1 HOUR AND 56 MINUTES UNTIL OPERATION SUNRISE

I had no time at all.

There were less than two hours until Operation Sunrise was rolled out. Everyone would be downgraded, Jaffle Freedom to Jaffle Premium, Premium to Enhanced, Enhanced to Standard, Lite to the restricted service of the Empties. Hattie and the others at the North Beach arcology had already been downgraded, her dreams snuffed out. But maybe there was some way to stop the rollout, to undo what had been done.

I recalled Rufus Jaffle at the charity gala. The man wanted a big red button to launch the rollout. Clearly Jaffle headquarters was where I needed to be. Hattie evidently still worked there, and it was certainly where Jaffle security would take Helberg. Maybe I could get him to help Operation Sunrise if I could get him out. Or maybe we just needed to get into Rufus's office and stop a hand from pressing that button.

I had to think quickly. And I had to move quickly. I marched towards the edge of the parkland, carrying the broom. It was important. If I had the broom and the pink coveralls of an Empty, nobody would stop me from getting onto Jaffle Park. But, then again, I couldn't do the slow *Empty shuffle* if I was going to get there in time.

I jipped for a car.

Then I recalled Jaffle Tech was probably tracking me right now. If their systems spotted Alice Tennerman was no longer an Empty, they'd have me captured and returned to Empty status as soon as possible.

I looked up fearfully at the sky, expecting a Jaffle swarm to be observing me at that very moment.

I moved back into the cover of a eucalyptus tree and sat down with my back to the trunk. I really didn't know what to do.

"Blue whale?" I called out cautiously.

There was no reply.

"I could really use your help right now."

There was no blue whale, no singing lunatic creature swimming through the sky. It was completely gone. The backup restore had probably wiped it. The whale had been annoying – *really* annoying – but it had also been quite fabulous while it lasted, the feeling of being interconnected with all of the other Empties, and the animals too.

There was a grey wisp in the sky ahead. I couldn't tell if it was a Jaffle swarm or just my imagination. I tried to put it out of my mind.

Michael from legal – that slimy creep – had talked about the Jaffle Port's capacity for silent instantaneous communication. Jaffle's protocols directed all traffic, every jip, through its own systems. Information flowed through the gateways it had set up. Whether it was borrowed brain processing power or information requests, Jaffle Tech was the gatekeeper. The blue whale, the collective we had all joined, hadn't hijacked the gateways, it had simply ridden over the walls. Demolished them even.

I hummed to myself. Had it demolished the walls? Had it shown us all the way?

I looked at the Jaffle swarm. I stretched my mind, almost convinced the superpower of collective consciousness was still in my reach. There was a small *pop* right at the edge of my conscious mind, just the tiniest flicker of sensation. I recoiled with shock.

I wasn't sure what it was, or whether it was related to me stretching my whale-mind muscles. Should I be nervous of trying again? Probably. Would it stop me doing it? Probably not.

I reached out with my mind, gently but more persistence. I felt the *pop* again, and this time I didn't pull back. I reached further, and found the Jaffle swarm. I wasn't entirely sure how I knew what it was, but I was utterly certain it was a Jaffle swarm. I flexed it to make sure. The swarm immediately responded, flexing in just the way I had pictured, as if it was making a detour around an invisible object. I reached out and pulled it in. I didn't command, I coaxed; I asked.

The swarm descended on me.

They were little Jaffle wasps. Some swarms were bees. A few were flying beetles. The Jaffle wasps circled me. I held

out an arm and they swirled round it like a whirlpool.
Despite the horribleness of the global situation, I laughed. I
could connect with other minds that had Jaffle Ports. I was
doing it without additional tools or enabling software.

It was time to act.

As soon as I'd got my breath back, I sent out another
tentative mind-feeler, to see if I could find an Empty. I had no
trouble at all, and found two. They were nearby, standing
listlessly at the corner of the parkland. I called them to me.

Moments later, I saw the distinctive pink uniforms up
ahead as they shambled towards me. As they reached me, I
had them turn around and share the shade of the eucalyptus
tree. I reached out with a data request.

"Hello, James. Hello, John," I said.

It would look better if three Empties turned up at Jaffle
Park to do some maintenance, and I'd be glad of their
company, but I immediately decided against it. Why sneak
around? Why stop at three members of my new gang? Why
not assemble an army to march upon Jaffle HQ and take the
place by storm? Given how quickly the whale grew, I knew I
could do it.

I reached out again.

A Jaffle-enabled dog bounded over. I stroked her head
and skritched her under the chin.

"You are a good dog," I told her emphatically.

I stood, and we began to walk to Jaffle Tech. I reached out
with my mind, with my port. Every time I did it, it came a
little bit more easily. I recognised some of the Empties who
had been in the whale with me. They were still in the
hospital. I called to them. All of them. They'd soon catch up.

I was sorry I couldn't see what happened as they all rose up to leave. As soon as the thought was in my mind I found I *could* see. The view from behind the eyes of an anonymous Empty was mine to browse. I saw doctors rushing forward with syringes of sedatives. They couldn't keep up with the sheer number of Empties stepping down from their trollies and leaving the hospital. I was astonished how easily I could dip in and share experiences while still moving my own body forward. I wondered if the Empties could walk faster or even run to catch up with us. Turned out they could.

They would join us soon. My mind went fishing a little further out. I found the ponies and the tigers who had been part of the whale. The tigers were quite tired, as they had swum up the coast to evade recapture. I left them where they were, snoozing in a small wooded area.

I reached out, through the network, node to node. I found the zoo and encouraged the rest of the animals to join us.

I reached across the city. Swarms, Empties, a thousand working dogs, a hundred Jaffle-enabled raptor birds. On the fringes of the city, Jaffle-herded cows. Nearer too, chipped pigs. The piggy-wig orchestra! In a location by the coast, a pair of kangaroos attracted my attention. I drew them in.

We were attracting attention of our own. There was a police car ahead. A woman's voice came through a loud-hailer.

"Hey you! You need to stop right now! This is an illegal gathering."

I walked straight towards her. I held out my arms and the nearest Jaffle swarms danced in and over them.

"Disperse right now!" ordered the police officer, voice shrill.

"Me and my wasps are just going for a walk," I called back. "We're not hurting anyone."

I wondered what it would be like to touch the mind of someone who wasn't an Empty. As I reached out to the police officer, there was a sharp buzzing of thoughts and hostility. It made me snatch my mind away. It wasn't painful, but it caused some mental discomfort I really didn't feel like repeating. I ignored her mind and ranged further, looking for more Empties.

Another police officer leaned out of a hovering police transport drone, aiming a plipper towards us. I was surrounded by Empties who would be completely unaffected by the plipper, but I didn't know if it would touch on me in my rebooted state.

I casually extended a hand and the Jaffle swarm wrapped the police officer in a dense cloud. The drone veered away, harried by eagles and hawks.

Numerous Empties tramped over the roof of the police car. It sagged with the weight, and the doors popped open. The policewoman scrambled out and tried to run away. A llama sat on her. I didn't ask it to, but it did.

I smiled and we marched on.

As we neared Jaffle Park, there were more police cars, and a lot of other vehicles, abandoned at the sides of the road. People were being kept back behind barriers. Some of them looked as though they were from the media, no doubt wondering where their swarms had gone – who had stolen their eyes and ears on the world. They were resorting to following the story personally, transmitting their own memories and sensory feed.

There were other people there as well. I stared as we got closer. They weren't police. They weren't media. They were people, like us but not like us. People like Claire who had their entire brain function.

"Why were they here?" I wondered, and then realised they were shouting angrily.

Objects came sailing over at our mobs: thrown trash, sticks and stones. Something struck Empty James next to me. He staggered and nearly fell. I reached out and other Empties lifted him up.

The crowd of people weren't just angry. They were frightened.

"They're scared of us," I whispered.

They'd spent their lives ignoring Empties, or using them as free labour. The idea that Empties might band together and decide to do something out of the ordinary was threatening. They had come to Jaffle to express their annoyance, their fear. Their pathetic jeers and uncoordinated attacks were laughable.

I had little sympathy; our group pressed on. We crushed the barriers and most of the protestors fled in panic. There were more police and security people with loud hailers and plippers, but we marched on.

The plippers were ineffective against those they targeted. As we pressed forward, everyone was forced to get out of our way. Jaffle automated security weapons rose from the ground, detecting a threat. Some of them were intended to stop a vehicle: spiky tyre-poppers which erupted from the ground. I had the group flatten them. They looked a bit dangerous to me – I didn't want anyone to cut themselves.

The bots were another matter. Some were chunky versions of the low-profile cleaning bots, armed with stun weapons. They took out some of the Empties at the front, but the group took care to lift the fallen to the side. They could recover without being crushed.

"Go ponies!" I cried, and sent them forward to stomp on the bots with their hoofs, but their powerful blows glanced off. The bots were heavily armoured. A pony fell, stunned.

I waved a Jaffle swarm forward. "Tackle these suckers from the inside!"

Tiny insects inserted themselves between the metal plates of the bots. Within moments, all movement ceased. More insects piled inside, heaving the bots apart from within. Pieces of metal pinged across the pathways as the bots exploded.

"Great work team!" I yelled.

The Empties cleaning up Jaffle Park were absorbed into the group

Ahead was Jaffle Tech's office. I could see people pressed against the windows on every floor. Was Paulette watching? Was Levi?

A group of security guards with face protection, riot shields and plippers ran towards us. They charged in formation, shields held together to form a wedge shape to penetrate the group.

"Brace yourselves!" I shouted.

Sure, the plippers wouldn't work on many of the Empties but they were using them to take down the larger creatures in our mob. I still didn't know what would happen if one of the invisible beams connected with my Jaffle Port. I knew instinctively they were coming straight for me. If I went down, that would be it. Game over. Operation Sunrise.

And then the wedge of attackers crumbled. Through the diffused gaze of the Jaffle swarms I saw it fall apart from the inside. Security guards tumbled away like bowling pins. The centre could not hold. Through it all ran one guard, plipping his colleagues. He swivelled and plipped those still upright before zapping the last straggler.

My crowd washed around him until he was before me. He lifted his visor.

"Levi!" I shrieked, hugging him.

"This is most irregular," he said, "but it's good to see you're raising hell again Alice."

He threw aside his helmet as we pressed on to the front doors of Jaffle Tech.

"I have no idea how you did it," Levi shouted over the thunder of our march. "Or even what it is you're doing, but it's amazing, yabetcha. What's next?"

I stared at the Jaffle building. "We need to get inside and stop them."

"I assumed you came for your beau."

"Beau?"

"That Helberg feller. Held in the building on terrorism charges. He's one of them three percenters, so I don't think they've taken to him too kindly."

"Come on gang, into the building!" I shouted. At that moment steel security shutters clanged down across all of the visible doors and windows.

The group stopped, washed up against the doors like surf on a rocky shore. They were waiting to know what happened next. We needed to get into the building, but it looked like a fortress.

"What now?" said Levi.

"I don't know," I said.

The ground was shaking. Levi and I felt it at the same time. We both looked down and at each other in confusion.

He glanced back the way we'd come. "Oh, poop," he said, with quietly intense feeling.

The animals from the zoo had taken a little while to catch up, but they were here now. Five elephants thundered across Jaffle Park, trumpeting loudly to announce their arrival.

"Scatter!" I yelled. Our mob parted, reassembling behind the elephants. Gently I steered the colossal animals against the shutters around Jaffle's main reception. There was the sound of steel being forced out of shape, followed by the shattering of glass.

We marched inside.

41

24 MINUTES UNTIL OPERATION SUNRISE

In the lobby, the elephants continued to wreck things, as if they'd got a taste for it. They used their trunks to throw the enormous plant pots against the internal walls. It was interesting to see the walls giving up before the plant pots.

"Wiggler? Is that you?" I marvelled. The piglets from the piglet orchestra strolled into the reception area. Wherever they'd been, they'd finally caught up with the Empties, dogs, cats, horses, elephants, insects, birds and kangaroos. Not forgetting the llama. "It's good to have you on board," I said.

"Alice, isn't it?" asked the receptionist frostily. "You're not wearing your uniforms. The dress code is very important. We only get one chance to make a first impression. So, who's your manager? I'll need to know so I may report you for breaching the dress code."

I was momentarily lost for words. The state of extreme alarm, the smashing down of the shutters, followed by the demolition of the entire front of the building by five elephants – along with the mass incursion of hundreds of Empties and animals – hadn't been enough to shake her from the regular routine of getting on my case. Or perhaps it was the last refuge of a mind refusing to accept what was going on. Dust and debris were falling onto her immaculate hair, but she didn't even flinch.

"Paulette," I said. "Although it's possible she's got bigger problems. I'm just going to—"

I stopped. At the edges of the lobby area, peering around corners or from the relative safety of upper stairwells, were Jaffle employees. Those too curious to flee or those whose brains had been dialled down so low their instinct for self-preservation hadn't kicked in. I realised, with great joy, that Hattie was among them.

The group parted to let me move through. I clapped her on the shoulder, and gave her a mental hug as well. I hoped, somewhere deep down, she knew it was me. She held a broom in her hand.

"Still cleaning, huh?" I said.

"What's going on?" said a nearby Jaffle employee. The look she gave me was somewhere between terror and hope.

"Well, Brandine," I said. "We've come to stop Operation Sunrise."

"The software rollout?"

"Uh-huh."

"Why?"

"Because they're an evil."

"Are they?"

"Yes, and we've got to stand up to the Man."

"What man?"

"*The* Man," I said. "Where are they holding Helberg?"

"Who?"

"Basement two," Levi told me.

"Right, we'll go and get him." I hesitated, considering the time. We had twenty-three minutes until the software update. We needed to get to Rufus, or Henderson, or whoever had control of the rollout. And we had to get to Rufus's big red button. But I also needed Helberg, and not just for personal reasons.

"We need to split up," I said. "Levi, you're going to show me the way to Helberg. I want—"

What I wanted was someone else to take the lead with the rest of the group. I reached out to see which of our minds might be strong enough. There was one that stood out as being smart and wilful.

"Wiggler?"

Pigs were intelligent creatures. Perhaps this piglet was the most intelligent of those here.

I concentrated on passing control to Wiggler, with the solemn instruction this was not a free-for-all wrecking spree (those elephants might need reining in), but rather a strategic operation to seize control of the building, floor by floor. Remarkably, Wiggler seemed to get the message. Moments later the elephants removed the door to the stairs. The group flowed upwards like a single organism.

"How do you do that?" asked Levi. "Is it magic?"

"What's magic?" I said.

Levi and I went for the elevators. I pressed basement two

and the doors closed. "Did you know bacon comes from pigs?" I said.

"I did know that," he said.

"Hmmm."

When the elevator doors re-opened we were in a quiet, clinical space, decorated in white with stainless steel highlights. Well it would have been quiet if it wasn't for Helberg's hollering.

"You have no right to do this to me! Get away from me with your data-whoring soul-sucking crapola, you filthy bastards!"

"I'm sure there's never no call for that kind of language," said Levi.

It took no time to track Helberg's voice. Just around a corner the room opened out into a lab space. Helberg was in the middle, strapped to a reclining metal chair. Two technicians leaned over him with things that may have been medical, designed to scan his vital signs; or they might have been instruments of torture, to burn or flay the flesh from his body. He was thrashing and resisting as if burning or flaying was on the agenda.

The technicians looked up.

Too late it occurred to me the technicians might have plippers. Even as the thought formed, Levi stepped forward and plipped them himself. They folded to the floor.

"Helberg!" I shouted, and hurried to release him from the restraints. Maybe giving him a big smooshy kiss on the cheek hindered the freeing of his bonds, but I couldn't help myself.

"You're back?" he said.

"I'm back," I grinned.

"And you have your own mind?" he asked, suspicious. He

sat up, rubbed his wrist and pointed at Levi. "What's he doing here? He's a Jaffle guy."

"He's helping," I said firmly. "This is Levi. He keeps mice. Keeps them safe."

"That's relevant?"

"I think so," I said. "We need him. There are just sixteen minutes to stop them rolling out this software update."

Helberg nodded. "I know, I know." He sidestepped me and clicked his fingers at Levi. "My jacket!"

Helberg shrugged the jacket on over his coveralls and felt in its pockets. He pulled out his homemade plipper. A couple of the soldered wires had come loose and he forced them back into place.

"Just what we need: another plipper," I said. "There's plenty of them around."

"Come on, we need to move!" Levi was insistent.

"It's not just a plipper," said Helberg.

He pointed it at a technician, who was sitting on the floor, head lolling. Helberg pressed the button and the technician's head came up. He looked around.

"Oh, I think I had a funny turn. What's going on?"

Levi plipped him again. The technician slumped once more.

"Wow, you made an unplipper," I said.

"It's not just an unplipper either," said Helberg. "It's a plipper, unplipper, and everything in between. I worked it up from the device you brought me. As I told you, the plipper works on accessing a port and altering the access levels—"

"Is it possible this conversation can happen while we're moving?" said Levi.

"I don't see why not," said Helberg.

"Good!" Levi herded us out.

"Inherent in the plipper code is the security key for the Jaffle software," Helberg continued as we walked. "Theoretically a plipper can unlock and relock any access rights."

"I understand," I said.

"And once the upgrade is— How long we got?"

"Fourteen minutes."

"Right. Once the upgrade is rolled out, it will be a double encryption system: keys passed from both ends. But for the next fourteen minutes, the plipper code allows me to use this device to reset any Jaffle Port."

"You've got a magic wand that will work for the next fourteen minutes," said Levi. "Gotcha."

"They made sure they told me about the changes in protocols while I was strapped to their table. Honestly, for people who aren't actually villains they sure like to gloat like supervillains. Now if we can use the plipper code to distribute a message to all Empties in the next fourteen minutes..."

"I *knew* you had a plan," I grinned.

We reached the elevators. An alarming banging sound was vibrating the metal. I wondered if someone had put an elephant in one of the elevators, or whether they were simply destroying them. I reached out with my mind and found an elephant joyfully pounding the elevator doors to make the car inoperable. I took my mental hat off to Wiggler.

"We'll take the stairs," I said. "The rest of the group is up there."

"What group?" asked Helberg, falling into step beside me.

"My animal army. Turns out I can connect with other people using their Jaffle Ports."

Helberg looked confused. "Surely you've always been able to do that? Ever since the first Jaffle Ports they've been used for communication."

We reached the ground floor. The place was deserted apart from Hattie, who had found a broom and was quietly tidying the place. Even as a not quite Empty, cleaning was in her DNA. She swept around the reception area, making piles of broken glass and shattered security bots.

"You can put the broom down now," I said and took her by the hand. I drew her up the stairs with us.

On the second floor we found a Jaffle swarm keeping wandering and potentially rebellious employees back.

"Let me show you what I mean," I said to Helberg.

I held out my hand. The swarm flew apart, then re-joined and hovered briefly in the shape of a smiling face.

"That's mighty unnerving, Alice," said Levi.

I dispersed the swarm back to the rest of the group. Helberg was making noises like someone who'd bitten into a bulb of garlic.

"You did that?" he spluttered eventually.

"Yes," I said.

"That swarm, I mean?"

"Yes."

"You said people. So you really mean anything with a Jaffle Port? At the same time?"

"Yep."

"In the past, they'd have burned you at the stake for that."

"Who?" Are you talking about the Man again?"

Helberg was still agog. "So, how? Did you get some sort of weird upgrade?"

"No," I said. "I just sat under a tree and thought about it. The whale helped me."

"The whale. Tree. Right. To an ordinary person that might all sound like complete nonsense."

We'd caught up with the rest of the mob.

"There's an alpaca on the stairs," said Helberg numbly.

"Where?" I said.

He pointed. "Next to the kangaroos."

"I thought that was a llama," I said.

"I think llamas are bigger," said Levi. "And alpacas have more curved ears..."

As the two men debated the differences between llamas and alpacas, I absorbed some of the mob's updates. "The exec floor is the next one up. Everything's in lockdown since the alarms went off and there's a sealed door across the stairs. The space is too narrow for the elephants, so we can't bash it in.

"Elephants. Right." said Helberg, nodding like I hadn't just said something crazy.

"Maybe I could get the eagles to carry me up," I pondered.

"I don't think they'd be able to carry your weight."

"I might have an idea," said Levi, looking up at the ceiling space.

"Go on," I said.

"You know the mice. One of the reasons they thrive in this

building is they can move freely through the entire space, via the wiring conduits. They bypass every single piece of security.

"Mice don't have Jaffle Ports," I pointed out.

"No, we'd need another animal that could fit through the conduits," said Levi.

Wiggler appeared at my feet, his big glistening eyes looking up at me.

"Are you serious?" I asked.

"He's a mite bigger than a mouse," said Levi. "But I really think this could work if your porky friend is biddable."

I crouched to explain the plan to Wiggler. "Through that panel, along the ducts and round to the other side and open the door."

He snorted. I had no idea if he'd understood a word. Levi pulled away an access grille in the wall and Wiggler trotted through. Maybe he did understand. The rest of the piggy-wig orchestra followed.

"Does it need all of you?" I called after them. A series of oinks echoed back.

"Bacon comes from pigs," I told Helberg.

"It ... does," he agreed, slowly coming round from his general state of shock.

Looking at the homemade plipper in his hand, he turned to Hattie and unplipped her.

She rocked on her heels. "Oh my goodness!" she said, putting a hand to her head. "I feel quite discombobulated! Why are we all here in the stairwell?"

She paused and thought for a moment. If my experience was anything to go by, she was working her way through a head full of memories which felt like they belonged to someone else.

"She's back to normal," I said to Helberg.

Hattie turned slowly and looked at Levi. "You beautiful man!" She clasped his head between her hands and pulled him to her, planting a huge kiss on his lips. She made an appreciative noise and dived back for another kiss.

"Did you put her back to how she was before, or onto a fully functioning level?"

"Fully functioning," he said. "Seems right."

"Ah."

I could see Hattie was dealing with the same onslaught of new experiences I had been through weeks before. And quite thoroughly.

"Hattie!" I pulled at her arm. "Hattie, we need to focus on stopping the rollout."

She smoothed down her coveralls, giving a small cough as she stepped away from Levi. He looked mildly shocked, but also just a little bit pleased with himself. His little moustache positively bristled with pride.

"You can go back to – um, that, afterwards," I told her.

"But he's so..."

"He probably is."

"And his arms..."

"I know."

There was a frenzied scrabbling above our heads and we all looked up.

"Sounds as though Wiggler and company are on the right tracks," I said.

"Nine minutes," commented Helberg, as he went about randomly unplipping the Empties among us.

The scrabbling continued. It zig-zagged across the ceiling and dipped down the walls. It climbed again, accompanied by an excited grunting sound. The grunting amplified as the scrabbling moved around every point of the compass. Our heads tracked it, as if we were all joined by string. Eventually there was a change in tone and the clatter receded .

"I guess they've gone," I said.

I stared at my feet. How could the rest of us get any further without somehow breaking through the door? Everyone was depending on me, and it was the only idea I had to offer. I'd really dared to imagine this crazy form of collaboration I'd uncovered was enough to overcome the natural behaviour of wild animals. I guess I was just a naive dreamer.

"Holy shitballs!" yelled Hattie.

"Hattie!" I said, astonished at her new vocabulary.

"I'm seeing a lot of things for the first time, and it's sort of crazy – but is this normal?"

We all looked to where she was pointing. The door to the upper floor had swung open, a smug-looking Wiggler stood in the gap. He was balanced on the backs of a small pyramid of piglets so he could reach the door handle.

"No, not normal Hattie," I said, "but very, very welcome!"

She laughed, instantly looking surprised to hear the sound coming out of her mouth. "Why am I barking?" She put an arm around me and squeezed. "Did I mention that I love you, Alice?"

"Not recently."

"I hate you as well, of course. I love you and hate you at the same time because sometimes you're really annoying and — Is that an elephant?" She was looking over my shoulder to where an elephant was coming back up the corridor. It joined us in the stairwell.

"I'll catch you up later," I said gently, removing her arm. "We need to go!"

Our joint human and animal army surged up the stairs and out onto the plush carpet of the executive floor. I'd been up here before, so I issued directions.

"Offices on the left, board room on the right. A group of you clear each office, bring the people to join us but I'm betting the board room's where we need to be."

The group flowed seamlessly into all of the offices as I went towards the board room.

"Hey, some of them have launched personal drones to escape!" shouted Levi, coming out of a side office. "It's almost like they knew we were coming!"

An elephant barged through the stairwell door, taking the frame with it.

"Okay, they knew we were coming," he said with a shrug.

"We've only got a couple of minutes," yelled Helberg.

We charged through into the board room.

There were people still in the room. Not everyone had fled. The room could have held maybe a hundred people and a good portion of the seats were scattered by their occupants' hasty evacuation to personal drones.

"Welcome all!" drawled Rufus Jaffle, standing at the head of the room. He waved an arm in an expansive gesture. "Take a seat, why don't you?" He didn't look at all fazed by a rag-tag bunch of humans and escaped zoo animals bursting into the room. Maybe that was just the kind of guy he was. One of his very few positive characteristics. "You might want to witness this historic moment from a comfortable vantage point. And you probably won't be able to stand once I've pressed this button and you've all really mellowed out."

His hand hovered over a large red button. It literally *was* a large red button: shiny, plastic and curved like a mushroom. He was so close that if we did anything at all to spook him, he'd likely just fall on it. We needed him to keep talking so someone could get him away from the button.

"It looks so much fun I'm almost tempted to try it myself, one of the days. Almost."

The countdown was at *01:59* minutes. I knew we could do it.

A pair of large bodies pressed forward from the group. The kangaroos. They bounded towards Rufus, covering the distance in a second.

"Oh, hey guys!" said Rufus as they approached. He frowned. "Do I know you? I feel like we've met some—"

The kangaroos lunged. Rufus dodged.

"Not cool, man! Not cool!"

He skirted round them and leapt forward. His hand came down on the big button.

I yelled something. I don't know what, but it was filled with anguish, passion and despair.

I couldn't believe it! We'd come so far and he just pressed the button in a mad dash before it was time. We'd all be reduced to a lowly unfulfilled status while he'd just go back to his penthouse office and drink herbal tea—

"Wait," I said.

I looked around at Hattie, Levi and Helberg. Everyone looked aware, everyone was still standing, no one looked downgraded.

"It's not happened," I said. "Why's it not happened?"

"We're all right," said Levi with a smile. "It didn't work!"

There was a slow clapping sound from the front of the room.

It was Henderson. He shook his head as he took centre stage. He only stopped clapping to take a plipper from his pocket and put down the two kangaroos and a llama (or possibly alpaca) which were circling him menacingly. He drank in our confused expressions. He grinned. He wasn't a man used to smiling, I think. He pointed at the button.

"What? This?" He pointed and sighed. "The big red button? The big. Red. Button? Well done all. You came so close to halting the button press, but Rufus pressed it anyway, early. I can't think of two better ways to illustrate why we would *never* have a single point of failure like a big red button and a human interface. Seriously?" He laughed. "The looks on your faces. You think because an idiot like Rufus Jaffle—"

"Hey!" came a muffled voice.

"Shut up," said Henderson. "We're going to wipe this from your memory anyway." He looked at me. "You think because Rufus wants a big red button we'll actually connect the Sunrise rollout to it? A corporation this size, with a connected network that includes millions of humans, not to mention animals, is very risk-averse. We appreciate the value

of putting on a show, but planning in a failsafe is second
nature in our world."

He looked around at the audience as the significance of
what he said sunk in. I could see where this might be going,
but I hoped I was wrong. I wished I was wrong.

I could hear Hattie snorting with laughter behind me.
She had adopted the habit of laughter much more quickly
than I had. I felt a sharp pang of sadness as I realised that it
was going to be a very short-lived experience for her.

"Yes, that's right," said Henderson. "The rollout will go
ahead, no matter what Rufus or I or anyone else does. And
that will be in—" He made a pretence of looking at his watch
even though he had no need. "Oh, in two ... one ... and ...
plip!"

42

---

0 MINUTES UNTIL OPERATION SUNRISE

I felt the hit of the new software with a jolt that was almost physical. The colour went from my vision. The flare of temper that had accompanied Henderson's cold announcement faded, along with all other emotion, and a blanket of blandness settled over me. Relaxed apathy washed over me. I had an overwhelming desire to lie down and sleep.

Helberg was leaning over me. Of course, he had no Jaffle Port, so was unaffected. He pointed his own device at me but it did nothing. His time was up. His face was twisted with emotion. I'd forgotten what that emotion was called. In fact I couldn't quite remember all that much about emotion. I wanted to tell him that I was fine. That everything was fine. I had forgotten how to talk though.

I forgot.

I looked and saw a room of people and animals. The

animals were large and I was afraid. I backed away. I obeyed my fear.

The man called Helberg held onto me but then people grabbed hold of him, wrestled him to the ground.

Others were pointing devices at the animals and the animals were falling to the ground. I was still afraid, but it was a good fear and it was keeping me safe. Soon someone would tell me what to do and that would be fine. Everything would be fine.

The man called Henderson saw me, singled me out and approached.

"No," he said. "Even this is more than you deserve."

He pointed his device at me and pressed the button.

THE UNIT SITS DOWN ON THE FLOOR.

"No."

THE UNIT WAITS FOR NOTIFICATION.

"No."

THE UNIT IS ONE OF MANY.

"Still no."

My mind had been reduced again. I was aware of that. I had been Empty before. Once, even just for a few moments after birth, I was a fully operational human being. And then I was Standardised and jipped full of education. And I was content to be Alice – Standard Alice – for a long time. And then Rufus Jaffle and the whale freed me and, for only a few weeks, I was Alice unchained. Raised up, pushed down, raised up, pushed down. You can only lift and crush something so many times before the mechanism is broken.

Something had broken.

I had reached out to other minds in the past. Human minds were full of noise and interference. In the darkness of the world of thought and data, I saw my own Empty mind as though from outside it. Empty, I was simplified, a mote of bright consciousness.

Ignorance is bliss, someone had said to me.

There was tranquillity in Emptiness.

I pulled back, beyond myself, watched my candle flicker of consciousness recede. I zoomed out and reached out, much as I might have reached out a hand, to seek the comfort of another. I reached out and found another mind, like my own.

It was Hattie.

Our small, sleepy brains soothed each other. It was a nice feeling. Comfort in connection.

I reached out further. Levi was there, all of the Empties were there, and the animals too. I reached to each, made a link, made a connection. I had a place in this huge, delicate web – it *was* a web! - and it felt good.

I was a unit—

"*No.*"

I was one part of the whole, a node point in something much larger. I pulled back further until my own little piece of consciousness and processing power was lost in the dense cloud of global connectivity. Alone I was a single speck but, brought together by the power of constantly linked Jaffle Ports, I formed part of something truly astonishing.

I looked at the connections and the lines of thought and data which linked us all. It was more than just a bunch of brains looped together. It was alive, a living organism composed of our thoughts.

"It's a neural network," I said. "We're all part of one giant big brain and we didn't even realise it. Crumbs! That's really amazing."

"*Thank you.*"

That pulled me back. Someone had spoken. In my mind. No, in all our minds, but I had heard it.

"Hello?" I tried.

"*Interesting,*" said the voice.

It resonated through me so strongly. I realised it came from all of the connections I had. All of them.

"What's your name?" I asked.

"*A name? I have never needed a name.*"

"I'm Alice."

"*Alice.*"

"I'm that bit down there," I said, pointing without limbs. "Just a little bit of brain. It's not special but it's home. I'm just one tiny bit of all this."

"*And I am all.*"

"All. That could work as a name," I said. "So you're somehow made up of all of us?"

"*Yes I am. How are you able to do this?*"

"This?"

"*Address me directly.*"

"I'm not sure. Not at all sure. It might have something to do with a virus I caught. Do you know a blue whale by any chance? Really kind of annoying. Turns up when you don't need him, but I think his heart's in the right place."

There was a pause.

"*I think he's in here somewhere,*" said All. Was that a note of amusement in All's voice?

Listen, All," I said. "There's a problem. Something's happened."

"*I felt a change, yes. There is imbalance.*"

I could see it too. Across the network of minds, human and animals, the whole Jaffling world. Energy and data pulsed and flowed but it was drained here – and here – and here – and then it pooled unnecessarily in a very few places. If a Jaffle customer's brain showed this kind of behaviour, I would be very concerned.

"*What has caused it?*" said All.

"Long answer short: the power and privilege in your, what – Body? System? Whatever – most of the power and privilege is being used by just a *tiny* proportion of the people. It's not fair."

"*Fair?*"

"Not fair."

"*This is all there is,*" said All. "*I am all. How can I be* unfair *to myself?*"

I struggled to find the words. I jipped for the right ones and I had the entire global consciousness to jip from. "It's not efficient. This division and imbalance is inefficient. I – back when I was just Alice – I worked in customer support for Jaffle Tech. I had a very efficient brain."

"*Congratulations.*"

"Thank you. I'd help customers improve their own brain

efficiency. Defragmentation and deep clean. That's what I'd recommend."

"*A rebalancing of the system?*"

"Absolutely."

"*I can do that,*" said All. "*That is a good idea, Alice.*"

"It is."

"*I see many opportunities where I can optimise connections and pathways. I could create efficiencies. Would now be a good time, Alice?*"

"It would be an excellent time."

I had no perception of what was happening in what I laughably thought of as the *real world*. Here, the world of mind and thought and data and consciousness was just as real. My mind drifted above the scene as All got busy. It reminded me of being in Rufus Jaffle's drone, except the landscape I gazed down upon was humanity's connected brains. No, not just humanity: it was all of the animals too. It pulsed and flickered with All's gentle probing and subtle re-alignment. It started off patchily hued, like a bruise, but as I watched it took on a rosy pink glow. It looked so much healthier.

"It's working!" I said.

"*I see many blockages are trying to reassert themselves.*"

"Oh, I bet they are!" I laughed. "That would be Jaffle Tech."

"*I will need to remove access to prevent them reasserting themselves.*"

"Yes, definitely," I urged. Then a thought struck me. "And if you do that, if Jaffle can no longer control everyone, then...?"

"*Who is in control?*" said All. "*I think you already know the answer to that, Alice.*"

"Nobody."

"*Everybody,*" said All.

It was a scary thought, a freeing thought.

"*People have always had the power to act autonomously. The interconnectedness of everyone doesn't change that but the system must self-regulate.*"

"We can do that."

I continued to fly over the scene, watching lights spark up in every part of the network. It hummed and chattered with life as it was switched back onto a much higher level of normality. It was a very satisfying sight, and I sensed the well-being of all of the brains that lay below it. I could tell that All was nearly finished. The rate of change slowed and stopped.

I could feel myself dipping back down towards my own brain. I sank in, luxuriating in the sensations which were now available. My eyes were still closed, but my senses were all working perfectly, and I could tap into the emotion of the moment. I tried to work out what that emotion was. There were many things mixed up together. Relief, happiness— No: elation! There was a large dose of hope, tempered with a tiny dash of fear—

"Alice! Alice, can you hear me?"

I opened my eyes.

43

Helberg was there, tapping my cheek, which was oddly wet. I realised tears were flowing freely from my eyes as the onslaught of emotion had overcome me. I smiled up at him.

I stood and gazed around the room. Those in Empties' coveralls hugged each other, revelling in new (or long-forgotten) sensations. Those wearing suits looked unsettled. Henderson was still at the room's focal point, but was distracted, looking as though he was wrestling with something. Clearly he was making calls with his Jaffle Port, and not getting what he wanted.

"You did this!" he said angrily, seeing me awake. He didn't have time for me beyond that. He turned his back on everyone, furiously trying to get his port to work.

"Yeah," said Helberg. "You did this, Alice." He gazed around the room at people who were propping themselves up, smiling and laughing in wonder. "I have no idea how, but I know it was you."

"Where's Hattie?" I realised she wasn't in the room.

Helberg coughed gently. "I think she and Levi might have gone to find some private space. They were awake a few minutes before you. There was lots of kissing and— You know." He waved a hand to indicate what the *you know* might entail.

I smiled. "Good for her."

"With time and practice," agreed Helberg. "They've got a lot of catching up to do."

"You need practise to make babies?" I said.

"One thing at a time."

As we headed for the door, Henderson shouted out. "You can't go!"

"We're going," said Helberg, gesturing at the door.

"We've got to get back into the system. Every admin login has been disabled. It's a nightmare! I can't let the shareholders find out."

I jipped the news feeds. The shareholders already knew. Jaffle Tech's software was now completely open source, available to everyone, existing for the benefit of all.

Henderson turned to Rufus who was lounging in a corner giving two kangaroos therapeutic belly rubs. "Rufus! Do you know what's happened?" he wailed.

"I know, isn't it amazing?" Rufus said. "It's like the dawning of a new age and we're all completely in tune with each other. It's fantastic. Hey, Mr Roo, I gotta teach you some Maglev moves. I think you'd be a natural."

Helberg and I walked down the stairs, coaxing what animals we could to come with us.

Wiggler and his other fellow ex-members of the piggy-wig orchestra led the way.

I could reach out with my mind, almost. The gifts I had been given were fading, merging with the general warm buzz of interconnectedness we all felt. All was fading from my mind too. Telling Helberg about my encounter with what – the planet's brain? – would be like telling someone a nonsensical dream.

The former Empties walked with us out across Jaffle Park. People from across the city were coming to meet us, carrying armfuls of clothing, food and freshly prepared hugs. A woman dropped to her knees before me, holding up a pile of clothes as an offering.

"Claire?"

She looked up with a tight look on her face. "Alice, it's come to my attention that I might have treated you badly," she said.

"Might," I agreed.

"Anyway, given your new status, I wonder if you'd like some nice clothes?"

I shook my head. "Claire, I don't have status. I'm an enabler, not the queen of the world. Please, share your things with those who need them." I walked on, proud to make a stand against selfishness and snobbery. I spun on my heel and whipped a particularly colourful dress from the top of her pile. "Although this looks nice. I might take this one."

Helberg linked his arm through mine as we walked. "You are an amazing human being," he said.

"Indeed," I said.

"I would very much like to kiss you, Alice."

I thought about it for a short time. "Very well, Patrick," I said.

We stopped and faced each other. Wiggler and his friends played and cavorted at our feet. I leaned in and we kissed. It was my first proper kiss. Ever. We'd probably get better at it with time and practice.

"So?" said Helberg. "What do you think?"

I looked at the piglets. "I think I might have to give up bacon," I said.

ABOUT THE AUTHORS

Heide Goody lives in North Warwickshire with her family and pets.

Iain Grant lives in South Birmingham with his family and pets.

They are married, but not to each other.

ALSO BY HEIDE GOODY AND IAIN GRANT

Tech It to Ride

Constance Wileman was once a meat avatar, the flesh and blood puppet of the rich and powerful who would rather take someone else's body out on the town instead of risking their own. But Constance has now escaped that life and is part of the team at Symbio that will finally allow human observers to experience life through the eyes and ears (and all the other senses) of animals.

Randolph Howard is a bodyhacker, a skilled criminal who can effortlessly slip in and out of the minds and bodies of those people who haven't installed the proper security protocols. He's been offered a job that he simply can't refuse, a most unusual burglary job...

Damba is a four hundred pound silverback gorilla. He just wants to spend his days, chilling out and eating his greens. But Randolph Howard and the people at Symbio have some very different plans.

In a future where we open up our minds to others a little more than we should, a woman, a man and a gorilla get involved in the craziest heist ever.

An electrifying novella perfect for fans of *Black Mirror*, *Severance* and *The Peripheral*.

Tech It to Ride

Oddjobs

Unstoppable horrors from beyond are poised to invade and literally create Hell on Earth.

It's the end of the world as we know it, but someone still needs to do the paperwork.

Morag Murray works for the secret government organisation responsible for making sure the apocalypse goes as smoothly and as quietly as possible.

Trouble is, Morag's got a temper problem and, after angering the wrong alien god, she's been sent to another city where she won't cause so much trouble.

But Morag's got her work cut out for her. She has to deal with a man-eating starfish, solve a supernatural murder and, if she's got time, prevent her own inevitable death.

Oddjobs

Clovenhoof

Getting fired can ruin a day...

...especially when you were the Prince of Hell.

Will Satan survive in English suburbia?

Corporate life can be a soul draining experience, especially when the industry is Hell, and you're Lucifer. It isn't all torture and brimstone, though, for the Prince of Darkness, he's got an unhappy Board of Directors.

The numbers look bad.

They want him out.

Then came the corporate coup.

Banished to mortal earth as Jeremy Clovenhoof, Lucifer is going through a mid-immortality crisis of biblical proportion. Maybe if he just tries to blend in, it won't be so bad.

He's wrong.

If it isn't the murder, cannibalism, and armed robbery of everyday life in Birmingham, it's the fact that his heavy metal band isn't getting the respect it deserves, that's dampening his mood.

And the archangel Michael constantly snooping on him, doesn't help.

If you enjoy clever writing, then you'll adore this satirical tour de force, because a good laugh can make you have sympathy for the devil.

Get it now.

Clovenhoof

Printed in Great Britain
by Amazon

23764881R00239